A-Z Guide to Arranged Marriage

Rekha Waheed

MONSOON PRESS

First Published in the United Kingdom in 2005 by Monsoon Press

Monsoon Press
Oxford House Arts Centre
Derbyshire Street
London E2

Book Produced by AuthorsOnline Ltd, 40 Castle Street, Hertford, SG14
1HR

ISBN 0-7552-1500-1

AKNOWLEDGEMENTS

I dedicate this book to the precious, wonderful and crazy Waheed family.

Abdul and Suraya Waheed, you are my heroes. Reba and Parvez bhai, your unwavering support brought this book to life. Jeba, for your determined encouragement and all the late nights, I thank you. Sakib and Rakib, the biggest Waheed hearts, here's another reason to go feast!

Nadia, Huma, Denise, Rabina, and all my friends – let there never be an end to the laughter, happiness, counselling sessions, bad dancing, fattening food, and one too many chocolates.

Thank you to my team at Monsoon Press, Kirsten and Pippa at Oh! Arts Centre, my agent Rebecca Winfield and Helen at Penguin– all your hard work, guidance and enthusiasm has made this a reality.

And finally, to the Almighty, thank you for giving me a second chance.

CHAPTERS

THE BRIT-ASIAN LINGO GUIDE

Akika - Circumcision ceremony
Alaap/Ristha - Marriage proposal
Appha – Sister
Ayjay - Hey
Bachoa - Help/save me
Bamieh: Middle Eastern okra dish
Barfi - Dry Indian sweet made of condensed milk
Bhabhi - Sister-in-law
Bhai/ bhaya - Brother
Bhangra - Asian music
Bhethi - Daughter/ woman
Bendoo - Naïve traditional man
Chaadhis - Underpants
Chacha - Paternal uncle
Chachijhi - Paternal aunt
Dadhijhi - Paternal grandmother
Dhakayan - Bengali with origins in Dhaka
Foopi - Paternal aunt
Gorafied - Derogatory term to define an Asian who tries to act white
Gulapjaman - Rose flavoured Indian sweet
Halal - Lawful act or food permissible for Muslims
Henna - Asian hen night
Jinn: Spirit- (good or evil)
Kala/ kalama - maternal aunt
Kheer - Tapioca dish
Kismet - fate
Korma - Indian chicken dish
Lajja - shame
Londoni - British-Bengalis
Mastan - Don Juan type character
Moharani - Queen of queens
Paan - Beetle nut leaf
Pagul - Crazy
Pathro - Male suitor
Rani - Queen

Rasagullah - Indian sweet in syrup
Rangeela – Glamorous forward woman
Shaadhi - Marriage
Shalwaar Kameez - Tunic trouser outfit
Shish taouk - Lebanese grilled chicken dish
Sidda sadda - Straightforward and honest
Sunnah - Recommended Muslim practices
Sylhethis - Bengali with origins in Sylhet
Wallahs - Owners
Walimah - Reception thrown by groom after the wedding
Zakat - Charity
Zindaghi – Life

A: Adopt Arranged Marriage But Avoid All Atrocious Alaaps

My name's Maya Malik, and I'm a twenty-eight year old SLAAG. That would be the 'Single Lonely Aging Asian Girl' brand. And if there's one thing worse than a slag in the British Bengali community, it's a SLAAG. I buy every issue of *Asian Bride* in preparation for my imminent yet all-too-distant wedding, I hide when my mother meets someone, knowing that her first question will be 'do you know of a good boy?' and I sit through patronising pep talks from well meaning friends who tell me that I will find a man *one day*. For a professional Bengali woman, my biggest fear isn't being overlooked for promotion to Lead Consultant with Chambers Scott Wilfred International. It's the realisation that I have to find a husband from a diminishing stock of eligible bachelors that increasingly consists of mommy's boys, closet gays, and the emotionally disturbed. Now I know that it's going to get worse before it gets better. The Bengali community has consigned me to the spinster league, the bitch called Age will continue to whore for Time and I will pay extortionate Fitness First gym fees to bribe Age to buy me Time's favour. So I'm going to give this sophisticated cute as a button, family oriented, sidda sadda girl a break. I'm going to find me a husband, at any cost, using any means and that includes having arranged introductions.

Arranged marriages are for most families a legitimised, and free, dating agency. They also provide our under-worked, overweight, and hyper-vigilant aunties with an endless supply of gossip. Take, for instance, my latest alaap or wedding proposal that my auntie, Chachijhi Fauzia, delivered to my mother a few weeks ago. She in turn instructed my married twin sisters to prepare me for this suitable boy.
"We've found you another victim." That's how they broke the news to me.
"Put on a decent shalwaar kameez and not the short sluttish ones you like." Meet Jana and Hana, my silhouette slim sisters. Both are model beautiful, practise medicine and, with doctors for husbands, have the ultimate status symbol in the community.
"Abu Ahmed's a stock broker trading in commodities, the older of two boys and he drives a Z3," Jana listed, walking across to my wardrobe where Hana rummaged through my shalwaar kameez collection. Ummm, he sounded scrummy. Would this be my super confident man who could fill a pair of CK boxers like Markie Wahlberg and have a taste for sophisticated living?
"He lives with his parents…"
"…so you're going to have to seduce him into buying you a separate home."
"And he's so loaded you don't have to worry about keeping that job of yours." Goodbye career, hello sex untapped! This stockbroker sounded better by the minute.

1

"So what does he look like?" There's always a set back, but when the twins turned to look at me with wide white grins, I knew his looks wouldn't be it.

"Like someone you need to make an effort for." Both laughed at Jana's comment, but I was already imagining my Devdas-inspired wedding to the designer accustomed Bengali broker.

"Amma insisted that we prep you for this alaap since you messed up the last two." Hana explained, shaking her head at two of the outfits Jana held up. She replaced those and brought out my matt bronze trouser suit in raw Japanese silk. Jana squealed with delight.

"You bring me a dwarf and then a man known only as ugly, and you say I messed up?" But they weren't interested in my reasons, they were already accessorising.

That's how I ended up in my parent's bedroom, crouching by the bay window to peek through the net curtains to see Abu Ahmed's arrival. My entire kandan had turned up for this promising alaap, which is why my parents sat in the living room with my eldest brother and his wife, along with my three sisters and their respective husbands making polite conversation. I, on the other hand felt super elegant in the designer bronze outfit and black stilettos that made the most of my Wonderbra amplified 32B boobs, slim waist and legs that could do with being longer. Jana had blow-dried my hair into a black silken curtain and Hana went light on the make-up to give me sultry brown eyes. I was to put it simply, a sophisticated woman ready to impress and end my stint at spinsterhood. And then I saw them arrive. Only there weren't four family members as expected. Instead five adults carrying gift stuffed fluorescent 'Everything for £1' carrier bags and bunches of 'two for the price of one' flowers brought from the nearest corner shop, dragged and cajoled three suited children towards my house. Nowhere in sight were the boxes of Ambala ludhoos, or the exotic arrangement of roses, lilies and tropical leaves that broker salaries afforded. Worse than that was the unmissable presence of wide boy style cheap polyester suits in a mixture of green, maroon, and brown partnered by luminous saris and huge golden jewellery that said two things: tacky and tasteless. My designer clad sensibilities rioted in outrage and my super confident man of the world stockbroker was missing. The impostors were making their way to my home with the intent of transforming me into a paan-chewing housewife with no colour co-ordinated dress sense. Suddenly, I realised I couldn't leave my perfect family to join that brood of shameless penny pinchers. I raced downstairs to convince my parents not to answer the door, to pretend that we weren't home, to pretend that we'd emigrated once and for all.

At least I would have done, if I hadn't been wearing Jana's stilettos. I would have done if I hadn't slid all the way down the stairs on my arse screaming at the top of my lungs just as my parents opened the door. I stopped screaming when I landed with a heavy thud at the bottom of the stairs and sat in mortified shame. Then chaos descended in the Malik household. In an instant, my family were each touching, pulling and patting one of my limbs.

"Oh Allah, what have you done?" Amma cried.

"Is it hurting?" Jana asked.

"You slid all the way down!" Hana sniggered.

"Don't move if it hurts, where does it hurt?" Jana cut in.

"And this is Maya I assume?" And through the many enquiries of concern, Abu Ahmed emerged from the outside world. There he stood, all five feet eight inches of him, casually dressed in black chinos and a black cashmere v-neck that clung to every sculpted sinew of his chest. Scrummy, he was.

"Yes, I'm Maya. Thank you, I'm fine…"

"Maya, can you get up?" I looked down at Umar, Jana's husband, before looking at my family who continued to flex different parts of my body before my husband to be.

"Really I'm fine." I muttered reclaiming my limbs to scramble up before Abu Ahmed and his watching parents. Amma wasn't convinced and carried on massaging my lower back as she ushered me through to the dining room. That wasn't quite the entrance I planned. As I looked back at the grinning broker, I knew it was one neither of us would forget.

"What were you thinking of?" Jana's concern disappeared the moment Amma closed the door behind us. "That was your entrance?"

"You think I chose to introduce myself like that…"

"Maya, don't talk back!" Amma for some reason was still massaging my back.

"But I could've died…"

"Oh, here goes Ms Melodramatic… Hello, it's so nice to meet you. I'm Jana, Maya's older sister." Jana's personality changes were seamless. One minute the bullying older sister, the next the perfect host. "Come in, please sit down."

"We saw Maya's fall and wanted to make sure she was fine." It was hard to make out which of the two women was Abu Ahmed's mother. Both were short and dumpy, with red paan-stained teeth and saris that screamed flowers of every known living and extinct variety. More to the point, both were checking me out from head to toe.

"I'm fine thank…"

"She's fine. Just a little bumpy ride, but she's fine," Amma said, pulling my chiffon scarf over my head before sitting in front of me. No, Amma wasn't going to let them inspect me like some filly they were buying for breeding.

"This is Auntie Ahmed, Abu's mother and her sister, Auntie Jaya," Ayesha, my oldest sister said, as three children raced into the dining room to play 'catch me' around the table.

"So Maya, do you plan to work after you get married?" Mrs Ahmed went straight for the jugular. She was testing my levels of ambition, and by default whether or not I'd make a neglectful wife. Little did she know that I hate my job and would give it up in a flash to be pampered by an ultra rich husband.

"I'd certainly like to make the most of my opportunities." I had no problem becoming the brunch and lunch wife, but for now I refused to concede that that would be my only fate.

"But there's a time for working, and a time to be a wife. And well let's face it, you've worked for quite a while now, haven't you?" She was good. One question, two nasty jibes. She would make one tough, hard to please mother-in-law.

"If Maya's half as good a wife as she is a consultant, then her husband will be very lucky!" Ayesha countered both protective and proud. She is my role model, a perfect doctor, a perfect wife and the best sister you could have to cover your back.

"You work in fashion don't you?" But Mrs Ahmed wasn't happy with Ayesha's rebuttal. "With those shameless models and women-like men?" She didn't wait for an answer, but along with Auntie Jaya raised her palms heavenwards in a dramatic but silent prayer of forgiveness.

"I write reports about the money side of the industry. It's really very academic."

"But I hear you travel to Italy, France and New York all by yourself?" Auntie Jaya added, content to fuel the fires of disapproval about my career and thereby my suitability.

"To gather information and data from senior executives in the companies I review..."

"To be travelling alone in such a market is worrying for a woman. If I had a daughter, and I know Allah didn't give me one for good reasons, but if he had, there's no way that I would let her travel alone in this big unsafe world." Mrs Ahmed had a strong penchant for melodrama.

"Nobody knows what can happen," Auntie Jaya put in, as if she was more than aware of the untold adventures of the travelling executive. We waited for more, but she sat back, happy to have made her point.

"The upside is Maya gets to travel the world and stay in five star hotels. How many Bengali girls can say that they've done that?" Ayesha asserted with a smile while handing out a platter of somosas.

"Done what?" He, Abu Ahmed 'the Svelte', appeared behind Ayesha in all of his groomed wonderfulness. He wasn't drop dead gorgeous, but he had that confident man of the world edge to him that made the hairs on the back of your neck stand to attention.

"Jet set around the world alone meeting strange men," Auntie Jaya exaggerated, causing Abu to look at me with concern. Who could blame the Ahmed family's misgivings about the fashion industry? But this really was too much.

"I sit behind a computer tracking financial performances and investment decisions of designer houses with pie charts and Venn diagrams. That's it." My crisp explanation stopped all further slurs against my career decision. Mrs Ahmed raised an eyebrow at my tone and looked to Auntie Jaya who shook her head. "I'm a consultant for the designer industry, my job takes me to…"

"Just like me, I'm a broker for TJ Fitzwilliam in the city and that takes me to a few foreign parts of the world." His polished public school accent made him sound like a sell-out Asian.

"Your uncle said you trade in the commodities market…"

"Yes, yes, I've come to specialise in the coffee market. It's a very competitive market between the Africans and South Americans these days." He had interrupted twice but was totally oblivious to this trait of his. As such, he carried on talking for a further ten minutes beneath the adoring gaze of his mother and aunt.

"So what does your brother do?" I didn't know if it was my interruption or the question itself, but they stared at me with disapproval.

"He works in the public sector," Mrs Ahmed revealed with a nervous laugh. "Abu's my real achiever." Ooh, badly answered, and the darting looks between my mother and sisters told me that further investigation into Abu's family background was needed. I knew stockbrokers' love of the fast lane clashed with all things puritanical, so I wondered what caused Abu to take the traditional arranged marriage route. There was more to this family, and I was about to discover exactly what that was.

"That's nice," Amma returned as Mrs Ahmed cut the ludhoos and pistachio barfis into small squares. I tried not to stare, but Mrs Ahmed had me captivated when she turned to Abu the Svelte and spoon-feed him. Yes, that would be spoon-feeding a thirty-year-old man who brokered million dollar deals, in my dining room, in front of me and mine. I looked to Ayesha and Jana but they carried on as if it was the most natural thing in the world.

"These are my rajahs. Ronny, Johnny and Sonny," Auntie Jaya said, feeding her children who lined up before her. This was worse than any saga on Bangla TV. This was real life. More to the point, this is my life. Only it didn't end there. Mrs Ahmed wiped Abu's mouth before sharing her cup of tea with him. One sip for him, and one sip for her. And then again, one sip for him and then one sip for her. Ayesha had brought out the gold-rimmed white bone china set we had imported from Dhaka for use only on special occasions and we had enough teacups for thirty guests. Still, mother and son shared one cup until they finished.

"They're sharing the food!" I whispered to Jana as Abu the Svelte asked his mother to feed him another ludhoo. I didn't mean to be heard, but the still silence told me it was the wrong observation to make. I looked to Jana, but she was already shaking with repressed laughter. Beneath the hard stares, I stemmed my bubbling laughter. "I mean, have another ludhoooooo!" I didn't mean to squeal, or burst out laughing, but I did. Before long, loud, unrepentant, hooting laughter filled the dining room.

Suffice to say, I was given a serious ear bashing by Amma, who insisted that mother-son habits changed after marriage. I knew that was why Abu the Svelte Ahmed was single. But no matter how much I told Amma he wasn't the one, she wouldn't listen. Then Baba discovered that Abu the Svelte's younger brother was doing time in a public sector prison for small time drug dealing. But even if Abu's brother had been fine, I wouldn't have accepted this alaap. I mean, which self-respecting stockbroker dresses designer, but lets his parents walk around in cheap East End suits and five pound saris? More importantly, if I married him, where would I fit in with the tea-sharing tradition? Would I replace his mother, would his mother expect to be included, or would I be excluded from the tradition?

Whilst intriguing, I haven't held out this long to accept one of society's weirdos. That's what we, SLAAGs, are offered and because we're older than the average Asian bride to be, we're expected to accept any maladjusted bachelor that walks through the front door. For now, I'm happy to say, give me my freedom. I can deal with atrocious alaaps. I'll get used to my old age for marriage. I will even compromise on my non-existent ambition, but I will not compromise on my soul mate for life.

B: Bet On Bendhoo Bridegrooms

Asian girls never wander alone. We've inherited our parents' paranoia and so form tribes for any and all social outings. Every Asian girl walking along Hounslow High Street, Commercial Street or Wembley's Ealing Road, carrying knock-off Louis Vuitton purses and the latest mobile phone, has a best friend or four. Tanya, a loud Muslim activist, Sakina our corporate rat, and Tina and Rosie who live in much- envied wedded bliss, formed my tribe. They were my best friends and that's why Sakina disturbed me during Fashorama, the fashion industry's weekly business documentary that I used as out of hours market research.

"He's seeing someone else. The shit's two timing me!" I stared at the phone and could still hear Sakina's long heartbroken sobs. 'He' being Raj 'the Arsehole', with his flashy but used Toyota Celica and his smarmy personality. I lowered the volume and hit the teletext button.

There were five rounds of "Why...?"

Followed by two rounds of "How could he?"

And then "How could I have been so stupid?"

More crying followed, and while my heart went out to my dearest friend, I have to say I was not the least bit surprised - or disappointed. He was the type of man who never appreciated what he had. So whilst Sakina spent hours and plenty of money making sure she was perfection incarnate for him, Raj the Arsehole spent his time playing the SLAAG market.

"But Maya, he's... the... ONE!" Sakina breathed out before another deluge of sobs arrived.

"No he isn't sweetie."

"But he is!"

"No he isn't..."

"He is, he so is."

"So why did he cheat on you?" I felt awful for Sakina as she sniffled and tried to control her emotions.

"How could he Maya? I gave him six months of, of... my... liiiiiffffffee!" And off she went again.

"He's a bastard..."

"I thought he was the one for me." The silent admission tore at my heart and I wanted to convince Sakina that maybe she had made a mistake, as I had no doubt that Raj was the cheating type.

"He's an arsehole who's cheated on you!" I hated being the 'wake up and smell the coffee' girl in her hour of emotional need, but she needed to realise that she was better off without him.

"How am I ever going to trust another man again?" Poor Sakina was hitting thirty and being burnt now was the last thing she needed.

"There are good men out there..."

"How do I know they're not all the bloody same?" I knew where this was going. Sakina wanted me to join in with her 'despise all men' mood. But I couldn't. "Are you going to see that barrister Tanya lined up for you?"

"Yeah." I had to believe that there were good men out there because I had to marry one of them, but the silence that followed my answer was unforgiving. I felt as if I was betraying Sakina, but I bit my tongue to avoid making false promises about banning men and all things male from my life and future. So I held out the olive branch to Sakina. "Do you want me to come over?"

"No, dad will realise something's wrong." This is another sacred fact about Asian girls. No matter how old, how worldly, how experienced we become through secret relationships, we remain forever snow white perfect in our parent's eyes.

"Maybe you should tell your dad so he can go kick the shit out of the Arsehole." Sakina laughed for a millisecond before her laugh turned into strangled crying. "How did you find out that he was cheating on you?" I asked, before the whys and the hows started up again.

"Tanya met her brother's best friend's sister who told her all about her boyfriend who only turned out to be MY BOYFRIEND!" she shouted. Sakina had seen Raj for six months and how her parents hadn't found out about her relationship remained a mystery.

"Small world." And it really was. The twenty-first century virtual information highway had nothing on the Asian gossip channel.

"Maya, what am I going to do?" The quiet question melted my anger and in that instant I realised how alone we singletons were. I gave up all hope of watching Fashorama, and spoke with Sakina until she stopped crying. After our conversation, I felt despondent about men. Men, potential husbands, and arseholes. Of course there were the exceptions. Dads, brothers and then there was Jhanghir. Jhanghir and I had met at Waterstones bookstore in Gower Street where I had worked evenings to finance my studies and he took on shifts after he blew away his father's allowance. He was a striking but laid back Hilfiger clad medic from Harvard Medical School on a one-year exchange programme at University College, and we couldn't have been more different. He was from a rich Dhakayan family based in Manhattan, and at that time I lived in a Mile End council flat with my Sylhethi family. As we stacked the shelves, browsed through the stores and then disappeared with books to laze around in Regents Park, we argued about everything. Politics, religion, identity, inter-race racism, family responsibility, the ethics of medical research, art, ambition, love, marriage and every other topic we could think of. I hated his lifestyle but loved his charm and wit. He hated my origins but loved my unaccommodating attitude. He was engaged and I was puritanically single. Truth be known, we fancied each other rotten, but were both too proud to build that particular bridge.

"Yeah?" As always, the sound of his voice made everything good again and I understood why pride was destructive.

"It's me." It was late evening in Manhattan and he sounded tired, but I wanted to talk. "I wanted to check how you are."

"You ok Maya?" Jhanghir knew me well enough to read my moods. Detached from my family, friends, and life, he was the one person I relied on wholly. With Jhanghir, I didn't need to have the answers, or fill in the gaps. He just knew, and that was enough for me.

"I'm fine Jhanghir, but you sound tired."

"It's the same-old, Maya. What with graveyard shifts at the hospital, rotations and exams, I feel like the walking dead. What's going on out there?" he asked. So thinking that he half-slept, half-listened, I told him about Abu the Svelte and my unforgettable entrance. I told him about my continued singledom, and then about Sakina. And then he called Raj an arsehole and without knowing it, Jhanghir showed me that there was still hope.

"He's here." I had a direct line to Tanya by the time I raced into the ladies' room. "Bilal, your barrister, my date tonight, just called to let me know that he's here, and he's early."

"Are you ready?" The bright lights were unforgiving and I needed more than five minutes of repair work.

"No! My hair resembles a hedgehog on Viagra and my skin's…"

"Relax Maya. Brush your hair and line your eyes. Put on some lip gloss and blend in with your liner." I opened up my essential make up bag and up ended it onto the counter.

"Fill me in on him," I prompted before I followed Tanya's instructions.

"He's driven, very very ambitious and wants to make it to judge. He lives in Chiswick…"

"And you've no idea what he looks like?" I applied the lip-gloss and then the liquid liner.

"No, but you don't find many Bengali barristers Maya, so don't drop him if he's not a Clooney clone…"

"I'm ready." I cut in before Tanya started her 'take this seriously' routine. I grinned at my improved reflection, before remembering the sacred conditions of blind dates. "You and Sakina can't call my home as I'm having dinner with you. And don't forget to call me after fifteen minutes to give me an escape route if I need one."

"What are you wearing?" I stopped grinning and looked at my boring suit.

"My arse-hugging navy suit with white shirt…"

"What about shoes and bag?" Tanya strongly believed that women who wore sexy shoes were by nature sensual love goddesses. Now, given Tanya is a strong Muslim activist and still single, I don't know how she had tested her theory. Still, I looked at my flat black shoes and couldn't help but feel dowdy.

"Black loafers and black case… "

"That's really going to get him excited!"

"Tanya, I'm going from work, so I'm not going to turn into some rangeela for a stranger…"
"But you knew you were meeting a barrister…"
"So maybe he'll be interested in what I have to say as opposed to the shoes I'm wearing!"

I should've listened to Tanya's wisdom. The moment Bilal, the barrister, pulled up outside Farringdon station in a brand new spanking metallic Jaguar XK coupe, I knew shoes and bags were important. Pushing past the army of commuters, I jumped in and put my case at my feet to hide my ugly shoes.
"Hi, nice to meet you." Thirty-five year old Bilal looked like a cross between Danny De Vito and George Hamilton, with Imran Khan hair. But most of all he looked like he was just small.
"Hi," I returned turning in the soft grain leather seat to face him as he pulled out into the crazy rush hour traffic.
"So, you have a good day?" I watched him drive and then noticed his hands.
"Fine. Busy." They were small, like a young boy's hands. In fact they were abnormally small for such a grown man. "How about you?" Bilal talked about caseloads, hearings, and how incompetent everyone, with the exception of himself, was. I tore my gaze away from his hands and looked at the car's satellite navigation system, hi tech sound system and plush interior. The perceptive dwarf picked up on that, but misread my thoughts.
"She's fine, isn't she?" I gave Bilal a small smile and nodded. "Yeah, you see this baby makes the other judges question how this coolie joined their ranks. She makes them ask who's the daddy. And you know who the daddy is, don't you?" He grinned like a Cheshire cat, and waited until I pointed at him to shout out in laughter. I stared in horror as he brayed with such force that his hair billowed around him. "So what car do you drive?"
"Renault Clio… the 'Baba' car." My French-accented take on the 'Papa' ad and my car failed to impress him.
"Do you know what I had to go through to get to where I am?" I shook my head. "I had to graft hard, and I grafted harder than they expected. Now when they ask for representation, Bilal Bakr is who they ask for. They know who's going to win and I win. Who wins?" Once again I pointed at him and he hooted in self-adoration. I smiled, but wondered whether the black barrister's gown worn in court swamped him or whether he had his gown custom made. "What do you think?"
"About what?" I looked away from him as we crawled at snails pace down Wigmore Street.
"Any suggestions or restaurant preferences?" Bilal repeated.
"Marhabah." He looked confused. "It's a great Lebanese restaurant just up ahead." Bilal nodded and looked for parking spaces.

"Maybe I should find an NCP. Car crime's particularly bad in central London and I don't want to risk …"

"Here! There's a spot here." Bilal jerked to a stop and glared at me for shouting. I smiled but he looked away to ease into the parking spot. "And it's after 6:30 so parking's free." But Bilal wasn't convinced. He walked around his baby three times to judge its proximity to the other cars, and then read the parking time conditions until I pointed out the time zones. At that point I realised just how petite he really was. In my flats, he was taller by an inch and he had a slimmer frame.

"It'll be fine there, right?" I nodded, but he continued circling his 'baby'. Exasperated, I walked on ahead refusing to be overlooked for a hunk of metal.

Once inside Marhabah, the waiter showed me through the warm fragrant Lebanese restaurant to a table. As I studied the menu, Bilal appeared, evidently put out at being stranded.

"Wow, you don't hang around do you?" I smiled at Barrister Bilal's icebreaker and promised to give him a chance. I had to focus on the positives and so I started. He appeared to be perfectly groomed, dressed in an open necked starched white shirt and charcoal grey Sisley trousers, and he was confident. Those were good starting points.

"This restaurant is one of my favourites. I love Lebanese food, are you a fan?" He shook his head and looked thoroughly unimpressed.

"Can't say that I am." I continued to smile despite his attitude. "So how long has Tanya known Marie? I can't believe she arranged this date! She didn't have much to say about you, only that you were a professional Bengali girl, and let's face it, there aren't really that many!"

"You'd be surprised, there are more of us out there than you think!" I countered.

"I really wouldn't know, I'm not tapped into the Bengali community." Oh, of course he wasn't.

"We've got quite a community in West London. It's nothing compared to East London, but it is growing." He remained unconvinced.

"I live in Chiswick, it's full of exclusive houses, fashionable cafés and classy cars. And let me tell you, there are no Bengalis there." Now he was beginning to annoy me. "Nope, nothing catches my interest." I also looked down at the menu and prayed for patience.

"You must see something that you like here?" He misunderstood my question as a lame attempt to hit on him. "I meant on the menu…" But I'd done the damage. "I didn't mean me, I meant on the…"

"Are we ready to order…"

"Yes! Yes we are!" I ignored the waiter's darting looks at Bilal. "For starters, I'd like black olive hummus and the ladyfingers dish…"

"The Bamieh?" I nodded at the waiter and caught Bilal reviewing the menu.

"The shish touk is great here, I'd strongly recommend that." Bilal looked at me and then shook his head at the waiter, indicating that he needed no such advice. "Then I'll have the shish touk, thank you." The waiter took my menu with an understanding smile.

"I'll have the lamb shwarma and we'll have a bottle of mineral water, thanks." Bilal held out his menu dismissively and looked at me.

"So, where are you from originally?" I hoped my light hearted question would lighten the mood.

"Medway Village, Berkshire." First sign of a Bengali coconut is that they think they originate from England.

"I'm sorry, I meant in Bangladesh." Bilal skimmed his hair back from his face and smiled.

"Jogonathpur, but I'm sure you haven't heard of it." The second sign of a coconut was denial of origin.

"Surprise! I do!" I gave up hoping that we would at some point find that we had something in common. "Have you visited Bangladesh recently?"

"Oh, I wouldn't go back to visit! I'll either get married off or come down with some God-forbidden tropical disease, and I can't afford to do either." The waiter arrived with our mineral water, and basket of bread with hummus and bamieh. Bilal was an 'ignoranus', both ignorant and an arsehole, and I didn't want to keep trying to connect with him anymore.

"You don't know what you're missing!" He guffawed at my reply. "The shopping, the breathtaking landscapes..."

"Poverty, vulture-like families, corruption, bribery! Give me Rome or Stockholm any day." When he laughed, his eyes screwed up into small glinting beads that reminded me of Babe the pig. "Have you been to either?" Bilal didn't let me answer. Instead he assumed that I hadn't, and rambled on about the beauty of both cities.

"I love Stockholm. I stayed at the Diplomat, which looks onto the The Grand Palace. There's something magical about the Palace. The architecture and hidden cobbled streets remind me of the fairytale stories we were told as children," I said, helping myself to the breadbasket. "But Rome, it's masterful in different ways..."

"You've been?" Bilal was so surprised he put his glass down to stare at me. I wanted to empty my drink over his gorafied expression.

"Surprised again?" I didn't want to justify myself, but the man needed a reality check about British Bengali girls.

"That's unbelievable! It's hard enough to come across educated Bengali girls, but Bengali girls who've travelled. Now I am surprised!"

"You don't know very many Bengali people do you?" Bilal stopped at my question.

"Not unless I'm bailing them from jail..."

"I hope that doesn't include your family and friends!" Bilal didn't find my comment amusing so I stopped smiling and helped myself to more bamieh.

"We only see them when they need help with filling forms or advice." I wished Tanya would call me to give me a reason to leave. "How many Bengalis do you think I come across professionally?"

"Fewer than the number of Bengalis you come across in Chiswick!" Once again he ignored my attempt to lighten the mood, and stared at me until I replaced my smile with a thoughtful expression.

"I help new Bengali barristers find their way. I tell them how it is. Last month, this bendhoo from Mile End walks into my office in a fifty pound Mr Byrite suit, and do you know what I did?" I hated to imagine, but I shook my head and waited. "I took him aside and I said, 'Brother, take out a loan if you have to, but if you want to have a career in my firm under my tutelage, go and have five suits custom made for you in Saville Row'. And that's me giving back to the community, that's my zakat." He wanted a standing ovation for his contribution to the community, and all I could think of was, for a small man, he had an ego bigger than his Jag.

"That's, um, good advice Bilal." I muttered before turning to the waiter who arrived with our main dishes.

"How about you? Are you in the thick of the Bengali community?" I knew Bilal's type and I knew what his worst nightmare would be.

"Yup, smack bang in the middle of it. We hear everything about everybody and some of the stories you hear about what our generation get up to are shocking, unbelievably shocking!" Bilal paused and cleared his throat, but I continued. "Dating, drinking, and would you believe it *sleeping around!*" He didn't replicate my mock outrage and I shook my head with a maturity of which Abu the Svelte's mother would have been proud.

"For a modern educated girl who's travelled the world you have very traditional views about relationships."

"Don't you think it's important that we maintain our integrity, principles and family reputation?"

"So do you know Chiswick at all?" He wasn't prepared to entertain a serious discussion and instead offered me a further serving of bamieh.

"Well enough to know that you have a lot of Bengalis in the area." In turn, I wasn't prepared to entertain him anymore. My serious response caught his attention.

"Really? Maybe I should take more walks, you know bump into one of them!" The novelty of the idea left Bilal beaming.

"One of them?" He seemed confused by my question and I wondered at which point he forgot that he was one of us.

"Well, maybe I could get to know one of them well enough to hire them to cook and clean for me. That'd be a way to get a few of them off benefits!" Very few things in life put me off my food, but this particular ignoranus did.

"I'm sure they'll be queuing up for the privilege!" He missed the sarcasm and laughed in agreement.

"So tell me about your family?" I couldn't believe he still expected me to qualify my family.

"Why are you here, Bilal?" He was thrown off guard, and it was the first time he realised that he didn't impress me. "I don't understand why you're considering a Bengali girl for marriage when you judge British Bengalis so badly."

"You think I'm a coconut..."

"No!" I answered a millisecond too fast. He raised a brow and sat back to watch me. "Ok, well yes I do, but just a little and not in that horrible mean way..."

"Of course not." He was offended and I wished that I had just answered his question, paid for the meal and taken the tube home. "I don't know that you can call someone a coconut and intend for it to be a compliment."

"Seriously, there are some confused Bengalis out there who would take it as a compliment..." Bilal's silence told me he wasn't one of them. I looked down at my meal and waited for him to say something, anything, to break the awkwardness between us. But he didn't, so I peeked up at him and caught his stony cold expression.

"How's your meal?" He wasn't interested in my attempts to make amends.

"It's not to my liking." I nodded at his cold answer and watched as he threw his napkin onto the table, marking the end of yet another one of my introductions. Blind dates and heart-stopping funfair rides, they go hand in hand. You wait hours for the most exhilarating rush of your life, and before you know it, it's over.

Sakina looked awful when we met up for a coffee the following evening. I was late and the girls had already started on the update in the Goodge Street coffee house.

"Last minute client meeting." I explained as I hugged Sakina on arrival and before we even sat down, there were tears in her big brown eyes. The humiliation of being single post 25 and dumped had changed my once glamorous friend into a gaunt shadow of her former self. She looked, to put it bluntly, betrayed.

"Has the barrister called?" Tanya asked as I took off my jacket.

"No, and he'd probably ask me to cook and clean for him if he did!"

"That's what sell-outs do. Once they forget who they are, they believe every stereotype out there." Tanya threw in with disgust.

"And you parted ways at the restaurant? Not even a ride home?" Sakina asked quietly.

"No, the shit worried that he would get carjacked driving his Jag through Ladbroke Grove. But that wasn't the worst part. The worst part was when he pulled up outside Edgeware Road station and leaned across the seat to kiss me goodbye. He just sat there, eyes closed, lips puckered, so I bolted." Whilst Tanya and I laughed at the incident, Sakina wiped at her tears. Our smiles faded.

"What an idiot," Tanya muttered, standing up to order our coffees. "Maya, what do you want?"

"It's been a long tough day at work, so I deserve a Vanilla Machiatto with extra cream…"

"Why didn't I guess?" Sakina whispered. "All those times I asked him to meet my parents, all those times he rearranged meeting you guys… You know, NOW I understand why he wouldn't take me to Green Street, because she bloody well lived there!" Sakina had spent every night since finding out about Raj beating herself up for being so trusting. I took the large mug from Tanya and watched her split a huge portion of the Devil's chocolate cake into three.

"He's an arsehole," I contributed, looking at Tanya with concern.

"He's a boil that grows on an arsehole," Tanya added.

"He's the puss that erupts from a boil that grows on an arsehole!" Tanya and I laughed, wrinkling our noses at the disgusting thought.

"He's the one." Both Tanya and I quietened at Sakina's whisper. I handed her a clean tissue to replace the soaked raggedy one she clutched, and watched her take a large mouthful of the Devil's cake.

"That's good," she muttered, working her way through her portion as she repeated Tanya's discovery of Raj's cheating ways. We kept the supply of cake flowing, and as she started on my portion she broke down. "He always gave me his chocolate cake…"

"And now we're going to find you a nicer guy who'll give you his chocolate cake…"

"I don't want a nicer guy!" Sakina cried as she wiped at her tears.

"You don't want a cheating good for nothing loser either," Tanya stated.

"I'll never feel this way again. I'll never love like this again. Never, ever again," Sakina whispered shaking her head.

"Sweetie, you'll meet a guy who'll make you feel like the princess you are." But Sakina wouldn't believe a word of it. "You deserve better than Raj, why can't you see that?"

"You've never felt it, have you?" Sakina asked looking at me with a sorry smile. "You've never known what true love is."

"The guy cheated on you and I know that can't be true love. He doesn't deserve a single tear you're shedding…"

"You have no idea what it is to love someone unconditionally, whilst hoping against all hope that they may love you back."

"I know what it is to love a man…"

"Really? When was the last time you were in love, Maya?" I held Sakina's eyes and struggled for a reply. Only Jhanghir came to mind.

"You know I've been introduced to guys, some of whom I've gone out with several times…"

"And then dumped because they couldn't live up to your mate Jhanghir…"

"He has nothing to do with this Sakina…"

"Do you love Jhanghir?"

"No!" I answered too quickly.

"I went to dinner with you guys once, and I can categorically say that I've not seen two people more instinctively suited than the two of you," Sakina stated.

"You're being ridiculous…"

"You were connected. You watched out for each other without realising. He knew what you liked without asking and every so often he'd ask to make sure you were ok. And when he looked at you…"

"Stop it."

"He looked at you like you were the most precious thing in his life," Sakina sighed. "Did you ever make out? Are you holding a secret light for him thinking that he doesn't love you…"

"Sakina, he's engaged to another woman!" But Sakina refused to accept my response.

"So why is he still in your life?" This was ludicrous! I looked to Tanya for support, but she seemed to be equally interested in the answer.

"He's a friend!"

"Why? No bloke lasts as a friend…"

"Jhanghir is and will remain as one." Sakina leaned forward, held my face and looked directly at me.

"What's the attraction to Jhanghir, Maya?" I held Sakina's wide brown eyes before pulling away from her. It was too hard to explain what Jhanghir meant to me, too complicated to describe what we could have been but ultimately chose not to be, and it was impossible to explain how we could still mean so much to each other and still be friends. So I met Sakina's eyes and smiled.

"There is no attraction. We choose to be friends." Sakina shook her head and searched my eyes. I realised that Sakina was searching for hope. If I let her believe that Jhanghir and I were meant to be and would one day be, she could hope that Raj would be hers again.

"That's just it Maya, you don't get to choose who you love." Sakina's heartbroken admission told me she had just lost all hope. She forced her tears back and cleared her throat. "I remember the plans we made, the home we dreamt of, and the children we hoped for. I think of him last thing at night and first thing when I rise, I think of him at every turn and I can't help myself. I want it to stop, I promise you I do, but I don't know how." I reached across to Sakina and pulled her into a warm hug. She rested against my shoulder and cried her heart out. Tanya smiled sadly before going to buy another round of Devil's cake. I pushed Jhanghir to the back of my mind and refused to think about the questions Sakina had thrown at me. Sakina's love for Raj sounded like the stuff magical Hollywood romances were made of, but this was real life and Sakina wasn't going to get a happy ever after.

The polar opposite of Bilal, a coconut go-getter, is the bendhoo bichara. Bendhoo bicharas are new to England and hard working. They form the group of men your parents would never consider when you're at your marital prime. The further you move away from your prime, the more regard desperately-seeking-groom parents have for this reserve army of potential suitors. Now there's nothing wrong with ambition, as long as it doesn't constitute taking advantage of the oversubscribed SLAAG's market to get that all too precious red passport.

"You're seeing this all wrong, " said Taj, my younger brother, trying to soften me up for an alaap with said bendhoo bichara.

"Of course I am." He ignored my sarcasm and opted to answer his mobile. Taj is the family capitalist. Having completed his biomedical science degree at Kingston University, and refused a transfer onto a medical degree, Taj embraced the world of pharmaceutical sales with passion. Three years on, he was on thirty five thousand base and a commission that had afforded him a brand new spanking Audi.

"What's wrong with a guy making his life in England?"

"Nothing. In fact, I'd respect anyone who can make a life in England. My worry is getting a guy who expects an easy ride guaranteed by my passport and the benefit system..."

"That it? You're worried about some man marrying you for your passport?" Taj looked disgusted by my attitude.

"It does happen, Taj. We know that it's a problem in the community..."

"Like we'd marry you off to someone who'd do that..."

"There are hundreds of girls in East London who are living that life and I'm sure none of their families intended for them to end in desperate marriages," I pointed out as we entered Whiteley's in Bayswater.

"Three years ago, you'd never marry me off to a bendhoo."

"They don't all wear polyester green trousers, satin shirts and speak with an accent." Taj said as we took the escalator to the third floor.

"I'm sorry, but I don't want to be the main breadwinner until he's established enough to support me and a family..."

"When's the stag night Raz?" Taj shouted out as he spotted a college friend taking the escalator down.

"We're thinking Barcelona, you know, do a weekend in the sun and clubs." I raised a brow at the reply. Bengalis don't approve of clubbing. In fact, Bengalis believe clubbing, drinking, sleeping around as just one big sin. That's not to say Bengalis didn't do any of that, it's just that no-one admitted to doing it openly. No-one except Taj that is.

"You need to book Barca's Buddha man, we hit that club and you got a kicking stag night." I stared at him as he held up the latest mobile he had imported from Malaysia. "Just buzz me, and I'll get my mate in Barca to hook us up in the VIP lounge."

"Yea, yea man, that's real of you. I'm feeling your luv, bruv." At that point, Raz spotted me and froze.

"Congratulations Razzaq..."

"I'll be round to invite your family to the traditional stuff, you know the important dos," he clarified with apologetic sincerity. "The clubbing's just for the lads."

"Of course it is." Taj glared at me to drop my disapproving big sister act. Raz looked uncertainly to Taj. As he neared the end of the escalator, he cleared his throat.

"Ok, well Taj, let me know how your mate can hook us up in Barca. And it's nice seeing you."

"No probs bro, consider it done. I'll buzz you." Taj overcompensated before stepping onto the third floor. "He's getting married." Taj explained as we joined the queue to go and see the latest action film he'd set his heart on watching.

"Clubbing in Barcelona? Baba is not going to like that..."

"Baba doesn't need to know." I stared at Taj until he sighed. "Look, it's a guy thing ok. You girls can stay real and pure, and everyone will praise you. But us guys, if we don't party for a mate who's getting married, we look like fags or fundamentalists..."

"That's rubbish!" Taj responded with a snort of disbelief. "Bengali girls can choose to party as much as you guys. We have stay at home good girls and the 'push the boat out' adventurous girls..."

"Yeah, that no decent guy will touch with a bargepole..."

"Taj, what's with the double standards? It makes no difference if a guy or a girl goes clubbing, the community just doesn't like it." Taj shook his head and chuckled.

"Sis, you don't know what goes on in clubs. There's a lot of bumping and..."

"Spare me the details."

"...and no man wants a girl who's happy to bump and grind with any Joe Bloggs who asks her to dance." The queue moved forward.

"But it's ok for you guys?" Taj let out an exasperated sigh and stood back.

"Stop turning this into an equalities issue!" He derided. "Men and women are not the same..."

"You're a hypocritical sexist..."

"What's that famous saying about women?" I shrugged and laughed as Taj tried to justify his beliefs. "If you're not a mother, a wife, a sister or a friend to a man, then you're nothing." I stopped laughing and shook my head at his double standards. Before Taj could convince me otherwise I changed the topic.

"Is Raz marrying Tina?" Taj sputtered in disbelief, as if mentioning the name of Raz's girlfriend was sacrilegious. "Is he seeing someone new?" I frowned, as Taj laughed and shook his head.

"Please! He's going back home to marry some pure honey his parents have found for him!" I couldn't see what was so funny.

"Why... why would he do that? What was wrong with Tina? Aren't there enough Bengali girls here for him to choose from?"

"I hate to tell you this sis, but there aren't that many Bengali girls here that don't put out." My look of outrage made Taj reconsider his words. "And good girls like you scare guys into thinking they won't live up to high standards..."

"So they opt out, and go pick the prettiest of the crop back in Sylhet?" I felt Tina's pain, and I felt personally slighted.

"Why settle for easy girls with no morals when you can have a fair, pretty untouched honey?" Taj believed his explanation was totally reasonable, but then he would. He had no idea what it was to be me.

"What about adjusting to lifestyles, language barriers, mixing at corporate dinners with your colleagues…"

"Between an easy girlfriend or a city woman who demands the world and shows no gratitude, I'd take the innocent pure girl from back home to be the most important teacher in my kid's life any day." Despite my anger at his cynicism, I couldn't help but see Taj's rationale. We were at the cinema now, and Taj paid for the tickets before we went on to buy the popcorn.

"And the girlfriend, the one that guys like Raz make an emotional commitment to, what happens to her?"

"She gets the same privileges if she goes back to Sylhet." I led the way into the darkened hall, silent and lost in thought.

So, the girlfriend who puts out isn't good marital material. Loose morals aren't good qualifiers for men who expect the highest standards from the woman who'll raise their children. Yet we sophisticated, city-savvy smart women, exceeded these standards, and still our men opted for the fresh-faced village girl. It was twisted male logic, but an accepted one. So whilst these bastards become bridegrooms in Bangladesh, we simply become a bigger brigade of the unwanted and the dumped.

C: Curse Crap Careers And Community Comparisons

Every morning, I made the forty-five minute journey to a job I hated with a passion. It was during my arduous journey to Chancery Lane one morning that I realised I had sold my soul for a corporate pay packet. I had never dreamed of being a 'Luxury Brand Trend Analyst' for the designer market. I never imagined that my days would be spent behind a computer, manipulating sales and turnover figures in charts, tables and high resolution graphics for my manager to no doubt pass off as her own work. And I never imagined that I'd stop caring about having a career because marriage and painting would become my *chosen* career. I loved painting, but as Amma put it, painting pictures wasn't a real job. The closest I came to being a painter was studying at Central St Martin's. But, it wasn't good enough to just study Fine Arts, as it lacked any business application. So I studied Graphic Design and specialised in advertising, which as Amma put it 'set me up' for an acceptable career. Now, as I jostled in the sardine packed tube with executives and students for a seat every morning, I dreamed of producing Rothko inspired work that combined the bold styles of Howard Hodgkin and Ben Sulemi with the richness of Indian tribal colours, materials and a hundred and one other variables.

"Excuse me!" Snotty nosed bitch, did she have to be so loud about making her way to the exit. I drew my legs in and ignored my fellow traveller who glared at me for breaking the sacred peace. I, in turn, glared at the suited city slave who made her way to the exit at Oxford Circus. It was then that I caught the eyes of a groomed city slicker. He was watching me. I looked either side of me, just in case I had got it wrong. But I hadn't. On my left sat a grungy unwashed student, bewildered at being awake so early. On my right sat an overweight, balding and already sweating businessman. Discreetly, I looked ahead and there he was, looking straight at me. I must be looking pretty good if this hot shot was checking me out. I caught his dark eyes for the briefest second and stopped myself smiling at his audacity. He wasn't half bad himself. Stocky, dark haired, with that blue blooded corporate rat look. We pulled into Chancery Lane and I flashed a grin at the groomed city slicker as I stepped off the tube. And when I passed the ticket machines and took the stairs up to street level, I caught more interested glances. I felt good and couldn't resist grinning. I had a skip in my stride, and a smile wider than Julia Robert's. This was going to be a good day. It was then I felt the cold rush of air against my bust. The stares I received during my ride into work weren't because of my drop dead gorgeous looks. They were generated by the generous display of my 32B bust, provided courtesy of my gaping shirt. This was going to be a bad Monday.

"Aah, there you are." Bitch Brenda was a piranha, who lived to set report deadlines, improve client retention rates and increase client spend. She always wore her hair back in a severe bun and a single-breasted Onassis jacket over a short fitted skirt, usually black. She was also my manager.

"Yes, here I am," I returned, as I put my jacket away and switched on my computer.

"Clare's feeling unwell today. I want you to take her meetings." I hated meetings. I froze in meetings and no matter how logical my thoughts were, my contributions always sounded naive, uncertain and inexperienced.

"Aah, what's wrong with her?"

The real answer was a weekend of heavy drinking and a bastard of a hangover, but Brenda said, "Stomach bug."

"And Nicole can't take any of the meetings because..." She might as well have said, 'Because you're the only mug who'd take the extra workload', but she opted for;

"...because Nicole's late with her report." Brenda didn't like to be questioned, so she pinned me with her icy stare and waited. "Is that going to be a problem?" There it was, that tone she used to make you feel like an unworthy minion.

"Let me just check my diary." I looked away from her piercing glare to log onto my mailbox. The program opened up to reveal the fifteen odd emails sent by Tanya and Sakina with titles including 'What to do with a Cheating Bastard', 'Six Ways to Make a Cheating Bastard Pay', '...You forgot to mention Castrate him' and 'Am I ever going to get married?'. With Brenda standing behind me, and my friends' documented bitterness before me, I clicked open my calendar and silently cursed at my client free day. So my excuses started.

"But I won't be able to attend the team meeting..."

"I'll make apologies for you." She smiled, expecting total acceptance.

"I have a conference call at three o'clock, I can't take Clare's meeting then..."

"Can you make the necessary cancellations?" She was going to draw this out.

"I have a report review with our consultants in New York and a deadline for Thursday. I can't reschedule." I wasn't going to prioritise Clare's work over mine despite Brenda's raised brow. "Also, I can't take her five o'clock meeting..."

"But you don't have a meeting at five o'clock." The Bitch had already checked my calendar.

"I have a private event this evening that I can't rearrange." Most corporate rats aiming to double their forty thousand pound income would never put their personal life before work. Given that Brenda knew I had no such work ethic, she didn't need to know that I was again meeting up with Tanya to console Sakina.

"I'll just have to take it." Her acceptance of the meeting was resentful and angry.

"Great, so we're all covered." Brenda didn't crack a smile, or mutter a 'thank you' before she strode away in her three-inch alligator stilettos. And then reception called to say the clients for Clare's first meeting had arrived.

At eight o'clock that evening, I sat alone at a balcony table in Rajah's. I had bailed on Tanya and Sakina, as my family had arranged another alaap, one that came from Rafi Karim, a bendhoo bichara from Bangladesh. I stared down at my family who sat in a close huddle discussing the boy's suitability before his arrival and I wondered why I hadn't been snapped up already.

"Can I get you another drink?" The waiter broke through my thoughts. I looked up and stared into the most stunning hazel eyes I'd ever seen. "...or anything else for that matter?"

"I'm... I'm sorry, uh I mean, yes please." I could barely speak, and paused with an embarrassed smile as I found myself gawping like a teenager. "Diet coke with lots of ice." I finally answered. He grinned and I grinned back. I liked the effect this man had on me.

"I know your father, he asked me to look out for you. He said that you have an alaap this evening." I didn't understand a word he uttered, but nodded. "You've been frowning ever since you arrived and I can't work out why."

"What would you like to bet that the man who walks into this restaurant is either a social reject or a chancer who's got a white girl on the side?" Catching the waiter by surprise, I grinned and raised a brow in challenge.

"I'm not a betting man..."

"I'm Maya." He sat down and narrowed those stunning eyes. "So how about it?"

"You're a beautiful girl, chances are that things will go your way." I refused to acknowledge his compliment and maintained a straight face.

"That means you win..."

"Win what?" I liked this harmless flirtation and threw a passing glance at his hand to make sure that there was no sign of a wedding ring. With none present, I smiled.

"How about dinner on me?"

"That it?" That's not quite the reaction I expected when I offered to take a man out for dinner.

"At a restaurant of your choice." But he was gorgeous, so I persevered.

"I get to choose the restaurant that you will take me to if you meet your future husband today?" he asked with half a grin.

"Let's just say, I like to share my happiness!" I was actually flirting with this man, right before my family introduced me to my prospective husband and it felt good. His deep rumbling laughter made me laugh and I smiled into his alluring eyes.

"And if he doesn't turn out to be the man you want as your husband?"

"Then you grab today's bill…"

"Your father tells me that he has high expectations of this match."

"Aah, insider information," I murmured with a smile. "So, are you on?"

"We're on." He agreed. Then he looked beyond me, and I knew that they had arrived. He grinned at me before standing up to leave. "Good Luck." I wanted to ask him to stay and keep me company as he walked away, but protocol demanded otherwise. With a heavy sigh, I turned to look down at the envoy of men and women who greeted my parents with over-exaggerated salutations and hugs to seek out my prospective husband.

"Hey, you ready to make your entrance?" I looked up at Ayesha's question, and felt nervous. We loved Raja's because its split floor design gave me the advantage of seeing my prospective groom before he saw me, but on this occasion I couldn't make out which one was Rafi Karim.

"Which one is he?" I asked Ayesha. She sat beside me and pointed to a man who sat with his back to us. "Is he cute?" Ayesha refused to look at me.

"He's nice, so try and give him a chance."

"I always give people a chance…"

"No you don't. You judge people on their appearance. Stop dismissing people on the basis of their looks and start enjoying their company. And I don't mean laughing at their expense!" We took the stairs down to the ground floor. "Promise me now, give him a chance, he's a nice bloke…"

"Oh Ayesha…"

"Just give him a chance," Ayesha pleaded, taking my arm to lead me to the table. "This is Maya, Maya, this is the Karim family." Everyone stopped to stare at me and I gave them a blinding smile. They kept staring and I kept smiling. And then Amma broke through the awkward silence to laugh at nothing in particular. I looked around the table, and when I spotted Rafi, I felt the blood drain from my face. I looked from Rafi my intended, to Baba before returning my gaze to Rafi. With the faintest of smiles, I pulled out my seat and sat before him. I struggled not to stare at the dark, scrawny man with the terrible squint and horribly protruding teeth. I wasn't sure if he was looking at me, although I knew that one of his eyes looked in my general direction. And then he looked away to giggle behind cupped hands.

"Maya, we've heard plenty about you. My name's Mukta, and it's lovely to meet you." Turning to one of his sisters, I returned the greeting. "I know these introductions are really embarrassing, but we're an open family. Asim stop belching and STOP PUTTING things in your nose!" I jumped at the high-pitched order, but the scrawny six-year old kept his finger locked in his left nostril. "As I was saying, don't feel intimidated by this, we just want to know what you're like. Would you like some shaag gush?" I barely nodded before Mukta served me a royal portion of the dish. "I love this restaurant, the décor, the atmosphere, and to think, I didn't even know it existed." Mukta's commentary was endless. I looked across at Ayesha who helped herself to my favourite lamb tikka dish. I caught Baba's apologetic expression and decided to make an effort with Rafi, despite having made my decision.

"This must be awkward for you?" I said, breaking the silence between us.

"Yeah, most of the time." Rafi was, worryingly, blessed with his sister's high-pitched voice and a strong Bengali accent. "I was told you were old. So I was thanking God that you're not also ugly." I thanked him for what I took to be a compliment. And it didn't get any better. Rafi giggled again and sat before me, content to just smile.

"This is our favourite family restaurant. We come here all the time." That's the only thing I could think of saying as I helped myself to a large serving of chicken tikka.

"You like your food innit?" Rafi observed with a squeaky laugh whilst pointing at my plate. "You're lucky you're skinny, because I don't want a fat wife." I looked at the man in disbelief. And then I held one of his eyes before giving myself a second serving.

"Rafi, are you sure you won't have some more chicken tikka?" Ayesha asked, but Rafi made a show of holding his plate away and shaking his left hand.

"Oh, no, no… One of us must make a point of not shoving every dish down our mouths." Ayesha put down the dish and smiled.

"I'm thinking, you know, that we should catch the cinema some time." Rafi continued. Who used lines like that these days? I swallowed awkwardly and gasped as a chunk of chicken lodged itself in my throat. Waving my hands, I started to choke and hacked away to dislodge the lump. Ayesha jumped up, and poured me a glass of water before patting my back.

"Bachoa! Bachoa!" Amidst the chaos, I heard Rafi's melodramatic cry for help, and coughed out in laughter. The chicken flew out of my mouth and landed with a pathetic thump on the table. Everyone stared at the piece of chicken in silence. "Take some water! For the sake of our marriage, drink some water!" I looked to Rafi as fits of laughter overtook me until I gasped for breath.

"Maya, are you ok?" Amma asked with that look of warning all mothers shot at their erring child.

"I'm fine, I'm fine!" I rasped, wiping the tears from my eyes. "I'm sorry, excuse me." Clearing my throat, I looked at the concerned Rafi and smiled.

"You shouldn't eat so much. Your parents must spoil you. Don't worry, we'll change these bad habits." Rafi was still under the impression that we were going to get married.

"You must be careful." Rafi's heavyset mother added between large mouthfuls of chicken jaalfreezi. "If you must shove food into your mouth at once, you must chew everything before swallowing." In two sentences she had swallowed five times and I looked at Ayesha who stifled a laugh.

"I should do as you do and not as you say?" Ayesha's smile dropped at my words and she shook her head to stop me. "Or should I do as you say and not as you do?" I asked Rafi's mother whose look of confusion was quickly replaced with one of outrage.

"Maya, is your throat ok, bhethi?" Baba intervened. There was no room for amusement at the table, and I nodded as Rafi's mother huffed and puffed at my audacity. "Why don't you go upstairs, and I'll get Sulaiman to bring you up some ice cream and coffee." Before I could refuse and make amends, Amma encouraged my departure and left me with no option but to do as I was told. I made my excuses to Rafi, who now refused to look at me. With a regretful smile, I took the stairs and made my way back to my overlooking table.

That evening, I was summoned down in my pyjamas with a ready apology that my family expected. My father rarely summoned us, but when he did it was worrying. I hesitated by the family room and then walked on towards the kitchen.

"Maya, we're waiting for you." Amma's super sonic hearing picked up on my light footsteps. I found Baba in his armchair, surrounded by the rest of the family so I found my place on the floor by Ayesha. "We thought that went well." Amma began and I frowned at her expectant tone. Had my parents reached the pits of groom-searching hell that they were considering clueless Rafi? "His parents were nice, his sister, well she has a big heart." Yes they were, they actually were.

"And a big mouth to go with it." I regretted my comment as soon as I felt the force of Amma's glare. I didn't want to disappoint my parents because I cherished them. And I, of all people, knew how difficult it was to find a suitable man for someone of my age. Yet, I couldn't relent to their pressure to accept Rafi.

"Maya, what did you think?" Ayesha asked to ease the oppressive silence. "If you like him, then we can prepare for another meeting..."

"He's not quite my type. And I don't believe I'm quite his type..."

"Of course you are!" Amma insisted as if the alternative was unimaginable.

"I tried to speak with him and all he did was tell me how he'd change me..."

"He was nervous..."

"I didn't like the way he looked..."

"You never do," Amma cut in angrily. "You always judge people unfairly. Do you even consider that they may do that to you?"

"I should hope so, but I didn't sit there and insult his habits..."

"Only his mother's," Baba pointed out. "Finding a boy from a good family is not getting easier Maya." I heard his concern and wanted to cry, but I didn't.

"Do you know how hard it is to find a good family? People snap these boys up for their daughters!" Amma cut in. "And you, you dismiss them for others to snap up!"

"Then I wish them all the luck." The words escaped before I could recall them.

"You are twenty-eight years old Maya. Nobody looks for a twenty-eight year old bride, so don't sit there holding cards on yourself..."

"I'm going to bed," I announced, ending the discussion.

"You can't hide from reality," Amma said, stopping me from leaving. "So you go to bed. Just remember that tomorrow morning you're going to wake up to your on-going single status." I slammed out of the room and stormed up to my bedroom. I refused to let anyone see me cry, so I fell onto my bed and buried my face in my pillow.

"Maya?" I cleared my throat and wiped away my tears before turning to find Tariq stepping into my room. He had returned from his restaurant early to discuss how the alaap went. "Are you ok?" I nodded at my oldest brother, but fresh tears stung my eyes. "They just want to see you happy." And with that I burst out crying. Tariq came forward to sit beside me as I covered my face with my hands and shook with the depth of my sadness.

"I'm sorry, I just, I just don't know what to do," I cried as Tariq pulled my hands away and tipped my face up. "I can't just say yes, I want to. I want to make everyone happy, to just get married, but I haven't seen anyone I've fancied." Tariq didn't say anything. He simply pulled me forward into a warm hug. "I know I have to get married. I want to get married because no one knows how hard it is to be single. To have it rubbed in your face at every event and outing. Everyone thinks I'm being difficult or that I'm being fussy, but I have to smile through it all. I have to ignore the gossip and pretend not to hear the whispers." As I ranted on, Tariq rubbed my back until I quietened down and leaned against him. Then he pulled back and cupped my face.

"You need to be stronger than this Maya." More tears blurred my vision, but Tariq refused to let me look away. "You have choice, which is more than I had. You have me and your sisters to help you, and that's more than Ayesha or I had. And believe it or not, you have Baba and Amma trying their hardest to find their baby a good match..."

"Well maybe they shouldn't give me a choice, maybe they should just arrange my marriage without my input..."

"Pagul!" Tariq laughed, sat back against the bed head and stretched out beside me. "I married Shireen after seeing her once at the age of seventeen just after I started at Baba's restaurant. We went back to Bangladesh and I knew they had a girl from a good family lined up for me. I didn't know any different, so I accepted Shireen." Tariq never spoke of his choices in life, so I watched him. His dark brown eyes stared into the past, and I couldn't tell whether he wanted another life.

"Would you have it any other way?" Tariq looked to me and the haunted look disappeared. "Would you change anything now?"

"Baba needed help at the takeaway, so I helped. Nani said Shireen would make for a good match, so I trusted her judgement..."

"But that's not what I'm asking bhai." Tariq grinned and the corners of his eyes creased with amusement.

"I know what you're asking Maya. I don't regret helping Baba at such a young age, because we saved his takeaway. We then went on to buy our restaurant in Paddington, and he got to retire early. I don't regret marrying Shireen. She's a good wife and a good mother to my beautiful children..."

"But would you change any of it?" I persisted, and Tariq looked away.

"I did the best I could with what I had." Then he looked at me. "The thing is, I wonder if you are?" I was surprised by his question and he faced me to elaborate. "You gave up your dreams of becoming a painter when you accepted a position with Chambers Scott Wilfred and you did that to help us buy this house and move out of Mile End ..."

"Bhai, we bought this dilapidated semi together, and turned it around. I don't regret that."

"But you don't have to do that anymore. Taj and I can cover the mortgage, you can start painting again. You were always so excited, always going to new exhibitions, starting on new ideas and following artists that you loved..."

"Giving up my professional career to become a poor painter will not get me married!" I teased as Tariq watched me.

"Maybe, if you used painting as an outlet, you wouldn't get so sad about the problems we're having finding you a husband."

"You'll end up with a portrait collection of all the men we rejected!" But Tariq didn't smile.

"Maybe you wouldn't expect so much of the men we introduced you to..."

"That's not fair bhai." I sat up and looked at Tariq, but he was serious. "You've seen the guys I've been introduced to..."

"And I've seen you judge them harshly for superficial reasons. By your standards, I'd never even get past the selection criteria because I don't have a city-savvy profession or grand vocation. But there are guys like me with humble average jobs. They may not be highly educated or drop dead gorgeous, but they're decent, hard-working and responsible. They deserve more respect and consideration than you give them." He was right, but I still wanted the whole package.

"I've given up painting bhai, I've stopped entering stupid competitions that I never hear back from, and I don't want to go back to it." Tariq looked at me for a while. I was being stubborn, but I had a right to be. Surely he could understand that.

"Nani said that people weren't created to fulfil your dreams, she said that they were created to help you achieve them." I was eight years old the last time I saw my grandmother in Bangladesh. She was a tiny woman, traditional and hardworking, and I remembered that she had the wisest, widest brown eyes that always saw too much.

"I just want to get married." I was tired and felt the whole world failed to understand me.

"If that's all you want, why haven't you accepted any of the alaaps? Take Abu Ahmed for instance. Besides getting spoon fed, there wasn't really anything significantly wrong with him…"

"Because his family were, were uh…" I struggled to find the right words to describe them without appearing too judgemental.

"Traditional. But he had the career, the status, even an exclusive lifestyle you would've enjoyed. Why didn't you marry him?"

"His brother's in prison, that's a disreputable family…"

"You're making excuses. We all know Taj is hardly a saint, but I wouldn't tolerate anyone slandering our family name. Why didn't you seriously consider Abu Ahmed?" I stared at Tariq and struggled to find a sensible answer. All I knew was that he wasn't the one. "Maya, your problem is that you're looking for a man to make your dreams come true…"

"Surely that's what falling in love and getting married is all about?" He chuckled and looked at me as if I were a naive young girl.

"And that's it? With all the skills, freedoms and talents you have, that's all you want from life?" He made my dream sound silly, but I nodded. He shook his head and sat up.

"And a nice house, and kids of course, but no more than three. I want financial security, but doesn't everyone? I guess a nice car and a couple of holidays a year wouldn't go down badly…"

"You sound like an airhead." I looked at my brother, affronted, and he laughed. "Marriage isn't a dream Maya. For you, it's a right of passage…"

"I want kinship and companionship bhai, I just want what you all have with your partners." I wanted Tariq to understand that I wasn't a vacuous bimbo holding onto Bollywood dreams. "That's not too much to ask, is it?"

"But Maya, you only get kinship and companionship through shared thoughts, experiences and dreams." We were looking at marriage from two opposite perspectives with little chance of coming to a common resolution. He reached out, tipped my chin up and smiled at me. "Have dreams Maya, otherwise you won't recognise the man who'll help you achieve them." Tariq ruffled my hair and kissed my forehead as he always did. I watched him leave and close the door behind him. I didn't want to think about Tariq's wise words, I didn't want to think about my untouched paintings and pastels that stood stacked up in the garage and I didn't want to think about getting married anymore. I turned off the light, got into bed, and wrapped myself up with the warm duvet. I stared at the dark ceiling, tired and at odds with myself. This getting married business was much more complicated that I had ever imagined it to be.

"Leila and Mina are both younger than you, and your cousins are both going to this party." Amma was on a mission to get me married and nothing was going to get in her way. And when things became tough between us she used family comparisons to drill her point home. If it wasn't comparisons about my single status, or my job, it was always about what my cousins did that I didn't do. "Do you want people talking about how they got married before you because you refused to go to parties?"

"This is a baby's akika party!" But that made no impression on Amma.

"And there'll be mothers with single brothers and proud fathers with single friends there."

"Every single one of them we know, and they know us..."

"So you have another opportunity to impress them." She had lost all her senses.

"Amma, they're going to circumcise the baby. How on earth am I going to impress people at a circumcision party?"

"That's it, get all defensive Maya, but that won't help you get married!" Amma disregarded my question as she did my emotions. And then the comparisons started up again. "Sama is celebrating her son's first birthday and his circumcision today. She's the same age as you and she has three children! Do you realise how far behind you are?"

"Not until you point it out..."

"Don't talk back! You're the oldest single girl in the community. Ayesha was never this picky. Lord knows I didn't have to worry about the twins finding themselves a husband. But you, what do you think the community's saying about you?"

"I'm sure you're going to remind me..."

"Leila's now getting most of your alaaps, her mother tells me that she'll be engaged by summertime and she's eighteen months younger than you," Amma listed before putting her hands on her hips.

"That's great for Leila..."

"No, it isn't!" Amma cried out in frustration. "She got better grades then you at GCSEs, then outdid you in your A-levels, and then did a biomedical degree like your sisters, while you decided to paint squares and circles. Thank God I have your sisters." My mother paused to look into her palms to thank God before looking back at me.

"But she will not out do you when it comes to weddings. No, I've made a pact with God that you'll have a bigger, better wedding before her so that at her wedding, they'll say 'Maya's wedding was better and bigger!'" Mercifully the phone rang and brought my mother's dramatic vow to a premature end. She picked up the receiver in my room and looked at me.

"Walikum asalaam bheta, how are you?" That was Jhanghir. My mother always spoke fluent Bengali with a patronising tone when Jhanghir called. I grinned at the thought of speaking to my friend and waited impatiently for Amma to pass the phone to me. "And your parents?" She had never forgiven him for not marrying me because of our different cultural backgrounds. And that's why she handed me the phone and said pointedly: "You have five minutes and then I want you dressed and ready to go."

"That's some order!" I chuckled at Jhanghir's comment and watched Amma rifle through my wardrobe to select an appropriate shalwaar kameez for a pre-circumcision party.

"You know your charm doesn't work on Amma!" I grinned at the sound of his laugh. Amma snorted in derision, intent on getting me off the phone. I mouthed five minutes to her and walked out of my room.

"I've always loved her for it!" And I laughed in return before making my way downstairs. "Preeya's in New York for the weekend, I'm taking her out to dinner tonight." Preeya is Jhanghir's long-standing fiancé, a San Francisco based software programmer by day and a model daughter-in-law to be by night.

"That's nice, where are you going?" I found Hamza watching Saturday morning TV in the living room, so wandered through to the dining room where Baba read the paper. Shireen-bhabhi chopped away at vegetables in the kitchen so I stepped out into our small garden, passed Amma's herbs and vegetable patch and headed for the garage.

"Meixcana, it's a noisy joint midtown. She likes tacos and…"

"How are you getting on at the hospital?" I knew stick thin Preeya was not a fan of food at all.

"I've got clinical responsibilities, residents to manage, rounds to do, conferences to attend and host, and I'm drowning!" I frowned at the amount of work Jhanghir carried and wished that there was some way I could help him. "Maya, I'm struggling to coordinate the extension of the Childhood Diseases research program as well as prepare case presentations whilst doing my rotations."

"Isn't there a way you can delegate some of your work to the junior medics?"

"I'm fifteen months away from getting this fellowship," he breathed. "The hospital's part funding my research and I can't compromise that now…"

"You sound like you're putting yourself under too much pressure." I looked to where my paintings and pastels were stacked up against the wall, and envied Jhanghir's dedication. "You're a fantastic paediatrician Jhanghir, and the hospital's funded you because you will be a specialist consultant. Hospitals strapped for cash don't just invest in flaky research programs or sub-standard medics. But if you find that too tiring, you can always come over here and join my sisters' general practice!"

"I may just check out their practice when I'm over for Professor Gardiner's seminars in the summer…"

"You're coming over?" I cut in, delighted by the thought. "Have you got firm dates? How long will you be here? Where will you be staying? You have to warn me when so that Bitch Brenda doesn't send me out on a consultancy project in Europe."

"It'll be good to see you too Maya." I smiled at his words but refused to comment. He laughed, and I twirled with excitement before pulling off the sheet covering my work. "What's the latest with you? And, hey, how's your friend Sakina doing?" I updated him on Sakina and her broken heart and listened to his advice about giving her time and space to recover. I even told Jhanghir about Abu Ahmed, Bilal the barrister and Rafi, and laughed as he teased me about my single status. And as we talked, I looked through my collection of drawings, paintings and pastels. Some pieces were unfinished, some lacked imagination in their use of colour, but a Rothko inspired piece, an experiment with Arabic calligraphy and a couple of life drawings caught my attention. They weren't bad at all.

"Jhanghir, did you think I was a good artist?" Jhanghir was surprised at the sudden change of conversation, but Tariq's words haunted me. "I mean, I knew I was never going to be a great painter, or even a commercially successful one, but I produced some pieces that..."

"...were remarkable." Jhanghir finished. "Remember I stole that sketch you did of me asleep in Regents Park. That was you doodling and it was good. In fact, it was more than good." I smiled at Jhanghir's words and looked down again at the canvasses. I wanted to experiment again with colours, styles, and images. "Preeya's got that picture." The mention of his fiancée made me pause and then I pushed the pieces back against the wall.

"What's going on with the two of you?" I didn't want to know, but he raised the issue and I had to ask.

"That's why she's flown in from San Francisco. There's no reason to put off getting married."

"No reason at all," I accepted, and pulled the sheet over the pieces. Who cared about paintings when I was still single? Things changed, people moved on. I wanted to be thrilled for Jhanghir, but I wasn't. The silence between us was ripped apart by his door chime.

"She's here Maya, I gotta run." I closed my eyes and felt at odds with his eagerness.

"Jhanghir!" I called out before he could hang up.

"Yeah?" I wanted to wish him luck and congratulate him like a genuine friend would.

"Promise to keep me posted about your wedding developments?"

"Yeah." The reluctant admission came just before he called off. The thought of Jhanghir's relationship propelled me into making an effort to find my man. I closed the garage behind me, walked back into the house and up to my room. Amma had laid out a shalwaar kameez on my bed and I smiled at her selection. No more judgemental attitudes and no more premature dismissals of good alaaps. I put on my long white tunic with the bunched chooridar shalwaar, pulled my hair back into a bun and applied bronzer to turn myself into a sun kissed goddess. Or at least I tried to without the skills of Hana and Jana. Only Amma didn't tell me it was a smart casual event for adults. So, there I stood dressed in white chiffon and gold, amongst my jean and sweater clad peers. Bad choice for a circumcision party, bad choice given the garden was filled with mucky, screaming kids. Bad choice as everyone smiled in understanding of what a SLAAG has to endure.

D: Dread Dashing Doctors And Other Disasters

Asian parents rear their children to become doctors. In short, it's the silent but universal passport to community respect, and a fixation I've never understood. Lord knows I'm a tortured soul as I never followed my brilliant sisters into the overrated profession. Ayesha and Jana were GP's, and Hana a dentist. Baba dreamt I would join their leagues so that he could manage the first Bengali female clinic in London, but after I failed my maths GCSE and achieved an E in double science, Baba tragically accepted that I wasn't 'doctor' material. He went into mourning and lost his appetite for two weeks. Only when Ayesha convinced him that I could still marry a doctor, did he start eating again.

Ten years on and, true to her words, Ayesha delivered an alaap from 31-year-old Shah Akbar, Brain Surgeon in training from Gants Hill, London. In fairness, he appeared to be focused, directed, and exactly what I was looking for. His bio data showed us that he had two sisters, both educated and married, and one brother for whom they suspiciously failed to provide any details. Despite promises from Amma and Baba that there were no expectations about this alaap, Amma hadn't stopped praying for Allah to bless this union. In fact, she hadn't even told her friends in case they jinxed the proposal. So it was no surprise that I returned from work to find the laminated floor in the hall covered in ASDA shopping bags.
"Baba!" The excited chatter behind the closed kitchen door stopped. There was little doubt that they had already married me off to Shah.
"What's wrong?" Baba asked, stepping between the bags into the hall. He had shopped to feed the world's starving, and he stood there asking me what was wrong?
"Who's coming for dinner?"
"The Doctor and his family are coming tomorrow evening. We thought we should buy a few things in preparation..."
"A few things?" Baba nodded as if the sea of shopping extending from the entrance all the way down to the kitchen passed for a 'few things'.
"Why don't you get changed and then help us put away the shopping..."
"How many people are coming...?"
"Oh, Maya, do as your father says. We'll manage the rest." Amma was wearing more gold than usual and was grinning from ear to ear.
"Amma, you promised me that we would keep this simple. That we wouldn't have any expectations until we met his family for tea..."
"That's exactly what we're going to do." She was using that placating tone, the one where she pretended to listen to you in spite of the fact that she'd already decided when and where the wedding would be.
"But, you've shopped to feed half of Bangladesh!" I pointed out.

"Maya, would you stop over reacting!" How bloody ironic. One introduction, one boy, two hundred pounds worth of shopping and she says I'm overreacting.

"You've cleared out ASDA for one alaap…"

"Well, we don't want to appear to be tight-fisted."

"How many exactly?" Amma stopped grinning and looked to my father for support. I looked to Baba who opted to take the shopping into the kitchen. This was serious.

"Just the doctor, his sister and their parents." I looked at the shopping, confused, before looking back at my parents.

"You've done all this shopping for four people?" My family had made their minds up.

"Well, you've been emailing each other so much and the signs are so positive that we want to be able to impress them…"

"I sent him two emails, one that confirmed I was me, and the second telling him I'd talk to him when we met!" My outburst made no impression on Amma.

"Why don't you go upstairs and relax?" Aarrggh, do all mothers have this in-built ability to make you want to implode? "I know this is hard and you're tense, as you should be…" I didn't wait for her to finish but stomped up the stairs to shut out my world behind me.

"Bellevue Paeds department, how can I help?" Sakina and Tanya were stuck on the tube, and I needed to vent.

"Dr Khan please." So I called Jhanghir who was five hours into his A&E duty in New York.

"Who's calling?" Oh please, I was in the middle of a life crisis and she wanted verification.

"This is Dr. Malik from Wembley Hospital in London, England. I have some test results for a patient of his." It always worked and I listened to the bleeping tone as she transferred me.

"Hello Maya." Just hearing his dry amused voice made me smile. God, I wished he hadn't left. "I have three minutes, so whatever crisis support you need, talk fast and be coherent." There it was, that bloody patronising Doctor Syndrome, trivialising every real life crisis.

"Life crises are incoherent by nature, Jhanghir."

"Spill!" He wasn't buying and I missed him even more.

"My parents have found me this brain surgeon…"

"A brain surgeon no less! You sure you can handle him…"

"That's real funny Jhanghir! Listen, he's turning up tomorrow night with his entire kandan and everyone's already decided that I'm marrying him. But he could be squinted, goofy toothed, and dog ugly for all I know!"

"And then again, he may not be." Had everybody turned against me? Did no one understand my dilemma?

"But how can I make a rational decision with all this pressure? I mean so what if he's a doctor? A surgeon even! Just because I'm 28, it doesn't mean I'm going to accept a look good on paper doctor ..."

"Are you just scared that you might have to make a serious decision?" Jhanghir knew me better than most and at that moment I wish he didn't. It felt wrong for him to be telling me to consider other men. "Don't tell me that you've just realised you're commitment phobic!"

"You think I should consider this seriously?" I listened to him laugh and my stomach churned at the thought of doing so.

"Maya, you're hitting 30..."

"But I've still to find myself, what I want out of life, who I want to be..."

"Well, if you don't know who you are now, you need to be getting married to a brain surgeon! Maya, what are you waiting for?" He was using that tone where I couldn't tell if he was talking about us or me in specific. I wondered what he would do if I told him that I wanted to be with him. He would laugh and tease me until I would hang up on him. "Maya?"

"George Clooney..." I replied.

"For Christ's sake, Maya!" Of course, it would be far too stupid to complicate things between us now. "Listen, you may meet the man of your dreams tomorrow night. You just have to give the guy a chance and trust yourself." I had called Jhanghir to vent, to get his wisdom and to calm down enough to give this alaap a fair chance. "Promise me that you'll give it a go?"

"I promise." Now that I had spoken to him, I felt more uneasy about the alaap.

"Good, listen I gotta run. You keep me posted on how it goes." He called off before I could ask him how he was doing. But that was Jhanghir, around long enough to make me feel better. Only this time it was different.

My parents spent hours in the kitchen cooking up a culinary delight. First would come the samosas, spring rolls and spicy potato wedges served with cool, freshly squeezed Mango lassi. Then kheer, flavoured with ground coconut followed with Indian sweets, rasagullahs, gulapjaman and barfis. Cardamom infused Indian tea would wrap up the alaap. And just in case we got on well, my parents had cooked lamb pillou, kebabs, chicken jalfrezi, dhal and fried vegetables for dinner and brought out the best china from the showcase. This was my family's way of keeping the process 'simple'. They had even banned everyone from the house besides Ayesha, Samir-bhai and Tariq, my oldest brother. Even Jana and Hana had been kept away. And whilst my parents did this to keep the pressure off me, I couldn't help but feel that such strong measures only enforced how serious this alaap was. In fact, I had gotten into work extra early so I could leave early, but that only exposed me to the heightened excitement of my happier than usual mother. By the time Ayesha led me into the living room, I was actually trembling from a heady mixture of fear, pressure, and anticipation. Here he was, every SLAAG's dream, a bloody brain surgeon no less. He was a good five feet eleven inches with a sturdy square build. But the first thing I noticed was Shah's receding hairline. I didn't mean to, but it happened. I was predisposed to picking faults as I resented the fact that he had my future in his hands simply because he was a brain surgeon.

"How embarrassing is this?" Shah asked, his sparkling eyes framed by cow lashes that any girl would readily kill for. But despite his easy nature, I couldn't relax.

"It needs to be done." Surely that haughty snooty catty reply hadn't from me? It had.

"Yes, I suppose it does," Shah muttered shifting in his seat. "I don't think I'll get used to these introductions so it's good to meet someone who's not daunted by them."

"Oh, I hate these introductions too. I don't know what could be worse than choosing your life partner after one conversation."

"So decisiveness isn't one of your strong qualities?" I laughed nervously at his quip. I listened as Shah told me all about his decision to specialise, but I couldn't get engaged enough to ask him a single question. He was trying hard to ease the tension but I couldn't shake the feeling that my life would be stolen away in a flurry of engagements, nikkas and marriage if I indicated the slightest interest towards this nice man. Lord knows I wanted to get married as soon as possible, but not like this. Not resenting this participation in my life, not dreading having to make a decision, not accepting him simply because he was a brain surgeon. And then I had one thought, one that I couldn't shake.

'He'll be bald by the age of thirty-five'. I appalled myself.

"So what it is that you do exactly?" I felt like a deer caught in headlights, thinking horrible pathetic thoughts that I couldn't shake.

"She's a consultant in the fashion industry," Ayesha replied, as she brought in the kheer and Indian sweets. Samir-bhai walked in close behind her and I caught his look of concern as he sat down beside me.

"I don't really know what that means... uh, do you get to go the fashion shows?" He was humble and genuinely interested.

"No, we handle most of the intelligence that directs market strategies, season assessment, cycle throughputs and couture ratings." I personally did a fraction of that stuff, but I was damned if I was going to tell him I assessed the fashion market using boring Excel spreadsheets, made tolerable only by occasional trips abroad to interview the key decision makers in fashion.

"That sounds important." He laughed it off, but I had the distinct feeling he was close to giving up on me.

"She's the black sheep of the family!" Samir teased covering for my cold attitude. "She turned her back on medicine when all her sisters excelled at it!"

"Sounds like she made the right choice, and is doing something far more glamorous and interesting." Shah was actually complimenting me and I smiled. Maybe I had been too hard on him, maybe I hadn't really given this man a proper chance, and now he was checking his watch. God, maybe I had blown this and he was wondering how long the ordeal would go on!

"Oh, its not that glamorous at all!" I laughed, but it sounded forced in the silence that followed. "Uh, so uh, what do you do... in your spare time?" I finished, ignoring Ayesha's slight frown and pensive look to Samir-bhai.

"I don't get that much time off to be honest, and when I do, I guess I help out my parents." Good answer. He sounded responsible and mature without being pretentious.

"And why now?" He looked confused and I cleared my throat before clarifying myself. "Why do you want to settle down now?" Everyone looked stunned by the question that I thought was perfectly reasonable to ask. Shah grinned and shook his head.

"It's the right time." He didn't sound convinced by his answer. "I guess my parents think it's the right thing for me to do." He paused and looked at me as he chuckled. "You know, I've not asked myself that question, I guess it's the right thing to do."

"I understand." I smiled and so did he. We were both doing this for our parents and for a moment we had a connection.

"And you?" Neither of us stopped smiling. Maybe there was something here.

"Besides hitting twenty-eight and having a mother who's close to having a nervous breakdown..."

"She's not really," Ayesha corrected, frowning at my comment, but Shah was looking at me and grinning.

"The same reason really, it's the right thing to do." And so, here we were. Two adults making our families happy and it seemed to be the first time that we both seemed to be enjoying it.

"Maya, why don't we go into the dining room?" NO! I needed more time with Shah. I looked to Ayesha, and gave her a wide smile to indicate she should stop. Shah and Samir-bhai misread the action and chuckled in understanding, but I wanted to melt with humiliation. "Don't be worried, we all have to go through this." Thirty years of growing up with this woman and she had yet to master my silent instructions. Shame on her.

"It's been a pleasure to meet you." Shah stood up as I rose to leave. He was a gentleman! A brain surgeon gentleman! He was articulate, polite and had the nicest eyes ever. I gave him my flashiest smile and felt stupid when he frowned at my enthusiasm. "Good Luck," he added as I left. I didn't know whether that was 'good luck' as in power to you for meeting the parents, or 'good luck' as in finding a decent husband. My smile disappeared.

Either way, it didn't matter because I was determined to bowl his parents over. At least I was, until I met his father. He had come dressed in a Punjabi suit, wore the traditional topee, had a long greying beard and red beetle nut stained teeth. He hadn't said a word, and I knew he was the type to run his house with prison-like authority. And any woman who married his oldest son would have to answer to him for as long as he was around. In short Mr Akbar, Shah's father, was a bastard. A hard nosed, ignorant, bastard with a mean glint in his eyes.

"Your mother tells me you work very hard." In contrast, Shah's mother was an absolute angel. Her serene face was surrounded by a cream headscarf, which made her look almost angelic and I warmed to her immediately.

"It's not too bad. Everyone has to work hard in this country to live well." She smiled at my observation, but Mr. Akbar's chuckle grated on my nerves.

"How much do you earn?" he asked, killing all comfortable banter in the room. I looked to Baba, who looked to Tariq who looked to Ayesha for help.

"She earns enough to live comfortably," Amma answered with a sparkling laugh as she brought through the tea and biscuits. "She's prudent with her income and isn't frivolous in the slightest." Mothers always came up trumps and this was my mother's way of telling him that I controlled my earnings and it would stay that way.

"Our family has an integrated approach to controlling bills, finances and payments," Mr Akbar informed us with a cold smile.

"So do we," Tariq stated without hesitation. He had dropped out of school to help Baba with his restaurant. I knew at times he regretted that decision, especially with our brood of doctors, but Tariq would never let anyone speak against our family. "And, we also respect our women's right to control their own finances as directed by our sunnah." Gold. He might be least educated amongst us, but my brother knew more about controlling situations than all of us put together. Mr Akbar didn't push the conversation any further, but he wasn't happy. Instead, he turned the conversation to religion, how adherent we were, and more specifically how adherent I was.

"Do you pray five times a day?" he demanded.

"Often," Amma said, but the truth was rarely.

"Do you fast during Ramadan?"

"Every one she can," Amma added, which was true because it helped me to diet.

"Do you plan on doing Hajj or umrah…"

"Ah! Maya's father and I went two years ago for the second time. What an experience!" Amma replied, distracting Mr Akbar with her own experience. The reality was that the Muslim holy pilgrimage scared me to death as Hajj represented the sacrifice of all things worldly. Small white lies go out of the window, Q-News replaces Celebzine, and catching up on missed prayers is replaced with regular punctual prayers. Don't get me wrong, I loved my faith, and knowing that Allah has my back in every situation was the securest feeling in the world. I just wasn't ready to stop appreciating George Clooney, Thierry Henry or Nicolas Anelka yet.

"So what do you think?" Ayesha nudged me as she waited for an answer. The evening had ended with high expectation. We were both standing in the upstairs hall peeking over the banister to watch both fathers shake hands and agree to meet up again, while our mothers hugged and laughed happily. Shah shook hands with my brother and grinned at our parents' antics.

"I'm scared that if I say anything positive, Amma will start planning the wedding."

"Did you like him? You know, he wasn't that bad and he seemed to be the type of guy who could handle most situations."

"I liked everything about him," I replied. And that was the truth. I liked the fact that he was going to be a brain surgeon, it told me that he was ambitious, focused and driven to be successful. I liked the fact that, as his wife, I could introduce him as my brain surgeon husband and get a kick out of the instant respect that would afford me.

"You didn't fall for him?"

"I'm saving that for when he puts his scrubs and gloves on!" Ayesha chuckled at this, but I knew that was exactly it. I didn't fall in love with him. I just got to the point where I would like to see him again. I didn't know how arranged marriages happened. How women knew when they'd met 'the one' or knew that like would turn into life long love and loyalty. I felt no instant karma with Shah that left us staring at each other like in the Indian films. Nor was there powerful chemistry to make us jump each other as they do in Hollywood films. There was just that feeling that he'd be a great person to grab another cappuccino with at Café Nero's.

"Do you want to face the family?" Ayesha asked as Baba closed the door to lead everyone into the living room.

"I'm scared Amma will call everyone in Bangladesh to announce a wedding if I said I'd like to see him again." Ayesha smiled in understanding. Whilst Jana and Hana had met and married their university sweethearts, Ayesha married the first man she had been introduced to. Samir-bhai was a GP from an educated family and after one meeting, Baba had asked for a simple yes or no. When poor Ayesha agreed, because she was expected to, despite her reservations, she was married within a matter of weeks.

"He's a good prospect, Maya. I like him, and if you promise not to pick trivial faults in him, I'll cover for you," she offered with a grin.

"I promise." I sat at the top of the stairs as Ayesha went down into the living room. She left the door open, so I could hear everyone's opinion. Amma loved the brain surgeon and threatened to kill me if I declined this offer. Samir-bhai admired his calm and mature disposition, as did

Tariq. Ayesha took comfort that the mother was kind and gentle which would be of benefit to any new bride. But Baba was noticeably quiet. He agreed with most of the opinions, but refrained from speaking. This is why I think Baba's the best of men. He rarely spoke badly of anyone, until his suspicions were confirmed. And his concerns, serious enough to curb his enthusiasm, made everyone else pause.

"What does Maya think?" I could tell Ayesha was taken by surprise at his direct question.

"She needs another meeting to decide." Since I had never asked for a second meeting, Amma started clapping in delight. Baba put a stop to her celebrations.

"I want to discover more about the family..."

"But we know what there is to know. The boy's father was open about his problems back in Bangladesh, and let's face it, who doesn't have problems back home?" Amma cut in.

"If this turns into a serious prospect, as I suspect it might, then I want to know everything about the family my daughter will be joining," Baba repeated.

"Of course you do, but you make it sound like a threat and not an invitation..."

"Consider it to be both," Baba said in a tone that invited no further questioning. "We'll wait for them to come forward and then we'll reconsider our options."

Now it's customary for feedback to be provided within a couple of days of an introduction. As nobody liked to be eager, very few families responded instantly or the following day as it reduced their bartering power when it came to setting the dowry. Since expectations were riding high on this alaap, Baba, who was now retired, manned the phone on the second day, but the Akbar family didn't call. He read the *Surma Bengali* newspaper, watched the lunchtime news and then prayed. He then rang each one of us in turn to make sure we were all fine. Furious with expected rejection, Baba took to weeding the garden with the trusted cordless in his pocket.

Ayesha called me at work just before I shut down my computer.

"I've just spoken with Baba and he's furious. Do you want to come round to mine tonight?"

"I don't know who's worse, Baba or Tariq. At least Baba's vents his anger. Tariq keeps bringing me home leaflets about art competitions and exhibitions to distract me from Shah's rejection..."

"They haven't rejected us," Ayesha corrected. "Tariq's being overprotective and means well, but he hates the thought of you getting hurt."

"I'm not a little girl, I can handle rejection." I opened up my diary and looked at the pamphlets Tariq had given me. There was information on the Sharjah Prize for Cultural Art, the Laura Ashley Fellowship Awards, the International SlowArt competition by New York's Limner Gallery, and the Khan-Ali Art Foundation Awards.

"I know, and still Baba rages because the Akbars haven't had the decency to call, even if it is to reject the alaap." I closed my diary and put all thought of the competitions aside. The humiliation was crushing. Here was one guy I was willing to see again and he didn't like me. How dare he?

"Maybe we should call and reject them?" The thought made me feel better even if it was self-defeating.

"Maybe Shah's been on call for the past forty-eight hours and he hasn't had time to talk with his parents," Ayesha suggested.

"How angry is Baba?" I looked to Clare who was in deep conversation with Bitch Brenda.

"We're talking rejecting his baby girl angry." I smiled warmed at Baba's protective nature.

"I think I'll go home and keep him company. I'll cheer him up by picking up his favourite apple tea brew from Whittard's."

"Oh, by the way, Jhanghir called." Just hearing his name made me grin. That's exactly what had happened when we first met. He had swaggered into the library as if he owned it, which made me grin at his cocky confident nature. I bet he was dying to know what had happened with Shah. Hah! I hope Amma told him I was going to get engaged to a *brain surgeon*. That would show him!

"Amma told him you said yes." The mischievous thought died. He would be furious that I hadn't called to tell him myself. But what could I say? How could I tell him that I'd been rejected when he had perfect, beautiful Preeya on his arm?

"What else did she say?"

"Uh, that you fell in love with the guy the minute you saw him…"

"No…"

"I'm kidding! She just said that it was very promising and he should book a week off in the summer to come to the wedding." Great. Fantastic. I had no groom, no wedding dress, and no hall booked, but my mother had told my best friend to book his holidays to come to my wedding. "Don't stress Maya, we'll have you married by the summer even if it isn't to Mr Brain Surgeon." That's what she thought.

"Everything ok Maya?" I peeked through my hands to find Clare watching me. The buxom brunette looked around to make sure Brenda wasn't around.

"She's gone," I confirmed. Clare walked across the office and pulled up Mark's chair. "And we're working late so she couldn't say anything even if she was here."

"Hey, thanks for covering for me this morning." I smiled as Clare sat down to face me. Clare was the jolliest person in the office, but her recent split with her partner of six years had left her tired and haunted looking. She needed to talk as much as I did. "I keep wondering what went wrong with us and I can't stop crying." I saved my work and gave Clare my full attention.

"You need to give yourself time Clare." She struggled to keep her tears at bay. "And you need to stop living it up and partying hard. You've got to deal with the break up, not pretend it didn't happen…"

"I hate being alone, Maya. I can't stand going home to an empty flat or going to sleep in an empty bed." Clare shook her head and her curls fell in disarray around her moon-like face. She looked up and I met her teary blue eyes. "You think I could get myself an arranged marriage?"

"Where do you think Internet dating evolved from? That's Indian. You have to tick all the things you like and instead of an auntie finding you a match, the computer does it for you!" We burst out laughing and I reached across to hug her.

"I could never marry anyone after three dates Maya, that's one leap of faith I can't make," Clare chuckled as she pulled back.

"You mean three official dates?" I grinned as Clare raised a brow and I nodded. "You can't believe we can get to our late twenties and still be blind to temptation?"

"But you don't ever end up living together? Your family would never accept it."

"I wouldn't ever accept it. I know it's not easy to hear Clare, but I believe women sell themselves short when they do that…"

"But I wanted my freedom too…"

"Why? Every other investment that you make is bound by contractual agreements, and yet you don't see fit to protect the most important relationship in your life. You've both made emotional investments in each other, why wouldn't you want to protect that?"

"Maya, we have different lifestyles. Marriage isn't the be-all and end-all for us…"

"It is for me." Clare laughed, and then stopped when she realised that I was serious.

"It can't be that bad." I raised a brow to defy her.

"I'm closer to thirty than my early twenties, prospective in-laws can't handle that. They want a young, impressionable innocent girl to mould into the family fold…"

"And you can't marry out of your culture?" Clare asked frowning.

"It's not that I can't, it's that I don't want to…"

"But what choice will you have if you're running out of time and options in your community?"

"Well, as of this Tuesday I have an option…"

"You've had another introduction, haven't you?" I nodded. "And it didn't go well?"

"No, for a change, it went right and I actually like this guy…" I stopped at Clare's shriek of delight. "He's a surgeon…" I continued.

"Oh my God, you get a man coming home to you in scrubs! Do you know what a turn on that can be?" Then she settled down with a worried frown. "Are you attracted to him?"

"Yes..."

"But how do you know? How can you tell if you've never... you know?" Clare asked raising a brow suggestively. I recalled the way Shah and I had come to a common understanding and smiled.

"To start off with, he's cute and charming, and if things ever get boring, I'll get him to wear his scrubs!"

"So what's the problem?" she asked. I stopped smiling.

"They haven't come back to us." Clare's surprise was genuine and she pulled her curly hair back from her face, lost for words.

"I don't understand. Didn't they visit your home because they were interested in you?"

"Maybe he didn't take to me in person ..."

"Oh come on Maya, what's there not to like about you?"

"That's the only explanation Clare. They came over, which means that they liked my family background and history. Since his family haven't contacted us again, it can only mean that he's told them not to pursue this." It was Clare's turn to reach out and hug me.

"You can't force love, Maya," she said as she sat back down.

"But Clare, this isn't about love. Not yet anyway. This is about compatibility, this is about finding someone with potential and being able to believe that together you can build a happy future. Love and attraction are bonuses." I stopped as Clare stood and walked over to her desk. I heard her open a few drawers before returning to her seat where she held out several jumbo size bars of chocolate. "It's been a while since I've seen that in a man," Clare snorted, and ripped open the wrapper.

"It's sod's law Maya. The minute you think you've found a good man, he finds a better woman." I took a giant bar of Dairy Milk and peeled back the wrapper. I felt personally slighted, and Clare's words rang true. In short, he thought I wasn't good enough for him.

"Without the scrubs Clare, he wasn't all that!" Even though she raised her bar in agreement, I knew I was deluding myself. I didn't like being overlooked or rejected. I looked at Clare, and though she looked like she was thoroughly enjoying her bar of chocolate, I knew she dreaded going home to an empty flat. More than anything else, I decided that I didn't like the thought of being lonely for much longer.

On Sunday, the fifth day after my introduction to lovely cow-lashed Shah, my father called the mediator who had given the alaap to Ayesha. Every member of my family was present. Jana and Hana sat on the floor by their husbands. Tariq sat with Samir-bhai and Ayesha, while bhabhi looked after the children in the garden. It was one of those situations where everyone felt awkward, but knew they had to be there to support me, the single unwanted rejected sister. I didn't want Baba to call, but he was on a mission to teach the mediator and the Akbars the protocols of alaap engagement. I sat beside Amma who was in mourning at the thought of her baby girl giving her heart away only to have it returned crushed into fine powder. She was trying hard to be strong for me, so that I didn't take the rejection too personally. Of course, I wanted to ask how dare they refuse me, how dare they turn me, a beautiful and intelligent woman, down, but in all honesty I felt relieved. And I didn't want to share that thought with anyone. This way, I had them all on my side, batting for my cause.

"Rahim-bhai, what's this family playing at, turning up at my doorstep, eating with my family and then disappearing without a word?" When Baba got started, it was hard for anyone to get a word in edge way. But then he went quiet. No doubt Uncle Rahim had explained to him the reasons for the Akbar's rejection of the alaap. I looked down sadly as I felt Jana and Hana shoot concerned looks at me and then at Amma and Ayesha. Inside, I wanted to hoot with delight at the relief of finding freedom from indecision, fear and ultimately compromise. But then, I couldn't believe it. My dad was laughing! It started off with a deep, rumbling, low laughter then turned into bellowing shouts of disbelief. We were all mystified. He ended the call, turned around and looked at me directly. I wondered if he had read my thoughts.

"I didn't do anything!" I retorted as Amma glared at me and Baba doubled over roaring with laughter.

"You nearly killed the Shah's father!"

"What?" Amma demanded of Baba.

"She gave him a heart attack with her talk of independence a...and..." But Baba couldn't finish as the laughter shook his body. Soon enough I couldn't help but join him. And before long, everyone was laughing with him.

"This... this will ruin her!" Amma declared rising in anger. "Who will want a girl who could kill her in-laws? She's tainted, she's ruined!" Poor Amma, she couldn't see the funny side and since she didn't have a single supporter in the room, she stormed out and left us roaring with laughter.

As it turned out, Mr. Akbar had a heart attack as soon as he left our humble home and stepped into his son's Toyota Corolla. I hadn't shocked him into it, but debts exceeding half a million pounds and the imminent loss of the family home had propelled Mr Akbar's admittance into the emergency unit. Whilst his father recovered, poor Shah worked every conceivable hour and sacrificed everything to keep his family above water. I was drawn by Shah's dignified demeanour, and more so now that I realised the burden he carried. But this alaap wasn't to be. Shah's family felt slighted that we hadn't enquired after Mr Akbar sooner, and my father blamed them for not informing us that he was ill in the first place. Needless to say, the alaap came to a swift end. But this time, I wasn't to blame. I blamed the pride in protocol.

E: Expect To Be Advertised In *Eastern UK Eye*'s Matrimonials

Imagine my suspicion when I entered my living room to find Ayesha, the twins and Amma in hysterics over the *Eastern UK Eye* newspaper.
"What's going on?" The simple question caused a flurry of activity that ended with Amma hiding the paper behind her. Jana had other ideas. She grabbed the paper from Amma and raced across to me.
"You're going to be famous," she told me with a wide white smile.
"What do you mean?"
"They're doing a..."
"We put you in *Eastern UK Eye*," explained Hana.
"*Eastern UK Eye*?" I asked, shaking my head. The ultimate humiliation was upon me. I looked from my mother to Ayesha, who in my eyes was the paragon of virtue and sensibility.
"Yeah, *Eastern UK Eye*, in the matrimonial section," Jana added as she opened up the paper to read from the relevant section. "'28 yr old Bengali Sylhethi Muslim female graduate, from good family, slim, pretty with cute bubbly personality. Seeks educated Muslim male with GSOH, with balanced East/West culture. Must be ambitious, caring, honest and hoping to marry'."
"Oh my God, I've reached the bottom." I mumbled, slumping onto the sofa. They were advertising me for a husband. Amma and my over concerned sisters had advertised me like a jilted bride's unused wedding dress in the unholy matrimonial section. Things were bad.
"You've advertised me like a non-refundable summer sale item."
"Oh, it's not that bad Maya..."
"It's not that bad? I've been reduced to a fifty-word advert! Cute bubbly personality? You've turned me into a twenty-eight year old Shirley Temple!" Amma didn't look too happy and I caught her slipping a letter behind her back, but not before I had seen the Channel 4 logo on the corner of the envelope. It dawned on me that my humiliation wasn't yet over.
"What does Channel 4 have to do with this?" I asked suspiciously. Even Jana and Hana had the grace to realise I wasn't amused. They all looked at each other, so I looked to Ayesha for an explanation. "Why has Channel 4 responded to my advert?"
"They uh, they're doing a documentary on Arranged Marriages, and they want to follow your progress for a husband..." Now I understood why the four banes of my life had been laughing hysterically. Amma handed me the letter. The documentary was called 'Arranged Marriages: Sleepless in Singledom'.
"And I've had no other response?"
"It's still early days..."
"Great! Bloody great! Not only am I a flipping discounted bride-to-be that nobody wants, but my humiliation is now going to be prime time viewing!" This couldn't have come at a worse time. I hated my career, I hated my uninspiring life and I hated my single status. Fearing an

imminent onslaught of Niagara Falls, I slammed out of the room and ran up to my bedroom. But I didn't make it to my bed in time before my tears began to fall.

Good school grades. Graduation followed by two years of employment. Engagement and then an all-out glitzy glamorous wedding with all the trimmings. That's the script for Bengali girls to follow. Somehow my scriptwriter forgot to bear in mind timelines for me. I want to be in love with a man who's right for me. Not because I'm surrounded by fifteen intimate family members watching my every expression. Not because I have a funkier fifty word description in the *Brides R Us* matrimonial section. And not because I'm twenty-eight and in the overlooked bargain bin of spinsters. Opening up *Eastern UK Eye*, I stared down at the matrimonial section with distaste. A niggling thought wouldn't go away. Was he in there? Was my man reaching out to me through an ad because, however embarrassing it was, this was communication, and maybe, just maybe, he was in here. I opened the paper at the relevant section and read through the ads.

'Smart intelligent good looking 28 yr old Bengali Prince searching for his princess. If you're out there, please stop hiding and walk down the aisle with me.'

'Bargain offer! Very fit male 30 yrs, great body, loves wining and dining. Guaranteed to make you smile. Write today for a limited only offer!'

'Divorced, separated, unhappy with present life? Need some fulfilment in this short life? Look no further, I'm very handsome and can make your dreams come true. Don't delay and waste another day. Write straight away!'

The deluded, the unwanted and the downright hopeless made permanent singledom tempting. Putting the paper away, I turned on my bed and stared at the ceiling. I wanted to call Jhanghir but I couldn't. I hadn't told him about the disaster with Shah, and I certainly didn't plan on telling him about my recent humiliation with the *Eastern UK Eye* matrimonials. I was a sad spinster and I couldn't stand the thought of him thinking that of me.

Three days later, I stood outside Bond Street station waiting for IT technician Motin to turn up. Motin was the first and indeed, the only, respondent to my ad. As such, Ayesha jumped at his interest to arrange an introduction. Only, it took several rounds of emails and many more telephone calls to convince Motin to travel into central London for dinner.

"I'm here." That was Motin's text message. Given I'd never met or seen Motin before, his message was as useful as a chocolate teapot.

Looking around the entrance to Bond Street station, it was impossible to determine which of the waiting Asian men he was.

"So am I," I texted back with a small smile, and before I could count to ten, he called.

"Are you waiting outside Dorothy Perkins in the tight black jacket?" Our eyes locked before I could disappear without his knowledge. Motin was tall and rake thin. Just like his physique, his features were skinny and long and with the weight of his bushy hair, he looked like he would topple over.

"Hi," I smiled and as he walked over, I silently changed our dinner plans to a quick coffee session. "How are you?"

"Fine, good to meet you." We shook hands.

"You're the type of girl who'll make a man spend money!" His assertion made me laugh and I looked at him, confused.

"What makes you say that?" Nope, no sparks from the touch of palms, just tense awkwardness as I led the way.

"Well, I tried to arrange this meeting in Zone 2 so that I wouldn't have to buy a ticket to come into town. But your sister insisted that I come in. I really was left with no choice." As Motin spoke, I tried to imagine myself with a man who thought he was 'splashing out' when he bought a train extension ticket. I couldn't. I picked up the pace, weaving through late night shoppers and diners at St Martins Square until we entered Café Rouge.

"Coffees aren't cheap here, are they? You could buy two jars of Nescafé Gold Blend at these prices!" I nearly missed the chair the waiter held out for me. I smiled at the young waiter who stared at Motin unimpressed.

"I'll have a cappuccino, what will you have?" I asked Motin, refusing to let the waiter leave so that I could get through this introduction as fast as possible. But Motin hovered over the menu and I could see his eyes skim over the price list time and again, until he finally made his decision.

"I'll have a hot chocolate," he announced, handing back the menu to the impatient waiter.

"So Motin, what's driving you to settle down?" If I went on the offensive, maybe, just maybe, I could scare him into an early departure from my life.

"It's expected isn't it! I've got the perfect job that I'd be happy to stay in forever, but I'm the oldest of eight brothers and sisters so I've got to start the marriage trend!" Motin's idea of forever seemed like a life sentence. As the oldest housewife, I would inherit an adult family with a never ending stream of family duties. "What about you?"

"Well, now that I've done the career bit, I'd like to settle down as soon as possible."

"Is that because of family pressure or because you're getting old?" Cheapskate Motin was too dim to realise he'd just insulted me but I kept on smiling.

"Time to begin a new chapter in my life," I replied. The waiter brought my cappuccino and Motin's hot chocolate, and left without looking at us twice.

"I quite like open chapters. Take my job for instance, I've been with Newham Council for seven years and I have no intention of leaving..."

"You've had the same job for seven years?" What happened to ambition, climbing up the ladder, moving onto bigger and better things? What happened to man being the main breadwinner?

"A job for life, if I have anything to do with it!" I smiled in muted understanding. "I've got the best manager who gives me the best projects and as long as I complete those on time, it really will become a job for life."

"And you have no itchy feet, no urge to do something different, try something new?"

"Why give up something good for the unknown?"

"Because it could be exciting, and maybe more rewarding." Motin didn't look impressed.

"Hand in hand with more stress, accountability and responsibility?" I gulped down my cappuccino. Isn't that what motivated men? Weren't they by nature of cavemen genes driven by the desire for power and control? We sat in awkward silence, forced to watch fellow cafenisters chat away.

"Have you had many alaaps or responses?"

Motin nodded and finished off his hot chocolate. "My sisters keep lining up girls for me, but they all want a house, a car, and a nice cushy life." I frowned at his logic and waited for more, but it didn't come.

"But Motin, every girl wants to feel like she'll be looked after."

"Not at my expense."

I wondered if he'd actually thought through what he was saying. "Wouldn't you want your sisters to feel secure with their husbands?"

"I think women should make men feel more secure, instead of treating them like personal bank accounts." Motin sure had a sting in the tail. "There's nothing worse than a woman who expects her husband to be the main breadwinner while she sits around on her backside all day." That was the final straw. Motin had unintentionally gunned down my ambition and by default killed off any remote improbable future we would have had. "Would you like another drink?" I shook my head and watched him review the menu.

"Three pounds forty-five for a side order of chips, they're one forty-nine in McD's!" Motin's outrage was sincere and I indicated to the passing waiter to bring the bill quickly. But the manager called him away and I was left with a menu-engrossed Motin. I couldn't wait for our waiter to re-appear.

"Why don't we pay on our way out?" I didn't wait for Motin to agree, instead I grabbed my jacket and bag before making my way to the counter.

"Hope you enjoyed your coffee. That'll be six pounds sixty-eight." Motin looked at the bill, and deep in thought, produced his wallet. Then he turned to me. "How should we do this?" I heard the question, but stared at him. "I'm sorry?" Maybe I had misunderstood his intentions. "The bill, how should we take care of it?" "Oh, you want to split six pounds seventy?" "Yeah, uh, some women take exception to having a man pay for them." Nope, I had perfectly understood his intentions. "Lucky you! I'm not one of those women." It took a couple of seconds for my meaning to sink. When it did, he stared at me in disappointment and then handed over a ten-pound note. Suffice to say, I wasn't Motin's type.

The run up to the month of Ramadan meant one thing. Shopping. Shopping for food, shopping for fine Eid outfits and shopping for presents. But Baba hogged the grocery shopping for Eid, and when Baba shopped, he really shopped. And he did it well in advance of Ramadan to miss the price hikes by occasionally savvy halal butchers and 24hrs Indian fruit and vegetable shops. "He's throwing money away! He has no idea of what's needed, but your Baba has money in his pocket and he's intent on getting rid of it." Amma muttered as we carried several bags of shopping back to the car. "How am I meant to cook avocados?" "Jana likes avocados…" "And I like diamond rings, but I don't see your father rushing to buy me half a dozen." "I don't think you'll find five diamond rings going for a pound!" She wasn't amused. Amma's conservative shopping style was always overshadowed by Baba's generous nature, and after thirty-nine years of marriage there was still no meeting of minds. "Appha!" My heart froze at the call, but Amma didn't hear it so we continued walking. "Appha!" Chachijhi Fauzia refused to be ignored and used her burly frame to push her way through the crowds. "My God! Why are you walking so fast!" She demanded, breathing hard and reaching out to hold onto Amma's shoulders for support. "Your brother's going to empty the food markets if we don't put the shopping away and get back to him!" But Chachijhi was in no such hurry and continued to pant as if she'd just completed the London Marathon. "You mustn't over burden your body like this. Offer your auntie some drink, Maya." "No, no, I'm fine." Despite her refusals, Chachiji took the carton of Rubicon Mango juice I held out to her. Chachijhi had something to say. She always did when she moved too fast for her burly body. So Amma and I put our shopping on the ground and waited. "I think we've found Leila a good match." Amma looked like she had been slapped with a wet fish. I was older than Loose-Leila, and protocol required her to wait until I married. Chachijhi was breaking protocol.

"Congratulations, is he someone we know?" My attempt to break the silence was ignored. Amma gathered up her shopping bags to walk back to our car. Chachijhi rushed to keep up with her, but I was at her heels, unwilling to miss a single word of their exchange.

"Ramadan is virtually here, we should delay such discussions until after the holy month." Amma was buying time with religion, God forgive her.

"You should use this month to seek guidance as to whether he's the right boy for our Leila..."

"But he is, if there's one thing Leila's father's good at, it's getting information about..."

"Did Leila's father seek counsel about this alaap with your older brother, Maya's father?"

"No, but that's why I'm here, we'd like you to see the family..."

"After you've made your decision." Chachijhi looked at Amma, and then looked back at me as if I'd put her up to this. Then she leaned in close to Amma.

"I understand that you're worried about what people will say about Maya, but we can't compromise our remaining girls for her sake."

"You need to consider what people will say about you overstepping Maya..."

"People are already speaking of her inability to get married, that isn't a new matter." I didn't miss the loud and angry whispers.

"Being ignored by your family is." Chachijhi stopped Amma and looked at her directly. I kept my distance, put my shopping down and played with my mobile to avoid her glare.

"They're saying there's something wrong with her, that's why she can't get married."

"They've been saying Leila's had boyfriends since she was at secondary school, but we choose what we believe." My mother, the tigress, would not back down easily.

"They say someone's put the evil eye on her..."

"Astagfirullah! May Allah protect my daughter from such evil jealousy!" Amma breathed out. "Who said that? I want to know names..."

"They can't understand why a pretty thing like Maya can't find a man, any man, to marry. Now they say that a spurned suitor may have cast the evil eye and that's why none of the alaaps work out for her." Evil eyes are spells cast on the envied to prevent them from a particular blessing, and though I knew Chachijhi had a tendency to exaggerate, she never lied.

"This is too much, this is unacceptable!" Amma muttered as she sat down on a low brick fence. "Her age, the quality of the suitors..."

"People are worried that she could pass on her misfortune and I want to protect my girls..."

"You don't believe that nonsense?" Amma demanded, her eyes widening as Chachijhi hesitated.

"Well, that poor doctor's father did have a heart attack..."

"I'm not a witch, I'm just single!" I told Chachijhi as I handed Amma a mango juice carton.

"This is not a matter for you to concern yourself with, Maya." I looked at my auntie.

"I'm not possessed, I think I'm quite capable of telling you that myself..."

"What if it's speaking right now?" Chachijhi accused, as I cried out in exasperation. If anyone had been possessed, it was my aunt.

"Oh for God's sake Fauzia! People speak nonsense all the time. No-one's cast an evil eye on Maya," Amma muttered before finishing off her juice.

"This is why I need for you to speak with Maya's father before I do. He's my brother, but he's Maya's father first..."

"Can we get back to the evil eye thing, as in who's been spreading these rumours?"

"That's not for you to know or rectify," Chachijhi retorted as Amma gathered the bags to walk on. Chachijhi gave chase and I followed close behind stunned by the rumours. Amma extracted the gossipmongers' names on condition that she spoke with Baba. I missed the murmured names, but the look on Amma's face told me she was up to no good. We put the shopping away in the car, and returned to baba where we watched Chachijhi take full advantage of his good nature. I wanted to shout that he hasn't come yet. He, the man I'll share the rest of my life with. Not some socially inept tightwad with no ambition. Am I expected to accept that these are the cards I've been dealt in life? I refuse to accept that is my lot. I want a new deck of cards. But life didn't work like that. I knew that, and sadly enough, so did Amma. She stood beside me, equally stunned and silent.

F: Fight Fate With Faith

Fasting is universally misunderstood. Every year Muslims around the world give up food, sex and all base desires for a month of religious observation. Whilst the month of Ramadan teaches us self-discipline, self-control and empathy for the poor, I think it's probably the only detoxifying regime that leaves you actually feeling on top of the world. Each time Ramadan comes around, I plan on rediscovering my seven stone figure, but the rich servings of kedgeree, bhajhis, somosas and chana at sunset tempt me to achieve anything but. This year however, it was all going to change. I wasn't going to pray for anything as materialistic as the perfect figure or a thoroughly deserved pay increase. No, this year, I was concentrating all my prayers on something that really mattered. A husband. And if there was any month to ask for help or a sign that my fortunes were about to change, this was it.

So everyday after work, I joined Tanya at Central London Mosque for the extended prayers, along with most of the city's Muslim professionals. I was as devout as I have ever been. And more so, as the chance for an encounter with a potential city savvy suitor on the way in or out of Mosque was high, and what man could resist a good professional woman who was equally God conscious? By all accounts, I had a month's worth of daily opportunities in which to reap my reward.
"You're finally here!" Tanya muttered as I joined her on the balcony in the Mosque's Women's section, which was packed with women of all ages and sizes covered in long gowns and headscarves. I slipped into the first row between Tanya and a tall Somalian woman who was all of eighteen stones and then some.
"The tubes are seriously messed up." I said before greeting the Somalian woman who stared at me. "Did you break your fast properly?"
"I hooked up with Javed and we grabbed a pizza." I grinned at Tanya and gave her a cheeky wink.
"Javed eh? You two seem to be getting a little cosy..."
"There's no foreplay going on Maya, nobody's going to get laid..."
"Did I say that?" It didn't matter that I've known Tanya forever. Her frankness still shocked me, and now my Somalian neighbour, who prayed for our forgiveness.
"Javed's the only guy I know who can string a few words together into something intelligent. It really is no big deal..."
"You fancy him rotten!"
"Sisters, I do not think your conversation's appropriate for the mosque," my Somalian neighbour whispered to us with strong disapproval.
"You don't think Allah can hear me outside the mosque?" I glared at Tanya to stop her being provocative, then turned to my neighbour to apologise. But I was too late, she seemed to be cursing us in Somali. Thankfully, the imam began his call to prayer. We all stood up,

shoulder to shoulder, feet by feet. The hefty Somalian woman jostled, and with each jostle I was pushed against Tanya.

"Did you see any cuties on the way in..."

"Ssshh!" Tanya was seriously testing my neighbour's patience.

"Don't worry, we'll take a stroll in the men's section and find you a cutie..."

"Sister!" I was already praying by the time Tanya let out a dirty laugh.

After the extended prayers, Tanya and I took a bus from Baker Street to Edgware Road still laughing about my Somalian neighbour who gave up trying to admonish Tanya and had found another prayer spot.

"Have you heard from Sakina?" Tanya asked as we entered the popular Beirut Express and queued for a table.

"Yep, she's still smarting about Raj, 'the Arsehole'." Having been dumped by Raj, Sakina had sworn off men for the foreseeable future.

"Well don't tell her I'm matchmaking you with someone that Javed recommended." I put the menu down and laughed at Tanya.

"We're supposed to be fasting, you know maintaining a degree of self-restraint ..."

"He's a city banker, twenty-nine, and good-looking. The best thing is that he's serious about settling down." I looked around the overcrowded Lebanese restaurant and wondered why Tanya wasn't more discreet in a place filled with fellow Muslims who were now enjoying their meals after a long day fasting and a longer evening of prayers.

"Why's he still single?" I finally asked, as Tanya grinned. He sounded too good to be true.

"That's not a question Javed's going to ask, Maya." Point taken. We were fifteen minutes away from getting a table, so Tanya and I ordered fresh smoothies from the drinks counter. "So shall I arrange a meeting?"

"It's Ramadan Tanya. We're meant to be abstaining from base desires..."

"I'm asking whether you want to meet the guy Maya, not mate with him!" I ssshed Tanya and smiled apologetically at the couple ahead of us. "Maya, I'll come with you. We'll grab a coffee after prayers and have a simple chat." In my bid to curry the Almighty's favour, I didn't want to test His good will. "C'mon Maya, Javed's said good things about him that tell me he's worth checking out."

"Ok, I'm up for quick coffee." Tanya laughed with accomplished delight.

"But only if it's totally informal. Promise me it will be."

"God, that's a relief! We're having coffee with him and Javed tomorrow in Baker Street."

"Tomorrow?" I remembered the message from Jhanghir and looked at Tanya.

"Don't tell me you have another date?" I shook my head and watched a waiter lead the couple before us to a hastily refreshed table.

"Jhanghir wrote today." We hadn't spoken about Jhanghir since Sakina's probing about my relationship with him. Still, I couldn't help but smile. It had been four long years since we'd last seen one another and now that he was actually flying in, I couldn't believe I'd see him so soon. "He's flying in tomorrow for a family wedding and I'm going to surprise him at the airport. Could we rearrange for Friday evening?"

"Maya, everyone has plans for the first Friday of Ramadan."

"I don't have any plans, I can do Friday evening..."

"Hang on, how come you're surprising him at the airport if he's already told you that he's flying over?"

"Well, because he just said that he'll be in London for the weekend." It didn't sound convincing, but I held Tanya's confused look.

"So how do you know when he's flying in?"

"Because I spoke with his flatmate Eddie, who gave me Jhanghir's flight details..."

"But Jhanghir didn't give them to you, nor did he make plans to meet you, but you're still going to surprise him at the airport?" I refused to accept Tanya's point and she shook her head. "I really think you should meet this guy tomorrow Maya."

"I can't make tomorrow evening."

"You're going to meet an engaged man instead of sowing the seeds for your future?"

"I'm not giving up anything for an engaged man! I'm just giving my past and my friendship a future."

"Why?" Tanya asked, refusing to buy my explanation. "You know when Sakina had a go at you about Jhanghir at Café Nero's, I kept my peace, I stayed quiet. But this, uh, this relationship you have with him, I don't get it. What is it about Jhanghir that you can't let go of?"

"He's a good friend..."

"Don't kid yourself sweetheart. Nature doesn't understand platonic relationships between man and woman. Sooner or later, she'll have her way and the lines between friends, soul mates, and lovers become blurred."

"Ladies, I have a table ready for you." Tanya followed the waiter, and I remained where I stood, frowning at Tanya's comment. The thing was the lines had always been blurred for Jhanghir and I. But aren't the lines in all relationships blurred, isn't that always the way?

"Maya!" I looked up at where Tanya stood beckoning me, and walked across to the table, which looked out onto the Edgware Road.

"You've got us wrong." I told her, as we took off our jackets and gave our orders to the attentive waiter. "Its not like that."

"If he's everything that you say he is, I bet that it's exactly like that." There was no convincing my friend, but I stared at her until she laughed and raised her palms. "Listen, on all accounts, the guy is gorgeous, he's a doctor, and he looks at you as if you're the most precious thing..."

"Enough already!" We laughed at her repetition of Sakina's words and then she looked at me seriously. "Ok, tell me what it's like then."
"Are you for real?" I asked wondering if she was being mischievous. But she nodded and waited without the slightest hint of humour. I cleared my throat and frowned at how I could explain something that I refused to understand myself.
"Any time today Maya." Tanya's dry comment made me grin and we tucked into the hummous with fresh pitta bread.
"Its like we're more than friends but less than a couple..."
"You mean like brother and sister?" I choked at the disturbing thought. I shook my head vigorously whilst coughing to clear my throat. "So it's not like brother and sister. There's chemistry between you?"
"When you know a guy for as long as I've known Jhanghir, you move beyond that..."
"So there was chemistry between you...?"
"Yes... No... that's not the point!" I told Tanya, who sat back in confusion. "He's different from me..." I sighed, as I sat back and looked at my friend who shook her head at me. "We were at Regent's Park one day, sitting down and watching the world pass us by. And then out of the blue, he just pulled me back against him, and wrapped his arms around me. We sat in absolute silence for what seemed like an eternity. It felt like the most natural thing in the world and I'd never felt so wanted on so many levels. At that point, he was everything I wanted but couldn't have."
"Spare me the details. Did he feel the same way about you?" I nodded and dipped my pitta bread into the hummous.
"He felt the same, but he had to honour his father's promise." I put the pitta bread down and looked at Tanya. "Mr Khan had promised his business partner of forty years that Jhanghir would marry his daughter Preeya..."
"I know Jhanghir's no angel." I frowned at how Tanya knew so much about Jhanghir, so she explained. "Javed's cousin studied biomedical studies when Jhanghir did his internship. I know he partied with the hardest, out-drank most students and played around..."
"But he changed." Tanya looked at me in disbelief. "It's why we never got together. He was too Western, uh, American, you know, hard headed and arrogant. He mocked me for being Sylethi, but I wouldn't concede to his way, and he knew that he had met his match."
"I still don't get why you didn't get it on." I took a deep breath and looked at Tanya.
"He's Dhakayan Tanya. His community look down on Sylethis for being uneducated and insular. Even being religious or traditional is enough for them to ridicule us." Tanya still couldn't understand, so I continued. "We lived in a four bedroom council flat in Mile End, nine of us. Ayesha was about to get married, and Tariq was struggling to buy the second restaurant. Jhanghir comes from an affluent elitist family who encouraged him to become Westernised. He's from a background that

refuses to understand me and my world. I couldn't open up my world for it to be derided..."

"But there was something there for you to be telling me this now." I looked at Tanya and nodded.

"He wanted to change his father's mind, but Preeya's father passed away five years ago, and Jhanghir felt bound by the promise." I remembered it so clearly. I felt as stunned by the turn of events now as I did then and shook my head.

"So what happened then?" Tanya looked as shocked as I felt. Our meals arrived and I was thankful for the brief distraction. "Maya?"

"I couldn't ask for any more, Tanya. He was honouring his father's promise..."

"That's it?" Tanya asked in disbelief before tucking into her shish taouk. "You just accepted a platonic relationship?"

"Four years ago, he found out Preeya was seeing his cousin. He broke off the engagement and caught the first flight out to London to ask me to marry him." Tanya choked on her food and gulped down her drink before staring at me in shock.

"And you never told us?" I had never revealed any of this to her, in fact I hadn't confided in anybody. "How could you not tell us...?"

"I cried and cried and cried, until I had no more tears to shed. What was there to tell?"

"Maya, he asked you to marry him!" By now Tanya's outrage caught the attention of most of the diners at Beirut Express.

"And I said no." Before she could ask me I explained why. "He was on the rebound, I refused to be his temporary stand-in..."

"H... how on earth could you know that? He didn't even fight for her, he just got on a plane and flew half way around the world for you..."

"But he flew right back, accepted her apology and had another engagement party to show his community that all was good again."

"But that's because you turned him down..."

"If he was serious about marrying me Tanya, why would he readily take Preeya back? Do you not think he had the perfect opportunity to prove himself..."

"Maya, you're talking as if men are sensible human beings. They're not." I ignored the men on the table next to ours who stopped talking at Tanya's comment. "They have this thing called an ego, as well as their God-given tool to control. When either is offended, logic comes a poor third in their world of priorities." The men lowered their heads and resumed eating. "When did you start talking again?"

"About a year and a half later." I took a bite of the chicken and thought about Jhanghir.

"Who made the first move?" I smiled and raised my hand. "No! How could you?"

"I really offended him." Tanya stopped and stared at me with a naughty smile. "I had to apologise!"

"How offended?" I grinned and raised a brow.

"Enough to get him on the first flight back to Manhattan." Tanya burst out laughing, and I laughed along too until I remembered Jhanghir's hurt expression after I had turned him down.

"And there's me thinking that you're just a cold bitch who thought she was too good for all her alaaps!"

"I am too good for all the alaaps!" I retorted looking up to see Tanya's smile fade.

"No, you're just scared to let go of the love of your life." I avoided her eyes, but smiled and shook my head. Tanya read my mind and put her hand on top of mine. "Do you regret it?"

"It was the right thing to do." I replied. "What if I'd said yes and he went back to the states only for Preeya to win him back?"

"You did the right thing." Tanya told me. I nodded and pulled my hand away.

"This way, I get to keep my friend and my dignity." I knew Tanya wanted to present a dozen other scenarios that could have played out, the main one being that he could have stayed true and faithful to me, but she didn't. She knew me well enough to know I had thought that very thought countless times. She also knew me well enough to know that I had too much pride to wait for him.

Just after seven thirty the following evening, I felt ecstatic, anxious, nervous and a hundred other rioting emotions as I stood waiting for Jhanghir. Virgin JK001 had landed, the baggage was in the hall and Jhanghir would appear from behind the sliding doors. I loved Heathrow Airport's busy International Terminal. It was always full of people from every corner of the world waiting to be reunited with their loved ones. There was even a group of good-looking young Bengali men in the waiting area opposite to where I stood. Now normally, I'd definitely have checked them out, but not tonight. Not with Jhanghir arriving. I hadn't felt so happy in a long time and I realised how much I had missed him. I didn't know why I needed to see him. All I knew was that I had to. I leaned on the handrail and watched new arrivals push their trolleys before racing to embrace their family. I looked back at the group of Bengali boys and wondered from which part of the world their friend or relative was flying.

"Jhanghir!" I heard the shout before I saw him and my heart raced. There he was. My friend. My bloody good-looking friend. My bloody good-looking friend who had his arm around a twiglet, otherwise known as Preeya! I'd forgotten just how attractive he was, so I waited excitedly for him to spot me. But he didn't. This was the man who could sense my presence without a word. Only now it was different. Now, he failed to realise I was there, as he had failed to inform me that he would be here all. I watched him push his trolley across to the group of waiting friends and draw them into warm embraces. Things had changed. I stepped back behind the barrier and disappeared amongst the bustling arrivals.

F: Fight Fate With Faith

Each year, in the first weekend of Ramadan, my parents opened our house to virtually everyone in the community. They refused to accept that our four-bedroom semi could only hold so many guests and despite the fact that we had friends and family congregating in the hall and sitting on the stairs, this year they insisted on inviting more people. Worse still, as the youngest of six children and as yet unmarried, I was at the beck and call of everyone.

"Maya, one glass of phani please." I nodded at Jana's mother-in-law's request, as I passed a bowl of somosas and aloo bhajhis to Ayesha's sister-in-law.

"Hamza, get Rhinni auntie a glass of water!" I shouted across to my nephew, before catching my mother look in despair at my behaviour.

"Could you get Hamza to get me some mango juice?" Hana's mother-in-law asked, competing with Jana's mother-in-law for everything. I didn't miss Amma's glare as she dared me to repeat my unladylike behaviour. "And I'd like some more of that lovely fresh mango we had for dessert." Without a word I left to do their bidding. Walking over aunts, around cousins and past friends I made it to the kitchen where Loose-Leila, my cousin, engaged everyone about her wonderful fiancé. I hated nights like these, where everyone had someone to speak to about something, and all I did was think of Jhanghir.

"…and then he took me to Falkredines off Park Lane. It was beautiful, we had the best table, the entire restaurant was dimly lit and he pulled out the ring." I'd heard the story a hundred times, so I poured out the juice and diced some fresh mango into a bowl to take into the women's room.

"Maya, you have a guest," Shireen called out from the front door. My heart leapt. Leila caught my fearful anticipation and narrowed her eyes. Jhanghir couldn't have turned up without an announcement. I gave Hamza the water and mango juice to take through and cleared my throat. My heart thudded a million beats to the second as I smiled at Leila before making my way through the crowded hall to the front door.

"Sakina!" I called out, pulling her into a hug so that she didn't see my disappointment.

"Tanya can't make it. She's at a work dinner and she said something about not chancing an inflatable airhead to ruin her good work." She stood back and held out a covered tray full of iftari offerings to celebrate the breaking of the day's fast.

"She's with Javed, isn't she?" Sakina grinned and so did I, as nothing more needed to be said.

"Maya, I can't stay either…"

"Please don't tell me that. I've only Hamza to chat with and he's five years old," I begged as she shook her head.

"My Chacha's having a dinner that I'm already late for," Sakina explained, as she toyed with her car keys and checked behind me to ensure we had some privacy. Then she leaned forward and whispered. "Has Jhanghir called?"

"No, but I'm alright," I lied, taking Sakina's tray. "Give me two minutes."
I left Sakina to transfer the food she had brought onto a dish before
refilling the tray with our homemade somosas, bhajhi's and kebabs. I
refused to think about Jhanghir's slight on our friendship as I covered
the tray with foil to take back to Sakina.

"Has the Arsehole called?" She shook her head with a sad smile. I
knew she felt as unwanted as I did and after she hugged me goodbye, I
caught her tearful eyes.

One call, that's all it took. Men just didn't understand the power of one
call.

"Maya, it's for you!" I didn't bother moving and asked Hamza to find the
cordless phone. It was late and all the girls huddled in my room to
watch Kuch Kuch Hota Hai, Bollywood's answer to 'Sleepless In
Seattle'. It didn't matter that everyone had seen it, the movie was a
timeless chick flick that left every girl wanting Shah Rukh Khan. I
extracted myself from the huddle of sisters and cousins as Hamza
brought the phone to me.

"Tanya, you weren't at the dinner were you? You might as well admit
you were with Javed..."

"Sssshhh!" I frowned at Leila's demand before walking out of my room
to sit on the top stair.

"I certainly didn't spend the evening with Javed." I could hear all the
elders in long, drawn out conversations below. I could hear my aunts
laughing about old times. But above all else I heard my heart thud
slowly.

"Hello Jhanghir."

"I'm in London Maya."

"I know." His silence was as telling as my lack of enthusiasm.

"I spoke with Eddie." So that's why he was calling, because he felt
guilty at being found out. I put the phone down and held my head in my
hands. Even my best friend was letting his side down. The phone rang
again, and I refused to answer until everyone shouted at me to take the
call.

"Don't hang up on me Maya..."

"You should've called Jhanghir..."

"Hey, you tell me about an alaap you had from a doctor, and then I
hear from your mom that you're getting married in the summer. You
don't even call to let me know you're getting married Maya..."

"You could've called me to find out, you know, showed some interest in
my life."

"That's cheap Maya, that's real cheap." I felt like crying.

"And how many times do you call me to let me know what's going on in
your life Jhanghir?" Something had changed, and I didn't know how to
get it back to the way we were. "I went to the airport to meet you. When
I realised it was inappropriate, I stepped back. But at least I tried
Jhanghir. Can you say the same?"

"Then let me repay you by taking you both out to break fast tomorrow."
Both? He meant Shah and I, the couple that never existed.
"I have plans..."
"I can't make dinner because I'm flying out at seven..."
"I can't make dinner either."
"What do you want Maya?" He asked after a long pause and I feared the worst.
"Nothing," I whispered, unable to be honest with Jhanghir for the first time in my life. I felt so alone I wanted to disappear. We didn't speak for some time, just sat there listening to each other's silence. I wanted to be me, the regular Maya who bantered with Jhanghir without a second thought. I had accepted his engagement to Preeya and now he dared to make me feel guilty for choosing a husband. That was unfair at best and downright selfish at worst. Everything had changed, maybe Tanya was right about platonic relationships. Maybe they all had a shelf-life.
"Life's changing us Maya. Break fast with me tomorrow for old time's sake." He was saying goodbye and my eyes stung with unshed tears. I agreed and we made plans to meet in Southall. After we ended the call, I sat on the top stair for a long time. Jhanghir caused many conflicting emotions, stirred many thoughts and memories that I wanted to repress. Still, the thought of losing him for any virtual husband made me miserable.

"Hey." I was late and found Jhanghir waiting at our agreed meeting spot.
"Hey," he returned with that slow grin of his. He looked even better close up and I looked away from his piercing hazel eyes.
"I'm sorry I'm late. We had a massive iftari yesterday, and I was still running after family this morning, tending to their every need!" As we headed towards Lahori's, I stole a glance at him and he seemed surprised to see me.
"You look good Maya." I stopped babbling and met his eyes. The truth was I'd spent most of the afternoon changing my mind on what to wear before deciding on the simple cream trouser suit. I wore my hair straight and had put on a touch of barely there make up. Where were my throwback remarks, the sarcastic cutting replies to check his ego? I felt awkward and I had to ease up before he realised.
"Thank you." I didn't give him another look as we walked down the Broadway. The truth was he looked incredible. Jhanghir had always been good-looking, but the years had given him authority and conviction. "You didn't bring Preeya?"
"You didn't bring your fiancé." I stopped and looked at him. I took in his golden chiselled cheeks, brooding eyes, stern jaw and grinned. We didn't miss Preeya or my pretend fiancé. We didn't want it any other way.
"It's been four years Jhanghir. I can't believe you're here." I felt like a wistful grinning teenager so I avoided his eyes as we walked. "The last

time I saw you, you told me I'd made the worst mistake of my life for not marrying you and then you stormed off." It was the wrong memory to recollect and he watched me. "You can't be that busy at Bellevue, if you're stealing weekends to jet over here for weddings!"

"If only! It really wasn't my choice," Jhanghir chuckled, and the throaty laugh made my tummy churn giddily. "You remember Mohibur from UCL?" How could I not? Mohibur had been Jhanghir's closest cousin since childhood, and he was also the man Preeya had had an affair with four years ago. "Well, it was his younger sister's wedding. Preeya and I had were required to show our faces, keeping the family united and all that. And now, it's back to the madness of rotas, research and managing residents..."

"How could you forgive him for what he did to you?" Jhanghir grinned but it didn't reach his eyes. His resolve and sense of duty had driven him to face his cousin before the entire community and that made me respect him even more.

"I forgave you." I stopped at his comment and frowned.

"I didn't cheat on you." He gritted his jaw and walked on. Neither of us wanted to discuss our turbulent past.

"It doesn't seem like you've been gone at all, yet it feels like everything's changed!" I laughed, trying to lighten the mood.

"Everything has changed. We're both getting married. Everything changes after that." I frowned, downcast at his reminder. All the unimportant things we had spent hours arguing over seemed unnatural under these circumstances, and yet I wasn't ready for anything heavy.

"What time's your flight?" But now I sounded like I couldn't wait until he was gone.

"Seven, I've got to grab a ride from you straight to Terminal 3." I nodded as he held the door open and we entered Lahoris. We were shown through the busy bustling restaurant to a table for two, and I watched Jhanghir take off his duffle coat. He wore baggy Abercrombie and Fitch chinos with a tan fitted sweater. His dress sense hadn't changed and I smiled at the ribbing I used give him about it.

"Something funny?" I shook my head as I looked at the menu.

"C'mon, share your thoughts and lighten the mood." Jhanghir's grin burned me and I felt my smile falter.

"I was, eh, I was just thinking about how I used to rib you about your clothes." There was something wrong with me and I felt ill.

"Don't start that one! I'm in white coats most days, then in a tie and button up shirts for meetings so I get to do casuals on holiday!" I grinned but remained stumm. "Alright, what happened to your jeans and baggy sweaters?"

"Don't be reflecting back on me..." I countered.

"Cop out! When did you start looking like a sophisticated elegant woman?" I gasped in mock outrage, before narrowing my eyes at him.

"You complimenting me Jhanghir?" He stopped and looked down. In the old days we could have kept this going for hours. In the old days we moved seamlessly from one topic to another. Now, we faltered with every conversation, struggling to move onto the next. We gave our order to the waiter who had appeared at the right time, but the moment he left we sat in silence.

"So how's your research going?" That was good a topic. Neutral and safe. One where I could sit back and listen. And as Jhanghir spoke, I saw his passion for his profession. I nodded and smiled at the right places, and imagined how wonderful it would be to be with someone who had so much enthusiasm for life. He'd be the type of husband who'd keep you interested in life because he was interested. I imagined waiting up for him to return from the hospital with a ready dinner, or seeing him off in the morning...

"... and your job? How's that going? Maya?" Jhanghir looked at me in confusion.

"Uh, it's going fine." My cheeks burned red hot, and I couldn't believe what I'd been thinking.

"Your job? The one you've told me you hate every single day of your life?" I avoided his eyes and cleared my throat.

"Oh that job!" Our drinks arrived and I took a long hard gulp of the icy diet coke to cool me down.

"It's not time to break your fast..." I spewed out the drink in his direction and covered my mouth but it was too late. I handed him a napkin. He used it to wipe his neck and jaw, but I wanted to do it for him. Shaking my head, I couldn't believe what had overtaken me.

"I'm so sorry!" I breathed out, as Jhanghir shook his head and frowned at me. "I, uh, do you want another napkin?"

"You haven't changed at all Maya." I frowned at his comment. "You appear to be very cosmopolitan, but you were baffling back then, and you're still baffling now." I didn't want him to think that. I wanted him to want me, to realise that he fancied me as I did him.

"Well that's not what Shah says..."

"Shah?"

"My fiancé." I couldn't believe I was lying while fasting, but I refused to let him walk away thinking I wasn't a smart sophisticated woman who was unable to catch herself a man.

"And what exactly does he tell you?" Jhanghir smiled, but again the smile failed to reach his eyes.

"He says that I'm a smart, articulate young woman with a lot of potential."

"That's not very romantic..."

"There's no single universal guide to romance." I didn't mean to snap, but his smirk irritated me. "I get flowers, and chocolates and we have lovely dinners..."

"That's not romance Maya..."

"That's not your kind of romance," I corrected. I checked the time and agreed with Jhanghir that it was time to break our fasts.

"It's not your kind, either," he said, serving me a good portion of the sizzling mixed grill.

"Does he surprise you with tickets to private views?" I avoided his eyes again and ladled chilli sauce onto his plate.

"Shah's very busy at the hospital..."

"You still collect Hodgkin posters..."

"I don't have time for art these days and Shah doesn't need to buy me posters..."

"Do you impress him with impromptu Julian Opie-inspired portraits?"

"I impress him in other ways."

"And he doesn't whisk you off to Paris, take Sunday morning strolls down Spitalfields Market, or follow you around like a love sick puppy when you lose afternoons in the National Portrait Gallery...?"

"That works when you're all of nineteen Jhanghir. But when you're part of a working couple with responsibilities, regular romance is more than enough." We ate in silence. He had remembered everything and it saddened me to think that even 'regular romance' seemed out of my reach. Tanya's words of wisdom churned in my mind. My emotions raged and everything I wanted from Jhanghir had changed.

"Have you started experimenting with your pastels again?" I shook my head, refused to meet his eyes and searched for cuttings of lamb tikka on the sizzling dish. "Do you scour the galleries for inspiration...?"

"There's no need to." I couldn't find any pieces of lamb tikka.

"But you still visit the Tate Modern, the Hayward and the Brunei Galleries, right?" I didn't want to remember the days we whiled away as we moved from one exhibition to the next.

"I don't have time." I didn't want to recall how he had teased me as I made sketches and took notes of the old, new and bold masterpieces.

"Maya, I don't get you. You hate your job, but you do nothing to help yourself get back to doing something you love..."

"I need this job Jhanghir..."

"No, you don't," Jhanghir corrected, passing me his servings of lamb tikka.

"Says the man who has everything..."

"Dhakayans help each other achieve our dreams." There it was, our world of differences. The differences that had stirred our pride enough to keep our relationship platonic. "Surely, it's time for your family to support you..."

"Don't judge my family, Jhanghir."

"I'm not judging."

"Yes you are. I may not come from a family with trade ties going back three generations, or one that can finance my dreams indefinitely, but my family have never asked me for anything. I chose to work to help Tariq and Taj move our family out of our Mile End council flat and into our beautiful home. I helped my parents pay for the twin's wedding, and I'm helping to keep my dad in his well earned retirement..."

"So who helps Maya Malik?" I put down my cutlery and sat back to watch him.

"Don't patronise me. I choose not to leave a well-paid city job to become a poverty-stricken artist..."

"Your dreams shouldn't be that cheap." I chuckled at his judgement, but he looked disgusted. "You Sylhethis sell out too easily..."

"That's an interesting take on being responsible, but I expect nothing better from an elitist Dhakayan..."

"This has nothing to do with me being a Dhakayan, Maya..."

"You mean Dhakayans don't look down on Sylhethis for being less educated, more traditional and more religious?"

"Sylhethis sell their sons into the restaurant trade before they can finish high school and marry their daughters off before they can begin to live their own dreams..."

"You're so full of bullshit!"

"Really?" I held his eyes and though I knew he was angry for me, I wouldn't concede to him. "What happened to Tariq's dreams? In fact, what happened to your dreams?" I looked around for the waiter, ready to end our meal. "Maya, what happened to your dreams?"

"Dhakayans may not understand this, but when we Sylhethis work hard to take our family out of a crime ridden, run down, damp council flat into a comfortable secure home so that our parents can live without fear of crime or assault, we're actually making dreams come true..."

"What happens to the dreams you had for your life?" Jhanghir refused to let the matter drop. I shook my head and smiled at him.

"I dreamt new dreams Jhanghir. You of all people should now that." He dropped his napkin on the table and checked his watch. There was that ego Tanya had pointed out and there were still the ingrained stereotypes and prejudices that meant we alone weren't enough.

"I don't know what the traffic flows are like, but maybe we ought to head out for the airport." Jhanghir beckoned the waiter and I felt ill. He was about to fly out, and all I wanted to do was go back an hour and leave him with happy fond memories of us. He took care of the bill, and I collected my bag. We walked back to my car in silence, both totally aware of the other for all the wrong reasons.

"How are your family doing?" I asked, pulling out to join the traffic heading towards the A312. It would only be a ten-minute drive, that's all. I had ten minutes to fill before he left and I could return to my normal senses. I listened to Jhanghir talk about his father's business and how Ayub, his brother, was being trained up to take over despite the worries they all had about Ayub's abilities. But my thoughts were on other matters. Would I say goodbye from the car or at the departure gates? What would he expect? Would he care? Would Preeya be waiting for him expecting him to dismiss me in her presence? In that moment, I knew I couldn't live without Jhanghir in my life. It broke my heart to think that he could want a life without me in it. I felt my eyes fill up with tears that threatened to spill over.

"Maya, are you ok?" I nodded quickly and wiped at my eyes.

"Contact lenses, they're... uh, irritating my eyes." I joined the M4 and headed for Heathrow knowing it wouldn't be long.

"Why won't you tell me what's bothering you?"

I looked at him briefly before looking straight ahead. The motorway was busier than I wanted, but that was to be expected owing to the many businessmen who flew out on Sundays for long haul flights. As I took the Terminal 3 exit and pressed down on the accelerator, I hesitated over my response. I didn't want to make myself appear vulnerable.

"Some things are better left unsaid."

"The old Maya would never be so pragmatic."

"The old Maya grew up."

"To become guarded?" The traffic lights forced me to slow down, causing me unnecessary delay so I looked at Jhanghir. I looked at his face, committed every feature to memory and smiled.

"You're always with me." One simple sentence, but it was strong enough to leave Jhanghir speechless. The lights changed, I took the roundabout, and then the tunnel before heading for the drop off section.

"I got you a present for your wedding..."

"Don't do this," I laughed, as I pulled up outside the terminal before leaning across him to open the door.

"In case I can't make it to your wedding Maya, I want to give it to you now." I sat back and shook my head.

"You're being stupid Jhanghir. Just save it for my big day and give it to me then." I closed my eyes when he grabbed my hand and pressed a small box into my palm. He covered it with both of his and tears seeped down my cheeks.

"You're always with me too," he whispered, before slamming the door shut behind him. I dropped the box on the passenger seat, put the car into gear and drove off with one backward glance. I drove for as long as I could without a single thought about Jhanghir. I headed straight for Central London Mosque, knowing that I'd make it in time for tarawiya, the extended prayers. If I concentrated on my prayers, if I asked long and sincerely enough for the strength to bear his departure from my life, the almighty would hear my prayers. When I pulled up by Regents Park and turned the engine off, I looked down at the small grey box. Slowly, I reached out and opened it. A single square cut diamond sparkled up through my tear filled eyes. I touched the small pendant before gently picking up the necklace. Timeless. Some friends came and went. Others you'd love forever.

G: Gamble On Getting A Gorafied Gay

Accountant Salek Joynal Uddin, with one brother and three sisters (all married), was a stranger until Samir-bhai handed me the biodata with an attached photograph. I looked at the photo.

"He's gay."

"What do you mean 'he's gay'?" That's not the response I expected from Samir-bhai, but there in the picture, sat perched on a stool in top to toe designer labels while staring into the distance, was the campest Bengali guy I had ever known.

"You know, 'gay'." I repeated, holding a limp wrist against my side. But he stared at me blankly. "You know, gay, same-sex oriented, homo..."

"How do you know he's gay?" Samir-bhai liked the latest alaap and found it difficult to accept the reality of Salek Joynal Uddin's sexual preference as I presented it.

"Because we worked together for a year at Waterstone's when I was at uni..."

"And you saw him making out with another guy..."

"No!" I cut in before Samir-bhai could go into detail. "I just know... I can tell."

"But he could just be effeminate," Ayesha pointed out, bringing mugs of coffee into the dining room.

"Joy, Gay Joy, that's what we used to call him." She wasn't convinced, so I continued. "You want me to marry someone who everyone will end up calling 'Campman'?" Ayesha failed to appreciate my fears. "What would the community say? I'd become the poster girl for the 'Marry early, get a gent, marry late, and he'll be bent' campaign."

"And why would he be considering an alaap if he was gay?" Samir-bhai asked.

"There are tonnes of ads in *Eastern UK Eye*'s matrimonial section where gay guys confess to wanting a convenience marriage..."

"But how do you know Joy's after a marriage of convenience?" Ayesha asked.

"I don't, I just think he's probably terrified of coming out! It's not exactly the easiest revelation to make to your mom and the Bengali community..."

"You're overreacting..."

"Which part of 'he's gay' don't you understand?" Ayesha looked to Samir-bhai. Then they both looked at me. "Listen, from what I remember he was a great guy, a good laugh. But he's gay."

"If he wasn't gay, would you like him?"

And then it hit me. The problem wasn't that Joy was gay, it was that they didn't know how to explain to our parents what being gay meant and why that was a good reason to pass over an alaap.

"Would you?" Ayesha asked as she looked down at the photo with a frown.

"Listen, it doesn't matter that he's short or that he probably has better taste than I do, but if he admires George Clooney in the way that I do, there's an issue we need to address."

"But he's an accountant..."

"Could you accept Samir-bhai, your husband, dreaming about Brad Pitt..."

"And he has his own house and just his parents to look after." Samir-bhai finished.

"And why would a thirty year old 'apparently straight' successful accountant with his own home, sports car and just his parents to look after want a twenty-eight year old spinster when he has the pick of the crop?" They stopped at my question and had no answer. Samir-bhai stared down at the biodata, disappointment marking his every feature.

"He sounded so good on paper." He muttered like a child who'd had his toy taken away.

"How do we break this to mom and dad?" Ayesha asked. "We're meant to be seeing them tomorrow in Brighton..."

"The gay capital of England?" Samir-bhai sat shaking his head in disbelief. "Why Brighton?"

"Because Kala brought his alaap and she lives in Brighton, and her place makes for a suitable meeting point. And since she's your mother's younger sister, we can get all the dirt on Joy's family from her and your cousins." Samir-bhai explained.

"What if I told Amma that he had a bad reputation?" Ayesha queried.

"Given Maya's age, I think Amma will still welcome him in with open arms!" Samir-bhai returned with half a grin.

"What if we said he had a secret lovechild with a white woman?" I suggested, ignoring him.

"That'd be lying," he said, as if finding an excuse that wasn't the truth would be anything but lying. We went through several rounds of 'what-ifs' and exhausted each idea until we were left with the only choice. "That's it."

"That's what?" I asked, nervous of the look that passed between my sister and her husband.

"We'll just have to go through with it..."

"Through with what?"

"The alaap," Ayesha stated, as if it were the most natural assumption to make.

"You can't expect me to set up home with a man who has a better skin care routine and dress sense than I do. I am not doing this."

"Listen, if he is as camp as you say, Amma and Baba will reject the alaap..."

"What if he acts straight, and they love him to bits? You'll just have to tell them he's gay." Both Ayesha and Samir-bhai shook their heads.

"Maybe they'll realise when they see him. They've lived here for fifty years, so they're bound to know what it is." Even as I said it, I knew that my parents had no clue what being gay was.

"I'm not telling them," Ayesha stated, sitting back to fold her arms.
"What do you want us to say Maya? Joy fancies blokes and blokes who fancy blokes like to..."
"Amma will react in two ways. She'd either take her slipper and beat her educator for telling her such things or she'd faint. Once recovered, she would take to the Quran to seek strength from the fact that not only was her daughter single at twenty-eight, but attracting men who fancied other men," Ayesha pointed out without the slightest hesitation.
"Ok, Ok, I understand." I looked at Ayesha and Samir-bhai who were both looking to me for the answer. We decided the least painful way to end this alaap was to let my parents meet Joy and realise he wasn't my type, or rather that I wasn't his type.

So Baba, Amma, Ayesha, Samir-bhai, Taj and I packed into my dad's Nissan Primera with gifts, including two boxes of mangoes, one watermelon, three pounds of oranges, apples and bananas, as well as our suits to change into before Joy and his family arrived. All because it was cheaper to travel like cattle in one car than take two cars. Baba and Samir-bhai sat in the front, which left wide hipped Amma and Ayesha taking up most of the back seat. Taj insisted on leaning back against Amma, which left me perched on the edge of the seat holding onto Samir-bhai's headrest. The two hour drive to Brighton seemed an impossible mission, one that got harder each time I slid off the seat and into the squat position behind the passenger seat. Baba and Samir-bhai discussed the current costs of an Indian wedding, and every so often, Amma would butt in with 'Ooph! Nobody knows the value of money these days." I, on the other hand, stayed out of the discussion. I wanted a small, intimate ceremony with fifty of my closest family and friends. There'd be no anonymous faces, no kids racing around in frou frou princess dresses or adult mini-me Teflon green suits. No grand hall, no overdressed, over jewelled or over made up doll. Just a simple, elegant and wistful ceremony where we'd take our vows, dine with our guests, then disappear to the Maldives. The Maldives, that's where Jhanghir said he'd take us, back in those days where we spoke about everyone and everything.

I smiled, remembering the second year of my degree, when I had taken on extra shifts at Waterstones. The last minute Christmas shopping madness had passed, so I lost myself in books about the lives of the old masters of art.
"Did you miss me?" Just the memory of his voice sent shivers up my spine.
"When did you get in?" I asked, putting aside my book to look at Jhanghir.
"This morning," he said as he dragged his hair back only for it to flop back over his brow. "I've got my paper to complete, I couldn't get it done..."

"You missed me," I told him, and watched that grin appear. "So did you see your fiancée, fix a date, take your vows, you know finally do the deed?" The grin turned into a wide smile and he looked at me pointedly.

"Preeya is fine and she sends you her regards."

I laughed in disbelief and shook my head. "Liar. She hates me."

Jhanghir perched on the desk, his cashmere coat parted and I noticed his broad, square shoulders. He really was in fine form. I met his hazel eyes and forced myself not to dwell on how good he looked.

"You're assuming she has something to hate you for."

"She has. You promised to marry me if I wasn't married by twenty-eight."

"You'll be married long before then." He sounded so sure and I grinned.

"To some poor fool who was told he was getting a normal beautiful woman." At that time I thought so too, but I looked at Jhanghir, at his warm grinning face and needed to know.

"But what if I'm not?" He held my eyes, and I saw his grin fade.

"I'll marry Preeya the moment you tell me you're getting married." In that instant I knew Jhanghir was my soul mate. I had suspected it the moment I'd laid my eyes on him, but it was then that I knew that this man was created for me as I was created for him.

"And if I never do?"

"Then I'll have two round tickets to the Maldives waiting for you."

"And family and friends, who could never accept each other, who have nothing in common..."

"I'll make it two open round tickets to the Maldives, where we'd swim all day, walk along..." At some point, I'd become fixated on his Elvis Presley lips. They moved slowly, parting and drawing together, and I wanted to kiss him.

"Do you want to kiss me?" The effect of hearing him read my thoughts shocked me. I cleared my throat, pushed my hair behind my ears and laughed nervously.

"And you wonder why Preeya doesn't have something to hate me for?"

"You still think you won't be married by twenty-eight?" I met Jhanghir's eyes and I felt what I saw in him. It was then that I should have built the bridge from platonic friendship to passionate relationship. But I didn't. I didn't, because I never imagined that I would ever feel this lonely without him.

We were on the London Road. Baba and Samir-bhai were now talking about selling properties back home in Bangladesh, so that no-good money draining relatives couldn't claim it.

"I'll believe it when I see it!" Amma threw in dismissively before Taj placed his ear phones on her to distract her from the conversation. Ayesha leant forward to join in the conversation and I took the opportunity to squeeze behind her to stare out of the window. I was twenty-eight, single and going to see a gay guy for an alaap. I toyed with the diamond pendant and shook my head. It just didn't make sense. Jhanghir had promised long ago to wait with two round tickets to my dream honeymoon. So Jhanghir's parents would blame me and inevitably hate me for breaking up their son's long-standing well-known and envied engagement to Preeya. Preeya's family would turn Jhanghir into an outcast. Baba would hate them for hating us for being Sylhethis, and Amma, who would love Jhanghir for taking me off of her hands, would ultimately blame him for putting her through years and years of stress over my singlehood. But through all the chaos, all the rejections and all the melodrama, I would be with Jhanghir. All of a sudden, I knew I would leave my job, family and friends to be with him, Jhanghir, my soul mate. And more than anything in the world, I realised Jhanghir was what I wanted.

"Who are you grinning at?" Amma muttered, smacking my knee whilst leaning across Ayesha. I looked down at my mom and held her face between my hands and kissed her forehead. She stopped and stared up at me. Maybe she thought I was serious about Joy, maybe she thought I was pinning my hopes on him. Either way, it didn't matter. I knew she'd be smiling soon.

One hour later, after the third replay of Hason Raja's classic tape we rolled into Kala's drive. We fell out of the hissing Primera, ready to take the English Channel and never ever return to normality.

"You made eit," Kala greeted us in her Benglish accent, neither fluent English nor Bengali. "Where half you bein?"

"What time are they coming?" Amma asked her younger sister in Bengali.

"Do you think she'll ever look at a man in the same way?" I muttered to Ayesha as we stretched our legs.

"Shut up," Ayesha muttered, but it was too late. Kala had overheard me.

"Who look at man agayn?"

"Kala, you've lost weight! You're on a diet aren't you?" Samir-bhai distracted, as Kala, round and stumpy as ever, giggled behind her sari shawl. "It suits you…"

"Stop, I haven't lost no weight…"

"Yes you have," Taj, added as Kala slapped his back playfully when he lifted her up in a bear hug.

"When did he become a junglee?" she demanded of Amma who, unimpressed, walked into the house without a single word. "She's tense, she's been tense since she was born so ignore her," Kala told us, shooting a warm look in my direction.

She understood because she had received many of Amma's concerned calls about my singledom. I smiled back, wanting to tell her about Joy so that she could help reign in Amma's expectations, but then Baba gave me a watermelon to lug in. As usual, Kala's husband, five daughters - Pana, Mana, Kara, Zarah and Farah, and only son

Sadek - were on hand to welcome us all. And after the hearty greetings, nature took over and we retreated into our peer groups. Amma and Baba disappeared with Kala and Kalu into the dining room. Samir-bhai with Taj and Sadek switched on Sky to follow Pakistan's one day international against England. And we, the girls, married and unmarried, retreated to a large bedroom.

"You're looking healthy Mana?" said Ayesha, initiating the catch-up session to distract us from the real reason we had invaded their home on a crisp January weekend. Kala had successfully married off Pana, Mana and Kara, but stalled with twenty two year old Zarah and sixteen year old Farah in deference to my single status. I wanted to tell them it wouldn't be long, I wanted to tell them about Jhanghir. I wanted to practice dancing routines for my henna and plan shopping sprees for our outfits. But I stayed stumm. Although we had grown up together and they, along with Loose-Leila and Man-eater Mina, were our only blood relatives in England, I couldn't do that until I had spoken to Jhanghir. And then, then they could stop wondering why I wasn't married at the ripe old age of twenty-eight.

"Amma says you know him, that you worked together," Farah, the youngest, finally asked with teenage enthusiasm. "What's he like?" My humiliation would be unleashed when they all discovered that Joy was in fact gay.

"I met him a few times, too brief to really remember him," I lied.

"But was he nice?" Pana, the oldest and most romantic, asked.

"He was a nice guy, but not quite my type."

"What do you mean?" Farah cut in with a mask of premature disappointment as Mana and Zarah left to make the first round of tea and biscuits.

"From what I remember, he was smaller than the type of guy I go for."

"How small…"

"No, no no!" Pana breathed out, waving her hand before her. "You can't decide until we all see him and know what he's like," she insisted, looking straight at me. "Uh-uh, you have to be positive, you have to believe the man will be good for you and you'll be surprised." I didn't believe a word my die hard romantic cousin uttered.

"What time are they meant to be coming?" It was way past lunchtime and I didn't know if I could keep my silence until they arrived.

"Around four, that's what Amma's friend, who's his aunt, told us."

But four o'clock came and went. Baba and Kalu were watching Bangla TV and debated Khalida Zia's rule over Bangladesh. Five o'clock came and went. Mana and Zarah had served up the third round of tea and refreshments, as Amma and Kala discussed whether or not to find out the reason for their delay. They decided not to. Six o'clock came and went. Kalu started cursing Joy's family and Kala decided to call her friend to check whether she had the correct address, as a guise to get them to get their arses moving. Seven o'clock came and went. We changed into our functionary outfits and continued waiting. The girls didn't whisper a word about the embarrassing delay and, even worse, their rudeness for not even calling to explain the delay. Amma and Baba sat quietly hiding their disappointment at what was a rejection. Samir-bhai, Taj and Sadek were still watching cricket. And the moment I decide to go to the bathroom to scrub off my make-up was the precise moment that Joy and his family decided to arrive.

"They're here, they're here!" Zarah squealed, thumping the bathroom door. I looked at my half-cleansed face, before throwing all my paraphernalia into the make bag to race out into the excited mayhem.
"Get the air freshener!" Kala instructed, causing Zarah to race through the ground floor spraying Haze Spring Cooler far too liberally. "The living room, do the living room!"
"She's got it, she's setting it up!" Mana squealed, as I hurtled into the dining room from where I'd be taken in to meet Joy.
"Setting what up?"
"The video camera!" Kara pointed out. "Ayesha's setting it up on the windowsill so we can record what they say about us when we're not in the room!" There was a lot of wasted talent in my family- we should have been the leading detective agency in the world!
"Here they come!" Farah whispered as we huddled up against the parted dining room door to see Joy's family's entrance.
"Oh my God, I see him!" Mana muttered as I stretched up on my toes to get a passing glimpse. Then I caught a tall graceful figure but nothing more. That wasn't the Joy I remembered. Maybe I had it all wrong. Maybe there had been a mix-up of biodata with pictures. Maybe I wouldn't have to swallow my pride and ask Jhanghir to marry me. Maybe I'd show him I could get married to a successful, established accountant all by myself. I felt a shiver of excited anticipation race through me. Maybe, just maybe, this was my moment.

Twenty minutes later, I had changed into a forest green chooridar shalwaar kameez, slipped on enough green and gold bangles to reach mid-arm and pulled my hair into an elegant chignon. With the exception of Pana, the oldest, who kept me company, and Sadek who was to serve the refreshments, all the girls had disappeared to an upstairs bedroom to avoid any confusion with the potential bride to be. Nothing Pana said allayed my silent excitement at the thought of meeting a tall, successful and straight version of the short gay Joy. I'd have to be careful as to how I'd break the news to the still heartbroken Sakina about the handsome savvy accountant who was to be my *husband.*
"Your brothers are talking with him right now. But I've sneaked the camera out for you," Sadek told me as he rushed into the dining room. At once we surrounded him, as he pulled out the small screen panel from the camera, hit rewind and then play.

"Is that him?" I asked as the camera shot whizzed by a tall dark suited figure.

"No, that's his uncle. This is him." It was then that I saw Joy, who was immaculately groomed.

"And this is Maya." And that was the moment my Kala chose to introduce me to Joy's auntie. We stood stunned at being caught red-handed hovering around the camera, all eager and shameless in our attempts to see the prospective groom.

"I'll show you our trip to Paris later," Sadek improvised as he snapped the panel back into place.

"Yeah, sure, I'd love to see that," I replied with a wide smile before I turned to Kala.

"Maya, this is Salek's auntie."

"Asalamalaikum," I greeted, remembering to pull the chiffon scarf over my head. The rotund, chocolate brown woman with pug eyes and thick lips that revealed paan-stained teeth, stared at me. She didn't say anything, observed my respectful modest appearance and then nodded, unimpressed.

"Let me show you the rest of the house," Kala said as she led her out of the room. 'The rest of the house?' Did I look like I could be passed off as a part of the furniture? Did I look the type to be inspected and disregarded like a mass-produced art deco lamp?

"It's time to go in," Ayesha announced, entering the room as soon as they had left. "Do your scarf properly," she added, as Kalu hovered by the door to lead us in as the elder. Once my scarf was tastefully thrown over my head and around my shoulders, I followed them out of the room and into the living room. I saw his uncle, an old woman like many Nani's I've seen, and then I saw Joy. He looked stunned as I walked in, but then giggled with recognition. I looked away and was led to a chair beside Ayesha and Samir-bhai. Everyone had noticed our reactions to each other. Everyone was silent, and I knew they thought we had fallen in love at first sight.

"You must be Maya," Joy's fair and recently-imported from Sylhet sister-in-law said as she sat near us. "We've heard a lot about you and your family." The old woman was looking back at me. She was dressed in a white sari that covered her head, with Jesus sandals and oversized men socks. Her face was lined with a hundred wrinkles, but her wide watching eyes had lost none of the alertness of a spirited hyena. If every other faculty failed her, I knew her sight told her everything she needed to know.

"Thank you," I answered, distracted by the old woman who was staring at my feet.

"You worked with Joy?" Joy's nani was now looking at my legs, back down to my feet and then my legs again. "In London, you worked at the same bookstore during your degree."

"Yes, we met a few times during our breaks," I replied. The old woman twisted round to get a better look. She almost keeled over. Kala got to her quickly and was shooed away for her efforts, but still the old woman sat twisted, starring at me intently.

"What do you think about moving to Luton?"

"We've only really visited Edinburgh, not really had much of a chance to see northern England!" Ayesha returned, intentionally misunderstanding the question. Sadek brought in a silver tray with a bowl of kheer to serve up. I caught his eyes and read his question about Joy. I rolled my eyes, but stopped when the old woman caught me. Now she was looking at my chest, as if to weigh up whether or not I could nurture my kids, her great grandchildren. I wanted to cross my arms but that would be giving in. I looked away and smiled at the Sylhethi doll who smiled back.

"Why don't you have some?" I took the bowl from the sister-in-law, felt Joy look over at me, but avoided his eyes. I suppressed all expression and reaction to prevent anyone misinterpreting courtesy for want of this alaap. When I looked back, the old woman was still assessing my breasts.

"Pssst, Maya!" Kalu was beckoning me from the doorway. I excused myself without a second thought. "Why don't you go into the dining room? We'll bring him through and you two can have some privacy." I nodded quickly, burning with embarrassment and disappeared into the dining room.

Soon after, Joy arrived. I have to admit, he was beautifully dressed in his charcoal suit, open-necked black shirt and fabulously shiny miniature loafers. But close behind him followed his sister-in-law, his auntie, my Kala, Taj, Ayesha, and Samir-bhai to ensure 'private' didn't mean 'suggestive'.

"This is much better, much, much better," Joy's auntie pointed out with wide, staring eyes. "You can talk freely without the pressure of family watching you. Talking about pressure, what pressure? This isn't pressure. Pressure existed in my days, when we were married off without seeing our husbands. That's pressure!"

"Who's feeling pressure?" Joy asked with a quick giggle.

"Good, good. That's how it should be. There shouldn't be any pressure, no tension, no heat!" Auntie came to a stop with a rumbling laugh. "But it's getting quite hot in here and I think it may get even hotter!" Everyone, including Joy, thought her innuendo was funny.

"Maybe we should leave, let them talk," she suggested, moving to rise. "Give them some time together. Who knows what they'll decide. Things aren't what they used to be, kids aren't what they used to be. Everything's changed." Auntie was on her soap box and she changed her mind about leaving. "When I was young, I did what my parents told me. I married when they said. These days, the kids get married when it suits them and they're now directing their parents. The world has turned on its head. Let's leave them to talk," she repeated, rising again to leave. Only, Sadek brought through another round of refreshments, which made Auntie change her mind and sit back down again. Sadek handed me my much-needed cup of coffee and I threw it back like a denied addict. "She drinks coffee. I love the smell of coffee, but can't stand the stuff. It's like living in Bangladesh, I love the smell, my homeland, but I can't stand the crap that comes with it!"

"I'd retire there with my husband," Ayesha said, as she handed out the samosas. "Have one, in fact you can have two!" She added, teasing Joy who stared at her. He appeared to be confused, looking from me to Ayesha and then back again. Ayesha smiled uncertainly and held out the plate until he took one.

"You couldn't live there!" Auntie derided as she finished her somosa in two bites.

"When I'm retired I would," Ayesha insisted as she passed a tea cup to Samir-bhai.

"Let's leave them to talk." Finally Auntie got up to leave. As no-one protested or initiated any conversation, they left. Everyone, that was, with the exclusion of Taj.

"So Joy, how are you doing these days?" I asked, as he looked at me with his twinkling little eyes and cute white smile.

"How are you? I'm blown away! I can't believe you're here!" he said in one breath. "All I was told was that I had an alaap, I didn't have time to look at the biodata, but I'm so glad you're here. It makes this so much easier when you find a friendly face!"

"What are you up to, I hear you're an accountant." Friendly face? Surely he was here for more? He knew that I knew, and I wondered at what point he would acknowledge that.

"Yeah, yeah, but that's work. In reality, I'm an ac-tor." His pronunciation was drawn out and Taj looked at me with a frown. I hadn't told Taj that Joy was gay, but Taj would find out soon enough.

"Really?"

"Yes, I'm a thespian."

"A what?" Taj blurted out.

"A thespian. I tread the boards up north, ready to make my debut…"

"You what?" I added cutting into Joy's theatrical explanation.

"In the theatre, I act in the theatre," Joy clarified as if he was talking to philistines. "My play goes out in two weeks in Luton. I had no idea I had to be here until my mother called and told me to drive down to Brighton to see a girl. I can tell you that my director was sooooo annoyed that I missed rehearsals today. Still, I'll make it up to him." The naughty giggle that followed made Taj look at me with disbelieving realisation. "Actually, would you believe that I met the director way back when I worked in Soho to pay for my accountancy exams. That was after Waterstone's and he was one of my biggest tippers, but that's no surprise. Gay men tip very well, especially if you're nice to them. And I always was. But that's enough about me, tell me about you," Joy said, waving his hand at me. "How's your husband?"

"What?" Joy looked at me with a naughty expression and then wiggled his eyebrows, as if he knew some secret about my past.

"Your husband? Remember Samira, that Pakistani girl who worked in the International Relations section, well she told me you got married last year, so where's the lucky man?"

"What husband?" Taj asked.

"Your husband…"

"I don't have a husband!" Taj shouted making Joy jump and shake his hands.

"Of course you don't!" Joy laughed away. "Your husband?" he said, looking at me. This was worse than I could possibly have ever imagined. I get an alaap. From a gay bloke. Who doesn't even realise that I'm the bride-to-be.

"Just to let you know, I've got to split you up in a couple of minutes!" Ayesha said as she peeked her head around the door before disappearing.

"Joy, who do you think you're here to see?" I asked. Joy winked at me in conspiracy.

"She is very lovely and caring. So very considerate." Of course it could get worse. "If a little obvious when she offered me a samosa!" I looked to Taj, who looked stared at me in disbelief. "Oh come on Maya, you walked your sister into the living room!"

"Why would your aunt leave us alone to talk if you're the alaap for my sister?"

"Oh my Gooooood, it's you!" Joy's eyes were round as saucers, and he held his hands to his face in shock. "Oh my God! I had no idea!"

"No kidding!" Taj muttered.

"Oh my God, that's why you're acting all shy and ladylike!" He didn't know how close he was to getting smacked. "You should be on stage if you can pull off a performance like this."

"Could you wing me some free tickets?" Well, I might as well make the trip worth my while.

"You mean complimentary tickets?" He wasn't this patronising at work. "You know, that cuts into our profits, and whilst my role isn't minor, it's certainly not the lead. Did I tell you my good friend went for an audition to be in The Bill. He's very, very good, though he didn't get to be the corner shop keeper, he's ever so good." Surely he wasn't trying to make me jealous? Joy covered his face with his hands and peeked through his fingers to stare at me with laughing eyes.

"Oh, you can't tell anybody!" he said. "I'd be mortified!"

My fate couldn't be left to the likes of Joy. I would crawl on my hands and knees through sleet and snow and beg Jhanghir to marry me to avoid such a fate.

"Taj, would you give us a few moments alone?" It was time to confront the issue. I waited until my brother left before facing Joy. I held his eyes and watched his amusement fade.

"You haven't told them, have you? You haven't 'come out'?" He shook his head and looked utterly miserable. "How long are you going to do this...?"

"You think I enjoy doing this?" Joy asked with incredulity. "Do you realise how hard it is..."

"I don't and I can't begin to imagine how difficult this is for you, Joy. But what you're doing is wrong, you're misleading our families and that's not fair."

"It's not fair on me either Maya. I didn't choose to be this way."

"But you can choose how you deal with it." I sounded unsympathetic but Joy needed to hear this. "And what you choose to be is between you and Allah."

"I'm trying to do the right thing by my family." The admission struck a chord with me.

"I'm not wise or learned enough to give you advice Joy, but I know enough to tell you that duping a girl into a marriage of convenience is wrong."

"What choice do I have?" Joy looked defeated and I smiled at him.

"You're a smart, intelligent man with a to-die-for taste in clothes. You'll figure it out." He grinned before shaking his head.

"All the aunts are probably choosing wedding venues by now " I read the uncertainty in his eyes and knew he feared how much I would reveal to the elders. "What do we do now?

"Why don't you tell them I'm not your type? That I'm too old, too direct and as difficult as it may be to believe, even a little too pushy?" The relief in his demeanour was evident.

"You know it's not personal?" he laughed.

"Of course not!" I returned, pretending to be put-out.

"Because you are by far the oldest, most direct and pushiest girl that I've seen," he teased.

"And still I'm not enough for you!" We laughed at the exchange until we settled into a quiet moment. I looked at Joy. He had a struggle ahead of him, but he smiled at me.

"Thank you Maya." I nodded and patted his hand. "I maybe able to bag a few free tickets..."

"That's not necessary."

"Really, I want to."

"It'll take more than a couple of free tickets to ease the pain of your rejection!"

"You done?" Samir-bhai asked opening the door to reveal both families keenly hovering. "Joy's family are ready to leave." We stopped laughing and looked to my waiting brother-in-law to nod.

"You must give me your email. We must catch up, if only to chat about this mess!" he winked before making us sound like we had gotten on fantastically enough to be married soon.

"Make sure you write to me and not Ayesha!" I teased as I handed him my business card and followed him to the hall. Auntie, Kala, and his sister-in-law were smiling. Kalu sent Sadek upstairs to drag Baba away from Spanish football for the farewells. And then she was in front of me. The old woman. Standing in front of my like a ghost in white, chewing away on paan. She looked at me from my toes to the top of my head. Then back down again. I tried to ignore her as the farewells were said and watched Sadek lead them out to the car with Taj. The old woman was the last to leave, looking me up and down from head to toe and back again. Then she left. Without a word. Without a single word.

"Where was Baba?" I asked as we piled into Zarah's bedroom to talk 'potential', whilst Amma and Baba retreated with Kala and Kalu to talk 'decision'.

"Spanish football," Taj answered, as if it was a reasonable excuse to be absent from meeting your future son-in-law.

"So what do you think?" Kara asked as Sadek arrived with yet more drinks and slices of fresh mango and watermelon.

"I don't think it's a matter of what I thought." With the exception of Taj, they all looked confused. "I don't think he knew what to think."

"He's soft," Sadek supplied as he sat down with his drink.

"What do you mean, Maya?" Pana asked ignoring her brother.

"He didn't know who the bride was!" I covered, as Ayesha looked at me.

"No!" My cousins cried out in disbelief.

"I don't think he cared either way," Taj muttered.

"But he can't have been confused..." Zarah pointed out.

"You're lying," Pana said. "I know you're winding us up!" I waited until the denials stopped and then grinned at Ayesha.

"He must've known, there's no way he could not have known," Samir-bhai added.

"Who did he think he was getting?" Sadek looked suggestively at Taj who glared back.

"The one who offered him two samosas!" I burst out, making everyone collapse in peals of laughter as Ayesha screamed in denial. But our amusement was short lived. Everyone sobered up as Amma walked into the room.

"What do you think?" she asked Samir-bhai, who was her last hope at giving Joy the slightest bit of credibility. We all shared looks uncertain of how far we could push Amma. Samir-bhai struggled to find a reasonable excuse and paused.

"I don't think so Amma, he took a liking to Ayesha." Amma looked at me and then to her oldest daughter, before shaking her head in resignation. She walked out without another word. We all looked at each other, waiting for someone to break the awkward silence. Seconds later, uncontrollable laughter filled the room.

We left Brighton long after midnight with Pana, Mana, Kara, Zarah and Farah waving us off. Joy was an alaap that everyone, including Amma, was happy to pass on. As soon as we hit the A23, everyone except Baba and I fell asleep. In the back, we stopped caring about squashing each other, and leaned in a warm huddle. I was still wedged against the door, but I didn't mind. I stared out into the black sky and smiled. There were two more weeks until the end of Ramadan. Now I had something specific to ask the Almighty for. It would be easy to arrange with just his blessing. I would call Jhanghir. No, I would perfect what I wanted to say to him first, and then I'd call him. I felt a burning light within me and I couldn't stop smiling. He'd pick up the phone.

"Don't speak," I would whisper, "I'm calling to collect my ticket."

"Your ticket?" He would say in a voice barely above mine.

"I want you to join me in the Maldives."

"Why?" he would ask.

"Because there's only you. There's only ever been you." Was that too corny? It sounded pre-planned, scripted. I would definitely say 'I'm collecting my ticket'. But then what?

"I've missed you since the day you walked out on me. I miss you every time we speak and you hang up on me. I miss you every time I think of you and want you with me." No, no, no. It all sounded like a mushy B-rate movie. I'd start again and then say: "I'm calling to say I'm getting married." That would be followed by. "Congratulate yourself, I'm marrying you." Oh please, this was going to be harder than I imagined. We were a long way from home, but I had plenty of time to perfectly end my stint at singledom.

H: Hide All Hellish Heartbreaks

"Don't speak."

"Just listen to me."

"I miss you. I've missed you since the day you left. And I haven't stopped missing you. I thought I would, I thought that maybe over time it would pass, that it would lessen. But it hasn't. So, what I want to know is, is it the same for you…?"

"Will you stop bloody reading poetry in there!" I nearly jumped out of the bath buck naked at my sister-in-law's scream. "Hamza's covered in mud, Tariq refuses to leave the bathroom upstairs and I need to bathe him."

"I'm out," I muttered, as I dried myself with my old pink towel. Privacy, I had no privacy.

"You haven't washed the tub," Shireen accused as I walked past her and a bawling Hamza, clutching my essential body oils.

"I haven't used it," I muttered back before storming into my bedroom and locking the door. I could hear Shireen telling Hamza off and Amma shouting at her from the kitchen for her to go easy on Hamza. I could hear Baba turn the soil with his latest B&Q gardening gadget and bhangra thumping out of Taj's room. I could hear everything on this perfect February morning, except my own thoughts. I had practiced my speech over and over again, but it never sounded adequate enough to explain what I was doing, or rather asking for. Yet two weeks had passed since that long drive back from Brighton and I didn't have any reason to put it off any longer. There in my pink fluffy towel, with soaking wet hair and racing heart I called Jhanghir. At each dialling tone, I thought 'one more. One more ring and I'll hang up, I'll hang up and carry on with the rest of my life'.

"Yeah?" I'd woken him from his sleep. It was four o'clock in the morning in New York and I could tell he had been on a late shift. He sounded exhausted and I felt breathless and nauseous and a hundred other rioting emotions.

"Jhanghir, it's me." I sounded perky, too perky, but my heart was racing a million beats per second.

"God, Maya, do you have the faintest idea what time it is?" He sounded annoyed.

"I don't know, three, four in the morning…"

"Maya, I've had a really rough night." This wasn't meant to happen. He wasn't meant to cut into my perfected professions of true love and happy ever afters. In fact, he hadn't even greeted me with his tired mutter before rolling over to listen to me babble on like he always did.

"I'll give you a call sometime." And then Jhanghir did something he had never done to me before. He hung up on me! I stared at the receiver with confused feelings of outrage and disappointment. Something was wrong, but I didn't have the courage to ask him. In any case, I'd find out soon enough. He'd feel guilty about how he'd behaved and he'd send me a sarcastic email to make up for it. Maybe one of his patients passed away despite all his best efforts. Maybe he hadn't slept for forty-eight hours on the trot. Maybe it was best he hampered my plans. Maybe we were just never meant to be and this was Allah's way of making me realise. Just maybe we'll always be a Maybe.

Mid-morning, I logged onto my email account from Jana's study and realised that we would be a Never.

To: MayaM@Instantmail.com
From: Jkhan@NYMedics.com
'Hey you, I see the concept of time zones hasn't dawned on you yet. How's the brain surgeon - still holding onto the slippery little guy? At this end, Preeya's agreed to marry this charming medic which means I'll be married off by the end of the month. So unless you throw a spanner in the works Maya, we'll both be married by the end of summer. Seems like we're finally making adult choices - Jhanghir.'

I felt my world shatter into a million pieces and freefall into nothingness. My mind reeled, my heart pounded until I shook with the realisation of his words.
"Maya! C'mon, we're ready to go shopping!" Hana had turned up with Ayesha and Amma for our Eid shopping trip to Wembley. "Maya!" They didn't know about my feelings for Jhanghir. Nobody knew. How could they?
"C... coming," I managed as I scanned his words again. "I'm coming," I shouted out as I closed my eyes and forced myself to smile. 'Good for him.' I whispered. We were worlds apart. He just dropped it into the conversation as if I were a mere acquaintance. After all these years, I wasn't even worthy of an invite to his wedding. I felt my heart break.
"Maya, you have five minutes, and then I'm disconnecting the Internet." With that warning I hit the reply button.

To: Jkhan@NYMedics.com
From: MayaM@Instantmail.com
'Jhanghir, I wish you and Preeya all the happiness and joy in the world, Maya.'

I rolled the icon over the send button and clicked it. I watched the note fold up into an envelope and whiz off into cyberspace. I logged off the computer, shut it down and joined my family with the brightest of smiles. Nobody knew. Nobody needed to know. Even he didn't know. I could handle that.

The buzz of Ealing Road didn't raise my spirits. I trailed behind as my sisters and Amma searched for the best vegetable prices up and down Wembley's twenty-four hour grocery stores. You see, Asians don't shop like white people. We buy in bulk, at wholesale prices. If ASDA do bananas for seventy-five pence per kilo, Wembley Vegetable and Fruits will do it for nineteen pence kilo. If Safeway sells tomatoes for fifty-five pence per kilo, our friends in Wembley will undercut them by thirty pence. Of course, there was no eye-catching packaging or jazzy cartons of the uber-brands, but who wanted to pay mega pounds when the said snazzy packaging would end up in the bin? Yes, you were shoved and knocked about by sweet looking elderly nannis dressed in multicoloured saris with men's socks and open-toe sandals. It didn't matter that the open stores were badly laid out, or that we were probably buying over-sprayed, under-priced and a little battered groceries. That was all just part of shopping Asian style. Only, I didn't fancy it today. I didn't fancy anything today, I just wanted to hide away from the world.

"Maya, what do you think?" Ayesha was holding up a large cauliflower and pointing to the '3 for £1.20' sign. She didn't wait for my thumbs up, but began piling six large caulis into her basket.

"You haven't picked up a single thing," Amma chided as she frowned in Jana's direction. "No avocados, Jana. They have no taste and no use in Indian cooking."

"They're all picking up the right bargains," I told her, as Jana replaced the avocados and moved on to more exotic fruits.

"I'm getting kiwis, mangos and pink grapefruits," Jana stated, daring Amma to stop her. Jana and Hana had always been carefree and despite being married for two years and having successful careers, they were still prudent in my parents' presence, as if to prove their money management teachings hadn't gone to waste. In this case, Jana's obstinate tone drew Amma to review Jana's shopping list and compare prices.

"We need to go across to the Hindu grocers, they're doing ten kiwis for a pound," she advised, leading Jana out of the congested grocers. I wandered aimlessly with one thing on my mind. I had been in a seven-year coma and had woken up with the realisation that Jhangir was everything I wanted. And yet, I was too late. He was getting married in three weeks. I felt Amma's watching eyes. Her motherly sixth sense had kicked in and she knew I was sad. I smiled and grabbed a plastic bag to make the most of the five-for-a-pound lemon offer. I liked lemons. Keeping busy was what I needed to do to fill the numbness within me. That way I wouldn't feel so sad. That way I could make it through the day.

Eid-ul-Fitr transformed our house into an open party. Besides all my brothers and sisters and their spouses and children, we never knew who else would turn up. Sometimes most of our relatives through marriage turned up, but sometimes it was just Chachijhi and cousins Leila and Mina. Only on this occasion, it wasn't just Loose-Leila and Man-eater Mina who turned up. Most of Ayesha, Jana, and Hana's in-laws, along with several children and grandchildren to boot, arrived unannounced. And yet somehow we all fitted into the four-bedroom semi and we always had enough food to feed everyone.

"Given anyone a heart attack recently?" That was Leila's greeting as she swayed past me to walk through the hall. The bitch was dressed in a sleeveless black fitted shalwaar kameez, which showed off her perfectly toned, carbohydrate drained body. I didn't have the energy to throw back an equally cutting reply.

"Ignore Leila, you will find a husband one day." I smiled at Chachijhi and stood aside to let them through. I remained there in anticipation of more guests and listened to Leila and Mina giggle as they spotted Samir-bhai's youngest brother out in the garden. They were funny to watch, uninhibited and brazen. But then the door chimed and I was back on duty. After door duty came serving duty. After serving duty came washing duty. After washing duty came kids duty, as the elders crowded into the dining room to talk about the old days. I took to it all without a word and with the single thought of Jhanghir's imminent wedding.

"For God's sake Maya, stop daydreaming and playing with that necklace of yours! You're meant to be watching over the kids!" Shireen snapped, storming past me. I looked to where Hamza tussled viciously on the grass with Ayesha's two year old daughter and then watched as Shireen tore the two apart as they scrabbled to tear each other apart.

"Give it back!" Hamza demanded, trying to grab his F1 Ferrari from Zarah's hands.

"No, I want it," Zarah insisted holding the car out of Hamza's reach.

"Give it back, it's mine," Hamza threatened, as he wrenched his arm free and jumped at Zarah. Zarah's shrill scream jerked me out of my miserable reverie. Grabbing both the car and my little nephew, I walked through the house, upstairs and into my bedroom.

"Now, you have to protect me from getting into trouble," I said, handing him the snazzy toy as he grinned up at me like I was his hero. He promised, giggled in conspiracy and instantly went on door duty as I switched on my laptop. We were born with the instinct to fight for what was ours. Even four years olds knew that. I felt embarrassed by my own timidity. Jhanghir was mine. And I wouldn't let him go without a fight. That way whatever the outcome there would be no regrets, no what-ifs.

To: Jkhan@NYMedics.com
From: MayaM@Instantmail.com
'Choose me. Choose me because I'm right for you, because Preeya shouldn't have to be the dutiful choice and because we're perfect for each other. Like in "My Best Friend's Wedding", where Julia Roberts tries to win back the love of her life. Only we don't have to have the sad ending. It doesn't matter that we're from two different backgrounds where we speak with different accents and move in different circles. It

doesn't matter that I've tried to give you up since the first moment I saw you because I was too stubborn to admit I wanted you. All that matters is that you don't commit yourself to the wrong person. That you know that I am totally utterly and still absolutely hooked on you. Choose me Jhanghir.'

Honesty had no room for pride. I had never uttered those words at any time in my life, but nothing seemed truer than to make Jhanghir aware of my feelings. I was asking Jhanghir to break up a ten-year engagement and the plans for the biggest day of his life for me. To choose me. To marry me. I was exhilarated and shaking at the same time. It was the single most selfish act of my life, but he was the love of my life and I couldn't just let him go. Not without him knowing that he still had a chance, that we had a chance. Jhanghir would read my plea, and know how I truly felt about him. How could he not choose me? He would choose me, tell his family, ride out the commotion and family dramas and then come for me. All my aunties and extended family would gossip about my last minute attempts to rescue any hope of a future with Jhanghir. Already, I could see myself dressed in claret and gold watching Jhanghir walk towards me as the perfect groom. I would be, for some time, the favourite talking point of my community, but I would have the perfect man for the perfect wedding and I would live happily ever after. Who would have guessed I would find my man in this way.

Then an email appeared in my inbox.

To: MayaM@Instantmail.com
From: Jkhan@NYMedics.com
'Maya, when we fell out four years ago, you denied we had something more special than a simple friendship. You denied me. Us. A future. I will always have the highest regard for you, but I made a promise to my father and I have to honour that. You've promised yourself to Shah, you also have a duty to him and your family to honour that.
I won't dwell on what might have been. That will only turn sadness into regret. We have both made decisions not in our own interests, but mainly for the happiness of others, though they will never know that. But we're not kids anymore Maya. Shah and Preeya deserve better.
There are couples in this world that are meant for each other, but never meant to be. That's what we are. Take care Maya, you're someone special to me, in more ways than you'll ever know.'

"Happy Birthday to me! Happy Birthday to me!" It was Sakina. The following morning, I was in bed re-reading Jhanghir's response on my laptop. "Are you set for tonight? We've got the table booked, everyone's confirmed, and Javed's also bringing along a mate to introduce me to. I don't know if it's too soon after Raj. I guess I won't know until I meet Javed's friend. But don't worry Maya, I promise you won't feel left out. You're sitting right beside me." Thank God I didn't have to speak and ruin Sakina's birthday. Whilst she was all excited about beginning the next year of her life, I was looking ahead into my shattered, empty, rejected future. *'You're more special to me in more ways than you'll ever know.'* What the hell did that mean? What was I meant to understand by that line? All I knew was that he was rejecting me, us and our future.

"You know we're all wearing shalwaar kameez? Nothing jazzy, understated and simple."

"Ok." This was Sakina's way of making sure that cool looking friends surrounded her.

"Tina, Rosie and Shazia will be there with their husbands. Remember, tonight's about losing ourselves, forgetting our sad, single, rejected over-the-hill lives. We're going to dance the night away."

"Yeah." I'm glad she didn't think about the Arsehole, I'm glad she didn't pick up on my desolate tone. I'm glad it was a short call. I promised to meet her promptly at seven pm at The Mumtaz Bengali Restaurant on Ealing Road. I promised to leave all my worries and concerns behind. I promised to be happy. I looked at back at my laptop and hit the reply icon.

To: Jkhan@NYMedics.com
From: MayaM@Instantmail.com
'Give it to me for timing right? I remember you calling me your soul mate. I believe some couples are meant for each other and meant to be. I believe we can convince everyone to accept our decision if we really wanted this. But I don't believe soul mates go on to marry others without truly fighting for what they want and I don't believe you've done that. So by default, I no longer believe in you. All that's left for me to say is that I wish you the happiness.'

It was eight o'clock on Sunday morning and three a.m. in Manhattan. On alternate weekends Jhanghir worked the night duty. At this time, things were slow and he would be online. I waited twenty minutes and saw the incoming mail. I was numb but I hit the open button. I had to know how he could explain his betrayal.

To: MayaM@Instantmail.com
From: Jkhan@NYMedics.com
'How did you turn this thing on its head and make me the bad guy? I realise you're pissed off for finding out about the wedding like that. I told you once that I would marry Preeya the moment you told me that you were getting married, so you knew this was going to happen. And how does that change the fact that you too are getting married. Maya, I gave you up four years ago. We've known each other for over eight years. And I've made peace with the fact that we are not going to be more than friends.

Yes, Preeya is now my soul mate. I've made a commitment to someone I am more than happy to spend the rest of my life with and there's no contemplating what you've suggested. Are you really prepared to drop Shah and create gossip and speculation over your family honour just to get what you want? If the answer is yes, then I don't really know you at all.'

Maybe Jhanghir didn't know who I really was, or had become, in his absence. Maybe I had kept up the pretence of being the Maya he loved because he was the only one to still make me feel good about myself. Somewhere, somehow, I had turned into someone I never wanted to be. Somehow the girl who loved a challenge, broke convention and loved life had changed into an ultra traditional Bengali female with a pension. I hated my 9 to 5 job. I hated my repetitive, predictable life. I hated my singledom. And here I was begging this man to choose me like those desperate single women on Ricki Lake. He was still online, and waiting for my reply. I still had an ounce of self-respect, so I logged out, switched off and cried.

"What do you think?" I had spent the afternoon at RKC's Beauticians, paying the Sunday premium for a facial, eyebrow shaping, threading and hi-lo lights to be reapplied. I had breezed into Chachijhi's home and brazenly asked Leila for her black sleeveless shalwaar kameez after promising her two tickets to Jezebel's next fashion show. Once I got home, I locked myself into my bedroom to transform myself into a party girl. Tonight there was no room for subtle elegance or sophistication. Tonight I didn't want to be Maya, tonight I wanted to be reckless and carefree. Though Leila's shalwaar kameez felt a little tight, my tousled hair and dirty kohled come-to-bed eyes told the world that I was ready to hit the town.
"Isn't that outfit a little tight? I hope you're wearing a cardigan to cover your arms!" That's exactly the response I wanted from Amma, and no, I wasn't going to wear a cardigan. "I know Sakina and Tanya will be modestly dressed..."
"You look nice," Shireen cut in as she held a dozing Hamza. I caught her eyes. Somehow she had read my sadness. I smiled and walked into the hall, before I welled up, to search for Jana's stilettos. I could barely walk in regular heels, so this would be fun. I could already see myself sprawled on the dance floor, but who cared?
"Maya, it's for you." That would be Sakina making sure we were all on our way. I took the handset from Shireen, while searching the shoe cupboard for the stilettos.
"I promise to be there on time." I had thirty minutes to get to Mumtaz if I took the A40 to Hanger Lane. "Twenty minutes max!"
"Even by Concorde, that's not possible." It was Jhanghir. I looked up at Shireen who was walking back to the living room.

"Hi." It was all I could manage as I scrambled off my hands and knees to race up to my room.

"Hi." My heart raced, and I wished I had revealed none of it. That way I could still be the perky, oblivious, pragmatic Maya he knew. Surely I could come up with an intelligent, witty, mature line to make him realise that his decision would be the worst decision of his life.

"This is a surprise." Twenty-eight years of life, love and loss, and that was all I could think of.

"No, believe me, I'm the surprised one." And I'm the rejected one.

"Jhanghir, it was always on the cards."

"Not for me. Why now? Where did all that come from?" I could hear the smile in his voice. He had no idea how hard this was for me. The big empty hole in my chest was hard to bear.

"It came from a last ditch attempt at a joke," I made up and he chuckled. He wanted us to end on a good note. He wanted closure and he wanted me to make him feel good about it. "How are the wedding plans coming along?"

"You know me. I'll turn up on the day, put on the suit and do what I gotta do."

"Yeah," I whispered, feeling that empty hole fill up and shatter into a billion pieces.

"I've got my suit, I know it fits and that's all I'm doing." I imagined how handsome he would look and I wanted to cry.

"This is the biggest day of your life, you're meant to take more of an interest in it!" I told him with a light laugh like the old Maya. "You're meant to think about your speech, the rings, make sure the bride has everything just the way she wants it." Or I would have, if the world were a just, kind, loving place.

"That's what families are for!" he brushed it off. We were struggling with the light conversation, but I didn't want to talk about us.

"When's the wedding..."

"Three weeks. I'm flying out to San Francisco where we're holding the wedding in two weeks."

"So am I invited, Jhanghir?"

"You gotta be kidding."

"I know that it's somewhere in San Francisco."

"And have you turn a perfectly ordinary wedding into chaos? Who knows what you'll do?" That's right. That's what old Maya would have done. She'd have walked right up to Jhanghir, demanded he stop the wedding right there and then. But he didn't know the new Maya, the timid, accept what-life-gives-you Maya. I felt the cool trail of tears as I laughed with him.

"Hold on, my mobile's ringing". I picked up my Nokia. "Hiya, Sakina, I'm about to leave..."

"You haven't left yet?" She squealed in disgust. "Maya, Tanya's only turning up with a guy for me. And you have got to be there with me so it's not a clichéd introduction."

"I promise I'll leave in five minutes." And with that I cancelled Sakina's call and breathed deeply before picking up the handset. "Hey."
"You still painting the town red tonight?" His light hearted tone had disappeared.
"You know me Jhanghir, parties, concerts, exhibitions," I lied. But it felt good to know that he knew I wouldn't be depressed and crying over his rejection.
"That's good Maya. I'm glad we can..."
"I shouldn't have said those things Jhanghir. I know this is awkward for you, so I appreciate this call, and I really really do wish you all the joy in the world." There, I had said it. Confronted the rejection, and given him the closure he wanted.
"You have Shah, the man of your dreams that you're marrying this summer. You've got everything you wanted." I didn't correct him. There was no point. I didn't want to speak to him anymore. I wanted to be out there, dancing the night away, losing myself from me.
"Yeah," I whispered. "I have all that."

Things didn't get any better at Mumtaz. Everyone of my friends belonged to another, either permanently or temporarily. Tina and Rosie had been married for two years, and Shazia had been engaged for six months. They were all equally blissfully happy. Tanya was there with Javed, and he had brought along Shaj to introduce to Sakina. Everyone looked great, everyone chatted happily and everyone made special effort to include me in their conversations. I tried hard to be spirited and funny. I kept up the banter through the barely-warm Bengali meal, I laughed at the jokes that accompanied the pistachio kulfi. I even took a second helping of Sakina's birthday cake to prove how much I liked it. But then there were those moments, when those on either side of me were deep in conversation with their partners. Those were the moments that I felt overwhelmed by what I'd lost. How could so much and so little happen in the space of forty-eight hours? My whole world, my dreams and my desires had all vanished and no one but me was any wiser. On my third visit to the ladies, I froze and stared at my reflection in the brightly lit ladies room. The diamond pendant sparkled in the mirror to cruelly remind me of what I had lost and why I had lost it. Gone was the sexy, sultry woman. In reality, my tousled hair looked like an unbrushed mop and the over-the-top make-up highlighted the dark circles around my dead eyes. The black outfit served only to prove how much I needed to go on the Atkins diet. But it was too late. Too late to go on the diet, too late to change my outfit, too late for Jhanghir. I grabbed a tissue and soaked it in water to wipe off my make-up. Fresh faced, I returned to the dimly lit ballroom filled with professional Asians having a good time.
"Are you ok?" Tanya asked, concerned at my make up- free appearance. I smiled and nodded, fed up with being mollycoddled. She didn't ask about Jhanghir, but then she didn't have to. She knew

enough to understand my behaviour. At the back of the renowned restaurant, the in-house band struck up a classic Indian track and that was all the excuse I needed to get away from the 'couples syndrome'.

"You're not dancing alone to my favourite track!" Tina warned as she joined me on my journey to the dance floor. Rosie and Sakina followed suit and before long Tanya and Shazia joined us. We didn't often go dancing, at least I didn't. Years of conditioning against mixed dancing had left us dancing adequately. But what did it matter? We were a bunch of women dancing, laughing at each other and losing ourselves.

That too was short-lived. Shaj shimmied up to Sakina to dance away like a wannabe George Michael. It was hard to keep a straight face. Sakina looked horrified, but we all encouraged her to keep dancing. Tanya returned to our table to speak with Javed, whilst Shazia had given up on any modesty and snogged her fiancé near the back of the ballroom. Before long, the rest of my friends partnered up with their men until I stood at the edge of the dance floor. I checked my watch and caught Tanya beckoning me to join them. It was past midnight and I was exhausted by the pretence. I walked over to the table and picked up my clutch bag.

"I'm calling it a night guys."

"Come on, another dance!" Sweet guy Javed was covering for my embarrassing single status.

"I'm beat so I'm disappearing first. You guys stay on, I'll call you tomorrow."

"You ok to drive home alone?" Tanya understood.

"Yes, but I'd appreciate Javed walking me down to my car." And that's what he did. Javed was a gentleman, tall, slender and rugged looking. He was also totally smitten with Tanya, who for some unknown reason refused to commit to him. At that precise moment in time, I felt a strong kinship with Javed.

"How are you doing with Tanya?" I asked sensing that he needed some advice.

"She talks to you more than she does me." He was also a no bullshit type of guy.

"I know you feel strongly about her."

"I love her." I wanted to smack Tanya into realising what she had. "And she doesn't love me."

"Think about backing off, letting her figure it out herself?"

"And lose the chance of making the most of what I have for as long as I have it?"

"You sure you're not deceiving yourself about the inevitable?" The devil's advocate in me wanted to protect him, save him from the hurt that I shut away deep inside me.

"There is no inevitable, Maya. There's a chance I can convince her to marry me if I keep trying, but there's no chance if I give up." I thought about Javed's words when I drove off. I repeated them in my head as I took the A40 off the Hanger Lane roundabout. When I let myself in and crept into my bedroom, I realised what he meant. So I opened up my laptop and logged onto my email.

To: Jkhan@NYMedics.com
From: MayaM@Instantmail.com
'You know I wouldn't be me if I didn't at least try to get the last word, right?!
Despite all the camaraderie during our call, things won't ever be the same between us. Actually, in a twisted way I was happier when you were pissed off at me. I can deal with you being angry, but you being nice, consoling me and telling me I have potential - that I can't deal with. I'm tired of being polite, doing the right thing, effectively sitting on the by-lines of life. So I'm going to be honest.
Ever since you flew out over a month ago, I've been rehearsing what I was going to say that night I called you at 4am. I wanted to tell you that I was coming out to see you to ask whether you wanted to go to the Maldives with me. Countless days wasted to get one stupid question perfectly correct. I repeated it silently, at work, through my boring meetings, when I was with friends & family, when I was alone- just so it was perfect. And then I called and you were annoyed and of course, like life, things didn't go as planned.
Jhanghir, I don't have a fiancé and I have no wedding planned for the summer. I was introduced to a surgeon and Amma in her excitement told everyone that I had agreed to marry him. But he rejected me. I couldn't tell you because four years on I'm still in love with you. Four years on I regret allowing my pride to reject your marriage proposal and I regret being too stubborn to tell you that if you asked me to marry you again, the answer would only be yes. I've seen enough alaaps to know that I have something special with you that I won't ever have with anyone else. Tonight, I thought about all the times we won't have, the home we will no longer build, the children that will no longer be. And I now know that with you, I would live a dream. With anyone else I would have to create one.
So why disclose this now? Because I know I'll never be able to say this again. Let's face it, your days as a bachelor are seriously numbered!
And our conversation today ended something. I hated myself for apologising to you. I was back to the accommodating Maya that put everyone and everything before herself. And all I wanted to say was, could you still contemplate a future with me?
I hope you understand that I have to do this, that I need for you to know. If I didn't do this, I'd regret it. I'm hurting right now Jhanghir, so don't be polite or nice. I don't know what will happen after you get married, things appropriate now won't be then. Know that you'll always be with me, but for now I'm gonna let you go.'

"Foopi, you back already?" Hamza always sneaked into my bed when I went away for conferences and late business meetings. Now he sat up tiredly in his Manchester United pyjamas rubbing his eyes.

"Go back to sleep sweetie," I whispered, wiping at my tears as I put away my laptop.

Hamza wriggled back beneath the covers and I tucked him in and kissed him on the cheek. I waited until he drifted off, watching his beautiful face and wondering how wonderful life would've been if I'd listened to Jhanghir four years ago. If I'd accepted his proposal, would I have been tucking in our child and staring down thinking how beautiful he was? And now, now that would never be. I would never have Jhanghir's children, I would never tuck them in, or watch them grow. Turning away, I wiped at my tears, changed into my favourite comfort pyjamas and then pulled out my photo albums from beneath my bed. I flipped through them until I stared down at Jhanghir. We had gone to Hyde Park for a picnic with his research group and had grinned up at the camera with wide happy smiles.

"Yep," I whispered, tracing his features. "You'll always be with me."

I: Identify Insanity And Internet Idiots

Is this what happens when people fall in love? Do we lose all ability to reason or function? Jhanghir hadn't replied when I woke up on Monday to check my email. I kept my personal email account open all day at work in case he wrote. I cut short all my phone conversations just in case he called. I kept my mobile with me throughout all my meetings. I caught the bus home instead of taking the Central line so that I didn't lose any mobile reception. I jumped each time the phone rang, hoping against hope that it was Jhanghir and then feeling crushed when it wasn't. When Tanya and Sakina called, I asked Amma to tell them I'd call back, knowing we'd spend hours talking about Shaj. I couldn't do that in case Jhanghir called. I checked my personal account again before I got ready for bed. And as I got into bed I told myself, maybe he was so bowled over by my honesty, that by the time I woke up he would have landed at Heathrow. That's why he hadn't responded. That's why he hadn't called. It would take time to delegate his duties and talk through his decision with his family before he booked a flight. I understood that. And I smiled. He was on his way and he would turn up on my doorstep to steal me away to our perfect future.

On Tuesday, I checked all incoming flights from JFK and New Jersey. I called home every hour to check if there were any calls, messages, packages or person waiting for me. I still had my personal email account open all day and kept my conversations short. And I seemed to get through more of my projects than ever before. I don't know if it was the joy of knowing Jhanghir was on his way, or whether being in love just made me a lot more focused and determined. Whatever it was, my evil pretentious colleagues looked at me differently and I liked that. Tanya and Sakina definitely knew something was up, but I couldn't risk missing out on Jhanghir's surprise. As the day progressed, I crossed off each flight and stared at my mobile for the call he would make on arrival. My nerves were a jangled mess. My appetite disappeared, but I'd never felt more exhilarated. My life was a rom com and it would end perfectly. By the end of the day, I knew he wouldn't write so I logged out of my account. Why would he, if he was going to surprise me? On my way home, I brought some bright flowers at Farringdon Station because they would liven up our living room, you know, add a little panache to our staid but tasteful room when Jhanghir arrived. But there were no messages, calls or packages when I got home, yet it didn't matter because there were five more flights arriving from New York that evening. And on Wednesday, there were a further ten flights.

"What's going on Maya?" I would give Tanya five minutes as two New York flights had just landed. "Where've you been?"

"Working, there's a load on."

"There's always loads on. What's going on? What happened on Sunday night?" It was too much to tell at work, and in any case Jhanghir could now be disembarking.

"I played the perfect gooseberry and I'm not doing that again."

"Is that why you've been avoiding our calls?" Like I didn't have more important reasons for not taking my friends calls!

"No, you asked me what happened and I told you..."

"What's going on Maya?" Tanya had known me since primary school. She could tell I was holding back.

"I promise to call you tonight." But Tanya felt something big had happened, and it took a further five minutes to convince her it wasn't life threatening. Sakina called as soon as I hung up. Tanya had obviously emailed her whilst we spoke to tell her there was something wrong. Eager to get off the phone, I told Sakina the same thing, and promised to call her with a full explanation. I checked my email account just a couple of times, just to make sure Jhanghir hadn't written to explain why he'd been delayed. He hadn't. I took my afternoon meetings and switched off my mobile. I checked for his voicemail on each return, but there were none. I played with my lunch at four pm, and then chucked it away when it turned my stomach. And as I doodled on my notepad, Amma rang to tell me that she had made chicken jalfrezi, my favourite, for dinner. She was worried by my quiet behaviour, but I blamed it on the pressures of work. I took the tube home, sure that if he was going to surprise me, he would make his way to my home and not ruin it by leaving a silly voicemail. I even took some work home, so he would discover what a dedicated professional I had become. At least it kept me occupied throughout the evening and stopped the doubts about Jhanghir's arrival from taking over.

"Hi, my name is Maya Malik and I'm taking the meeting on behalf of Clare..."

"She no take meeting?" The De Niro look-alike in immaculate Armani was not happy.

"Unfortunately, Clare's unwell today. But I've been briefed about her report..."

"But we fly from Milan first thing to make this meeting," tutted Ricardo Maldini, Director of European Marketing, before turning to his army of colleagues who burst into an angry exchange in Italian. I stood by unaffected and stared back at my desk where my mobile lay. Then I saw Bitch Brenda peek out of her office and watched her until she disappeared.

"Sir..." My tired interruption made no impact on the raging argument that now involved the entire party. "Sir!" I had their full attention and refused to apologise again.

"Yes?"

"Why don't we head for the meeting room, where we have refreshments on hand?" Only they weren't interested in refreshments.

"And?" Only Ricardo needed to be persuaded that I was worthy of his time.

"And over coffee, I can update you about my coverage areas and our latest findings, as it may prove to be mutually beneficial." I didn't wait for his acceptance but began leading the edgy, chattering group towards Meeting Room Three. As we filed through to the meeting room, I flicked through Clare's client profile. With coffee in hand, I waited for coats to be shrugged off and laptops to be set up before taking my seat at the oval mahogany table.

"So, you work with Clare?" Ricardo pinned me with hard, unforgiving eyes as he stirred his black coffee methodically. He wanted me to validate myself and I obliged.

"We have overlapping areas of analysis, particularly in relation to the proliferation of the counterfeit luxury market and its financial implications globally..."

"The counterfeit market?" Bingo! We had a taker. "I'm Gianni Sallas, Global Marketing Executive. As a supplier to the couture houses, this is a critical area for us. I'd like to know what you can tell us about our competitors' strategies." I smiled and thought of Jhanghir, but I stopped thinking and looked at Gianni.

"Why don't we begin with introductions? My name's Maya Malik and as a consultant with Wilfred Scott Chambers, I'll begin with a brief summary of my coverage areas." I didn't know that it was so easy to take control. Trivial insecurities disappeared in the face of impending betrayal, so I passed out my business cards. They followed likewise, and with exchanged business cards we started again with secured credibility.

Thursdays were client meetings days. I hated meetings. I hated the niceties of starting a meeting, I hated the protocols of running meetings and I hated speaking at meetings. On this particular Thursday, I had back-to-back meetings with six Indian manufacturers, as my latest report had investigated the cost-quality ratio of cheap manufacturing. My take-no-bullshit threshold was non-existent, so it felt good to cut Mark's meandering feedback with some crisp, punchy analysis that made the clients sit up and for the first time realise I wasn't there as the token Asian consultant. In between meetings Mark wanted to discuss some of my thoughts. What he really wanted to do was pass off my hard work as his own. He just didn't realise I wasn't in the mood to accommodate his underhanded behaviour any longer. The truth was, I was too busy checking all my emails, voicemails and ticking off Thursday flights from New York that had already arrived.

"Maya." I stared at the flashing icon on my screen. There were no new messages of any consequence and none from Jhanghir. The truth was it had been four days since I had emailed Jhanghir and he still hadn't written, called or arrived. The truth was slowly dawning. "Maya, are you ok?" I jumped at Clare's question and looked at her. She had her jacket buttoned up, her case bulging with papers, and she was ready to leave. "I didn't mean to startle you."

"You didn't, what can I help you with..."

"Are you ok, Maya?" Clare repeated, and I frowned at her question. I had spent so much energy bottling up all my emotions and hiding my feelings from everyone that her gentle question nearly broke me.

"Yes, I'm fine." I tidied up the papers on my desk and adjusted my laptop. Clare put her case down, leaned against my desk and waited until I gave her my attention.

"Who is he?"

I smirked and shook my head. "Why does there have to be a 'he'?"

Clare smiled compassionately and I gritted my jaw. "Because the alternative would mean that you've rediscovered your love for this job." I frowned at Clare's assertion. "Maya, this week you've cleared all your research requests pushing your client service ratio to almost eighty-five per cent. The average on a good month is seventy-five. Mark's spewing with jealously because you've outperformed him. Face it, whatever's going on in your life, you're making the rest of us look bad and Brenda look good, so this has got to stop!" I grinned at her, and she leaned over and took my hand. "Whatever it is Maya, if I can't help, I can give you the names of the best pubs and bars in a five mile radius for you to lose all your worries in."

"I don't drink."

"I know, that's even more reason for you to get sloshed." I chuckled at Clare's logic.

"Has it helped you?" Clare had refused to stop partying since her split. Though her health and work suffered, she was big-hearted to a fault. "Have you stopped missing him or loving him?"

"What's happened Maya?" I choked up at the thought of Jhanghir's indifference. "Who is he?"

"Nobody," I blurted out, as I looked at her. "He's nobody. I wanted him to be somebody, but he's chosen to be nobody to me." She leaned forward to draw me into a hug, but I pulled back.

"Go home Maya..." I shook my head and laughed at myself. "They don't know, do they?"

"It's ironic isn't it? My life is so messed up right now that I find work to be a blessing!"

"It'll hurt for a while Maya, you can't afford to bottle this up..."

"I'm fine Clare. Really, I am. And there's the chance that I'll be proved wrong." I ignored her sympathetic, but disbelieving nod. I wasn't ready to go home. I wasn't ready to accept the inevitable. "I've still got my notes from today's meetings to write up and upload onto the client files, I'll do those before I leave..."

"It's after seven, why don't you and I lose ourselves in Salsa? By nine, the place is packed with city types moving to the Latin beat badly - and I mean badly!" Clare raised her brow suggestively but I shook my head.

"You're leaving me with no option but to take Mark!" she whispered with a look of disgust. The thought of buxom Clare and conservative Mark dancing the night away to the sensual and intimate rhythms of Latin music made us burst out laughing.

"I want to write up my notes," I told her when we stopped to draw breath.

"He's not worth it Maya. They're not worth a moment's sadness." I nodded, smiled and accepted her warm hug. "I've unlimited supplies of chocolate and snacks in my desk drawers. You help yourself ok?" Again I nodded and watched her head for the double doors. I turned back and looked at the flashing icon. There were no messages from Jhanghir in my Inbox, my voicemail or my mobile phone. Taking a deep breath, I pulled out my client notes, opened up a new e-client template and began to type.

"Let me out!" I was sitting in the back seat of Jana's Suzuki Vitara, deaf to her conversation with Hana and freaking out that I wasn't monitoring all communication sources. He could have arrived on the 6:16pm Virgin Atlantic flight and could now be walking up to my front door only to discover I was out having a blast. He could be calling my mobile, which I'd left behind deliberately to find how to get to my home, or he may have called home to ask me to go meet him for a romantic Friday night dinner. "Stop the car, I want to go home."

"What are you talking about?" Hana asked with a frown.

"I want to go home, I've changed my mind. I don't want to go out to eat..."

"It's Friday night, and we're going for a meal, Maya. Our husbands are already waiting there. They wanted to treat you, their baby sister-in-law because you've been so unhappy. So, it's settled, we're going to Wagamamma's," Hana told me firmly, as if she was talking to a little kid. "And you're going to look surprised and happy!"

"Drop me off at the nearest tube station, I'll make my own way back..."

"What's wrong with you?" Jana demanded fed up with my quiet behaviour.

"Nothing," I whispered, starring out at the bright lights of London.

"Amma doesn't know what to do with you. She's really worried, she says she hasn't seen you eat..."

"I'm on a low carb diet."

"So, what's with the attitude?"

"Nothing." It was too painful to admit the truth to my perfect sisters with their perfect lives.

"So, you're up for a night out?" Hana asked as I nodded with a bright smile. I was living in a dream world. Jhanghir hadn't called. He hadn't written. And he wasn't going to turn up on my doorstep to whisk me off to my perfect future. He was going to get married in two weeks. I had no hope. I felt numb. I didn't recognise me. And it was easier to pretend nothing had happened.

It was three o'clock on Saturday afternoon and there was a knock on my door. I just managed to wipe away my tears as Amma entered with my breakfast. But I couldn't stop the tears, so I turned on my side to let my already damp pillow soak them up.

"I brought you some breakfast." Amma had never figured out how to deal with emotional girls. She was so used to being strong and independent that all she could do was fuss around us with food and drinks. "Your father's asking after you."

"I'm just tired Amma." My voice faltered.

"Is auntie giving you a bad time?" She actually made me laugh. A sleepless night of tears and with one question my mother had made me laugh, God bless her. Four daughters, one daughter-in-law and being a woman herself, Amma still wouldn't say the word 'period'.

"No, work's just getting on top of me." It was easier to lie and save them the worry.

"You know your father's told you to apply for other jobs Maya..."

"I know. I will." I promised. Amma looked me over and didn't miss my puffy eyes and red nose. Just knowing that she knew I was upset brought renewed tears. "I j... I just want to sleep," I breathed out, refusing to break down for her sake.

"You can't sleep all day Maya. You'll be exhausted!" I didn't even have the energy to question her logic.

"You know, I never met your father before I married him." Amma placed a hand on my head and smoothed my hair back from my face. Tears pooled in my eyes at my mother's attempt to reach me. "My father's family were renowned throughout the region, and when your paternal grandfather heard that my father was looking to get me married, he came straight to our village to see me." Slowly I turned over and looked up at my mother. Tears seeped down the sides of my face and Amma brushed them away. I had heard the story a hundred times and still it gave me some hope. "He set us off all in a tizzy. Nobody arrived unannounced at our village. And certainly nobody arrived to talk about an alaap without forewarning. But arrive he did. My sisters rushed around to find the best sari, and get me prepared whilst your nani tried to placate your astonished nana. And all the way through the mayhem, your dada sat there drinking his tea, waiting to talk with my father and waiting to see me." She smiled softly and held my face. "He didn't even ask your father's permission. Your nana led me in to the room, I greeted your dada and then left. They spoke for an hour and it was agreed."

"Just like that," I whispered wistfully.

"Just like that I was promised to your father. A week later and with the exception of your nani who never left our village, my entire family headed for the telephone exchange in the Sunamgonj town centre. I was surrounded by my sisters and we were all concealed behind burqas so that your father's family couldn't discern which one of us was to be the bride and use it as a reason to stop the marriage."

"They were difficult even back then."

Amma nodded and laughed at the memory. "The line to London was so bad we could barely hear your father. And what with no less than thirty people crowded around one handset, the imam must have asked him half a dozen times if he accepted me, because we couldn't determine whether he had said 'yes' or 'no'!"

"Baba said that he kept saying no, but that nana had paid the imam to announce that Baba had agreed!"

"Of course he would say that!" I chuckled at Amma's derision. "I was asked three times and I accepted three times."

"Without seeing Baba, talking to Baba, or even being with Baba." Amma nodded and stroked my hair gently.

"You see in those day, we trusted our parents to make the best decision for us. Your father's family were widely respected, your father was of sound character and he promised me a future in thriving London. What more could a girl want?" And with that Jhanghir came to mind. Tears blurred my vision.

"I don't think I can do that Amma," I whispered. The pain of losing him again made me shake my head.

"I know this is difficult for you Maya and I know I can be tough on you, but you must let us help you." Amma had tears in her eyes and I reached up to hug her. I closed my eyes and held onto her for dear life. I wanted to cry, to let everything out, but it would be too much. "You know Sakina and Tanya have been calling all week." Amma cleared her throat and used the tail of her sari to wipe away her tears.

"And you're meant to meet Sakina and Tanya today. You love meeting up with them!" Normally, Amma did all she could to stop me going to my fortnightly weekend meals with my friends. Normally, she'd insist they come to our home, so I wouldn't have to risk my health by driving on the 'crazy unsafe' Saturday streets of London and waste my money on poor quality over priced meals. Today, my normally paranoid mother was prepared to push me onto the crazy unsafe streets of London just to see me happy.

"Yeah," I smiled, as she looked away from the tears slipping down my face. "Just give me a moment." Amma left with a worried smile. She would send in Hamza to keep me company and then rush downstairs to call Ayesha, Jana and Hana to try and find out what was wrong. They would come round and question me with sarcastic older sister jibes that I didn't have the energy to face. All I wanted to do was sleep. As predicted, Hamza charged into my room, but froze after one look at my appearance. Kids had a way of sensing situations, and Hamza knew his auntie was sad.

"I'll come back," he promised, like a little old man. How was it possible for kids to turn into adults and for adults to become kids? I cleared my throat to thank him, but was unable to speak. "You'll be ok," he said with a smile as he closed the door behind him.

"Yeah," I whispered as I stared up at the ceiling. "I'll be ok."

"You think you want to see him seriously?" I had scrubbed my face until it gleamed. I had pressed an icy cold flannel against my red rimmed eyes to reduce the puffiness. I had pulled my hair back into a neat bun and dressed in my customary bootleg jeans and black polo neck. I had driven down to Nando's for stodgy but scrummy pirri pirri chicken and chips, grateful for its modest laid back atmosphere. And as we sat waiting for our meals to be served, Tanya and Sakina knew there was something wrong.

"Shaj and I have spoken a couple of times since last Sunday. I don't know Maya, it's still early days." Sakina was downplaying her hopes of being in a couple for my sake.

"That's good, that's progress," I said with a bright smile.

"Yeah, he seems nice, but you know how long these introductions last for me!"

"Be optimistic! If he liked you enough to call you then..."

"You should've told me how you felt about last Sunday." They both spoke at the same time, and I realised they thought that I was still pissed-off at being the golden gooseberry.

"And what, miss your birthday?"

"Yeah, I'd rather that than have you feel awful," Sakina stated without hesitation.

"Your mom asked Jana to call us to ask if we knew what was bringing you down." And that's how the Asian grapevine worked.

"I didn't know whether to tell her that being single was getting you down."

"I didn't either, so we both said work," Tanya added. I smiled at my fellow conspirators and felt my eyes well up with tears. "Oh, sweetie, it's not that bad..."

"No, I know, I'm fine," I agreed, clearing my throat with a hard cough.

"What's wrong Maya, it can't all be down to my birthday?" Sakina muttered miserably. These were my friends at arms, my confidantes who suffered equally in the taboo world of the unmarried.

"I promise you, it's not because of your birthday." Our chicken dishes arrived, and we collected the paraphernalia of sauces, sachets, napkins and drinks from the self-service section.

"It's Jhanghir isn't it?"

"What about Jhanghir? What's happened?" Tanya ignored Sakina's question as I filled up and nodded. "Somebody tell me what's happened with Jhanghir!" Sakina insisted. I cleared my throat, and wiped away my tears, as Tanya gave Sakina a thirty-second summary of my relationship with Jhanghir. Her expression changed from one of disbelief to one of complete and utter sadness. Tanya caught me playing with my pendant and looked at me.

"He gave you that didn't he?" Nodding, I tucked the necklace inside of the high neck collar. "What did he say?" she added.

"He said that I'd always be with him and that he was getting married at the end of this month."

"Oh my God!" Sakina cried out as she covered her face and shook her head. "I was so mean to you about Jhanghir, I didn't know, I swear I didn't mean to hurt you..."

"You didn't know Sakina..."

"I'm so sorry, I just... I'm sorry," Sakina whispered as she gave me all her French fries.

"Why didn't you say something?" Tanya asked. She knew I was holding back and I looked at her.

"It was Sakina's birthday, I couldn't ruin..."

"But you always knew he was going to marry Preeya at some point..."

"We can fly to New York to stop him," Sakina cut in, in a moment of inspiration. "It'll only cost a couple of hundred pounds each, and we can find him and convince him you're the one for him!" she added with sparkling eyes and a big smile. And for an instant I felt her great sense of adventure. "We'll crash at Jhanghir's place. Tanya and I'll disappear to Fifth Avenue and you can sort it all out. Oh my God, I can see this working out for you!" But for all the excited planning Sakina indulged in, I knew that it wasn't going to happen.

"He says he's found his soul mate." I confessed to Tanya, who sat waiting to hear everything.

"Well good, so have you," Sakina pointed out, but I shook my head.

"It's not me. He's said he's not leaving her." Sakina gasped in disbelief, but Tanya held my eyes.

"You didn't ask him that did you?" Tanya and I were born sceptics, stubborn and full of pride. She could not believe this of me.

"What did I have to lose?" That wasn't enough.

"What did you ask him Maya?" Persisted Tanya.

"I asked him to choose me." Sakina and Tanya were both silenced. They had seen me when I had crushes and passing fancies. They had seen me control my emotions in such a way that even they were oblivious to my turmoils. They had dealt with my no nonsense attitude to playing around. But they had never heard me put my emotions on the line. "But he didn't."

"Oh Maya!" Sakina cried reaching out to hold my hands. Both Sakina and Tanya were at a loss with my confession. I looked at Tanya and for the first time in a long time, I saw her eyes fill with tears.

"I've lost him." I whispered and she nodded.

Hennas are the Asian equivalent of hen nights. I used to love going to hennas. I loved the bad singing of my mom and her cohorts. I loved dressing up in the latest styles, in shades of fertile green or hot terracotta with the trendiest hairstyles and accessories in anticipation that one day I'd be up there, being groomed with mendhi for my wedding day. Then the bride-to-be started getting younger, as did all her friends, and I realised that even the groom was younger than me. And they continued to get younger - or rather, I was getting older. More often than not, I started swapping trendy for elegant, and latest for classic. I danced less eagerly and stood further and further away from the front of the singing crowd. Somehow, through the henna seasons, my henna was overlooked. And what had once been a pleasure now became an ordeal. So attending Loose-Leila's henna to good looking (but short) computer analyst Abdul Raquib was going to be painful.

Red tinsel and green paper chains lined the wall, along with bows and hearts. Balloons lined the floor to keep the children occupied, as the adults jostled to get the best table in the hall. Leila had broken protocol by marrying before me, but as Chachijhi put it, 'Leila wouldn't be sacrificed to spinsterhood because nobody wanted Maya'. The insult was public and personal and despite dad mediating an apology from his sister, Amma boycotted all wedding preparations. Amma gave Hana and Jana full remit to scour Green Street and Southall to turn me into the talking point of the evening. Only, I didn't want to be pinned into a sheer, sun-kissed sari that draped around my body, or wear impossible to walk in high heels and heavy rajashtani antique bangles that covered both my arms. I didn't want my hair pulled back into a 1960s beehive, bronzed cheeks, honey stained lips and kohl lined eyes. I wanted to feel whole again, I wanted to smile without feeling the tears, I wanted to think without feeling Jhanghir's loss. Instead, I made my entrance behind Amma, as she walked in with a proud, strutting bravado, daring any soul to criticise her unwanted unwedded daughter. Spotting Hana and Jana up on the stage with Leila, who was grinning like an Oscar nominated star, Amma went to congratulate her, but I held back. Ayesha sat beside Leila on the hired chaise, as the eldest cousin over-looking the evening. In that moment, I knew fate was a cruel bitch. Had Jhanghir chosen me, I would have been on stage being pampered and preened and admired.

"When are we going to be dancing at your henna?" Chachijhi appeared to make amends, as my mother had with Leila.

"I'm sure you'll know before I do!" I returned with a tight smile. I didn't want to prolong the conversation with her, but I was scared that I'd be showered in paan spittle if I angered her.

"Your age is working against you and what's more, you're making your mother ill with worry." Unmarried girls weren't meant to ask for their marriage to be arranged.

"Then you must find me a husband!" Chachijhi Fauzia wasn't amused and I sobered up.

"Maya, you know you can't afford to be choosy at your age. Doctors, lawyers, engineers, they all want 'fresh' young girls," Chachijhi advised with wide, telling eyes that believed I was finally entertaining the revolutionary idea of getting married. "There's an age to be a bride, Maya, before the innocence disappears. Our boys like innocence, they feel like they've conquered unfound territory." She whispered to me, as if confiding some sacred female secret.

"Is that why Abdul Raquib is marrying Leila?" Everyone knew Leila had long lost her innocence. And every so often I had to remind Chachijhi, so she knew when she crossed the line between advice and condescension.

"And to think, she is getting married to a fine young man with a good city job, good prospects and a three bedroom semi in Ruislip, and uh, you're not." Chachijhi, like all mothers, would defend her own to the end. "Do you even know what you want?"

"A strong mochaccino."

"Eh? What you mean?" I finally smiled and looked towards the back of the hall where Taj and his friends began to play bhangra. I felt the thudding beat give me courage and I looked back at my confused auntie who chewed paan like a cow chewed its cud.

"I like my men hot and very very rich." I walked away before the red spittle could hit me. I could hear her coughing as if to bring up phlegm from the pits of her gut, and I really laughed for the first time in a long time. The thumping track drew the puritan out in Chachijhi Fauzia and she marched across the hall to warn Taj about the sin of music. Left alone, I stood by the corner of the hall, content to be invisible.

The aunties flitted from one table to the next, in their new saris, golden jewellery sets and clutch bags that never matched their outfits. Gossip moved even faster through laughter, hushed murmurs and fleeting glances that met for a millisecond of understanding before moving on. The newly married couples circled tables still glowing from their nuptials to declare they had passed the marital test. Young girls in bright shalwaar kameezes and stronger make-up fluttered around keen to make their presence known. Some self conscious, others brazen and confident at the interest they invited, ready to take the marital test. The young men in ill fitting suits and Ben Sherman shirts grouped in threes and fours to check out the talent. And oblivious to all this, the men, most with groomed beards, in finely pressed Punjabis or suits, huddled to debate about the merits of Mujibur Rahmans, the founder of Bangladesh's independence campaign. The natural order stayed the same. And I didn't belong here. I didn't have any peers in this natural order.

"Where are you going?" Chachijhi caught me at the exit.

"I left my... I uh, need to collect some hairspray from the car."

"We're about to get the dancing started. You have to join Zarah, Farah and Kara with the stick routine..."

"What about Mina...?"

"Mina can't leave her sister alone on stage to dance!" I looked over Chachijhi's shoulder and counted no less than twenty relatives attending to Leila's every whim. Standing in the cleared space in front of the stage, Zarah and her sisters prepared for the stick routine.

"I can't dance," I told Chachijhi who took my arm and marched me through the hall, around the tables, past all her hyper-vigilant guests and up onto the stage. "Congratulations!" I announced to Leila, as we came to a stop.

"You look lovely," Leila said, reaching up to give me a hug. She sounded genuine, so I patted her on the back in surprise. "Thank you for coming. Sit next to me and we'll show everyone what good genes we have!"

"Maya's refusing to do the stick dance Leila. She refuses to do the dance!" Chachijhi declared.

"You're not doing the stick dance?" The shrill demand was back, as was Loose-Leila. All expressions of affection were now replaced by deep outrage. "But you have to dance, all unmarried cousins dance." I had no doubt she had softened me up to stun me with that perfectly delivered line.

"I have heels on, I can't dance with heels on," I explained, taking a place behind the chaise to avoid further confrontation.

"Appha, your daughter refuses to dance at my daughter's henna!" Chachijhi shouted across the platform. "Why? Why does she deny me?" I felt the hostile stares of those on the first few tables who could hear Chachijhi and looked at Ayesha.

"Chachijhi, Maya's not been feeling too well."

"Oh, I know she's not. I know what her illness is!" Chachijhi shouted as Amma rushed onto the stage. I looked out at the hall and knew we had turned into a BanglaTV melodrama. Everyone quietened down to discover what my illness was. "It's called envy, it's called jealously!" The guests gasped in joint disapproval.

"How dare you?" Amma asked, perfectly poised at one end of the platform. Even the men had stopped debating and waited for my mother to deliver her next line. "I've done nothing but support you..."

"Asking me to postpone Leila's henna isn't support..."

"Stop, just stop!" Leila cried out standing up to glare at me. "You see, you see what happens when you don't get married young?"

"Don't blame her!" Hana defended, dropping her flower bouquet to stand between us.

"Why won't she dance at my henna?" Leila demanded. "Does she think she's too good..."

"What's the big deal if I don't dance?" I asked in confusion. "They can dance, you can dance, Chachijhi can dance, but I don't want to dance," I shouted in defiance. Only I shouldn't have shouted, because now Leila stood stunned, tears filling her eyes and her chin wobbling with pent-up sobs. Silent seconds ticked by as everyone waited for Leila's fall-out. And then it came.

"You're so selfish!" Leila screamed, before throwing down her bouquet to storm off the stage and out of the hall.

"You see!" Chachijhi accused, pointing at me. "You see what she's done!" In an instant, half the female guests emptied out of the hall and filed into the back room after Leila. Taj stopped playing his tracks so that the only sound in the hall was Leila's loud heartbroken sobs.

Amma and Ayesha followed the crowd as I stood beneath the awkward glare of the guests.
"You should go and apologise." I looked across the stage and saw Baba.
"But I don't want to dance." Baba only smiled with apologetic understanding.
"You still need to apologise to Leila." I wanted to stamp my feet and insist that I was in the right, that I didn't have to dance, that I didn't have to celebrate her henna.
"You don't want a reputation as the spiteful one, as well as the single fussy one," Jana added with a grin, which instantly disappeared when Baba glared at her.
"She's my sister's daughter Maya, I want to see her happy today." He was right. And with that, I walked off the stage to go and retrieve the 'melodramatic one'. I apologised, and Leila forgave me like a benevolent elder, before leading everyone back out to the hall without another tear in sight. Drama over, Taj hit the decks indicating the start of the stick dancing routine. I ignored Leila's smug grin as she handed me the colourful sticks.

The most important thing the Internet has given us Bengalis and Asians, is the new social phenomenon called Internet dating. This is where we, the ditched, dumped and unwanted, ended up. Of course, you wouldn't admit it to save your life. But let's face it, who isn't doing it? There's shaadi.com, asianweddings.com, musmat.com, ristha.com, meet-a-mate.com, find-a-pathro.com, brit-bengali.com, even asian-professionals-partner-finder.com. But that's just the tip of the iceberg. And where there's demand, there's supply. With Leila's henna humiliation and Jhanghir's brutal betrayal behind me, I was determined to find me a man, be it through cyberspace. So when Sakina passed on to me her annual subscription to shaadi.com, costing fifty pounds and offering the opportunity to contact fifteen potential suitors, I didn't think twice.

Before I started the process of selection, I locked my bedroom door and adjusted my Internet options so that the URL could not flash up unexpectedly at work. After logging onto www.matmus.com. I tapped in my preferences: male, fit, Muslim, Bengali, professional and England, and watched the four selections pop up. My matches included:

User ID: mabs Age: 29 **Height:** 5'5" **Education:** blank **Employment:** Management
I'm tall, dark and handsome. I have a goatee and a French crop. I like my Asians and they seem to like me (not trying to be big headed or anything but you won't be disappointed). So any sexy Asian females that wanna get in touch with me, flex me ur number and I'll flex u right back, if u're lucky.

User ID: Laasi **Age:** 38 **Height:** 5'10" **Education:** LPC **Employment:** Lawyer
Ambitious, attractive, charming, intelligent, cultured, and conversationalist. Born London, educated Cambridge/Boston Unis'. Pray a bit, but drink and smoke a little more. I feel short changed that my previous relationship did not work out. Separated after 6-year marriage. Now looking for best friend to love.

User ID: Uddin **Age:** 25 **Height:** 5'6" **Education:** BA/BSc **Employment:** Management
I'm fairly good-looking, medium build and of fair complexion who's honest and sensitive. I am looking for a wife who's seeking a legitimate relationship. I am seeking an honest, educated, God-fearing woman of at least moderate beauty. You will be willing to live with my parents. For those of you who have entered this site for means of illegitimate SEXUAL relationship, fear God, the last day and know that your sins will one day catch up with you.

User ID: mo love **Age:** 28 **Height:** 5'3" **Education:** BA/BSc **Employment:** Unemployed
Asalaimalaikum. I'm looking for someone who is an open-minded person, sociable and with GSOH, in between 5"1 - 5"6 and pretty. I'm not superficial/shallow, the fact is I'm just being honest- initial physical attraction is a factor, so to avoid potential embarrassment be honest with yourself. If you're cute with moral/Islamic values, then get back to me.

So from matmus.com's entire database of Bengali men across the globe, I get the local East end ghoonda, a drinking smoking divorcee, a religious psycho and a 5'3 unemployed twenty-eight year old looking for a Muslim Cindy Crawford. It didn't matter how many late night crying sessions I had, how many hennas I would now avoid, or how many Internet searches I ran, my heart was broken. And that was the truth of it. There was no five-step guide to mending broken hearts. There was no quick fix or rip and replace policy. The only way to deal with broken hearts, and I suspect this crosses all races, religion and sexes, is to carry on. Continue with life. Do all the things you'd normally do, like an automaton. Tick of all your to-do lists. That way, you fill every waking minute and stop yourself feeling the pain of lost love and lost dreams.

George Clooney. Tierry Henry. Nikolas Anelka. Stodgy chocolate cake with thick chocolate custard. Strong mochaccinos. Nothing. Nothing filled the hole in my heart. So I deleted all matched profiles, stared at the flashing cursor and knew what had to be done. I reached across my bed for my mobile.

"I'm going to New York." I was absolutely sure I had a chance to stop Jhanghir for my sake, if not for his.

"Are you serious?" Sakina's voice shook with excited anticipation. I couldn't tell Tanya because she would stop me. Instead I tapped in Expedia's URL and selected my travel options to New York.

"I've never been so certain of anything as I am of this." My heart was racing away and I just had to have faith that things would turn out well. "I'm going for one night..."

"But you haven't booked any leave, you don't have a flight..."

"I'm booking as we speak..."

"What about your parents?" I paused for a moment, realising that I would have to deceive my family. "We'll cover for you," Sakina offered.

"I can't lie to them..."

"Maya, be selfish. For once do the wrong, crazy, insane selfish thing. Your family need never know if it goes wrong, but if it goes right, can you imagine how happy your mother would be?" I smiled at the thought and clicked the confirmation icon.

"It's done. I'm going to New York to win Jhanghir back." When fate seems intent on taking a different course than you wanted, it's down to you to take destiny into your own hands. And that's what I was doing. I had a flight booked to JFK and I planned on changing Jhanghir's mind. I felt my heart fill up with happiness. It was insane. It was absolutely crazy, but I had to exhaust all hope. I had to, for my own sanity.

J: Justify Jetsetting

I believe that at some point in our lives, we all do something that defies logic. That for no reason beyond the compulsion to be proven wrong, you try one more time to change things for the better. And this was my moment.

"But this is so unusual." Amma helped me to pack my overnight bag.

"I know. I can't believe my company can't find any other representative to meet with the clients." I felt awful for lying to my mother, but an urgent business trip was the only explanation I had for disappearing immediately. I'd thrown a pair of jeans and a sweater into my overnight bag for a quick change as soon as I reached the airport, but for now the blue trouser suit I was wearing was pretty convincing.

"But you don't even have any details of where you'll be staying." Amma worried each time I had a business trip and expected an itenary of my whereabouts.

"I think it's the Marriott on Central Park, but I won't know for sure until I pick up my ticket at Heathrow." I looked at my mother who put away my cosmetics bag and smiled. She would beat me with her slipper if she knew that I was going to win Jhanghir back.

"You're not taking your laptop," Amma picked up as she looked at my case.

"No, I've got my notes and files in my carry-on case." Another lie. I needed to get out of the house before I confessed to my loving mother.

"And you'll call me the minute you get into your hotel?" Nodding, I took my case and bag, and headed for the front door. "Your father can give you a lift to the airport..."

"Amma, there's no reason why Baba should go to any trouble, I'm going to claim all this back from the company." She stopped by the door and hovered. I turned into her ready embrace and held on tightly, terrified of what I had to do.

"I know you'll be good," Amma whispered, stroking my hair before I stepped back. "I'll be waiting for you to come home." And with that I took my case and walked out to the waiting cab.

"I can't believe you're doing this." Sakina was waiting for me at Terminal 3 with my tickets. "Are you sure you want to do this?" I looked at Sakina and nodded.

"The first time Jhanghir swaggered into work, he made me smile from the inside. And he's kept me smiling ever since. I can't let him go Sakina, not like this." Sakina shook her head as we headed for the Virgin check-in counter and joined the queue.

"It might not turn out the way you want to." She sounded as worried and nervous as I felt, but I couldn't back down now.

"I need to know either way." Sakina watched me and then pulled me into a long, warm hug. "He's everything I want," I whispered, as she squealed in nervous excitement. Then she stepped back, held my face in her hands and looked me straight in the eyes.

"Have you got everything you need? Jhanghir's contact details and his hospital details? Are you sure he's still there and hasn't flown out to San Francisco already?" I avoided her eyes and checked my ticket flight details.

"He said he's getting married at the end of the month. So I'm hoping he's still in New York..."

"You mean you haven't checked?" I shook my head at Sakina's incredulity. "But what if he's not there?"

"Then I come home." We were at the head of the queue and stood in silence until I made my way to the counter.

"But I have a good feeling about this Maya, I know this is going to have a good ending." I laughed at Sakina's romantic nature and handed my ticket and passport over at the check in counter. "You're going to bowl him over, and he's going to take you to the Empire State Building to propose with a Tiffany square cut diamond ring!" she added, wide eyed with a big white grin.

"More like I'm going to be dragged across the floor trying to stop him marrying skinny Preeya!" The check in stewardess looked at me in disapproval.

"Either way, you had better keep me informed with what's going on, understand?" Sakina stared at me until I nodded. "I'm serious, you're on the biggest adventure of your life and I want to know every sappy, sickly, heart-warming detail!"

"Ok, ok!" I laughed before turning to the stewardess who waited for me to answer her security questions. I turned back to Sakina. "I tried to reach Clare this morning, but she's not in yet. Do me a favour, would you call my work and bag me a couple of sick leaves?" I looked back at the impatient stewardess as Sakina used the time to call Brenda.

"Hello, I'm Maya Malik's older sister. Yes, I know she's not at work." I could hear Sakina's condescending accent as she worked her way through to speaking with Bitch Brenda. "Yes, I'm Maya Malik's sister, I'm calling in to let you know that we've had an unfortunate incident in the family... No, I can't give you the details, but Maya is unable to come into work over the next few days. She's fine, but she's looking after my aunt in Hastings for a couple of days." The stewardess looked at Sakina before looking pointedly at me. "Yes I'm at the airport, no Maya isn't with me... I'd rather not go into details. Yes, yes, I will ask her to call in." I took my documents and passport, before leading Sakina to the departure area. "Ok, I will pass on your regards. Right, thank you."

"You should be an actress," I told Sakina as she called off.

"Do you want to grab a coffee?" I shook my head knowing my doubts and nerves would explode if we sat around trying to predict the outcome of my foolish trip.

"Go do what you have to do. Just be safe and make sure you call." I hugged Sakina with all the fear and excitement inside me. And when she stood back with tears in her eyes, I walked on without another word.

Eight hours in flight, one hour getting through customs, one hour through Manhattan's traffic and three hours camping outside Jhanghir's door later, Eddie appeared first out of the lifts. He stopped, spotting me, before walking on down the hall.

"Hello Eddie." I stood up gingerly as he nodded and opened up.

"You been waiting long?" I nodded and cleared my throat. Having spent a summer with Jhanghir in London, I knew Eddie well enough to know that he wasn't pleased to see me.

"Long shift at the hospital?" Nonetheless, he took my overnight bag from me and waited for me to follow him in.

"Yeah. You eaten?" I shook my head at his question and walked into the open plan living room as he went to check the large double-door fridge. "I'm ordering some take out, you fancy anything in particular?"

"Anything vegetarian." I wandered around the large room furnished only with a huge black leather sofa and a massive entertainment system. I sat down and looked through to the adjoining kitchen area where Eddie ordered up some pizza and drinks. "Has Jhanghir started his evening shift?" Eddie replaced the receiver and frowned.

"Shift? He's getting married Maya..."

"I know, I thought I could catch him before he leaves for San Francisco."

Eddie paused as if to consider what I had just said. Then finally, he looked at me.

"He's gone already." My heart stopped beating.

"Gone?" I felt light headed at his words.

"He left for San Francisco two days ago," Eddie explained, reluctantly breaking the news to me.

"But he doesn't get married until the end of the month, there's more than ten days to go..."

"Maya, he's taking his vows first thing next Wednesday." I shook my head to refute what he was telling me. "He wasn't meant to fly out until the weekend, but Preeya called him and he flew out as soon as he put the phone down."

"Right." Confused, I looked away from Eddie to the window and stared at the apartments across the road. I didn't understand. Why would Jhanghir mislead me?

"If you had called..."

"I know," I whispered. And then it dawned on me. He had anticipated this. Jhanghir knew I would try and stop him, he knew I was crazy enough to do just that. I felt heady and dazed, so I held my head in my heads.

"Maya, you ok?"

"I'm fine." My tone stopped Eddie in his tracks. He paced uncertainly in the awful silence between us, but I had nothing to say to him.

"I'm gonna grab a shower." Eddie shouldn't have been the one to tell me. It should've been Jhanghir.

"Right." The murmur barely left my lips.

"Maya." I looked up at Eddie's call. "He should've told you." I managed to smile at Eddie for his kindness and watched him walk down the hall. I felt more betrayed than at any point in my life. I don't know how long I sat there, but I felt my heart ice over. I played back every time that I had willingly taken the back seat, accepted Jhanghir's obligation and supported his predicament to make it easier for him. And with each passing thought, I got angrier at myself. The apartment buzzed to life with the pizza delivery. I grabbed my purse and walked across to the front door to pay.

"No, no I'll get that," Eddie called out as he jogged across the living room towel-drying his wet hair. I couldn't look at Eddie so I took the pizza from the delivery man without argument. Feeling stupid and foolish, I carried the warm box to the worktop where Eddie joined me. I opened the box and handed him a drink.

"I'm sorry you had to find out this way." Eddie was a slim, unassuming Puerto Rican who had worked hard to become a doctor.

"I should learn to take 'no' for an answer." He didn't smile, but I was past caring. "This happens when you watch too many Meg Ryan movies!"

"I have his number in San Francisco, you want to speak with him?" I finally met his eyes, and read the compassion in them. I looked away and shook my head. I took my soda and pizza slice and walked through to the living room.

"You shouldn't tempt me. He won't thank you for having me turn up to ruin his wedding plans!"

"He waited a long time for you." Eddie followed me to the sofa, put the pizza box on the floor and sat down facing me. "Even when you fell out, he waited for..."

"Preeya to come back and when she did, he took her back. What can I say Eddie? My halo became my noose." He looked uncomfortable so I grinned. "Why aren't you at the wedding?" He snorted and helped himself to another slice of pizza.

"I'm covering for Jhanghir. It's the only way he could get the extra time off for his wedding and that honeymoon in the Maldives." I felt like I'd been stabbed. I must have looked like it too, because Eddie held his hands up and apologised. That was the honeymoon he had promised for me if I hadn't married by twenty-eight. We sat through an awkward silence while Eddie finished up the pizza and I sat dizzy with disappointment.

"So, how long were you planning to stick around for...?"

"I'm not, I'm heading home tonight..."

"Don't do this Maya, you've only just arrived." He sat forward and looked straight at me.

"I've got to get back to work..." Who was I kidding? He knew I was running away. "I don't have any reason to stay." I closed my eyes at my reality. A reality without Jhanghir. I was prepared to give up everything in my life to be with the man I loved, but the man I loved was committing himself to another woman.

"Maya, you've come so far, why don't you call him..."

"I can't. I'd rather you never mentioned this to Jhanghir, Eddie. I accept his choice." I had opened my heart, I had pleaded with him to choose me and I'd flown half way around the world to convince him. Now I didn't have the will or the desire to want him back. "Do you mind if I use the phone to confirm my flight out?" Eddie shook his head, and switched on the TV as I took the phone. I wandered around the apartment, as I channelled myself through the automated options. I turned into a bedroom and found a framed photo of Jhanghir with his family on a desk. I checked behind me. Eddie was engrossed with the sports channel, so I walked in and sat on what would be Jhanghir's large bed as an operator took my call. I booked a seat on the last late night London-bound flight from JFK. I'd be back in London by lunchtime, acting as if nothing had happened. Instead of returning to plan my glorious, much celebrated wedding, I'd return to sardine-packed journeys to a job I hated and the SLAAG meat market that just kept getting bigger and bigger. I looked around the room filled with medical books and clothes strewn everywhere. On his bedside cabinet sat my leather-bound prayer book, which I had given Jhanghir after he had fallen out with his father. Things had changed forever. I felt it was time for me to reclaim it and in return, I unlocked the necklace he had given me from around my neck. Walking over to his desk, I opened up a drawer and placed it on top of his notes. I picked up the photo frame and stared at his handsome grinning face as he stood outside his South Kensington flat with his friends. Replacing the photo frame, I left his room and returned to Eddie. I found him snoring on the sofa, pizza in one hand, the remote in the other and smiled at this friendly, tired man. I left a thank you note, grabbed my bags and left without another word.

By the time I arrived at Heathrow I was too tired to feel anything. I had barely slept on the flight, but I sat on the Piccadilly Line into Leicester Square. Dressed in my jeans and sweater and with my overnight bag, I headed down Charing Cross Road towards Trafalgar Square. I took the stairs upto the entrance of the grand National Gallery, and then the right flight of stairs to the main floor. Degas and Van Gogh failed to evoke any emotion from me, and though Degas's La Coiffure always inspired me, I headed for the North Wing. There, in one of the small rooms tucked away in the juncture with the West Wing, sat Simon Denis's Sunset in Roman Campagna. Tourists, art lovers and art haters filed past me, but I stood staring at the stark white evocative sky and felt the fleeting but intense force of nature. The sky seemed so calm and yet you knew it was on the verge of breaking. But you couldn't tell whether the sky would break up with one last blinding sunray before the sunset, or if deafening thunderstorms would destroy the serene setting. That's how I felt at that moment. I knew that when Jhanghir took his vows with Preeya, I could no longer think of him as mine. He would belong to another, be some other woman's husband and no doubt be a good father to her children. For their sake, I had to get over him. From tomorrow onwards, I would stop thinking about Jhanghir. I knew I would return home to put away our letters and emails. I would, with a wry smile, read each one and then reread them. Then I would seal them in a padded envelope and bury them deep in our junk-filled attic. Some day when I'm old and reminiscing about my past I'll open up the emails and read them to my grandchildren. Read them and realise that it wasn't the real thing. Jhanghir wasn't the one and had only seemed to be because I had too much time and not enough work to do. In reality, I knew I didn't need the emails and the precious necklace to remind me of our times together. I would think of Jhanghir a hundred times a day, and when I didn't, a passing phrase, a wry comment or even a sleight of hand would bring him crashing into my thoughts. He would be my last thought before I went to sleep and my first when I rose for a long while. And until the pain of lost love and friendship numbed into nothingness, I would keep those letters, notes and emails stored deep away and out of sight, gathering dust until they were forgotten. For now I wanted sunlight in my life, so I stared at Denis's small painting through tears and smiled.

"Maya! You're back, so soon?" Amma's bright happy smile nearly undid me, and I held her tightly as she held me. "Maya, are you ok?"

"I'm just tired," I whispered, avoiding her concerned eyes. I looked towards the living room, where I could hear Loose-Leila's excited chatter. "The client cancelled the meeting…"

"A wasted trip?" Amma knew there was something wrong, but didn't pursue it.

"You're back already?" I looked up as Tariq raced down the stairs ready to start the evening shift at his restaurant. I nodded as he pulled on his shoes, kissed Amma and stepped out of the house. "Maya, I sent photos of your work to some of those art competitions for you…"

"Bhai, I don't want…"

"Don't thank me just yet," he yelled back before slamming into the Primera. Amma closed the door and sighed as she looked at me.

"Your father's throwing a dinner for Leila's wedding. She's here to talk about what she wants. Maybe you can help her?" I'd stepped back into the whirlwind that had no time or consideration for what I wanted. I wanted nothing to do with art competitions, marriages or dinner parties. But this was my family, this was my life and I had no choice.

"Let me just put my bag away and grab a shower." I was reaching out, making amends with Leila, and Amma smiled in gratitude.

"Maya!!!" The squeal of delight lasted for all of fifteen seconds as Leila ran down the hall to envelope me in a tight bear hug.

"Hello Leila..."

"I'm so glad you're not hiding in New York to avoid me!" I felt exhausted, haunted, betrayed, robbed and lost. And she had no idea how much I was hurting. "Now you can help me plan everything, and I've already got Abdul Raquib checking out all his friends and family to find you a husband."

"Leila, why don't you let Maya go and get changed," Amma suggested, offering me a chance to escape.

"No, I'm fine Amma." I don't know what possessed me, but I followed perky Leila into the living room. I hugged Baba, bhabhi and Taj before greeting my unforgiving Chachijhi Fauzia.

"So Maya, I told your family that I want Rajah's booked for the meeting of the families," Leila began as I settled on the floor. "And I want to have a banner saying 'Congratulations Leila and Abdul Raquib on your Engagement'!" Leila announced with a satisfied smile.

"That's a bit tacky, don't you think?" I didn't mean to offend anyone and as usual I did, but the idea was as naff as shoulder-padded power suits.

"Actually, I think it's very welcoming. A sign that we're embracing Abdul Raquib and his family," Leila defended with a frown.

"So, why shouldn't we have a banner saying 'Welcome to the family, AR'?" I suggested.

"Maya, do you always have to be so critical?" Chachijhi muttered with a deep frown.

"I'm not, it's my opinion..."

"Well, we're not as interested in your opinions as we are in your cousin Leila's plans." Baba spoke with the authority of a judge. I looked at him as he sided with his niece against me, and wondered why the world was turning on me. But Leila took it on herself to explain.

"As I was saying, we have this banner, then we get Baba, and Abdul Raquib's father, as the elders of both families, to exchange engagement rings to formalise the agreement."

"Why is that necessary? Haven't both families agreed to the engagement already..."

"But this is a formal agreement!" Leila spat out as bhabhi giggled at my naiveté.

"Why does there have to be formal agreement? Why can't we go for a nice meal so that both families can get to know each other?" Baba's deep sigh told me my point was unreasonable.

"We need to show Abdul Raquib's family that we're as good as they are, if not better..."

"And what happened to being grateful for having a decent guy?" I countered.

"Oh please, I don't want decent or someone who tries. I want settled and sorted!"

"Of course you would Leila, a man's bank balance is a very redeeming quality."

"You're turning green…"

"Oh please, over an IT-midget and a tacky poster…"

"Maya, why don't you help me with the tea?" Shireen interrupted as Chachijhi chastised Leila for inviting me into the discussions. Taj hooted with laughter that faded beneath Baba's glare.

"We are a well respected family. I will see Leila married according to our station," he stated.

"Our station?" My 'station' is exactly why Jhanghir didn't fight for me harder. Our 'station' is why his father would never have accepted me. Our 'station', his 'station', everyone's 'station', it was all a joke. "It's a sad day when our station is more important than our sense of self." Chachijhi refused to look at me, but turned to my father to object against my participation. Taj tried to diffuse the situation, but there was no compromise to be reached. I didn't wait to be excused or excluded, and took off to my bedroom. There I found Hamza asleep in my bed. I dropped my bag, changed into my worn pyjamas and eased in beside my nephew. Holding my little hero close to me, I closed my eyes against the cold hard world.

K: Kill Kismet With Kebabs And Kormas

I worked harder than I'd ever worked in my career. I hadn't slept well since my failed New York mission. And as if having my heart, my soul mate and our perfect future destroyed wasn't enough to deal with, the rajah of all blows came DHLing its way to yours truly two weeks after Jhanghir's wedding. First, Baba and Amma booked me on a round trip to Bangladesh to give me a break from my melancholic verging on tears sadness. And then Baba added to the injustice by saying:

"I've asked your mother's brother to arrange 'meetings' with suitable families."

"But... but I don't want to get married..."

"What do you mean you don't want to get married! Of course you want to get married..."

"...in Bangladesh! I don't want to get married in Bangladesh!" I finished.

"What's wrong with Bangladesh?" I knew where this was going, and I would lose.

"There's nothing wrong with Bangladesh!" In fact there is plenty wrong with Bangladesh, the gross poverty levels, the corrupt governing body, and the under-developed roads, sewage and water systems. But you don't say that to a man who knew every detailed development in Bengali politics since its creation in 1973.

"So what if we look at good families in Bangladesh..."

"Yes, but they're in Bangladesh..."

"Yes, exactly, I may finally get one son-in-law who can speak Bengali fluently!"

"And I may get a husband who can't string an English sentence together!" Baba looked insulted and glared at Amma.

"You think they're not educated in Bangladesh? You think just because it's a poor country, the people aren't good, aren't worthy of you?"

"No!" Why did I sound so unreasonable? I wasn't being unreasonable. Being advertised in the *Eastern UK Eye* and Internet dating didn't seem such a bad idea anymore. "I mean, it's going to be hard finding someone I click with..."

"What is this 'clicking' business you always go on about Maya?" Amma said, snapping her fingers before me. "It's temporary like this. You hear 'click', and then you don't. Is that what you want? Husband and then no husband, huh?" I wondered at what point my adult/child relationship with my parents had reversed. My mother's logic for going to Bangladesh was that 'clicking' didn't matter and my father's was that he wanted a son-in-law with whom he could speak fluent Bengali. There was no consideration of what I wanted, what I had lost, what I would never regain. The thought of Jhanghir brought tears to my eyes, and I burst out crying, there, in front of my incredulous parents.

"Oh no, no, no. The tears will not change my mind," Baba declared, turning his back on my shuddering snivelling form. "It won't work, Maya. You go to your room and cry your eyes out. Trust me, one day you will thank me for making this decision." Nobody understood that I wasn't meant to marry a stranger in Bangladesh. Nobody knew that I was meant to marry Jhanghir. Not even Jhanghir realised this fact. So, while being mosquito bitten, dehydrated with diarrhoea and being introduced to families, Jhanghir would be returning from my honeymoon in the Maldives. The more I thought about the golden beaches and Jhanghir bringing Preeya yet another cold drink, the harder I cried.

"I've booked the tickets Maya, and I'm not losing my deposit because of your crying!" Baba added before walking out of the room.

"He's only doing what a father thinks is best," Amma said as she sat down next to me. "There's no more boys in England left for us to consider, and we don't know where else to look, who else to ask, but family in Bangladesh." It didn't matter what Amma said. Now that I had started crying, I couldn't stop.

Further talk of my banishment to Bangladesh's SLAAG-shifting market was postponed for Loose-Leila's dinner and her short, bespectacled and not-so handsome fiancé. The only difference was, Baba refused to host it anywhere public due to my current emotional instability. Instead, he hired a large white marquee to hoist up in our garden in the middle of March. Tariq borrowed tables and chairs from his restaurants, Taj arranged the music and Baba took control of the menu. The super capable men in our house tended to everything, giving us women time to ready ourselves for the early evening dinner. Only, I didn't want to get ready or celebrate Leila's ascent into the married league when I had just lost control of my life. But Baba had no time for my self-pity.

"Maya, make the samosas." He handed me a large bowl of fried mince, a platter of rectangular strips of filo pastries and some flour paste. I took my ingredients through to the dining room and set to work. Mince in the middle, fold the filo three times and paste into a triangle. Mince, fold, paste. Mince, fold, paste. The routine was soothing and when the first batch of forty disappeared to be fried, more ingredients arrived for a second batch. Ayesha arrived early-afternoon, bearing a forest of flowers and a hyperactive Zarah who took straight to bothering Hamza.

"Maya, you're not ready!" Ayesha stared at my flannel pyjamas and unbrushed hair with dismay. She, on the other hand, looked like a classic Indian actress dressed in a beautiful burgundy silk sari with 1940s make-up. "Leila could arrive any minute and take to reorganising everything."

"Well then Loose-Leila and man-eater Mina can do it by their skinny little selves," I retorted. Mince, fold, paste.

"Why isn't she ready?" Ayesha asked Shireen-bhabhi who appeared in an equally stunning maroon sari and similar make-up. I sensed that Hana and Jana would dress in the same style and that I was expected to follow suit. But I resisted falling into the trap of taking on the unified 'family' look and carried on mincing, folding and pasting.

"She's making samosas…"

"I can see that, by why isn't she getting ready?" I caught Ayesha's raised brow and sensed something more than just a co-ordinated themed look going on.

"We're all wearing saris today. I'll pull your hair into a Hepburn fold if you want." I looked at Shireen before returning to my job. Shireen was as kind-hearted a sister-in-law as any family could be blessed with.

"I'm making samosas and then I'll get dressed." Ayesha gave me a bright smile. "I'm wearing my beige shalwaar kameez and I'm putting my hair up into a bun..."

"But we have Leila's in-laws coming..."

"Yes, not royalty Ayesha. Just more faces, with opinions and judgements."

"But Hana and Jana have brought you a sari too..."

"I don't do saris." The statement brought Shireen and Ayesha to a stop for that, like humans need oxygen, was a fact.

"You look beautiful in saris," Shireen offered, refusing to meet my eyes.

"The last time I wore a sari, it was at the Independence Day dinner at the Commonwealth Institute. I not only tripped on the train, but I entered a packed hall with the back of my sari tucked into my knickers..."

"But they were such nice knickers." My glare stopped Shireen short.

"Oh, nobody noticed Maya!"

"Amma screamed in shame from the upper balcony Ayesha..."

"But that was such a long time ago and this sari is so beautiful, you've got to try it."

"No..."

"Just put it on..."

"No."

"...and if you don't like it..."

"I don't want to wear a sari..."

"...you can wear what you want," Ayesha finished, as she handed my bowls of ingredients over to Shireen. "Now go have a shower and I'll be up in fifteen minutes."

The sari was indeed beautiful; black silk with stunning embroidery on the train. But there's a secret art to wearing saris in a manner that elongates and flatters even the dumpiest of women. And after forty-five minutes of wrapping, pleating and unwrapping, I realised I hadn't learned the art. Standing before the mirror in my blouse and slip and towel-wrapped wet hair, I started again. I tucked the end of the sari into my slip, wrapped it around my hips once, then pleated it several times at my abdomen before tucking the pleats in. I ignored the doorbell and pulled the sari around me once more, then placed the train over my shoulders to fall gracefully down my back. Done. Then I looked at my reflection.

"Aarrgghhh!" I looked pregnant and all of three foot tall. The pleats kicked out in a frou frou and the train fell all the way down to the floor. "Leila's here!" I screamed as the doorbell rang again and again.

Hoisting up my sari, I stomped across to my window and looked down at the marquee. "Someone's here."

"Get the door Maya!" Amma shouted back and I stared in amazement. I couldn't possibly be seen like this. I slammed my window shut and clutched the pleats against me as I walked out of my room and down the stairs.

"Everyone's in the marquee, so go straight through..." I froze as I saw Abdul Raquib and his kandan of family and friends before me. I yanked the train around me and stood grappling with the pleats in an effort to retain some dignity. Then I looked up at the silent family with a flustered laugh.

"We're a little early, we can come back if you're not ready..."

"No! No, come in!" I stepped back, still clutching my sari for dear life, to let them in. "Amma! Abdul Raquib's family are here!" I bellowed as they entered one after the other. I greeted each individually, ignoring their confused and yet more than amused expressions. Then the cute waiter from Rajahs entered and I wanted to melt away with humiliation.

"Come through, come through!" Amma sang out as she floated through the kitchen and into the hall with a ready smile.

"They're here," I repeated, as she stopped dead at my appearance. Her smile faltered before she looked away with a reapplied white smile. "If you'll excuse me..." I whispered, disappearing up the stairs and into my bedroom. I covered my face with both hands, only to burst out laughing when I felt the sari fall, soft as a whisper, to my feet.

After Hana and Jana were dispatched to turn me into the model of sophistication, I was determined not to screw up Leila's dinner. The marquee had been transformed into a warm, dimly lit Bedouin tent filled with flowers, Arabic music and conversation.

"Maya! You're finally ready!" I grinned at Leila's loud greeting and spotted a seat next to Sulaiman, the cute waiter. "Come sit by me and you can tell me all about the greeting you gave to Abdul Raquib and his parents!" My hopes of familiarising myself with Sulaiman disappeared as the rumble of laughter emerged from Raquib's family. I fixed a smile before taking my place beside my nemesis. Once again I greeted everyone.

"That was quite a greeting!" I looked to my left at one of Abdul's friends. He was all of five feet three inches and probably weighed in at seven and a half stones. It was just my luck that Sulaiman was sitting between Man-eater Mina and Chachijhi, whilst I was stuck between Leila and shortie. "I'm Jim by the way."

"Jim?" Brown face, white name. It never worked.

"My dad was a fan of Jimmy Hendrix," he said without hesitation. I nodded as if this was a perfectly normal thing for Bengali parents to do. "You must be Leila's cousin, I've heard quite a bit about you." And then it dawned on me. Leila's promise to match-make, the empty seat and Ayesha's insistence on the sari. It was all for Jim.

"It's nice to meet you." He grinned from ear to ear like a little chihuahua and I looked towards Ayesha who was preoccupied with Shireen. I could feel Jim watching me and I cleared my throat before turning my attentions back to him.

"So, how do you know Abdul?" I asked.

"We're old friends. Actually, the five of us here today grew up together in Upton Park. We all ended up going to the same schools, colleges and universities," Jim pointed around the table and included Sulaiman in his group.

"Really, so, what did you all study?" In an instant Jim had captured my full attention.

"Actuarial studies" he said, sounding rather pleased with himself. I had no idea what that was, but I nodded with an inane smile.

"I'm an actuarist by profession." I waited for more, but Jim was content to leave it at that.

"You mean you all studied the same thing?"

"Oh no, uh, Abdul as you know is a software engineer along with Feisal and Malik. Sulaiman, over there by Leila's sister, he's the only entrepreneur. He runs a series of fusion Indian restaurants." I turned to accept some pilau rice, grinning with the knowledge that waiter Sulaiman wasn't just a simple waiter, but a thinking man too.

"Can you believe the last one of your group is getting married!" I baited, as I helped myself to my favourite chicken korma dish.

"Oh, Abdul's not the last one," Jim corrected eagerly, as I looked at him wide-eyed in mute anticipation. "I am." What the hell did that mean? I wasn't interested in Jim, or his bloody marital status, I was interested in Sulaiman. I kept smiling, but waited and when it became apparent that Jim, the man of few explanations, needed prompting, I asked:

"So you're the only one left who's not married?"

My question reverberated in the silence that Baba had just achieved to make his speech. I heard Amma groan at the end of the table, Leila and Mina 'tsk' with muted laughter and saw Jim grinning like the village idiot who had struck it rich, as Baba cleared his throat to break the awkwardness. My timing for the humiliating was impeccable. I tucked into my chicken korma with full gusto and Baba began his speech. A good korma warmed me up like nothing else. Actually, a good korma's quite similar to romance. If it's too creamy and rich, like a schmaltzy corny romance, it makes you want to throw up. Alternatively if it's tasteless and watery, it leaves you cold. But if the taste and consistency is right, it just leaves you wanting more.

"Yeah, I'm the only one who's not married." I looked up as Jim leaned in to whisper against my ear. I wanted to slap him away like an annoying fly, but the implications of what he'd confirmed dawned on me. I looked down the long table at Sulaiman and as he nodded in greeting, caught his amazing eyes. But, he was married. "Why do you think you're sitting next to me?" I turned to look at Jim. Watery, tasteless chicken korma came to mind. I shook my head. It was true that all the good ones were either married or gay. I served myself another helping of chicken korma.

"...and the funniest thing was that the woman Sulaiman had never met, but had an arranged marriage with was my salsa partner." Jim had dominated the conversation since my embarrassing outburst, and no matter how hard I tried to engage with Leila, who was basking in the spotlight and Abdul's friends, she refused to entertain me. However, the conversation took an interesting turn. "She was very good, quite modern for a Bengali girl. Do you salsa?" Jim asked, with a little jig that made me want to slap him into adulthood.

"No I don't do salsa, I don't dance very much at all."

"Is that because your parents won't let you?" There he went again, leaning in close, as if we had something intimate to talk about. I leaned back and shook my head.

"I choose to follow the guidelines of our religion." Intimacy-creating Jim had to be stopped.

"So you're quite strict then? You know, with the book?" I frowned in confusion at his reference.

"The book?"

"Yeah, you know the holy book, our one." I stared at Jim as I lost the will to live. I couldn't believe that this man, a second generation Bengali Muslim, had such an identity problem he couldn't even bring himself to call the Quran by its name. "I skimmed through it a couple of times. Although I admit it has a few interesting things to say, I don't think it's quite relevant to our times." Oh no. I wasn't even going to be drawn into this one.

"So do you still salsa?" I asked with a bright smile and feigned interest.

"Well, not as much since Sulaiman separated from Nargis..."

"Separated?"

"Well, we're hoping that they'll get back together especially since they've had a baby girl, but things aren't looking good." I looked back down the table again and watched Sulaiman as he chatted easily with Chachijhi and Hana. I wondered what Nargis looked like. If he was anything to go by, she'd be a goddess.

"Why did they separate?"

"Like all men, Sulaiman wanted a naughty girl turned good. Only Nargis likes partying, and when their daughter came along, he gave her an ultimatum and she walked out."

I found it incredible that anyone would walk out on a man as stunning as Sulaiman. "So tell me, is there a bad girl buried deep down inside of your good girl image?" I stared at Jim as he grinned at me and wiggled his eyebrow suggestively. I leaned in close to Jim, with a warm smile on my lips.

"You make me want to stay a virgin for the rest of my life." I watched his grin slowly disappear. Jim cleared his throat, sat back and then turned away to talk to Jana. I helped myself to another serving of chicken korma.

"I can't get married in Bangladesh!" I cried to Tanya who met me at Café Nero after work on Monday. I took the tissue she held out.

"Lots of people get married back home Maya. It works out for them..."

"But I don't want to get married in Bangladesh, who's going to come to my wedding?" I explained, even though Tanya remained frowning.

"I think you should think about finding a good man before you plan the wedding..."

"But I want my friends to see me get married, I want you there, I want Sakina there..." I blew my nose and looked at my oldest dearest friend as new tears welled in my eyes.

"We'll be there for the wedding..."

"But I want my henna in the three-tiered hall at Ealing Town Hall, with Evergreen wedding caterers, a female DJ and a henna artist. I want to be fitted at Dhamini's and then shop for matching maid's outfits until... until..."

"Until you realise you may not get the wedding you dreamed of, but you may just get a good man..."

"I don't want to get married in Bangladesh!" It didn't matter how many times I said it, the reality was I was going, my ticket was booked and I could do nothing about it.

"Did Brenda give you time off?" I nodded and wiped at my eyes.

"I've booked three weeks' holiday and Clare has agreed to manage my accounts in my absence." I took a large bite of the Devil's chocolate cake before looking at Tanya. "Brenda's not happy about me taking my holidays off all together, but with all the overtime I've put in I still have one more week of annual leave left. Though there's hardly any point in wasting that looking for a man in Bangladesh."

"Listen, we're all out of men here in England. You said so yourself," Tanya pointed out, helping herself to the cake. "Take Leila's dinner for instance. You said that all the good men were gone and only the creeps are left over..."

"But we haven't searched every city or town!"

"Who's going to do that for you Maya? We're all out of ideas. Look at me, look at Sakina, we're going with what's out there, making the most of what's left. Now somewhere along the lines you're either going to have to accept that or broaden your search."

"But all the way to Bangladesh?" I cried out, unable to accept that this was what fate had in store for me.

"Maya, sweetie, there could be some lovely man who's waiting for you out there..."

"And all the aunties, they'll all say nobody wanted me here, so I had to go back and bribe some man to marry me..."

"They've probably got slappers for daughters..."

"And then when I come back, everyone will look at us and feel sorry for him for having a wife nobody wanted..."

"You've refused perfectly good alaaps, even ridiculed some for failing to meet your gold standard and you expect me of all people to feel sorry for you. That's not going to happen." Tanya's angry tone stopped me. As I was the heartbroken reject, I looked at her in confusion. "There is no one here Maya. Sakina's only been dumped by a cheating man, yet she's giving Shaj a chance and I'm seeing a man who's beautiful to me, but I know deep down something's missing. We're doing this because there's nothing else out there for our age." The thought of Jhanghir brought on a fresh onslaught of tears. Tanya crouched before me and pushed my hair back from my face. I looked at her through tear filled eyes.

"I still want him." Tanya smiled at my confession and held my hands.

"He doesn't love you, honey. He's made his decision, and now he's having an idyllic honeymoon with his picture perfect wife, so you have to move on." I shook my head and clenched my eyes shut, but her words hurt just the same.

"He's everything I want Tanya, I thought my kismet lay with Jhanghir."

"Kismet has other plans for you Maya." I frowned and stared down at my hands.

"How can I marry someone who I don't love?"

"Maybe that's why you should get married, that way you don't get hurt." Tanya sat back and looked at me. "That way, you can get yourself the best terms, the best set up and be in control." Tanya always made the hard decisions sound more rewarding.

"Maybe... maybe I could find a doctor..."

"No 'maybe' baby!" Tanya said, with a wide, white smile. "And just maybe, he might be an English doctor going back to get married..."

"Do you think so?" Maybe I would get myself a Bollywood love story. Maybe this was the beginning of my love story, and not the end. Tanya leaned forward, and winked mischievously. "No reason why the search can't begin on the flight out there!"

L: Leave Lost Loves For London's Lajja

And that's how my trip into an unknown future began. Like all Bengali fathers, Baba insisted on getting to Heathrow four hours before flight departure and an hour before the check-in counter opened because, as Baba said:

"They'll head out to Heathrow early from Manchester, Birmingham and Luton to check in first and we'll lose the best seats."

True to his words, when we arrived there were a number of Bengali fliers questioning why check-in wasn't open. Before I could say 'please don't', Baba spotted the queuing travellers and joined them to encourage the check-in counter to open up.

"Could you try and control him?" I pleaded, as Taj handed me the trolley to jog off after Baba.

"Leave him be," Ayesha muttered carrying my travel bag. "You'll be ok, you know that."

"Sure." My sisters all felt bad that Baba and Amma were whisking me off on my own. "I'll be fine." Ayesha looked away, already teary at the thought of my imminent departure.

"Remember, it's your life." We hovered by the check in counter. "You can say no."

"But I can also say yes." I reminded Ayesha with a grin, but she wasn't amused.

"Where are they?" Hana and Jana were still trying to find parking, and this was Ayesha's way of dealing with the possibility that I could make a decision without her good guidance. We stood in awkward silence, watching more and more Bengali travellers arrive to join the queue behind us. They arrived with trolleys loaded with brand new TVs, videos, irons, Hoovers and other appliances that could all be bought in Bangladesh. Then there were the suitcases that were way over the weight allowance zipped closed with three locks and triple strapped with extra strong string to make it difficult for Bengali baggage handlers to cut out hard earned goods. Then Ayesha called out to Hana and Jana who rushed with Amma, as if the final check-in call had been made.

"Are you in the queue?" I looked at the skinny twenty year old, with greased-back hair, big Aviator shades and ultra-tight fake Moschino jeans.

"Take a guess?" I smiled, but the twenty year old kissed his teeth and walked away.

"Is it time to check in?" Amma asked, all out of breath and flustered.

"They haven't opened the check-in counter yet," I pointed out as Amma looked around to find Baba chatting away with fellow travellers.

"That father of yours, rush, rush, rush! That's all he knows." Taj walked back to pull Amma into a warm hug. "Ayesha, make sure you feed my boy. It breaks my heart to leave my baby behind." The fact that Taj was hitting twenty-five made no difference to my mother. Taj lapped it up and grinned when Amma slipped him a fifty-pound note. "For when you get hungry."

"They've opened, they've opened!" Baba shouted, racing across to us as if we were in the Grand Prix for checking in. The staff had yet to switch on their check in equipment, but that made no difference to Bengalis. The two families before us were dragging their luggage to stand before the indifferent Bangladesh Biman staff members. "What are you waiting for? You're holding up the queue!" Baba shouted, taking charge of the trolley. Reluctantly, we followed him and stood before Counter 3, where Shumi the check-in stewardess tapped away on her keyboard.

"How many are flying?" I handed over three red passports but Shumi deemed us unworthy of even an acknowledgement.

"Three, just me and my parents." My loud clarification caught her attention and Shumi realised we would be acknowledged. Shumi looked at Ayesha, Hana, Jana and Taj. She took in our groomed appearance before gracing us with a forced smile.

"You're booked for a direct flight to Sylhet via Dhaka." Shumi's statement told me two things - that she was Dhakayan, and that she was definitely scoring points. "And how many pieces of luggage do you have?"

"Four." I returned her glacial smile. We had spent half the night packing and unpacking so that we met the thirty-five kilogram per passenger weight allowance. The rest we shoved into hand luggage we would carry on board. The family checking in to our left had already been asked to pay an excess baggage fee and, as a result, were frantically unpacking their case in full view.

"Just four?" Shumi's surprise was evident and we pointed to the matching, heavily- secured luggage. "And you packed those yourself?" Baba nodded before making light talk to soften Shumi into being polite. And he succeeded. "Sir, would you like any seat in particular?"

"Seats that are as far forward as possible and next to the window," he answered, as I looked back at the queue to see if there was anyone worthy of a second look.

"And any dietary requirements?" Shumi now had my full attention. Biman staff offering a choice of on board meals was about as likely as getting quality customer service at your nearest McD's, so I shook my head at Baba and smiled. Shumi issued our tickets and fastened our luggage with tags before sending them off on the conveyor belt. I looked back at the growing presence of sari adorned, paan chewing, luggage loaded Bengalis waiting to check in. By my calculations, there would be three hundred and sixty-odd passengers on the flight, a hundred and forty of whom would be parents, with a hundred and sixty or so pre teens. And with the exception of 'Fake Moschino Pants', that left about sixty fliers from which I could find a potential suitor.

"Who are you looking for?" Amma asked as Baba organised the tickets and passport.

"I thought I saw someone from college," I muttered as we headed for the lifts to the first floor café. "But I was wrong," I added as we stepped in and watched the doors slide shut. It suddenly occurred to me that Jhanghir could be passing through Heathrow on his return from the Maldives. I shook the thought from my mind and listened to Amma lecture my sisters. But the thought wouldn't disappear. What if Jhanghir was in the airport?

"How do I look?" Hana frowned at my question, but I had to be sure that I looked agreeable in case I bumped into him.

"You look pretty." Hana never said anything nice, so I paused at her comment. I had cut out a picture from *Asian Woman* to copy the look and hadn't known whether I had pulled off the look, until then. I had dressed in a sixties-inspired short cream shalwaar kameez with tan Greek lace up sandals and matching hand bag, but I didn't have the hair stylists or make up artists to transform me into a beautiful model. Instead, I simply pulled my hair back into a neat bun and applied lip-gloss and mascara. "That outfit really suits..."

"It suits your figure," Jana finished when Hana looked away teary eyed. They feared the outcome of allowing me to travel without them and yet I felt liberated by my independence. I reached out to hold Hana's hand and smiled, ready to greet life beyond my sisters' shadows.

My family and I sat in the café huddled around two pots of tea making small talk to pass the time caused by our early check-in. Amma fretted at the fact that Tariq hadn't turned up and whenever there was a lull in the conversation, Ayesha would remind us of yet another superstition to be careful of.

"Don't wear red."

"Don't let strangers take your photo."

"Drink only from bottled water."

"Don't walk beneath trees at night."

"Don't let Baba get involved with family politics or get into any fights."

"Always tie your hair in a bun, and cover it so that they can't put a jinn on you." Ayesha reminded us of the kinds of things that would scare the living shit out of any sane person until our flight was ready to board. At once the hordes scheduled for BG005 stood up. We made our way to the departure gates amidst my fellow polyester-suited restaurant wallas, with loud voices and bigger bags, and petite women in bright saris, chequered cardigans and black headscarves. And as always, the young girls bejewelled in too much gold and dressed in ill fitting shalwaar kameezes followed behind with their skinny barrow boy brothers.

"Tariq, you made it!" Amma cried when she spotted bhaya running across the floor. He swept Amma into a tight hug as she began crying. Baba hugged my sisters as I kidded around with Taj, refusing to cry.

"Take care of them," Ayesha told me, hugging me warmly. "Take care of you."

"I will," I promised with a bright smile, as the crying twins enveloped me. Taj joined in and I missed my family already.

"Speak to Shireen, Amma," Tariq said, handing her his mobile as he hugged Baba before turning to me. My oldest brother was a big man, a pathana bacha, broad and stocky, and he pulled me into a mighty bear hug.

"I'm sorry I can't look out for you," he whispered as I held on for dear life. "I've bought you a mobile, you call me day or night if you're not happy, do you hear me?" I started crying at his consideration and refused to let go.

"We have to go Maya," Baba said, patting me gently on the back as everyone sniffed and wiped at their tears. Slowly Tariq released me, but before he did, he kissed me on the forehead.

"Say bye to your bhabhi," he said handing me his mobile.

"Maya, you be careful out there. Did your brother buy you a mobile?" Shireen asked.

"Yes," I whispered.

"It's got international roaming so call, if only to stop Hamza from crying because he misses his favourite aunt. He's been walking around with your mobile thinking that you're going to call…"

"He's still crying?" I asked.

"And your friend, Jhanghir called…"

"He's here?" My loud shout brought everyone to a stop and I lowered my gaze but my heart jumped into life at the thought that he had come for me. "What did you say to him?"

"That you're going to Bangladesh to get married. He's at Terminal 3, he wanted to see you." And my heart sank at the realisation that he was en route home from his honeymoon. I was glad my sister-in-law had told him I was getting married.

"Do me a favour Shireen-bhabhi?" She agreed without hesitation. I looked at Tariq. "Stop bhai sending my work off to art competitions."

"We need to go Maya," Baba said, taking the phone from me. "Draw me some of the magical sunsets when you get time," Tariq said, handing me a big canvas bag. I peaked in to find the most glorious selection of pastels, artist pads, fixative sprays and putty rubbers, as well as a new mobile set. I looked at my brother in awe. "You go with what your heart tells you," he said, smiling at me. This was a man who, to help Baba out with the restaurant, had given up his dream. And now he was helping me with mine. I held onto him tightly as he pulled me into a final hug.

"I promise," I whispered. Bengali farewells at the airport were similar to funerals. Everyone cried. Not discreet crying. But long, hefty, loud, sobbing multiplied across all three hundred passengers and their families. So amidst the chorus of weeping, crying and sobbing we went through passport control to begin my new journey.

It was a longer flight than I could have ever imagined. Between paan swapping sessions, six year old Shamsuddin Miah throwing up every hour in his black suit, white shirt and clip-on red tie, and two year old Farhana Bibi Begum screaming at the top of her lungs, I was ready to concede defeat and return home. But there was no such luck. After twelve hours stuck in the children's vomit-zone, two arguments with rude airhostesses, and a flight transfer at Dhaka airport, we arrived in Sylhet, Bangladesh. From the moment we landed, there was pandemonium. Officials, baggage handlers, inspectors, and receiving families all shouted instructions, demands and greetings in what was a din of hyperactivity. Bewildered new arrivals joined slow moving queues for visa clearance, baggage handlers manhandled bags against the angry protests of travellers, and inspectors picked out the most lucrative passengers for checks and potential bribes. As such, I walked between my parents, happy to let Baba bellow and bumble his way through passport checks, baggage claim and then into the meeting point for families. There the volume of people and noise multiplied ten fold and in an instant, our family surrounded us to escort us out into the blaring, burning daylight of Sylhet.

"Are you ok?" Amma asked, as she joined me on the rooftop of our new home.

I hadn't left Baba's two-storey five-bedroom home in Talukgonj, an hour north of Sylhet, for two days. Family, friends, and acquaintances visited us from every corner of Sylhet, and despite my cousins' attempts to keep me busy with polite questions, the beautiful sunset called me to the roof with my pencils, pastels and pastel pads. Amma brought me a cold drink and a small plate of samosas. She stopped beside me to look at my work. "You were always very good at art."

"It's been a while, but look at how beautiful the sunset is."

"Are you putting your mosquito repellent on?" But Amma seemed more interested in inspecting the bites on my face. Then, in a sudden change of tone, she said. "Your cousins are saying that you're ignoring them."

"I don't think I'll be making best friends with people who live off Baba and then lie about it," I told her, leaning back from her close inspection of me to look out at the view. "I've met countless aunts and uncles, greeted even more cousins, and smiled inanely at elders who all arrive with stories of hardships, wrongdoings, and family politics that my parents by virtue of living in England are expected to sort out. Why do we have to solve the world's problems?"

"Maya, they only ask for good advice based on worldly experience." I shook my head at Amma's explanation.

"So why does Baba turn into a beast in the evening demanding answers about the missing income generated by his land, paddies and properties?"

Amma stalled, because there were no real answers beyond family need. Not desperate, urgent need, just the luxury of unbound greed. If my father's family could break his trust, I wanted no part in reacquainting myself with them.

"You're here for a short time, surely you can make an effort..."

"My moisturiser's missing, as is my conditioner and insect repellent," I told Amma who looked at me with disappointment. "Fifteen years ago, the same thing happened, I knew who it was then, and I know who it is now. I don't know how you expect me be friends with them."

"These people are your blood relatives. Moisturiser, conditioners you can replace, but family, good or bad, you can't," Amma said without the slightest hesitation.

"Ten years of rent from this property, five years of rice sales, and five years of financial support from Baba for my uncles to start up as fishmongers, and what do we have for our troubles? Nothing. In fact, Baba's youngest brother is now claiming this building as his..."

"You're a child, what do you know of these matters!" Amma dismissed, but I held Amma's eyes and smiled. It was easier for our elders to believe ignorance was the cause of our discontent back at home. "And you shouldn't bother yourself with these matters, we're here for more important reasons than your father's business dealings!"

"You're right Amma, I know nothing of these matters," I conceded. "I just like drawing my sunsets."

"Come in now, I don't like you being up here alone in the dark. There's too much talk of jinns and ghosts." Amma helped me collect my tools to pack them back into their packets. "Soon they'll be saying that you've been taken by a spirit!"

I was ill-prepared for the first of the alaaps that had been arranged for me. Having become the preferred meal for every mosquito in Talukgonj, I was covered in bites. On top of which, over the last few nights, I had become very well acquainted with the pothole toilet.

"Are you ready for breakfast?" It was Najma, Baba's favourite niece, who I couldn't stand. She had recently married a green card holder in America, and with a future in the States in sight, she now floated around with the grace of a Rani. Najma came into my room and sat down on the edge of my bed.

"I want to sleep in," I said looking at this slim, pretty woman through my mosquito net.

"Everyone's waiting for you, and I've been sent up to bring you down."

"I'm not very hungry..."

"I understand. You must be very excited about the alaap today." She knew. Every member of my family knew. And they all looked at me with that 'you'll be married soon' look. "Do you know what you're wearing?" Najma grinned with a coy look.

"Do you?" Her grin disappeared for a moment before reappearing.

"Well it doesn't matter what I'm wearing, I'm already married!" Najma reminded me all too effectively.

After Zuhr prayers, Najma arrived to lead me down into the living room. I looked truly hideous in the pink outfit that her father had brought for me, but I had to wear it as a sign of respect. It was just so big. The arms fell off my shoulders and the kameez swung around my ankles. In short, I looked like a deflated blancmange. Still, I dutifully followed Najma down the stairs. I could hear the sniggers of my younger cousins who hid behind partially opened doors and winked when one of them glanced out.

"Hold your scarf on your head," Najma instructed loud enough to be heard. I smiled and held the pink scarf in place. Baba rose at our arrival and shifted uncomfortably.

"Maya, this is Amir. Amir this is my daughter, Maya." That was as simple an introduction as Baba could manage. "Ah, Najma, why don't you stay with the kids whilst I join Amir's family in the dining room?" Baba bolted at the first opportunity and I stopped grinning as he headed for the door.

"Why don't you sit here Maya?" I looked at Najma unimpressed by her big sister routine. It was then I saw Baba standing in the corridor waving his hands around for her to get Amir and I to talk. He looked like he was directing a 747 to land. Najma in turn pushed me towards Amir. "Why don't you talk to him?"

"Assalaimalaikum," I said instantly, at which point I stopped. That was the first time I noticed Amir. Rather, I noticed his large white eyes floating on a face that had no discernable jaw line.

"Walikumasalaam," he stuttered, gripping his hands together, nervous and sweating in his three piece suit. "How are you liking Sylhet?" Amir spoke in English and I wondered why, with a population of sixty million people, my parents had to find the ugliest man in Bangladesh for me to consider.

"Very well thank you," I said with a pleasant smile. Najma poured me some juice and winked at me in mock conspiracy.

"You look very good to be searching for a husband in this country, no?" I smiled at the compliment. "Hai Haaaai! Hai Haaai!" Dear God, he was laughing as if the Heimlich manoeuvre was being applied to him. Each time he laughed, his shirt strained against the buttons that held in his bulging waist.

"It's the right thing for me and my family to consider." I answered, as he searched in his pockets and pulled out a folded piece of paper.

"This is my bio data," he said, shifting across to sit next to me. I slid as far left as I could until I backed up against Najma. Amir unfolded his biodata and scooted closer. With a fixed smile I looked down at his details.

"You see, I studied chemical engineering at Sylhet University after taking my intermediate at private college. My auntie lives in Bow in London and she tells me there is plenty of demand for chemical engineers there." At some point I stopped listening to Amir as he worked his way down the two-page outline. He looked directly at me and then stared at my lips. I looked back down at his details, repulsed by his sleazy look. I didn't want to wake up next to this man for the rest of my life. I wanted to scream. There and then. Scream. Was the world mad? Amir caught me looking and gave me a lopsided grin, interpreting my stare for instant attraction.

"Why don't I get you both some more refreshment?" Najma had caught the interchange and like Amir, misread the moment.

"I'm fine," I said quickly, gripping her thigh to stop her from leaving.

"Let me get some mango and pineapple," Najma insisted, unclenching my hand before leaving the room. I watched her leave with wide, betrayed eyes.

"So, you like living in London?" I turned to Amir and refused to respond to his leering expression.

"No, no I don't," I lied. "I actually really want to settle in Sylhet." He looked shaken.

"B... but everything's better in London..."

"No, it's hard work. I want to stop working, I want to raise children here and have a maid, a cook and a chauffeur." Amir could no longer disguise his disappointment, as he watched his plans of migrating fade before him.

"And you can adjust to the conditions here?" Amir didn't seem happy.

"If my husband has a good job here, then there's no reason to return to London." The seeds of doubt had been planted and Amir stared at me in search of the truth.

"Is there some reason why you don't want to return to London?" Now suspicion was setting in and I looked at him with feigned surprise.

"Oh no! Of course not, what would give you that impression?" But he now had a worrying impression of me. Amir folded up his bio data and slipped it back into his pocket.

"If you do not mind, what is your age?" He was making a last ditch attempt to find some virtue in me, so that he could overlook the assumptions he had made.

"Nearly thirty." Poor Amir's eyes nearly popped out of their sockets, but I looked down like a defeated, unwanted spinster. Najma returned to silence and looked from me to Amir and then back again.

"Please have some more," she said, serving up three dishes of fruit, but Amir declined and asked to speak with our parents. My cousin looked at me with narrowed eyes, as I took a serving of fresh mango. She didn't say a word before taking Amir out of my life.

Every image I gathered of Sylhet I drew from the rooftop. The wondrous dusky sunsets, the hazy mid-afternoon chaos of shrill riksaws and bleating cars and the sumptuous colours of saris that made my conservative colours appear drab, middle-aged and dreary. I felt inspired and copied Hodgkin's technique using giant bold strokes of colour.

"Ayjay, you've got a phone call." I turned to Najma's loud call and walked across the rooftop to her. I hadn't made friends with my cousins who called me the 'snotty one'.

"Hello?" I took the phone from Najma and watched her walk over to my drawings.

"Maya, is that you?" It was Tanya. The sound of Tanya's voice made me realise how much I missed her and my life in England. I turned away from Najma to wipe away my tears.

"Yeah, it's me." I cleared my throat and walked out of Najma's hearing range.

"How are you? How's it going?" She had a million questions and then some about my introductions, so I put a stop to them all with:

"No news Tanya. Nothing's changed."

"Oh." The disappointment in Tanya's voice was evident and I felt like a spoilt child refusing to adjust to the situation. "Well there's still some time. Are you getting on ok out there? Health, food, climate?"

"I've had diarrhoea since I landed and I'm the new feeding ground for the entire population of Sylhet's mosquitoes, but apart from that I've got a wicked tan, lost a little weight and the weather's fantastic..."

"Listen Maya, I can't hold it in anymore. I wanted to tell you when you returned, but I can't wait that long." The brash laugh told me that Tanya was getting married. "Javed asked me to marry him!"

"Oh my God! How did that happen?" I squealed in expected delight. And then it sank in. Sakina had Shaj. Tanya had finally got it together with Javed. So that left me. I would be the last of my tribe to marry. I would be the one everyone would commiserate with for having such a 'rough time' finding a man.

"Well, he just asked me and I've decided that a man with half a brain has got to be better than a man with none." I laughed at Tanya's logic but felt like crying. "The only thing is, we're getting married soon."

"How soon?"

"As soon as." My heart thumped slowly and we stood in silence. "The guy's waited a long time to sleep with me, and since he seems to be the kind of guy who won't be boring in bed, I can't see any reason to wait."

"No, none at all..." We both chuckled, but things were already changing between us. She was joining the Married League and I was about to be relegated to the All Star Spinster Federation.

"Well, we'll plan everything when you get back." I stared down into our neighbour's yard and watched the young cook chase a shrieking scrawny chicken for the evening meal. "And guess what else is hot on the gossip vines?"

"I've no idea." I didn't want any more updates. I wanted to have some news to share.

"Sakina heard some news about Jhanghir..."

"Yeah, I know. Shireen told me that he had called from Heathrow, wanting to appease his guilt no doubt..."

"No, that's not it." My heart stopped at Tanya's excited tone. "She heard from her brother's best friend who married Ruby who's Bengali and her cousin..."

"Tanya, what did you hear about Jhanghir?" I didn't mean to shout, but Najma, the young cook next door and the chicken stopped to stare at me.

"Princess, hold onto your chaadhis!" Tanya retorted, as I strolled away from the now alert and nearing Najma. "Well, Miss Impatience, our Jhanghir's marriage turned out to be a sham. Apparently, they've both been sleeping around with other people. Only they got a little too carried away, you know, dispensed with protection and our girl, Preeya, ended up a little preggo. Her parents obviously flipped out, assumed it was Jhanghir and demanded they get hitched to save her now less-than-white reputation." Tanya took a long deep breath.

"How do we know it's not Jhanghir's?" My heart raced and I rubbed my face with disbelief. I didn't know what to think.

"We don't, but that's not the end of it. The worst part Maya, is that they're saying Jhanghir convinced her to have a termination. We're thinking they came over here for the..."

"How much of it is true?" Even as I asked, I knew that was why Jhanghir had left early for San Francisco. The young cook in the yard below finally caught the chicken and with one twist of its neck, the chicken shrieked its last shriek.

"Even if fifty-percent of it is true, it's still very bad Maya." I stood stunned and unable to reconcile the man I loved with the man who acted as Tanya described.

"Prince Charming doesn't sound so charming now, does he?" She added. The young cook held out the limp chicken with a wide grin for my benefit. I smiled back, but empathised with the dead chicken that had run for its life but had still lost in the end.

"Jhanghir wouldn't do that..."

"Oh really?" I closed my eyes knowing what would follow Tanya's incredulous question. "Are you talking about the Jhanghir who happily strung you along for years and then neglected you when you needed him the most? Maya, wake up and smell the coffee!"

"Tanya, I'm being called," I lied as I stared through tears at nothing in particular. "I'll call you as soon as I have good news," I promised, blinking away my tears as Najma hovered close by.

"We miss you sweetheart and make sure you look seriously for Mr. Charming out there. He sure as hell isn't back here!" I laughed with her before ending the call.

"Is that your friend?" Najma followed me back to my sketches and waited as I picked up my pastels to finish off my drawing of the noisy, colourful landscape.

"I've known Tanya since we were babies. She's getting married when I get back," I informed the curious one.

"I meant Jhanghir." Najma asked watching my every reaction, so I continued with a bright laugh and shook my head. "You can tell me Maya. We all understand that you couldn't have gotten to this age without a boyfriend or some kind of affair."

"I don't have a boyfriend and I've never had an affair!" My indignation made Najma smile, and I wanted to slap the smirk off her face.

"Everyone does here, so it's not a big thing," she added as she leaned against the mid level wall overlooking our front yard. "Most marriages are love marriages. Look at most of our cousins. They met in secret through friends and cousins, before they got married." Najma didn't realise how close she was to seeing the yard face-first, as I was in no mood to divulge my love for a man who was now a stranger.

"We don't. Amma and Baba brought us up differently." I sounded like a puritanical prude and Najma stopped grinning.

"So Jhanghir is...?"

"A university friend in New York who's just got married." Even as I said the word 'friend' I felt my stomach turn. "He's in London with his wife and he was asking after me." The answer didn't satisfy Najma, who no doubt wanted to spread the dirt about the real reason I was still unmarried. She 'hmmphed', made her excuses and left. I sat on the chair and stared out at the late afternoon sky. The man I thought I loved had condoned, no, not just condoned, had recommended the unimaginable. I couldn't believe that of Jhanghir. Yet it fitted with the character of a man who refused to acknowledge my true feelings for him. Maybe Tanya was right. Maybe Jhanghir wasn't the man I thought I knew.

M: Marriage Is Not The Be All And End All

Several family members joined us for dinner the following evening. Baba's aunt Dadhijhi, an old wrinkled lady wearing a forest green sari, scuttled around with a walking stick shouting orders as her son, sitting back like a mastan with his big gut and thick moustache, stared at me. I wasn't in the mood to be trifled with, so I sat and stared back in silence.

"I remember the first time you visited. You were just five years old and you raced around with Taj and the boys refusing to play with the dolls and your sisters," he told me with a slow smile.

"She never liked dolls," Amma said, as the tea and dessert were brought through.

"She never followed her sisters career choices either. They're doctors and she's in some high fly company," Baba added, reliving his pain at my chosen profession.

"She hasn't stopped running round either, that's why she's not married," Dadijhi stated as she fell into the seat beside Baba, pointing her stick at me. "You're not a boy. Allah made you a girl and a girl has certain duties, first to her elders and then to get married." Mastan gurgled with laughter at his mother's logic.

"In London, they don't worry about marriage. They think about careers and money…"

"It's not a girl's duty to be the breadwinner," Dadhijhi cut in impatiently. "It's her duty to make babies, keep your home perfect and keep herself pretty for her husband, if she wants to be kept like a princess."

"We don't have servants and maids to do our every bidding in England."

"Your home is meant to be your castle, your pride of place." Dadhijhi belonged to the dark ages. "Anyone would think you all had palaces to clean and look after!"

"They have no time for that any more," Amma began as she served out the tea. "And who can blame them? They work hard and late. By the time they get home, they're so tired they have no energy to clean and cook…"

"Don't expect any sympathy. Women in your country sold out from being masters of their realm because they thought it to be demeaning." Dadhijhi was unforgiving in her judgements. "And for what? To become servants in the man's world with no control over their own homes or children. Now we read women in the west marry old rich men so they don't have to work. Tell me what has changed?"

"My daughters are all working women and are mistresses of their homes." Baba grinned with pride.

"In New York I'm going to work and drive," Najma announced proudly, not that anyone had asked for her opinion.

"And you must enter college and learn English. You can't survive without English," Baba advised, as Dadhijhi snorted and thumped her stick against the floor, demanding attention.

"You say they're masters of both worlds?" Dadhijhi was a feisty old battle-axe, but I was beginning to like her. "So why do you look after Ayesha's daughter when she's at work and why is Maya still unmarried without a man or family to call her own?" I didn't like the old crow quite as much when she dragged me into her debates. I sat back and listened, as they argued over tea and pan. However much Baba debated with Dadhijhi, I couldn't help but agree with her on the fundamental issue that women had given up the luxury of a protected life for one that was dictated by image, diets, bills and childcare, on top of housework, washing and cleaning. I was too young to join the bra-burning brigade when they 'emancipated' women in the seventies, but somewhere along the line women had been sold short and men had ended up with a three-for-one deal. Instead of having just a baby machine, now they had a money-making, baby machine, with a self-correcting feature to always look good. From this perspective, it wasn't too difficult to see who had got the better deal.

"You're not going out dressed like that," Amma rushed across the hall and up the stairs ready for my next alaap to take me back to my bedroom. "What will people say?"
"This is the latest look from India," I explained evading Amma's grasp to skip down the stairs.
"You can have one of my saris if you want to look decent." I stopped at Najma's comment and saw she was dressed in a gorgeous red silk sari. Anybody would think she was going to meet her intended.
"You look nice, Najma appha." I said. In comparison, my pastel-blue fitted trouser-suit with three inch strappy heels, seemed inappropriate. Even my nearly straight hair and light make-up looked out of place where tight buns, kajol-lined eyes and red lipstick seemed to be the norm.
"That's a nice suit, but maybe you want something a little more appropriate." Najma suggested in a more than patient, verging on patronising tone.
"This covers my butt and boobs. It's appropriate enough," I retorted before walking through to the living room where Baba waited with knotted nerves.
"Ah, you're ready." He fidgeted and then barked for some tea to be brought in. "You look nice bhethi." Baba thought he was already losing me and couldn't bring himself to look at me now.
"No she doesn't, she should change. She needs to change before people start talking about what she's wearing," Amma said as she entered the room and headed straight for me. "This sixties look is too advanced for this type of meeting..."
"She could wear a sari," Najma offered, following Amma into the room.
"I don't want to wear a sari, I don't want to change. I just want to go see this bloody boy!" It was the wrong thing to say and the wrong person to

snap in front of. Najma's eyes widened with relish and I looked with regret at Amma.

"There's no need to be stressed Maya. The car is waiting, your cousins will be there to support you whilst your mother and her brother will be there as your guardian." Najma disappeared to collect our cousins and update them on my latest outburst.

"Amma..." I said, but she left the room without a word and headed out to the car to join her brother, Uncle Rahman.

"She fusses over you because she cares so much." Baba's words made me feel worse than I already did. "You better join your mother."

Five cousins, all dressed in beautiful saris and too much make-up, joined us in the Litace space-wagon that Baba had hired for my first excursion into Sylhet. I sat between Najma and Hasina, who sang wedding songs all the way to Parjaton National Park, where we were to meet Mo, the engineer. Slowly, we made our way through the bustling city centre, filled with rikshaws, young men on fast bikes and people packed buses. London-financed, half-built gated mansions lined the roads that led to malls and shaanti stores selling everything from live chickens to Pampers nappies.

"We're going to have a wedding!" Hasina giggled before grinning at me. "We hear that he's a handsome man. A very handsome man." The emphasis wasn't missed and caused my younger and carefree cousins to giggle along with her.

"Girls, we're nearly here." Uncle Rahman, Amma's brother, pointed out from the front seat. I looked out of the window as we left Sylhet city behind and headed out towards what looked like hill tracks. "Maya's mother and I will talk to his guardians. Najma and the rest of you, follow close behind Maya and Mo. Give them enough space for a conversation, but not too much for him to feel like he can take liberties." The girls giggled at the full license he'd given them to stay on my heels throughout the introduction.

"We'll look after Maya appha," Hasina threw back, as our driver drove up a steep hill and came to a stop before the Parjaton hotel. My heels were totally inappropriate for what turned out to be the national hills and the most popular romantic spot in Sylhet. Uncle Rahman and Amma stepped out and walked to the hotel to meet Mo and his family. I sat oblivious to Hasina's excited chatter and looked at the strolling couples holding flowers with families trailing five steps behind.

"Here he comes!" Hasina squealed as Najma smacked her knee to reign in her excitement. Mo was the tall, slender fair man who walked back to the space wagon with my uncle. He had nice features and a Hilfiger-inspired dress sense.

"Maya, this is Mo. Mo, this is my niece." Uncle Rahman, introduced as he slid open the door.

"Assalaimalaikum," I greeted as I looked at the pleasant-looking man. He replied with a curt, "Walikumasalaam."

"Your mother and I will stay indoors with Mo's parents. Maya, why don't you take a stroll with Mo and see our national park?" I nodded at Uncle Rahman's suggestion and held back a smile as I stepped out.

"Excuse me!" I shrieked grabbing Mo's arm to steady myself amidst my cousins' giggles. It was as though I had stepped into quicksand. I straightened up, extracted each heel from the soft earth, and then looked at my uncle who closed his eyes in despair.

"I'll see you back in twenty minutes." He muttered before disappearing.

"Not very practical shoes," Mo pointed out, as he took long strides along the footpath. I struggled behind, each step sinking deep into the earth and taking twice as long to extract. "Let's take this route," Mo said, pointing to an inclining track.

"Mo, why don't we slow down?" I called out as he turned to look at me.

"Bad shoes for our national hills," he repeated, as I caught up with him. He spoke with a slight American accent, which told me he was a fan of American soaps and sitcoms. "Let's take a seat over there." I nodded when he pointed to a hidden bench that would leave my cousins standing around.

"I'm waiting to hear whether my application to Australia or America comes through." I frowned at Mo's icebreaker, but sat down in relief. "I can't wait to start my life abroad."

"So where does getting married fit in?" I smiled and looked up at him.

"It's the right time for me to settle down, but it's not my one way ticket out of Sylhet."

"And what do you plan to do abroad?" We conversed in English, as my cousins strolled around on the lawn in front of us. A skinny beggar boy, in a dirty worn-out buttonless shirt and adult size shorts held up by a piece of rope, appeared with sweets to sell.

"Bhaya, won't you buy appha a rose?" I smiled at the little boy and looked to Mo.

"Get lost!" I jumped at the bark and watched the boy scuttle away. "I want to get accredited in computer programming. That's where the money is, that's where I want to be." But I was barely listening. The poor boy was now approaching my cousins who redirected him back to us.

"Tell me, what's a pretty girl like you doing back here looking for a man to marry?" His question surprised me.

"We didn't find anyone suitable in England." The small boy was now heading back to us and I dreaded Mo's reaction. But he didn't seem to have noticed.

"You believe in arranged marriages?" he continued, and seemed surprised when I nodded. "You mean you've not been romantically involved with anyone?" Mo floored me with his question. I couldn't believe he expected me to answer that honestly without tarnishing my own reputation.

"Bhaya, won't you buy even sweets for..."

"I've told you before, get away from us!" Mo's aggressive nature bothered me and I reached for my purse to give the poor boy some money. "Put your money away, these people feed off charity like hyenas." I did as he asked to avoid confrontation. The boy hesitated and walked away. Mo looked at me waiting for an answer.

"We weren't brought up to date and have boyfriends. That's forbidden by our religion..."

"It's not just a matter of religion. It's natural to fall in love," Mo corrected. "It's natural to like someone, to be romantic and to feel pain when things don't work out. How did you get to your age without getting burned?" His words brought Jhanghir's betrayal to the front of my thoughts. I stared at him and released a nervous laugh.

"You sound like you've been burned, Mo." The deflected answer made Mo refuse the suggestion. "You really don't have to..." I stopped as I saw the poor boy approach yet again.

"Come here," Mo said, beckoning to the hesitant boy. I feared that he would strike out, but nodded as the boy looked to me. "Give me three of your sweets." The boy handed over the sweets with a smile. I looked at Mo and stared in horror as he chucked each sweet in three different directions. "Now go and fetch those and then I'll give you your damn money." The boy raced off to collect his day's earnings. I shook my head in silent disgust.

"These beggars, they're like vermin," Mo muttered, wiping his hands. I watched the boy search for his sweets in the lawns and flowerbeds, sickened by Mo's cruelty and my silence.

"Wait!" I called out, racing after the little boy intending to give him everything in my purse, but after my third step, I stumbled to my hands and knees as my heels sank into the lawn.

"Maya, what are you doing?" Mo demanded.

"Get off me!" Pushing away Mo's hands, I pulled off my heels and pushed my hair back before racing after the disappearing boy.

"Maya!" Ignoring Najma's scream, I held my stilettos close as I ran around the tall hedges and up the slippery track. The little boy picked up one of his sweets before taking a sharp left to find the other sweets.

"Stop, you'll get lost." Mo and my cousins were close behind me, but I needed to get to the little boy. He was small and fast and terrified.

"Just leave me to pay him!" I shouted back at them. The boy heard me, stopped and turned to look at me. "He shouldn't have thrown your sweets like that." We could hear the others approach and the boy watched over my shoulder ready to dart away. I opened up my purse and grabbed some notes to hand out to him. He stared at me with big round confused eyes and I felt ashamed for all my ungratefulness in life.

"Maya!" I looked back at my approaching entourage as the boy took the notes from my hands and raced away.

"What did he take?" Mo shouted.

"Oh my God!" Najma breathed out as they stared at me. "Oh my God, what did he do, what did you do?" She wiped at the drying mud on my cheek in disbelief. "Look at you, your clothes and shoes - it's all ruined!"

"Why did you run after him?" Mo demanded as he pushed past Najma. "Are you mad..."

"How can you treat a child like that?" I demanded. Mo snorted in derision. "He's a poor boy, a child..."

"He's a crafty con merchant!" Mo spat out. "He cheats people of their money..."

"No. He's a child and despite all the odds against him, he's making a living to survive," I hit out, disgusted by his lack of compassion. "He may need your money, but he doesn't deserve your hate..."

"Maya, you've said enough. Let's go to the hotel..."

"Pitying the beggars makes them even worse," Mo said, with a steely expression.

"I don't pity that boy, I pity you." Hasina started the first of the chorus of gasps. But I didn't regret my actions. Not even when Mo pushed past me to end our disastrous alaap.

Amma remained silent when we returned to the hotel to find that Mo had left with his family. She didn't say a word when I appeared bare-foot and caked in mud. She even refused to look at me when we all piled into the space wagon to make the journey back in silence. As soon as we arrived home, my cousins disappeared.

"Maya come with me..."

"Let her at least wash up..."

"In the living room now," Amma finished, ignoring her brother to stride into the house.

"What happened..." Baba's question faded when he looked at me.

"It wasn't my fault..."

"It never is!" Amma snapped, as she slammed the doors behind me.

"It wasn't my fault! Mo insisted on finding out the details of my non-existent love life, then takes these sweets from this poor boy and chucks them..."

"How on earth can you end up covered in dirt Maya?" Baba was incredulous.

"He said you insulted him and that you pitied him!" I nodded at Amma's accusation.

"He mistreated this poor boy, so I raced after the boy to give him his money and fell over..."

"What do you think Mo's family will say about your behaviour? Running around like some street girl! Have you no shame? No lajja?" Amma asked.

"Because I helped some poor boy..."

"You're not here to solve the poverty problem Maya, you're here to get married!"

"He treated this child like an animal..."

"And you show him to do otherwise by rolling around in mud?!" I stopped at Amma's demand. She was close to tears and even though I didn't regret my actions, I understood her. "I don't know what to do with you anymore, I don't know how to make things right for you." I saw a desperation in Amma that I hadn't seen before. I could deal with her anger, her comparisons, even her crude ploys to get me married. But I couldn't see her sad.

"Let Maya clean up..."

"No, she needs to hear this. She needs to tell me what to do, because I don't know any more, I don't know what to do." Amma wiped at her stream of tears.

"I'm sorry..."

"You're too old to apologise after the fact, Maya. What's wrong, what's stopping you getting married?" I wanted to confide in Amma, I wanted to show her the massive hole Jhanghir had left in my heart and cry the pent up tears deep inside me. But I wouldn't let Jhanghir hurt me anymore. I just couldn't.

"It has to be the right man..." I stopped speaking as Amma shook her head.

"You're not a maharani who'll receive proposals until your death bed..."

"I'm not some unwanted goods to be palmed off at the cheapest price. I'm Maya Malik, I'm educated and a professional, with a good history and an even better family..."

"You're an ungrateful, spoilt, vain woman who thinks she's too good for..."

"...the alaaps you've brought to me? Yes I am. Teethmen, cross-eyed, ugly..."

"Superficial maybe, but I never had you down for stupid," Amma finished. "You're going to your grandmother's..."

"You're washing your hands of me?" I whispered in disbelief.

"I'm giving you time to find yourself, because I don't think you know who or what you want anymore." I was stunned by Amma's perception and had no reply. I just stared at her. Amma started crying. Really crying in a way that made Baba draw her to the sofa to comfort her. I took my shoes and bag and left them alone. Slowly, I passed my cousins who hovered in the corridors, avoiding their eyes as I took the stairs up to my room. I locked the door behind me and went to sit on my bed. The truth was, I didn't know who or what I wanted anymore. I felt nothing but emptiness and saw nothing but emptiness in my future. The worst part was that without the Jhanghir I knew, I had no future.

Word spread fast amongst my family that stubborn, wild, reckless Maya was being dispatched to her Nani's. A five hour car journey, boat trip and half hour walk through dense forest later, I was ready to accept defeat.

"I'm sorry. I'll marry whoever you want me to." The strappy Greek sandals failed to give any support as I struggled to keep up with Amma along the narrow, uneven mud paths that opened up to a single-storey building. "I didn't mean that..." Amma had spotted Nani and raced off to hug my grandmother. Nani's home consisted of three interconnecting bedrooms with one bathroom and a kitchen at the back of the house. It had no electricity or gas, and a tube well provided water.

"Baba, I didn't mean to be rude or big-headed..."

"Not now Maya." Cut off, I fell behind Baba as he greeted Nani. I copied Baba but kept by his side. Nani looked as old as time, with crinkled leathery skin and wide owl- like eyes that saw everything. She nodded in my direction before leading us to her home.

"Baba, please let me come back with you. I won't survive here, I won't know what to do..."

"I've packed your pencils and pastels..,"

"I can't paint out here, I'll die of some illness..."

"You won't." He threw back unphased.

"But I've left my mobile behind. What if I get malaria or get bitten by a snake?"

"Grow up Maya," Baba muttered, before leaving me to join Amma and Nani. I sat on the veranda that overlooked the small clearing, which was dominated by a big black water pump. Chickens clucked around at leisure and ducks led their ducklings away to a nearby pond. People from nearby villages arrived in an endless stream. I greeted each one quietly. These were not rich people, but I didn't know them or didn't want to know them. Opening my bag, I searched for my mobile in the vain hope that I could get Tariq to convince my parents not to leave me behind, but it was getting dark and it was time for them to leave. Amma was already in tears when she looked at me. I wanted to beg them not to leave me behind, but everyone was watching. I refused to cry, or hold onto them in case I couldn't let them walk away. As they left, I waved them off, feeling as if my heart would burst. I was terrified, but I was determined to prove everyone wrong.

"Are you ok?" I found Nani beside me holding my arm and nodded. "Come inside." The big room was filled with the strong bed, cabinet, table and chair that hadn't changed since I'd last visited fifteen years ago. Kerosene lamps were positioned high at the room corners. I followed her and found hoards of people staring at me. I didn't know what to say or who they were. All I knew what that I wanted to run after my parents and beg them to take me back. "Where are my bags?" The question sounded like an order and my petite grandmother pointed to her cabinet. People started to leave, offended by my attitude and silence. Once the room had emptied, I sat on the high, hard bed.

"Are you hungry?" I shook my head, avoiding my Nani's eyes, afraid I would start crying. "I'll check on the kitchen." I waited until she left before wiping at my tears.

"What are we having for dinner?" I walked through the dark corridor and into the adjoining hut. Kalama, Amma's cousin, stoked the fire with dry wood just outside the hut, and Nani placed a bamboo mat on the floor for my comfort.

"Are you hungry?" I shook my head and looked around the big, basic kitchen. There were no mod cons, no dishwasher, no microwave, not even a sink. I took off my slippers and sat down, glad that my chic black trouser suit would hide any dirt I would pick up. "But you haven't eaten."

"I'm fine Nani," I smiled, hoping to convince her but the truth was that I was worried. Plates were washed in bowls filled with water from the water pump. Food was cooked in small amounts, as there was nowhere to store leftovers. And the mat passed for both table and chair.

"Not even a cup of tea?" I shook my head and watched Nani return to pluck and clean a small chicken that had prematurely met its end on my account. I felt my stomach turn when she cut out its innards with the foot bayonet.

"You really didn't have to kill the chicken." Nani laughed as she threw the unwanted bits to a waiting cat.

"And have your mother tell me that I didn't feed you properly!" I really didn't think I could eat anything in this place. All my pampered, hygiene trained sensibilities rioted against this form of rustic, albeit natural, living.

"I don't really eat anything at night time. Its part of my eating habit…"

"So tell us about your life in London," Kalama called out from the makeshift fire.

"There's not much to tell." The truth was that I didn't know where to start since we had no common reference points. And now that I had to re-adjust to basic living, I felt even worse for taking my life and all that went with it for granted.

"You live in wonderful London where you have everything and yet you have nothing to tell?" Kalama's disappointment was obvious and Nani looked at me with a faint smile.

"Why don't you tell us how Tariq and the rest of your brothers and sisters are doing?" Nani prompted, as she stopped cutting the chicken. But my update didn't take that long, and the silence that followed told me I hadn't satisfied their curiosity. Nani finished with the chicken and took to washing the rice, as Kalama crushed fresh spices for the chicken. Feeling redundant, I excused myself and walked through the house to the veranda. The glorious, golden sunset and the stillness of the surrounding overgrowth created a peace that money couldn't buy. I wanted to pull out my pastels, my boards and dusting brush, but I resisted the urge. Sitting down on the wooden bench, I thought about my future. Like the dense forest before me, it scared me. I knew I wouldn't survive in Nani's village just as I knew I wouldn't ever get over Jhanghir. I still carried the hungry ache in my heart and soul for him. Tears blurred my vision as Tanya's words came to my mind. How could he deceive me? How could I still love this man? Jhanghir had robbed me of my beautiful memories and had left me with a cold, predictable future. I knew that I would never trust myself to love again just as I would never venture out into the surrounding forest to discover its hidden, steely beauty.

Over the next two days I waited in vain for my parents to collect me. And whilst I waited, I offended Nani or Kalama in every possible way. I screamed awake when the cock shrilled the world to life and I shrieked whenever a chicken or duck waddled past me. I hesitated over the food I was given and I carefully chose where I sat down in order to protect my clothes. Since I knew nothing about plucking chickens or stoking fires, I hardly lifted a finger. None of this went unnoticed by Nani or Kalama, but I acted out of mod con-dependent ignorance and fear rather than laziness, which is how it appeared.

"Why don't you help me wash?" Nani finally asked, holding out an armload of clothes.

"Are we going to town to use the launderette?" I asked, excited at the chance of returning to my parents.

"We're going to the pond." I didn't want to leave the house in case my parents arrived, so I hesitated. "Give me a hand." Nani didn't wait for me to accept, but walked on ahead with a bucket-load of clothes. Taking the bundle she had left for me, I followed reluctantly and headed down the narrow, uneven path. I tried to keep up with my barefoot Nani, who held aside low lying branches and vines for me, but I slipped and struggled until she led me through the lush green jungle to point to the pond far below.

"We can't get down there," I announced, when I couldn't spot a safe path down.

"Don't be silly, that's where we all bathe. There's a fresh water source from the river..."

"I can't get down there, I'll break my neck..."

"You city people!" She was disgusted and started her descent without me. "You're full of fear. Fearful of the food we cook, the water we give..."

"I'm always fussy, I don't mean to be rude..."

"No, I know you don't." Nani took her time and kept her balance by using the plants and trees as support. "You're fearful that you'll spoil your clothes, dirty your hands and ruin your appearance. And all the while I wonder when you'll stop worrying and start living." I frowned at her words, but stepped forward to keep listening.

"I don't worry, it's just that this is all new to me." I checked a vine for creepy crawlies before holding it for support as I took a few steps down.

"Life is new Maya, but you choose not to deal with it," she shouted back. I couldn't see her through the large plants, so I moved further down. "You should marry." Even my Nani in the middle of nowhere, where civilisation had yet to affect, brought the reality of my world crashing down on me. I could hear the rushing water, and Nani sloshing the clothes against the wet stones. So I struggled down, step by slow step, until I ruined my kitten slippers and my blue trouser suit beyond repair. But I refused to let Nani have the last word.

"I will marry," I stated, spotting her at the base. "Everyone's looking to find me a groom."

"But are you?" Nani stood up to look at me as I stumbled to the bottom. I didn't know this woman very well and yet she spoke as if she was looking into my heart. "We can find you a hundred men, but it's pointless unless you open your heart and know what you want."

"My heart is open." We stood apart, looking at each other and I knew that she knew I had just lied. "I know what I want in my future." Nani took to soaping the soaked clothes before scrubbing them against a rough stone.

"Then what's the problem?" I closed my eyes and saw Jhanghir. I didn't want to think about Jhanghir, or his marriage, or my inability to move on.

"I'm just... I'm heading back." I dropped the clothes I had carried, before scrambling up on my hands and knees. The mud moved beneath my heels and I stumbled down. Gripping vines and plants made no difference, as the faster I tried to climb, the harder I fell.

"What are you running from Maya?" Nani appeared and eased my hands from around several vines. I stared at this kind old woman and felt myself falling back into the pits of my feelings. Lowering my head, I held back the tears and refused the hand she held out. Once again I tried to walk up, but fell on my arse, hitting the ground hard.

"I can't do anything right!" I shouted, holding back my hair with my filthy hands.

"Stop being silly…"

"No it's true. Everything about my life is wrong, I hate my job and I hate being a disappointment. I try to please everyone but I still get everything wrong." I cried, holding my head in utter defeat. Nani put her hand on my head and stroked my hair.

"Have you ever tried to please yourself?" I shook my head as I looked back into my safe, secure and sensible life. I felt ashamed of accepting my middle-class monotony, so I accepted my Nani's help. Slowly we edged to the top of the bank as I sniffed back tears. Once we reached the top, she looked straight at me. "You can only reject life for so long before life rejects you. Embrace life Maya, and life will embrace you." Nani didn't see me back to the house. Instead, she headed straight back down to finish the washing. But her words resonated through my head as I walked back. She was right. I was living in a world of self-pity, heartache, loneliness and frustration. I was tired of dreaming, thinking, planning, and hoping. I wanted everything: risks, experiences, challenges, passion. And I wanted to start now. I raced into my room and jerked open my case. I grabbed a change of clothes, toiletries and a big towel before racing back down the narrow path.

"Nani, I need to bathe," I shouted from the top of the bank.

"Wait! I'll come up to help you..."

"No, I'm fine." The steep path down was impossible, but I tried not to be fazed by it.

"You'll fall Maya, just wait." She was rushing up but I called out for her to stop, and she did. Nani stood near the base looking up with a mixture of fear and hope. "You'll fall, Maya."

"If I fall, I'll just pick myself up and try again." And that's what I planned to do. I was at the lowest point in my life. But the good news was that it could only get better from here on.

N: New Perspectives To Old Endings

Nani had a cure for neurotic women in this image-obsessed, man-hungry world. The cure was simply flab busting, muscle toning hard work that exorcised all self-indulgent, self-pitying demons. Maybe I could start a new business on my return. I would call it something like 'BrokenHeartsRepaired.com' and ship out my fellow SLAAGs for therapeutic hard work that left you too exhausted to remember just how bad singledom really was. For days Nani made me take several trips to the pond to wash saris, shalwaar kameezes, smalls, wiping cloths and every other piece of clothing that was marginally short of being clean. But I didn't complain. There was something soothing in making the lone trips and struggling down the slippery footpath to spend hours beating and sloshing wet clothes against hard, flat, stone surfaces. I had no time to think about straightening my hair, I made no effort to make the most of my appearance and more importantly I had no energy to while away my hours missing Jhanghir. The monotony calmed me, until my body screamed in protest at the exertion and I lay exhausted beside Nani. But it was at dawn, when Nani stirred for morning prayers, that my craving for Jhanghir left me in tears. Was it possible to love and hate one person with such intensity that all you did was want them even more? Without a word I would turn and stare out of the window at the dark forest, in despair.

"It's a good thing to pray, Maya." Nani said, one morning. I wiped away my tears before turning to look at Nani.
"I'm too tired." Nani chuckled and stepped off the high, wooden bed that we shared.
"Your grandfather loved morning prayers. He'd always be the first up." Nani turned to me and through the darkness I met her aged, wise brown eyes. "He would sit on the veranda and swear that every morning he witnessed a new world being brought to life." I smiled as Nani left to perform ablution. Turning around, I reached under the mosquito net and slipped open the wooden shutters. I could see every shade of blue and listened as the cockerel shattered the still serenity. Here was a new dawn and a new world, and I knew what I had to do. Gingerly, I crawled across the expansive bed and pulled my case onto the bed. Opening it, I drew out my canvas bag that held my pastels, stay spray and large drawing pad. I quickly pulled on my polo neck sweater and jeans. Slipping off the bed, I threw Nani's shawl over my shoulders and stepped out into the dark morning. The cold stillness in the middle of a forest at dawn was beautifully crisp.
"I'm just going to the pond," I told Nani, as she stopped washing her arms at the water pump.
"It's dark Maya, you'll fall and hurt yourself…"
"No, I'll be fine…"
"I'll come with you…"

"Nani, I'll find my way." My words stopped her, and she nodded without a smile. I walked on before she could change her mind. The waking insects and twittering birds kept me company as I carefully made my way to the pond. Step by step, I took the path down until I was half-way to the bank. I held my breath at the striking orange pond that reflected the rising sun against the black setting of its bank. Ripping off a banana leaf, I placed it on the floor before sitting down. I had to rush to capture this ethereal beauty before daylight stole the serenity of my haven. Placing my pastels, pencils, charcoals and paraphernalia by my side, I drew out a fresh pastel board. It was a new dawn and for now, that was enough.

"Maya, your Uncle Rahman's here to collect you." Several days later, I paused on the third version of the original sunrise that I had seen. I turned to find Kalama standing at the top of the bank. "You've been drawing all day, aren't you tired?"
"Will you help me take these back to the house?" I yelled up, spraying the fixative over my third pastel picture. I waited for it to dry as Kalama walked down to where I sat.
"These are beautiful!" she cried, staring at each in turn, before looking at the pond. "Maya, when did you learn to draw so well!" Laughing, I packed up my materials before rising.
"I only draw to get out of work!" I quipped, handing Kalama a rolled up picture to hold.
"Then I deserve one for doing all your work today! And I choose to keep this one." I regretted asking Kalama to help me, as she had just asked to keep my favourite sunrise piece. It would be totally selfish to refuse her, but Kalama looked at me as if she expected me do so. I nodded and watched her laugh giddily with shocked surprise. I smiled. It was the right thing to do, and I felt good about doing it.
"We should get back," I smiled, as I led the way up the bank.
"You know you made the next village happy with the cartoon drawings of the children," Kalama told me. "They can't believe you spent all that time drawing only to give them those pictures." I smiled recalling how the young children had giggled with disbelief when I asked them to pose.
"They're just pictures…"
"Some of them have never had their pictures taken Maya, and some may never have their pictures taken." I stopped halfway to look at her.
"Then maybe I'll do more of that whilst I'm here." The thought pleased me and I carried on walking.
"You must be looking forward to going back." Kalama bumped into me, as I stopped at the thought. "Maya, are you ok?" Turning around, I stared down the bank at my haven.
"No."
"No, you're not ok?" Kalama asked, touching my forehead and holding my arm with concern.

"No, I'm not ready to go back," I realised, looking to my aunt, who walked on around me.

"Don't be silly Maya, your mother has another alaap ready and you must return for it." I stared down at my pond, my rocks for washing, my seat for drawing and my peace from Jhanghir and I knew it wasn't time.

"Come on Maya!" Turning at Kalama's call, I smiled and followed her back to the house.

"There you are!" I heard the shout before being enveloped in a bear hug. "We've been worried sick about you!" Extracting myself from the overly-concerned Najma, I searched for Uncle Rahman and found him sitting beside Nani. "Oh, Maya look at your hands!"

"How are you?" I asked my uncle who laughed at my at my bedraggled appearance and threw me a rag to wipe my hands.

"Fine, your parents want you back with them." I took a tin jug out onto the veranda and reached out to wash my hands clean of pastel marks. Leaving the empty jug on the veranda, I dried my hands before walking back inside. "What are you doing roaming around the forest by yourself? Your mother would be sick with worry if she knew about it!"

"Isn't it wonderful that they're not angry with you any more!" Najma interjected looking her best in an ivy green kathan sari and terracotta embroidered kashmiri shawl that I would never have worn together. "But I'd really advise you make a real effort with this alaap."

"Another alaap?" I asked, turning to Uncle Rahman as Nani rose to bring through refreshments.

"Your mother worries about you and that's why she wants you back with her..."

"But there is another alaap?" Uncle Rahman hesitated and I looked to Najma, who grinned with pure satisfaction. "What do you think about this alaap?" I regretted asking my arch-enemy the question, but as soon as I said it, I realised that the answer made no difference to my decision.

"Well, it's come from the eldest son of the wealthy Qudus family in Sylhet, they own a mansion near the stadium..."

"I'd rather stay here," I cut in, moving across the room to sit beside my surprised Uncle Rahman.

"Maya, your parents want you with them..."

"But I want to stay here." Nani walked in with a small tray of tea and stopped at my answer.

"Your place is with your parents," she said, handing a small cup to Najma and Uncle Rahman.

"They will not be happy at all. I think you'd better speak with them directly," Najma muttered, searching in her bag and pulling out my mobile phone. I stared at her bare-faced cheek, then frowned, as she dialled my parents without the slightest acknowledgement of my outrage. "Chachi, your daughter won't come home. No, Maya refuses to see this alaap, she says she wants to stay..."

"Amma, why has Najma got my mobile?" I asked taking the phone before walking out onto the veranda. "Yes, I'm sure you only gave it to her to pass on to me. Listen Amma, I'm not ready to return to Sylhet. I don't want to return to the city."

"But we have an alaap for you and you're all alone out there," Amma returned.

"I don't want to see any more alaaps." I turned at the concert of gasps and caught Nani holding her head in her hands. Amma's silence worried me, so I cleared my throat.

"What do you mean when you say you don't want to see any more alaaps?" Amma asked. Uncle Rahman and Najma watched me closely, but for very different reasons. Najma's excited eyes couldn't wait to catch the smallest of developments, whilst my uncle looked troubled.

"I mean just that," I repeated, turning back to stare out into my forest. "I want to stay with Nani until we're due to fly back to..."

"What about getting married? When are you going to fit that into your schedule?"

"My heart's not open yet Amma..."

"Stop talking nonsense." I smiled at her order but shook my head. "I know this is hard..."

"I'm not seeing any more alaaps." I winced at the silence that followed, but I refused to break.

"Pass the phone to Rahman." There were no goodbyes or 'take cares', just a stern, angry order. Turning around, I walked across to Uncle Rahman and handed him the phone. I couldn't hear a word Amma said, but the grimace on my uncle's face spoke volumes. When he finished the call, he looked at me and shook his head.

"She wants you to know that she's booking the first flight home and that you're to do what you want..."

"She's just saying that!" Nani muttered, sure of her daughter's behaviour.

"No, she's asked Najma and I to return and for me to make flight enquiries at the travel agency on my way back." Uncle Rahman looked at me with a beseeching look and I started shaking my head. "Maya, just come back. At least see the boy and see what he can offer you before you say no. That should appease your mother." But I kept on shaking my head.

"I can't..."

"Just to make your mother happy!" Najma threw in with relish.

"Maya, maybe you should listen to your uncle." Nani suggested. I looked at everyone in the room and felt my stomach turn for all those I was disappointing. But I couldn't disappoint myself anymore. So I shook my head.

"I can't do this anymore. I can't give false hope when I know the answer already."

"Maya, what are you going to do? You need to get married." I smiled at Uncle Rahman's assumption and for the first time realised that maybe marriage wasn't intended for me. I felt a glimmer of hope disappear within me, but I held Uncle Rahman's eyes.

"If it's in my fate, it'll happen." Najma gasped at the implications of my words and Uncle Rahman shook his head with disappointment. "You should be heading back if you need to check those flights for Amma."

"Are you sure this is what you want?" I nodded at Uncle Rahman's question.

"I want to stay with Nani right now. In fact I'd like you extend my ticket by two more weeks. Is that ok?" Everyone looked surprised at the request, but I had never been more serious about discovering myself than at this point in my life.

"Is that what you want, or are you doing this to anger your mother?" Nani asked quietly. I looked at Nani and she knew the answer already. She turned to Uncle Rahman and smiled. "You tell her mother to speak to me if she's worried about Maya's welfare."

I didn't wait for Uncle Rahman and Najma to leave. Instead, I took my canvas bag and headed for the forest. I strolled around the bank a few times to find the best vantage point to watch the sun set and found an overhanging rock that nearly touched the water. There, I laid out my towel and sat down before calling Tanya on my mobile for an update.

"Where have you been?" Tanya screeched once she answered the phone.

"Well I'm missing you too!" I returned, with an ear-to-ear grin.

"Where are you? What have you been doing? Have you found a man yet?" I dropped my grin. "Come on, you've been gone forever! What's the gossip!?"

"I'm doing pastels again…"

"Don't kid around Maya, have you met someone?" I looked across to the pond and wished I had jumped in for a swim instead of calling Tanya. But then there could be snakes and eels and fishes and other unknown scary creatures swimming around waiting for a idiot like me to come along. Whilst not pleasant, it was a safer option to speak with Tanya.

"No Tanya, I haven't and I don't intend to, but I'm doing good pastels again. Stuff that could sell…"

"Maya, you didn't go to Bangladesh to find a new profession, you went to get married!" Tanya yelled back in disbelief.

"I've changed my mind…"

"You've changed your mind? Have you turned into a lesbian all of a sudden?"

"No!" The birds in the trees screeched in protest at my loud shout. "I'm not over Jhanghir, I tried, I really really…"

"Oh Maya, tell me you're not hankering after that disappointment of a man?"

"And you're sure that you've met *the* man for you?" I snapped back.

"Don't do this Maya. Jhanghir's a scumbag, who's even now trying to get back into his fiancé's bed. Why are we even talking about him?" Isn't it funny how the heart holds out for even the tiniest glimmer of hope in the direst of situations?

"Do you think it's possible to make a sound decision when you're on the rebound?"

"I think you need to invest in your future." Tanya stated. "Jhanghir missed his opportunity."

"Answer the question Tanya, you're a counsellor..."

"As your friend, I'm telling you not to waste any more time on him or on pastel drawings. You should be spending time finding yourself a good man." I frowned at the lack of confidence my closest friend had in me.

"Sweetheart, this is a good time for you to move on with your life."

"I am moving on with my life, just not the way you want me to."

"What does that mean?" She was offended, but I wasn't prepared to live by niceties.

"That everyone would be so much more comfortable when I'm off their hands, off the shelf and not left behind..."

"Is that why you think we want to see you married?"

"Yes." My answer made Tanya breathed out in exasperation. "But I don't think you realise that I feel physically ill because I lost this man. Sometimes I feel like I'm going out of my head with questions and feelings and memories. I still crave him to the point where I cry. You know that and yet you advise me to marry some poor stranger who I'll never truly love. As a friend, how on earth can you advice me to move on?"

"Let me remind you that I'm on your side Maya. I'm telling you that you didn't lose Jhanghir, he just didn't choose you." I cancelled the call at that nugget of brutal honesty. I didn't give another thought to Amma, to Uncle Rahman, to Tanya or to anyone who wanted me to live my life for them. I stared across the pond and smiled. I had nothing more to lose, no fear of disappointing, embarrassing or hurting anyone I loved, since I'd managed that all in one day. So, pulling off my sweater and jeans and without another thought, I raced to the edge of the rock and jumped into the deep inviting pond.

That evening, the sunset was breathtaking. I rushed to capture nature's fleeting moment in sharp lines and bold clean colours. And as the sun dipped out of sight, I sat back and looked at my sketch, contented. It was far from perfect, but I found peace in the strong image. Nani brought my dinner out to me and sat with me whilst I ate. We spoke until I convinced her that I wasn't hiding, just thoroughly engrossed in my work. Nani left me a kerosene lamp and I waited until she climbed out of sight before turning back to finish off my pastel. I felt exhausted. I regretted upsetting my mother and arguing with my friend. But still, I yearned for a man I had come to hate. So maybe I wasn't destined to have the perfect arranged marriage that every Asian girl expects.

Maybe I'd turn into one of those glorified bachelorettes who becomes renowned for her heart-broken, empty, but stunning and commercially-successful art. In any case, it didn't seem to matter anymore. I was beginning to care less and less, the more I lost myself in my art. I was exhilarated by my sunset. And soon there'd be a new sunrise, and another opportunity for a new beginning.

O: Observe Age-Old Advice

Now every Asian girl knows that mothers always get their way because the alternative is to live the rest of our lives being reminded of the consequences of not accepting their decision. Ten days after my refusal to join my parents in Sylhet, Amma ordered my return to London on the grounds that I was going marry a doctor she had waiting for me. I started packing as soon as Amma threatened to get 'Maneater Mina' to stand in for me just to secure the alaap. I could see Amma delighting in securing my alaap without me there to mess things up. This alone made me confirm my homebound flight. Only I had the small detail of thanking and leaving behind the very people who had saved me from a life of Prozac-dependent depression.

"Everyone's waiting for you." I turned to find Nani joining me on the rock in my haven.

"I feel like taking one last dive." I laughed. Nani placed an arm around my back and I held her close as we stared ahead into the pond. "Come on, you and me. One last swim..."

"Pagul!" Nani laughed as she patted my back. "You're strong enough to face your future."

"I don't want to go back." Nani chuckled at my reluctant admission. "I don't want to face the alaaps, my job, my married friends, my empty life..."

"Then fill it." I looked at my petite, beautiful Nani and smiled. She made it all sound so simple. And then her owl-brown eyes welled up and I drew my Nani into a hug. We stood there crying, I needed her support more than anything to face a life I had come to hate and needed to change. Slowly, we drew apart and made our way up the bank.

"I want you to have this," I said, taking off the slim gold bracelet that Tariq had given me on my graduation. We stood on top of the bank and I took Nani's small delicate hands to clip the bracelet onto her wrist, and then I handed her an envelope filled with taka notes. Now, whilst it was expected of Londoni's to bestow personal and financial gifts to all or as many family relatives rich and poor on departure, I was doing this because she had given me renewed faith in my future. But Nani shook her head, so I paused and looked at her.

"Maya, you must get married, so be stubborn about who you choose to marry. In your world you must work, so be fulfilled by your trade, and you must love your parents, so be generous with your trust." I accepted her advice and pressed the envelope into her hands.

"Please," I whispered to stop her refusing. And then we returned to the house where half the Island's residents waited to see me, the crazy artist, leave. I felt humbled by everyone's kindness and shamed by my initial selfish self-indulgence.

"Give our salaams to your parents."

"Pray for us and don't forget the needy back here."

"Crazy painter, send us back some photos of your pictures."

"Listen to your mother, she loves you and knows the best for you."
"When you come back, bring back a tin of baked beans." When it came to Bengali departures, there was no end to advice or requests. I passed each smiling radiant face, and to those I knew, I bade my farewells and handed out small gifts. Uncle Rahman walked ahead with my bags. He had two children from a nearby village carry my carefully-wrapped boards and drawings through the forest and into the clearing, whilst our island neighbours escorted Nani, Kalama and me to the dock.

"So you've packed all the tailored outfits for your sisters?" Kalama asked. "You got all the shalwaar kameezes that you asked for? And the presents for the boys?" She was filling time. I nodded, unable to speak at the thought of leaving my new home-away-from-home. And then the crying began as the riverboat drew nearer. First it was the sniffing. Then it was the hugging and crying. Then open weeping as we said our farewells. Thankfully, Nani was wise enough to cry less in order to help me down the steep stairs. I hugged her fiercely before stopping into the boat and then I turned away to embrace my future. I had no idea how or what my family or fate had lined up for me, but I was confident enough to face it.

We landed in Dubai for a three-hour stopover and I browsed through Duty Free eager to be reunited with my brothers and sisters. I picked up Chanel No 5 for Ayesha, Dune and Clinique for the twins and Coco for Shireen. Hovering by the Armani section, I debated whether I needed another bottle of Aqua Di Gio and it was then that I saw him. The fine looking Bengali I had noticed in Sylhet's departure lounge. He had cropped hair, roughly dragged back, thick lashed eyes and a broad jaw.

"Can I help you with those?" I tore my gaze away and looked at the perfectly groomed assistant who'd caught me drooling. I realised what I was doing. I was becoming the old Maya, intent on making everyone happy and acting like a teenager. Looking down at the perfume packages I clutched, I shook my head.

"No."

"No, you don't need any help madam?" The assistant asked with haughty indignation. I looked at the assistant and handed the perfumes packages to her.

"No, I don't want them." And with that I walked out of the Duty Free zone. I felt cleansed in a way I hadn't expected. Change was possible and I felt that I could do it. I smiled as I mingled with the gold buyers without buying a single ring, necklace or bracelet. And then I headed off to the Newsagents. I flicked through several glossy magazines before seeking out the latest copy of *Asian Woman*. Finding it on the top shelf, I stepped on the bottom rung to reach up for it.

"I'll get that for you." I jumped at the smooth voice behind me and stumbled backwards. It was the fine looking man from Duty Free.

"Thank you." It's Sod's Law right? The moment you decide against a decision, that decision turns up to tempt you.

"You're welcome." He had a strong American accent and an easy grin. "You heading out for London?" I took the magazine from him and nodded. "I envy you, I've got the four hour wait before my long-haul trip on to New York." I could come to like this man but, beyond suspecting that he was a little young for me, I didn't want to. "You're an artist?" He pointed to the large bag of drawing paraphernalia I was carrying.

"An amateur more like it," I told him.

"You get a lot done in Sylhet?" I paid for the magazine and we headed towards an open seating area. "Is that why you visited?"

"I went to Bangladesh to get married." I said. He checked for a ring and I laughed.

"Now there's a surprise! So did I." He was flirting. We both knew it.

"I'd be on the rebound," I warned him. His smiled faltered.

"So would I." My smile faltered at his admission. I looked at him to see whether he was joking, but he wasn't. I caught the flicker of loneliness in his eyes before he looked away. We both sat down and stared ahead. Then he got up, as if he was unsure of what to do or say. "I'm grabbing a coffee, would you like one?" I shook my head and smiled, understanding his need to escape. I watched him walk away with his backpack and felt bad for bringing up feelings he'd rather forget. I drew out my sketch pad, and did a quick caricature of him walking away head bowed. Once I finished that, I watched the travellers scuttling around like busy ants, all rushing to get somewhere, board some flight and head out. Grinning, I drew as many characters of travellers, information providers, and security guards as I could. Several announcements were made on the overhead Tannoy and every so often I checked on my flight details on the large board.

"They're pretty good." The American was back and as he looked at my drawing he held out a bottle of juice to me.

"Thanks." I took the bottle and he sat down. "I'm sorry about before..."

"Don't apologise. It's just bizarre to meet someone in the same position as yourself on your travels." He said as I took a long gulp of the fresh juice. "It's tough, isn't it?" And without explanation I knew what he meant.

"When you've loved and lost 'the one' and you find yourself trying to accept a replacement," I elaborated.

"Only the replacement gets a bum deal, because they'll never be 'the one' and you feel like you're cheating them from day one."

"It is very difficult," I agreed. I closed my sketch book and turned to face him. "What happened to you?"

"I own a couple of restaurants in New Jersey, nothing fancy. Zina and I dated for over two years and when I wanted to settle down, I soon found out that I wasn't good enough for her. It didn't help that she's Dhakayan, she said her family wanted her to marry a professional, not someone who worked in a restaurant." I grimaced. She sounded judgemental. She sounded nasty. She reminded me of me. I avoided his eyes and looked across at the flight information board. He asked. "And you?"

"We fell in love, even though he was promised to his father's business partner's daughter. She cheated on him and he asked me to marry to him. I refused him, thinking he was on the rebound and I guess he was, because he went straight back to her. Since then, I've begged him to reconsider me. He refused. He even booked a honeymoon to the Maldives, the same honeymoon he had once promised me." He winced at the round up and looked at me in disbelief. I nodded to assure him I spoke the truth. "Oh, and he's from Dhaka."

"That's painful." He opened a bag of crisps and we started on the crisps as we leaned back into our chairs. "There's no consolation, is there?" He added. I shook my head and chomped on.

"You're left feeling like you're not good enough, that you fall short..."

"...and the worst thing is you feel like you'll never be good enough."

"That's the ironic thing right? They get to move on and we're left here, confiding to strangers how we didn't do enough, when in reality it's they who failed to love us and be true to their words..."

"But we have no get-out clause. I've been in this position for over a year. I can still see her, smell her and feel her." I heard his disappointment and shook my head in disgust.

"He told me that 'I'm always with him'." He snorted with derision.

"'Always' meant until the little fiancée came running back, right?" I nodded and chuckled at his comment.

"Do you see her?" He shook his head at my question. We finished the crisps and he opened a big bag of Kettle sea salt and balsamic vinegar chips. "Does that help?"

"I don't know. Sometimes I crave her, do you know what I mean?"

"I know exactly what you mean!" I answered, with a wide smile. "Like you're going out of your head with the need to see them..."

"...and you can't focus or concentrate..."

"...and you can't eat or sleep..."

"...and you try to do things to stay busy so you..."

"...don't think about them all the time, but no matter what you do they're still there..."

"...and you wonder what they would do if they were with you, if they'd like the meal you were having, the company you kept..."

"...and you'd do anything, just about anything, to see them again." He paused at my words. "And you pray that if they saw you once they'd realise just what they had given up." Our excited exchange ended with the futility of our dreams and I looked at him.

"I saw him. It didn't change anything," I confessed. He smiled and offered me more chips. I obliged and we sat back to stare at the flight information board.

"Do you think we'll ever get over them?" I shrugged at his question. I had no answers.

"Do you ever wonder how we came to fall so deeply and pathetically in love with people who don't love us back?"

"You mean as in, if we knew they'd choose not to be with us, would we have fallen for them in the first place?" He clarified. "They say it's better to have loved, than to not have loved at all." I laughed at his words, but felt empty to the core of my being.

"I'd have stayed well clear of Jhanghir," I stated without hesitation and he looked at me, surprised. "The guy who came up with that line, that one that you've just quoted, he loved but he didn't lose."

"Because the pain of losing your love is that unbearable," he finished with a sad smile. "What are you going to do?"

"My mother's ordered me back home because she has a doctor lined up for me." He chuckled and I rolled my eyes.

"You ready to face that again?" I shook my head. It felt like I'd known him forever.

"Do I have a choice? What would I be waiting for?" I asked. He had no answers either. "What are either of us waiting for?" And with that, we sat in silence, lost in our own uncertainties and undetermined futures. A while later I heard the call for BG005 and we watched an exodus of Bengalis racing to be the first to get to the departure gate. "I have to go."

"I'll walk you to the gate…" But I shook my head and pulled out my sketch book. I turned back a page and showed him the caricature I had drawn of him walking away. "You gotta be kidding me!" He laughed. I ripped off a corner of the page and scribbled down my email address.

"For when you're feeling particularly low or lonely." He tucked the note into the back of his passport. Then taking the pen from me, he wrote his name, number and email address beside his caricature.

"For when you're going out of your mind and need to be distracted." I read his name and nodded before putting my book away.

"Thank you Monsur." He stuffed the half eaten bag of Kettles in my bag as I stood up to leave. "You're more than good enough."

"So are you Maya." I looked at this lean, friendly man. We could talk forever and we both wanted to, but this wasn't the time.

"Maya!" I turned back to look at Monsur. "Would you give him another chance?" I shrugged. It opened up the door to hope, but I had sealed, locked and double bolted that door shut to avoid any further pain. He said. "I hear you."

As I waved and walked away, I knew I had found a kindred spirit in that short time at Dubai airport. I joined the exodus of British Bengalis and queued for a ticket and passport check before waiting in the lounge. I took out my sketchbooks and smiled at Monsur's caricature as Biman started calling up passengers in seat order for boarding.

"That's a lovely drawing. Maybe it'd help if you drew him from the front," commented the old auntie with thick glasses, as she leaned in close to look at my drawing. "Did you marry him in Sylhet?" Normally I'd snap my book shut and put the auntie right, but I just smiled at her. It seemed to make her day, because she looked down at the drawing and chuckled mischievously.

"Our seat number! They've called our seat numbers!" I almost jumped at her husband's bark.

"Slow down! The plane won't leave without you!" she shouted back. The old auntie patted my cheek and smiled before turning back to her duties. I watched as she helped her ancient husband out of his seat. He in turn helped her up and together they rushed towards the queue. I'd bet everything that they'd never met before they got married. And decades later they were still there for each other. Being candid with Monsur didn't stop me from loving and hating Jhanghir in equal measures, but he did make me feel that it was ok to feel the way I did. Jhanghir had hurt me enough to make me give up on wanting the 'one', but I was now content to find someone. Someone who, like the old auntie and her ancient husband, wanted to build their future with me.

P: Prepare For Perfect Pathros And Pride

The wonderful thing about being Bengali was that a lift from the airport was never needed. You actually felt like a star when you walked through arrivals at Heathrow's Terminal 3. All your family would be waiting at arrivals to drag you back into the bosom of the family home and a warm ready meal. And when you push your luggage trolley into some six foot, tall, irate, white man who has to make it through the melee of hugging families, happy couples and excited united friends simply because there's no one to receive him, you realise the wonder that is called family.

"MAYA!" The coordinated shout wouldn't have gone amiss at a football stadium. Spotting all eleven members of my family, I abandoned my trolley to race into their open arms.

But once you get home, the realisation of returning to real life hits you. I walked into the living room with a mug of coffee. Everything seemed different. The rooms were smaller, the streets were quieter, and the concrete roads were barren of the lush trees into which I used to escape. In short, I missed Nani and her home. And then my family followed me in. No one referred to my disastrous alaaps in Bangladesh and for now that sat well with me.

"Did you get us suits like the one you're wearing?" the twins began.

"How's everyone? Did you leave them without complaint?" asked Amma.

"You're looking radiant, you do know that?" Shireen-bhabhi pointed out.

"Did you enjoy yourself?" Ayesha explored.

"How are the honeys back home in Sylhet?" probed Taj.

I answered each question in turn.

"Do you got a husband yet, foopi?" We all stopped at the question that everyone had tried to avoid. I looked at Hamza and drew my five-year-old nephew onto my lap. Amma cleared her throat tearfully, but I winked at her before pointing to my luggage sitting in the centre of the room.

"He's packed inside my case because they wouldn't let him in..."

"But he wouldn't fit in your bags with all my presents!" He looked confused and then giggled infectiously. "You're joking me foopi! You're joking me!" I laughed along with my nephew before hugging him tightly.

"Pressie time!" Jana chimed, clapping her hands with unabated excitement. "As long as I've got a few well cut shalwaar kameezes, I'm happy." I moved across to the first of my cases and opened it up as Hamza took his place beside me.

"You shouldn't have bought anything Maya, especially after your father and I brought back..." Amma stopped talking as I handed her the rusty gold balagonj sari.

"I'm going to borrow that Amma!" Jana called out, as Amma laughed with delight. She opened up the sari, threw it across her shoulder and stroked the soft garment.

"And Nani gave you this." I pulled out sealed jars of pure organic ghee and tamarind chutney. "She gave more, but I had to leave it behind, because..."

"Ok, ok! What about us!" Zarah shouted as she sat down beside Hamza.

"Get the kids out of the way!" Hana cried out, pulling Zarah onto her lap.

So I handed out the gifts. Punjabi suits with mujib jackets for all the men and Hamza, who beamed with macho satisfaction. Custom-made shalwaar kameezes for my sisters and niece. All oohed and aahed over their outfits, until the sari I had bought for my sister-in-law distracted their attentions. I looked to Tariq who was trying to swap his Punjabi suit with Jana's husband.

"I got you another present bhai." Everyone stopped at my comment. Tariq looked confused as I cleared out some of my clothes and pulled out my carefully wrapped canvas. "It's not that good, it's just a scene..." I stopped talking as Tariq ripped off the wrapping. He stared at the three-by-two pastel painting of my water-reflected golden sunset. "Anyway, that's it! There's lots of stuff for the house and..."

"It's beautiful," Tariq whispered, looking straight at me. It was the first time I'd seen tears in my brother's eyes since Hamza's birth.

"That's wonderful," added Amma, who used her sari to wipe the tears from her eyes.

"Maya, you did this?" I nodded at Samir-bhai, realising that they did in fact like it. "Do you have any more?" All the presents were forgotten, as everyone clambered to look at my amateur pastels of the magical sceneries I'd seen.

"Thank you," I mouthed to Tariq, who winked in understanding before bragging about his present. That's the fickle thing about modern-day presents. We slave away to buy tokens of mass-produced, perfectly-packaged, over-hyped trinkets and toys, but we forget that the person who gives it to us loves us enough to make us happy in the most unexpected way. Tariq and I didn't have the academic talents the others were born with, but we had other talents. Whilst few knew what Tariq's dreams were, he was helping me realise mine. As everyone chatted without a care amidst the torn wrapping paper, scattered clothes and opened cases, I felt my heart fill up. It was good to be home.

"It's good to have you back. We thought we'd lost you for a while." I grinned at Tanya's words. They were as emotional as she would allow herself to be.

"It's the best thing I could've done Tanya, and to top it off I've lost six pounds and I've got a radiant tan. Now that alone is worth the air fare out there!" I pinned the phone between my chin and shoulder, whilst reaching out for the mug of coffee Shireen-bhabhi had made for me. "How's Javed?"

"Well, he's finally got me to commit so he's over the moon!" I shook my head and stared at the open cases and presents abandoned on the living-room floor, as everyone sat in the dining room talking. "I'm sorry you weren't here for the engagement Maya, I missed you."

"I'm sorry too Tanya, but I've got some cute gifts to make up for it." And I was genuinely sorry that I had missed Tanya's engagement. "How's Sakina doing?" It would take time to convince everyone that I was content, but I would not return to wallowing despite the fact that we were well into the shaadhi season.

"She's still seeing Shaj and they're serious about each other. I don't think she was even this happy with Raj." Tanya pointed out.

"Good, I'm glad she's moved on." I knew Tanya worried for me. "She deserves to be happy after the ordeal she went through…"

"And what about you Maya, have you moved on past Jhanghir?"

"Yes." I answered without the slightest hesitation.

"No second thoughts, doubts, or niggling need to know questions in the back of your mind?" Tanya persisted.

"For what good? He duped, deceived and dumped me. Why would I have second thoughts?" Tanya hesitated and I frowned. "Why do you ask?"

"No reason, I just needed to know that you've moved on." Tanya was being uncharacteristically reserved. "But you sound definite, so that's a good sign that you've moved on…"

"Tanya, what have you heard?" I added.

"Nothing Maya!" The nervous laugh was a sure give away. "As long as you're definite about your decision regarding Jhanghir, then you can handle any of life's surprises."

But nothing prepared me for the shock that my family lined up for me. In preparation for the alaap, I quickly applied barely-there make up and pulled my hair back into a loose French pony, which complimented my simple baby-pink trouser suit. Ayesha and Shireen-bhabhi led me into the living room, but the brain surgeon in training and his heart attack survivor of a father were nowhere in sight. Instead, I found Jhanghir, looking every bit the rugged, handsome man that I knew. Everything ground to a stop and I stared at Jhanghir. I looked to a smiling Ayesha and blinked away my tears.

"Maya, aren't you going to salaam Jhanghir's mother?" I turned to Amma who was beaming with delight and then looked at his immaculately presented mother. Elitism emanated from her every pore. Whilst I took pride in our tastefully furnished cream room, she seemed out of place in our modest living room.

"Asalaamalaikum." Her expression told me that she wasn't here of her own free will. But she had little idea of how I had longed for this, and even less of an inkling about what I knew.

161

"Hello Maya." Jhanghir spoke before his mother could respond and I looked at him again. I stilled my racing heart and traced his every feature. He had had his hair cut into a close crop, which served to emphasise his strong eyes. "You're looking well."

"Thank you Jhanghir..." I grimaced at bhabhi, who pinched me for sounding overly familiar. Ayesha stepped forward and I followed her to the seat that had been kept for me. Baba sat beside Amma and Ayesha sat beside his mother. Tariq sat on a seat next to Jhanghir and I faced them all.

"So, how's Preeya?" My question had the same effect as a thousand pound lead weight falling onto a slim sheet of glass.

"She's just come back from Bangladesh, jet lagged but looking great! It makes you say unexpected things..." Amma trailed off, shooting Baba a concerned look. Then she looked at me with a forced smiled and pleading eyes. "Jhanghir and his mother have flown in for the weekend Maya. He flew in the day we left for Bangladesh." I doubted that Amma knew about Jhanghir's scandal and my anger heightened at his willingness to deceive her. I looked to Jhanghir and waited for him to answer my question.

"Preeya is back to full health and back at work..."

"Ignore Maya's question," Baba cut in with a nervous laugh before glaring at me.

"It's lovely to have you here, would you like some tea?" asked Shireen-bhabhi through the polite cover-ups. I stared at Jhanghir. I had never felt such anger as I did at that moment but he didn't waver from my look.

"What are you doing here Jhanghir?" I demanded. Amma started the Mexican wave of gasps in the room.

"Maya, apologise," Baba commanded pointing towards Jhanghir's affronted mother. But I remained silent. "Maya, I want you to apologise!"

"Uncle, she has cause to be angry..."

"Regardless Jhanghir, I will not have my guests offended with or without due cause..."

"I asked him to choose me three months ago, but he didn't even have the decency to acknowledge me." I only meant to whisper the truth but everyone stopped at my words. "Now he's here after a broken engagement to a ruined woman, a woman he advised to have an..."

"Jhanghir, we should leave." I looked at Mrs Khan and shook my head. She looked disappointed as she collected her bag and waited for him to lead her out. "Jhanghir, you don't need to hear this..."

"I see where you get the ability to disregard people Jhanghir..."

"Please stop!" Amma cried into her hands, as Baba stormed out of the room.

"Let me speak with Maya alone," Jhanghir asked Tariq, who looked at me. Only after I nodded did he leave the room. Shireen-bhabhi cajoled my sobbing Amma out. And when Ayesha led Mrs Khan out and closed the door behind her, I was left alone with Jhanghir.

"Why are you here Jhanghir?"

"I thought that was fairly obvious." I raised a questioning brow. "I'm here for your hand..."

"And what about the ruined woman you left behind?" I asked.

"Maya, you know better than to listen to gossip," Jhanghir warned, leaning forward.

"So, is it true?" I met his eyes. I could see that he was agitated.

"Is what true?" He returned. I noticed his gritted jaw and clenched hands.

"That Preeya wasn't the only woman in your life?" I wanted to forgive him, but I couldn't.

"Who told you the details Maya?"

"Was there someone else besides Preeya?" He stared at me.

"I'm not proud of never being straight with Preeya..."

"Did you advise Preeya to have an..."

"If the circumstances had been true, I probably would have..."

"So that didn't happen?" I demanded.

"No..."

"All of it, your affairs, the sleeping around, the pregnancy, it's all lies?"

"No..."

"Make your mind up Jhanghir, is it true or isn't it?" He refused to answer and in doing so, put an end to the terse exchange.

"You're not the man I fell in love with..."

"If you think I'm capable of doing all the things the Bengali grapevine pins on me..." He paused as I shook my head. Tears blurred my vision. I didn't know what to think or who to believe anymore. "What do you want me to take responsibility for? What do you want to know?" Jhanghir demanded angrily.

"I want to know what happened!"

"You want me to tell you that there was someone else besides Preeya?" He threw back.

"Is it true?" I whispered, staring across at him.

"Yes." I frowned, looking down at my hands. I didn't understand why he would do that. "And you know..."

"And Preeya?"

"Hear me out Maya..."

"Is it true about Preeya?"

"Give me a chance to explain..."

"I've given you eight years!" I shouted at Jhanghir. And suddenly I didn't have any energy left in me. "I've given you too much facility already. I can't give you anymore." He was stunned by my quiet admission. He gritted his jaw, shook his head and then stared at me.

"I set a date with Preeya after you told me about Shah." Jhanghir's admission shocked me.

"That was your decision..."

"I set the date after you confirmed you were getting married..."

"This is not my fault, you chose Preeya..." I stopped as tears fell onto my cheeks. "Is it true about Preeya cheating on you?"

"She started seeing Mohibur again." And with that, I chuckled. Four years on and he was back to playing rebound.

"Did she get pregnant?" I frowned at the thumping ache in my head, but I needed to know.

"Yes, but she came to me for advice..."

"That's enough." I couldn't look at him, I didn't want to even be the same room or house as him. "I've heard enough."

"That's the problem Maya, you haven't heard enough." I shook my head at his arrogance.

"You're in my house..."

"What does that tell you?" He pointed out, brow creased with frustration.

"...telling me I've not heard enough..."

"I'm in your house Maya, ask yourself why I'm here?"

"...when I have the truth from you..."

"You have partial facts that fit the gossipmongers' story." His audacity left me stunned. "Why am I here Maya?" He repeated.

"Because you probably think I'm desperate enough to take you back..."

"You really believe I would drag my mother through this..."

"I don't know!" He stopped at my outburst. "I don't know you anymore."

"You're too quick to judge Maya. It's not an attractive quality." He sounded tired, almost exhausted. I looked up to find him holding his head.

"I don't think you're in any position to tell me how to behave." Jhanghir looked across at me. "You ruined your family's name, and your cousin's dishonoured the family. I may be Sylhethi but I have my honour, my family is still well respected..."

"You being Sylhethi has never been the issue. My mother's here because..."

"Why wasn't she here before?" Jhanghir rubbed his eyes and shook his head at my question. "Because she thought you were too good for me. So what's changed? Does she think you've lowered yourself enough to make Sylhethi girls look like an attractive option..."

"You have too much pride Maya..."

"Tell me why your father isn't here? Or even your oldest brother? Where are they?"

"And your pride is blinding you to the obvious..."

"Where are my father's or my brother's counterparts?" We were having two separate conversations. He stopped and looked at me.

"Don't make the mistake of thinking we're from equal backgrounds Maya." He was absolutely serious. "I bring status and wealth that you don't have."

"There are several dozen pimps and drug-pushers on the Mile End road who are wealthier than us, but I'm not rushing to marry them Jhanghir."

"As there are many over-aged, single, pretty little women that nobody wants, but I'm not running after them." He returned.

"There's still time to find yourself an 'over-aged pretty little thing', Jhanghir."

"As there is for you to realise that even under the worst possible conditions, marrying into my family would still give you more respect and status than you could imagine." His arrogance left me at a loss for words.

"You've given me enough 'special respect and importance' to tell you that my answer is no." I said with finality. He watched me with steely silence, and then he shook his head and chuckled.

"Save your breath Maya, I've changed my mind." He always had to have the last word. I smiled and looked away as Jhanghir stood up to leave the room.

"You should've told her." I heard Ayesha's quiet advice to Jhanghir, and frowned at the hushed murmurs that followed. I couldn't be wrong. Pride comforts. It makes you feel right and leaves you empowered. It was a hard thing to be a SLAAG, but it was harder to pass up on a perfect pathro. He had hurt me once, and now he had abandoned someone in a far worse situation than me. He left me with no choice but to reject him.

Q: Fulfil Your Quarrels And Quitting Quotient

The quarrels started as soon as Jhanghir left with his mother. Baba started on Tariq, while Amma sobbed her heart out in the kitchen. Then Shireen-bhabhi shouted at Tariq for not stopping me from speaking. He in turn argued with Ayesha for failing to prepare me well enough for the alaap. All the while I sat alone in our living room listening to it all. Everyone had gone to a lot of trouble for me and I felt like the unwanted burden that Jhanghir had mentioned. Taking a deep breath, I held my head in my hands and waited for the anger to turn on me. I thought I'd never see him again and yet he looked so good. I rubbed my eyes as if to erase his memory. Using Nani's advice, I committed Jhanghir firmly to my past.

"It's no good crying now." I looked up to find my tearful, angry mother standing in front of me.

"I'm not crying..."

"Don't speak to me!" I was startled at the force of her anger. "I don't want you to speak to me..."

"Amma, please..."

"Don't you interfere!" she screamed at Ayesha, who had followed in behind her. Ayesha stood silenced. "She brings this on all our foreheads! With her Western ways, her uncontrolled behaviour! What was wrong with that boy?"

"You've never liked Jhanghir..."

"Because he didn't ever ask for your hand! And here he is asking and you throw him out?" Amma explained.

"He doesn't want me. He's here because he can't get anyone else..."

"So what?" Amma demanded, leaning forward to point at me. "You can't get anyone else either so what makes you so different? What gives you the right to judge him?"

"Because he still thinks we're not good enough for him!" Amma laughed at my logic.

"You stupid girl." Her laughter turned to tears that she wiped away with the sari I had brought her. "He thought all that, and he still wanted you." I refused to cry. My pride prevented me from accepting her words. I had sworn to never shed another tear for that man and I wouldn't.

"He's running from ill-repute..."

"And so are you. Don't you hear what people say about you?" Amma reminded.

"Please don't do this..."

"You need to hear it..."

"Amma, let Maya be," Tariq pleaded, stepping into the room with a mug of coffee. "Ayesha, I want you to go home and tell the twins to come round tomorrow..."

"I don't want anymore part in this..."

"Amma, we'll talk about this tomorrow..."

"What's there to talk about? She can ruin her life but I'm not going to watch her do it."

"Could we try and not be so melodramatic…"

"Shut up Maya!" Tariq shouted, as Amma stormed out of the room. He raced after her with Ayesha. And then the quarrelling started up again. Only this time, Amma turned on Tariq for standing by me, Tariq shouted at Ayesha for not calming Amma down and Baba yelled at everyone for every wrong in his life. I picked up Tariq's mug of coffee, sat back in the chair and listened to everyone's opinion about my disastrous life.

I left for work extra early the following morning so that I could avoid everyone in the house. But I regretted it the moment I logged into my inbox. There I faced the impact of Bitch Brenda's decision to reallocate my client accounts in my absence. It took three client meetings, four mugs of coffee and three wafer thin biscuits before I had the chance to catch up with Brenda in her office.

"It's good to have you back Maya." Brenda, as always had her hair pulled back and was dressed in her uniform black, single-breasted Onassis jacket and micro skirt. "I was beginning to wonder if you'd ever come back!"

"No need to wonder anymore!" Brenda kept her fixed white smile in place, but there wasn't any humour in my response. "What's happened to my accounts?"

"We rearranged the client base in your absence…"

"Why has my account value declined by thirty-five per cent, and everyone else's increased by fifteen per cent?" 'Cruella's' smile finally dropped and she speared me with her ice-blue eyes.

"The premise of the revised split was based on the future report schedule…"

"Report schedules change on a monthly basis and we both know that's not how accounts are divided." I was unhappy with her excuse.

"Are you questioning my motives Maya?" My colleagues quietened down waiting for my response. At this point, everyone usually backed down. She waited for me to do the same, but I looked at Brenda and raised a brow.

"Yes." I felt empowered by my disintegrating life.

"That's a bad move Maya…"

"Brenda, HR approved my leave, I ran two handover sessions with Clare and Mark before I left, and I return to find that you've taken my biggest accounts to give to Mark. What move would you like me to make?" My calm disposition rattled Brenda.

"I will not allow our major clients to be served on an ad hoc basis…"

"How do you propose that will improve when Mark's still a researcher? Everyone knows he's struggling to make Consultant grade, his reports aren't comprehensive and he requires more training. Can you justify why his accounts have risen in value by twenty-five per cent?" Brenda actually looked stunned by my outburst. She searched for an answer, shifted uncomfortably, then pinned me with a hard stare.

"You know that I do not discuss personnel issues of one staff with another, but since you ask a legitimate question, you should be aware that Mark's renewal rate is higher than yours..."

"With non-strategic clients that make up ten per cent of our client base ..."

"You were out of the office and I made the call and I stick by it." Brenda stated.

"That's a bad decision..."

"I will not be questioned Maya!" The Bitch slammed down her fist as if to mark the end of our conversation. And in that moment, I realised that not only did I not like my job, but I didn't actually care about it. I smiled at Brenda and knew what I had to do.

"And you expect me to complete my work-load on my previous accounts before I hand over to Mark, whilst accepting the incomplete workloads he hands over to me from his previous account?" Brenda was caught out by the discrepancy.

"As I understand, Mark's handover requires some administrative work..."

"Actually, there are two short reports and three analytical pieces to complete..."

"That'll help you familiarise yourself with your new accounts..."

"I'm not doing Mark's unfinished assignments." Brenda stopped at my directness.

"Are you refusing to take responsibility for your accounts Maya?"

"I'm refusing to accept the double-standards you're imposing in the office." She laughed at my attitude and I waited for her to finish. "If you don't rectify this situation, I'm taking this to Personnel."

"You have no grounds!" Brenda screamed, slamming her palm on her desk.

"Then you have nothing to worry about." I didn't wait for her finish but got up to leave.

"We haven't finished Maya. I will not have you..." I left the door open behind me and the entire office stared in wonder as Brenda's outraged demands continued. Only this time, I wasn't embarrassed by the attention. I felt liberated from Brenda's intimidation and I was proud of my courage. I walked over to my desk and listed down the contents of our conversation. I had nothing to lose, so I picked up the phone and quarrelled with Personnel.

Clare appeared with a mug of coffee and several bars of chocolate after I replaced the phone. I looked around the office floor and found Mark in Brenda's office, no doubt updating her on the details of my argument with Personnel.

"Welcome back Stranger, it is good to have you back." I accepted the coffee mug as Clare perched on my desk.

"Why didn't you protect my client base?" She looked shocked and folded her arms.

"Maya, you tell me you're going to get married back in Bangladesh, and then you extend your leave out there. How do I protect your base when I don't even know if you're planning to come back?"

"I have covered your back countless times Clare…"

"And I had yours covered until Brenda started giving my accounts to Mark…"

"So how do you end up with some of my core clients?" Clare looked at me and shook her head. "I don't get it Clare, why did everyone come out of it with a better deal than I did?"

"She was looking to make you redundant, Maya." The admission was reluctant and hesitant, but Clare refused to be maligned. "Brenda wanted to split your client base to make a case for your redundancy. A couple of girls and I told her we couldn't handle the work-load, and that's why you were given the dud clients." She had gone out of her way to help me, even made herself appear unable to manage her responsibilities.

"It was the only way you could force her to keep me on," I finished. Clare nodded and I felt my anger dissipate.

"I wanted to tell you over lunch, but you get the gist, right?" Clare didn't wait for an answer, but headed back to her desk. I held my head in my hands. Things were going from bad to worse, and I had no choice but to ride it out.

"How's everything at home?" Sakina asked as we met up at Café Nero after work.

"I haven't seen Baba for two days, Amma refuses to talk to me and the twins ring up to give me ear ache all the time." Tanya brought the coffees over to our regular couch and handed them out. She also bought a generous slice of Devil cake.

"I can't believe he just turned up after everything he did!" she muttered, splitting the slice into three pieces. "How did he look?"

"As good as the cake I'm about to eat!" And that was the truth, Jhanghir simply stole my breath away. "He looked scrummy, but I'm done being the mug, I'm done mourning over lost loves and…"

"And he told you the story straight, right?" Tanya's hesitant question caught my attention. "With all the details?" she added.

"Yes!" I stated and looked down at the cake. "With the facts…"

"It's just that I've heard conflicting stories…"

"Isn't that a surprise?" I laughed, catching sight of the sparkling diamond ring on her engagement finger. "They probably held a community dinner party and slandered poor Preeya's name…"

"No, but that's not the case…"

"Does it matter Tanya?" Sakina cut in as she nervously gave me her slice of Devil cake.

"They say she's still pregnant…"

"I don't want to know." I couldn't explain the aching loneliness caused by righteous pride or the nagging doubt over my actions, but I couldn't open myself to him again. "I heard his side of the story from him and the matter's closed. So tell me, how are the wedding plans?" I listened as Sakina and Tanya competed to explain their weddings to me. I nodded and smiled and aahed in all the right places. I agreed to the roles we would all take in the services, the outfits we'd be fitted for, the style of the weddings and the catering. And then I realised I had finished the entire portion of the Devil cake.

"My shout," I muttered taking my purse across to the counter. Taking the replacement slice back to the lounge area, I sat down to stony silence.

"What's wrong?" Sakina shook her head to prevent Tanya from answering my question. But nothing stopped Tanya from speaking her mind.

"Would you take him back?" Tanya asked.

"I said no to him..."

"But you look so sad Maya." Sakina asked. I felt the sting of tears, but shook my head. "Maybe you should talk with him alone..."

"He wronged me and he wronged his fiancé of eight years. How do I know who he is?" I reminded my friends.

"Do you want to give him another chance?" Tanya persisted.

"Let's get back to your weddings..."

"Don't change the bloody topic!" Tanya cried in frustration.

"Why can't I change it if you two changed it in the first place?!" I demanded. "I've sat here listening about your fantastic frigging lives for the past hour and not once have you asked about how I feel..."

"You've only just got back from Bangladesh..."

"And Jhanghir turns me into the biggest mug of the twenty-first century..."

"We don't know what we can do for you," Sakina defended helplessly.

"Then ask me! I'm here, right in front of you, aren't I?" I shouted, causing our neighbouring coffee lovers to glare at us.

"Hey, is it your time of month?"

We glared at the smug student and waited for Tanya to give him a piece of her mind.

"Do you really want to talk about my monthly cycle?" she hissed. "I mean, seriously, are you really interested in the gory details?" The student's grin disappeared beneath Tanya's perky but condescending tone. "No, I didn't think so," she added, when he shook his head and returned to his friends.

"That's why we're asking about Jhanghir?" Sakina breathed out as we returned to our coffee.

"Why?" We rarely argued, but this needed to be asked.

"Because Chinese whispers is a stupid reason to give up on the man you love." I stared at Tanya. I felt like crying. Really crying. Crying until every emotion, thought and memory of Jhanghir could be expended.

"I don't love Jhanghir..."

"That's bulls..." Tanya's exasperation stopped her from finishing. "You've suddenly stopped loving a man that you've loved for over eight years..."

"I can't sleep, I can't think, and besides this stupid cake, I can't eat. I can't concentrate, I can't stop missing him, and I can't even get him out of my head. But I don't love him anymore." I explained without hesitation.

"Just like that?" demanded Tanya, angrier than I'd ever seen her before. "And if you let your pride down for a moment..."

"This had nothing to do with my pride..."

"Really?" Tanya laughed. "Aren't you insulted by the fact that Jhanghir may have cheated on Preeya with someone else but you?"

"He never cheated on Preeya with me..."

"Yes he did." I shook my head vehemently and sat forward. "He gave me up for her, she knew that..."

"Is it that he cheated with someone else but you that has you enraged?" I glared at Tanya. "Is that it?" She repeated.

"Why are you doing this when you know what he did?" I asked in complete confusion.

"He came for you, not once, but twice. What if the other woman he referred to turns out to be you?" Several silent seconds passed after Tanya's comment.

"That's enough!"

"What if he took the slack for Preeya because he went to San Francisco to call things off, only to discover Preeya wanted to cancel too?" Tanya continued.

"I've heard enough of this rubbish..."

"But it's not rubbish..." She persisted.

"Then you should think twice before you spread rumours!" I shouted at Tanya who sat back in shock. "You were all too happy to bleat on about how bad he was, how he ruined Preeya, what he advised her to do. You delighted in the scandal, so don't give me the 'what-ifs' now, not now when it's too late." Both Sakina and Tanya stared at me, but I refused to back down

"But it's not too late for you," Tanya told me quietly.

"It's eight years too late..."

"Your life isn't tragic Maya, you just make it sound like it is," Tanya shouted, equally indignant. It was my turn to sit in stunned wonder. I stared at my 'Judas' friends. Only unwed SLAAG members truly understood what it was to give up on something so dear. They were no longer members. Both Sakina and Tanya belonged to the soon-to-be-married clan and I had no claim to that. I gathered my bag and coat and walked out on my deserters.

Tariq was my only salvation from my parents, friends and work. In the evenings he took me with him to view restaurants for his next venture.

He asked for my design opinions, we discussed clientele type, menus, prices, décor, entertainment and advertising strategies. I enjoyed it more than I expected. One Friday evening he took me to a closed down restaurant in Ealing that he had his heart set on.

"So this is it!" Tariq said as I looked at the large empty property facing the Town Hall. "This would put me in a different league," he shouted, racing to the end of the long wide room like an excited schoolboy.

"It's certainly big and it's close to the station..."

"It can hold anywhere up to two hundred people, if I buy the first floor too." I rushed to follow his disappearing form and clambered up the stairs to find him.

"But would you get the payback from an Indian restaurant?" Tariq looked offended.

"That's just it. I don't want another Indian restaurant. I want something better." This was Tariq's dream and he was trying to live it. "I want a fusion restaurant. Great Bengali cuisine influenced by Lebanese grills, in a contemporary North African setting. I want to take out this floor and put in an industrial-strength perspex floor that looks straight down onto the floor below. I want changeable mood lights, the latest technology and the fastest, friendliest, memorable service." He was bursting with ideas and beamed with unbridled excitement. I grinned with pride as he took me to the windows. "Just imagine that!"

"What's stopping you?" I asked, looking at him as his smile faded.

"Money. I need the capital," he muttered, rubbing the back of his neck. "Even with the twins' input, I'm still seventy thousand short. They're coming for a viewing too." Having avoided them successfully in the past week, I could no longer avoid them.

"Tonight?" The clatter of heels signalled their arrival.

"There you are!" Tariq grimaced as they greeted him, mouthed an apology and walked away to talk with the letting agent.

"I guess you're both going to tell me that I've made a stupid mistake?" They stopped at my light tone with displeasure.

"Amma hasn't stopped crying for a week and you're making stupid jokes?"

"She booked the bloody wedding hall!" I pointed out to them. "She lost the deposit, that wasn't my fault..."

"You're a selfish cow," Hana stated. "We want the best for you, why would you think we'd accept Jhanghir if he had a coloured past?"

"He admitted it to me..."

"What exactly did he admit?" Hana asked, as I defiantly held my hands on my hips.

"That Preeya wasn't the only woman, that... that he'd advised on a termination..."

"That's a lie, I've spoken to Preeya myself." Jana's admission surprised me.

"What does it matter? I've made my mind up." But the nagging doubt at the back of my mind had started to grow.

"Who filled in the gaps Maya?" Jana asked. I looked from Jana to Hana and frowned at their defence of Jhanghir.

"He rejected me three months ago when I begged him to choose me." I reminded them.

"You fell out with him four years ago, but he stood by you as a friend." He had got to them with details I had only ever told Sakina and Tanya.

"That's different..." Only it wasn't, but I couldn't go back.

"Of course it is. It's always 'different' for you." Hana threw back flippantly.

"That's not fair..."

"You've always thought you were better than anyone and acted as if the world owed you the best of everything, starting off with a perfect marriage..."

"No I have not!" I retorted, outraged by Jana's attack. "I've always done what's best for the family..."

"And only you can do what's 'best', is that right Maya? Only you know what's right?"

"That's not what I mean." But she wasn't listening.

"The entire family checked out Jhanghir and we thought he was fine. Yet you think he's not good enough. Why is that?" Jana handed her bag to Hana and walked over to me.

"You won't understand..."

"Make me understand." I caught her angry hurt eyes and looked away. I failed to understand how Jhanghir had convinced them that somehow he had been wronged. What could I say? How could I explain that I didn't want to be the second choice without sounding selfish?

"I can't marry Jhanghir. I don't want to marry Jhanghir."

"Of course, because you know better than all the experience and best wishes of your family put together."

"No, because sometimes there's no way back from..."

"Who are you going to marry Maya? You have every one of us running around bending over backwards to find you a groom." As I couldn't hold her eyes, I folded my arms in front of me. "For what? For you to reject them because they're to fat, or too poor or too bendhoo..."

"I'm trying..." I interjected.

"Oh please! Have you thought for one moment that the problem isn't the men you're introduced to but that it's you, that you're the problem?" I frowned at the accusation and shook my head. "What do you have to offer to a man?"

"What?"

"Think about it. We've brought you men who have a combination of family reputation, profession, status, financial security, looks, homes, futures. What have you ever offered them besides your caustic judgement and rejection?" I looked to Hana who avoided my eyes, and to Tariq who had stopped to listen to my answer. Then I looked back at Jana.

"I have me to offer..."

"So what! You're pretty, but there are prettier girls. You're educated, but there are far better qualified and successful girls in London. You have nice clothes and great dinners, but who doesn't these days? You're twenty-eight and, needless to say, you have a large percentage of younger Bengali girls at your heels. So what do you have that's so precious?"

"Jana, you've made your point," Tariq stated from the far end of the floor. But she was right. My sister had single-handedly put me in my place and my heart raced at the point she made.

"But that's not the problem." Jana hadn't finished and I looked up. "The problem is, you're too proud. You think you know what's best, you think you can handle everything by yourself..."

"That's not true..."

"Really? So why didn't you never confide in us, Maya, ask us for help? Do you for one moment think we'd give you wrong advice?" The disappointment in Jana's voice mirrored the tears in her eyes. "You never gave us a chance, Maya. You never give anyone a chance and that's why you're not married. That's why you're still single."

Every lunch I made the short trip to the National Gallery and sat in front of Degas's La Coiffure. The canvas was coarse, the red and orange colouring bold and strong, and in the middle of it, a girl leaned back to have her hair gently combed. Sometimes I forgot time, sometimes I failed to see the tourists and art lovers passing by it, and sometimes I felt as if Jhanghir was there, sitting beside me, staring at the same picture in silence. I wanted to be soothed in the midst of all the decisions I faced. The truth was that Jana's judgement resounded in my every thought. The painful truth of her words left me feeling ashamed and alone. The thing about a quarrel is that its cause becomes immaterial in comparison to the hurt inflicted by it. My pride had caused me to hurt my parents, embarrass my friends and disappoint my sisters. Despite my intentions to open my mind and heart to all since my return from Bangladesh, I had done the opposite. I had quarrelled with everyone I loved and respected, I had ignored the pain caused through my stubbornness, and most of all, I had lost Jhanghir all over again. But this time, I had only myself to blame.

R: Reconcile Realities With Risthas And Resignations

Over the next month, I alternated my free time between the National Gallery, the British Museum, the Tate, the V&A and the National Portrait Gallery. Bulemi's confident calligraphy and Hodgkin's Indian Views collection left me spellbound. I fell in love with Julian Opie's collection, despite hating his work during my time at university. I adored Don Barchardy's style. Boldini's dark, compelling Lady Campbell captured me with her confident stare while she reclined. Sometimes I raced out at lunch and forgot the time, as I tried to emulate the styles of the artists. On other occasions, I got to work early, and worked through lunch so that I could race off to the galleries with my charcoals and sketchbooks. But most significantly everyone, including my family and friends, backed off. I didn't know whether this meant that they had given up on me, or were simply giving me space, but for now that sat fine with me.

"The Bitch has been looking for you," Mark muttered as I passed his desk. "She ordered me to tell you to go straight to her office." I thanked the office do-gooder and rushed to my desk. Dumping my bag, I pulled out a baby wipe and cleaned the charcoal smudge from my fingers. Grimacing at the wall clock that told me I had taken thirty minutes extra for lunch, I took off my jacket, as I looked around to spot Brenda in her office. I sat down at my desk to check my messages. As expected there as one from Monsur, my email confidant and the only friend I currently had.

To: MayaM@Instantmail.com
From: Monsur1@NYmail.com
Dear Princess of Pride, whilst I'm happy to hear about your rediscovery of art, I have no idea who you're talking about when you reel off names like Degas, Rubens, Turner, Beechy or Rothko. Neither do I want a Dummy's Guide to Art. Be content to know that unless you mention Amitabh, Ashwariya, Shah Rukh, or even Amir Khan, this East Coast guy's not interested!
Now I can't stop thinking about your dilemma. Your doubts about the events behind Jhanghir's cancelled wedding may be self-created - or as you say, a manifestation of your obsession to believe Jhanghir's a good guy - but what if, Maya?
I understand you don't want to appear obsessed, or be hurt again, but I don't understand how you repress the need to discover the truth and reconcile that with the choices that you now have. Loosen the reign on your pride Maya, ask your friends or your sisters for the truth so that there are no more what-ifs. You owe yourself that much.

I reread the email and hit the reply icon.

To: Monsur1@NYmail.com
From: MayaM@Instantmail.com
*Dear Culinary King of Advice, Degas, Rubens, Turner and Rothko
could transform the appearance of your restaurant as well as the way
you prepare, cook and present your meals. Trust me, Bollywood glam
will NOT give you that hint of distinction discerning diners crave for!!!
I cried twice this week. That's nine times less than last week and a
whole fifteen times less than the first two weeks after Jhanghir turned
up in my living room. At this rate, I'll definitely be over him next month.
Seriously, my point is this. If I unravel the truth and discover it is as I
know it to be, I don't think I can stand myself for being so desperate, so
weak and most importantly so stupid. Even if the truth is other than I
know it to be, how would I begin to undo the pain, hurt and humiliation
I've caused? No, I'm sticking by my decision to move on. It is the safest
route forward.*

"Maya! So you've decided to turn up!" I looked back at Brenda's office,
from where she greeted me. "Let's review your client research
requests." I waved in agreement and looked back at my screen.

*p.s. I'm not scared of discovering that I'm wrong, I'm scared of
discovering that I'm right.*

I hit the send button and closed down my email account. Grabbing my
client information folders and my notebook, I headed for Brenda's
office. Pulling on my jacket, I picked up a pen and headed to the office
of humiliation.
"Good Luck!" Clare muttered, as I eased around her desk. "She's had a
bad day, avoid the handover," she advised. I nodded and knocked on
the open door.
"Maya!" The false surprise made me smile as I closed the door behind
me and took a seat in front of her desk.
"Mark mentioned you were looking for me." The look of surprise
disappeared and Brenda pulled up my client details on her screen. She
took several long minutes to review them. I watched her eyes race over
the figures and the data. Once she was satisfied, she turned to face
me.
"I'm concerned about your commitment to the firm." I looked down at
my notepad and started doodling. "I'm sensing a general lack of
interest and, uh, hard work from you."
"I've met all my client requests bar the two that are pending for today
and I plan to complete on those by the end of the day."
"Ok, Maya, I'll be more specific." Brenda clenched her fists together
and rested her chin on them. "You're not putting in enough hours."
"You're not happy with my work management…"
"No, listen to me. I don't like you skipping lunches, or doing the 'get in
early, leave early routine.' It sets a bad precedent." Brenda clarified.

"I don't take cigarette breaks or coffee breaks. I put in the hours required by my contract which also says that I have flexi hour permissions…"

"That's really for women with child-care issues." Brenda dismissed.

"I really think it's unwise of you to discriminate between us."

"I don't like you taking extending lunches…"

"For which I make the time up…"

"…or turning up looking like a uh…" She struggled to find the words and I waited. "…uh, like a malnourished student with refugee status." I stared at her, absolutely lost for words. So I no longer blow-dried my hair into a sleek glistening mane every morning, and my shirts weren't perfectly ironed, but the 'Bitch' had stepped over the mark.

"I'm going to end the meeting here," I decided.

"I haven't finished…"

"I think we have." I took my belongings and walked towards the door.

"I haven't finished," she repeated. I opened the door and walked out.

"Maya, I'm reporting you to HR…" I slammed the door behind me. Mark and every other colleague I passed stared straight at their screens, intent on being invisible. I caught Clare's eyes and she winked in a sign of support. I grinned before walking to my desk. I had had enough of this blinkered office, the terrified plebs and the abusive warden of a manager. I walked over to my desk, lodged my complaint with HR and closed down for the day. This wasn't my reality. This wasn't what I would accept from my life. Leaving my jacket hanging from the back of my desk, I grabbed my art bag, my purse and headed straight for the door.

Since everyone in the family had turned their backs on me, Tariq took me beneath his wing with a determination I had never seen. He made sure Shireen-bhabhi prepared my breakfast, he advised me on my deteriorating work situation and he called me every night from the restaurant to make sure I was ok. And then he went and did the very thing that everyone else had given up on. With Ayesha's help, he organised an alaap.

"Maya, this is Chacha Amjad, his son Sajjid and Sajjid's friend, Iqbal." And I was happy to oblige, all the while praying for a simple humble man I would consider as my partner for life. We stood by the outside tables at the entrance to Café Rouge in Bayswater's Whiteleys. I greeted them, before taking a seat beside Tariq and opposite the short, skinny, bespectacled man who continued to wear his summer mac at the table. I dipped some crusty Italian bread into the olive oil, balking at his appearance, as Tariq talked with Iqbal. Sajjid's hair was perfectly parted down the centre and slicked down with too much hair gel. Beneath the summer mac, he wore a West Ham football shirt tucked into his high waisted jeans. But I refused to negate his suitability on the basis of his appearance. In fact his eclectic taste made for interesting conversation and with that thought, I smiled. It was then that I noticed

Sajjid staring at me until I was forced to lower my gaze. I wondered if I'd seen correctly and sneaked another look at him. There he was, staring at me without the slightest interest or expression.

"Do you watch Star Trek?" With a mouth full of bread, I looked at Sajjid. "I'm a big fan of Star Trek. I watch every episode. Any episode that I miss, I tape and watch on Sunday afternoon." That was Sajjid's icebreaker.

Wide-eyed, I wondered how much latitude I could give this man.

"I have to say I'm more a 'Friends' type of person..."

"Although Captain Kirk's the best Captain ever, I have to say the technology these days is unbelievable. Did you watch last week's episode by any chance?" Sajjid had come to life for Star Trek. He was animated and confident. I, on the other hand, felt like dying. "I've seen it before, as I import the series from Malaysia, but that episode truly was outstanding." I listened and nodded at the right times, as Tariq encouraged Sajjid to express his love for the series. Half an hour passed and still Sajjid and Iqbal debated the evolution of the Starship Enterprise. Completely forgotten, I felt like I'd been transported to the virtual hyper-vortex planet of the Trekkers.

"You're being obstinate and you know it," Sajjid accused, checking the inside pockets of his mac. "I got this in the post today from Malaysia and I think you need to watch it." Incredulously, we watched Sajjid pull out the latest pirated copy of the Star Trek DVD and hand it over to Iqbal. I dropped a knife and jumped as it clattered against my plate. Smiling in embarrassment, I picked up my glass and drained all the contents.

"Maya, why don't you tell Sajjid about some of your hobbies?" Turning to look at Tariq, I wondered when my ordeal would end. Catching his look of encouragement, I didn't want to disappoint him. I cleared my throat and turned back to Sajjid with a small smile.

"I love drawing, I do a lot of pastel work when I can find the time." I didn't get any response, but I persevered. "I like going to the gym, well actually, not really. In fact I hate going to the gym, but I like meeting up with my friends and catching the latest movie." Silence followed my opening and I looked back to Tariq who frowned at Sajjid.

"Uh, I like dark humour and romantic comedies... 'One Fine Day' was great, Bridget Jones was hilarious, and my favourite movie is 'Out of Sight'. Have you seen it?" I asked. Sajjid shook his head before telling Iqbal to put his DVD away safely and to return it to him in exactly one week's time. He wasn't interested in a word I had to say, and I wondered if it would be best for Sajjid to settle down with a fellow Trekkie. I looked at Tariq who nodded at Iqbal to give Sajjid some encouragement.

"Sajjid does go to see the 'Next Generation' at the movies," Iqbal contributed lamely as Sajjid provided a list of 'Next Generation' movies that had been released in the past five years. And then I felt inspired.

"I forgot to mention, I like singing anthems. I'm not the greatest singer in the world but there's a song called 'Star Trekking' have you got that?" Seeing Sajjid's interest in my question, I ignored Ayesha's warning cough.

"No, I don't listen to music much, but I'd be interested to listen to that..."

"Oh, I can do a rendition..."

"Maybe at another meeting Maya," Ayesha said, struggling to keep her composure and then coughed to cover her laughter.

"Why wait?" I asked with a wide smile before taking a deep breath to begin the helium induced Muppet tune. I got past the first two sentences before collapsing into whoops of laughter, as Tariq and Ayesha guiltily covered their laughing faces.

"I think it's time I left..." Sajjid stated.

"Sajjid, Maya has a unique sense of humour..."

"Yes, one that's not to my liking." I stopped singing as Sajjid stood up to leave. "Good luck and thank you for your time." And with that Sajjid and Iqbal left, as the silent Chacha Amjad raced after them. Minutes passed as we laughed, coughed, and cleared our throats before we finally looked at each other.

"Tell me I was out of order," I asked, but Ayesha shook her head.

"I'm going home to my husband, I do not envy you with mom in her current state of mind." Ayesha leaned over and took hold of my cheeks to inspect my face. "You've lost too much weight. Are you skipping meals?" I pulled back out of her reach and frowned when she exchanged worried glances with Tariq. I shook my head subconsciously and finished off the fries.

"I'll drop you off," Tariq offered, paying for the drinks and nibbles.

"Maya, that wasn't fair on Sajjid..."

"He was a freak! C'mon, he deserved it," I insisted, as Ayesha stole some fries before pulling on her jacket. I cleared my throat and looked at Tariq. "What are you going to tell Amma?"

"Amma doesn't need to know!" I grinned as Tariq turned to Ayesha, who nodded in agreement. I developed a deeper respect for my brother. He had been given a trade, a bride, but carried the family responsibility without question. And though he never lamented his fate, he wouldn't consign me to his fate. It felt good to be listened to.

Soon after I discovered that it was also important to do the listening.

To: MayaM@Instantmail.com
From: Monsur1@NYmail.com
Dear Princess of Pride, I'm sorry that things didn't work out with Sajjid. But going by your account it sounds like you had a lucky escape from a life of Star-Trekking servitude!
I'm even sorrier that I've been unable to convince you to reconsider Jhanghir. I discovered that Zina got married to an economist based in

Geneva. I would've done anything to be in your position, to have one more chance with Zina. But I know now that's impossible. The Bengali grapevine tells me she's doing very well out there, but I couldn't tell you how I'm doing. I'm at a loss, that's the only way I can explain it. But I deserved better. That much I know.

I stared at Monsur's email until tears blurred my vision. Monsur had lost the love of his life. He had been cast aside and left with a hopelessness and a sense of worthlessness that would plague him from here on. I understood the pain he felt. And yet, how could I explain that I couldn't open myself up to Jhanghir again? I quickly wrote a response encouraging him to immerse himself in work, but deleted it for being too cold and hardhearted. I scribbled down my favourite prayer for him to recite for strength and deleted that for being too impersonal.

"Maya, EuroGrand have arrived," Mark announced as he returned to his desk and then added. "They're in the lobby."

"Thanks," I muttered, staring at my blank response. I had no words of consolation, for there were none in this situation. But I could give him hope, so I pressed the reply button.

To: Monsur1@NYmail.com
From: MayaM@Instantmail.com
I'm not sorry Zina has married, or moved overseas, but I am sorry that you discovered this development in the way that you did. But she has moved on. There is no more what-if for you. And the truth is you will never feel what you did for Zina again, because for you there will only ever be one Zina. So you must look forward to life's next, not a replacement Zina. You must hope for new experiences, new emotions and new dreams, because the heart forgets sadness in the face of new hope. Make a list Monsur, of things you want to do, movies, plays and concerts you want to see and places you want to visit. And focus on achieving those, and leave love to fate. For all her flaws, fate will do right by you.

I hit the send button and closed my email account. I sat staring at my screen, biting at the corner of my mouth. Make a list. That's what I needed to do. EuroGrand, whom I had inherited from Clare's old portfolio, were waiting, but all I wanted to do was make a list. My list. I checked Clare's calendar and saw that her afternoon was empty, so I turned to find her at her desk. She was searching Expedia to book her next holiday. Relations between us were still strained and it was time to mend bridges. I turned back to my screen and smiled. I printed out the client background and the update they required on our future reports schedule.

"Clare." She closed her Internet window and looked round at me. "I need you to take EuroGrand's meeting…"

"But you handle the account now…"

"I know, but I'm not feeling well so I'm going home." Before Clare could disagree I handed her EuroGrand's profile.

"Has Brenda been informed?" I looked at her and shook my head. She looked at me and smiled. "You're not going home are you?" I winked and she laughed.

"My days here are numbered already." I confessed. She nodded and took the papers I held out. "I want you to start familiarising yourself with the best accounts I manage."

"Is this you making the peace offering?" Clare asked with a reluctant grin.

I shook my head. "No, but I hope this will make up for my behaviour." Clare took the gift I had brought her from Bangladesh. I grinned and watched her draw out the red silk sari from the package in awe.

"Maya, it's beautiful," she whispered, gently touching the soft material. "I have no idea how to wear it, and since I don't want to end up looking like an overstuffed sausage you're going to have to teach me how!"

"I'm sorry," I whispered as I reached down to hug her. She patted my back and laughed.

"Now go, go do your thing. Just let me know when you discover what that is, ok?" I waited in the ladies until Clare had taken EuroGrand through the open plan office into the booked meeting room. As soon as they were settled, I raced out of the office and up Chancery Lane. It was a quick walk through Holborn to Russell Square. There, I shed my jacket and sat in the forecourts of the British Museum. I pulled out my sketchpad and started my list.

"What do I want?" I whispered to myself as I tapped my pen, lost in thought.

First of all, I needed to launch an all-out offensive to 'get married'. Jhanghir.

Which meant I had to 'find a husband'. Jhanghir.

As well as needing to 'just resign'. Jhanghir.

And I wanted to 'focus on my art'. Jhanghir.

That wasn't going to happen overnight, so I put down 'make Amma and family happy with me again'. Jhanghir.

I wrote 'to apologise to Tanya and Sakina'. Jhanghir.

I also needed a 'holiday vegging out on a beach'. Jhanghir. Jhanghir. Jhanghir. Jhanghir.

He was always with me. He was the only need that plagued me. I looked up from my sketch book and stared at the grand impressive Museum. My heart went out to Monsur. I still had hope and that's what he had wanted me to realise. I wrote JHANGHIR in big, bold, underlined capitals. And this meant I needed to 'discover the truth'.

"I want to see you now." Brenda didn't wait for a response but strode back into her office. Clare and Emma wished me good luck, as I picked up my notebook and followed her. Closing the door behind me, I turned to find Personnel sitting in the room.

"Do I need representation?" The grey suits of Personnel looked to one another before Brenda took control.

"Take a seat Maya, this is an informal meeting. One where we outline the options you have here." She wasn't happy. I sat back and enjoyed her discomfort. "You can then decide whether or not you need representation."

"We'd like to begin by saying 'thank you' for being open to this discussion. We appreciate that this is a difficult situation for you." I dropped my grin and nodded at Personnel, as Brenda breathed out in exasperation.

"Basically, you have three choices Maya." Brenda did not have Personnel's patience for niceties. "One, you can carry on working here under my terms and conditions; two, you can accept a transfer into a different department although we can't guarantee you the exact position or salary; or three, you can accept voluntary redundancy with six months tax-free."

This was better than I had expected. I was ready to hand in my resignation, but the voluntary redundancy would support me in the short term.

"Of course, we can discuss a combination of the options..."

"I understand the options." Personnel stopped at my comment. "You want me to leave with guarantees that I'll take no legal action."

"We'd like to emphasise that we've given you the option to stay on..."

"I understand," I clarified, looking straight at the Personnel representatives. "You realise that this conversation itself would be admissible in Court, if I pursued the discrimination claim." Personnel cleared their throats before looking to Brenda for direction. "Will I get the minutes from this conversation?"

"Maya, one comment does not make for a case..."

"Brenda, please..." But Personnel had no gagging powers over Brenda.

"Maya, you're not happy here. You're not committed..."

"Don't tell me how I feel Brenda. I've had no complaints from the clients or from my colleagues..."

"The issue is working practices," Personnel jumped, in trying to break up the exchange. "Maya, Brenda runs a tight ship. The management is happy with her performance, and though they're not unhappy with yours, we think your style may be suited elsewhere, like in marketing research..."

"I'm not a marketing professional," I stated before staring down at my notepad. I recalled my list of wants and realised that maybe, fate was doing right by me. Maybe this was the get-out opportunity I so wanted. I looked up at Brenda and curbed a smile.

"You realise that she's done this to others, forced others to leave through discrimination and intimidation?" I wouldn't leave without some mischief. I looked from an outraged Brenda to Personnel. "Bullying at work has become a serious crime these days, the company doesn't want its reputation to be tainted..."

"Slander is also a serious crime Maya," Brenda threw back.

"It's ironic that you feel the need to remind me of that fact!" I smiled.

"Didn't you call me a 'malnourished student on refugee status'?"

"Maya, we're fully aware of the issues that caused you to contact us. That's why we're offering you a transfer…"

"I want full medical cover for my redundancy period, an extra three months' pay for the short notice, a written guarantee that references will be positive and endorsed by this company…"

"Maya, that's not your only option," Personnel informed me.

"I'll have to start at the bottom in marketing, I'm not prepared to do that." They understood and nodded.

"We won't do the extra months, and we'd need to come back to you on your other points," Personnel stated, as Brenda smiled icily.

"I want the extra months, as stated in my contract, under item 14.g, so come back to me on everything." I was resigning, freeing myself from something I hated with a passion. Personnel agreed and I looked to Brenda.

"Thank you." She had helped me leave Chambers Scott Wilfred International. Brenda looked like she'd been slapped, but I had meant it. If it wasn't for her, I'd still be there, accepting the status quo, being overlooked for promotion, keeping the analysis wheel turning. "Leave the paperwork on my desk," I told Personnel before concluding the meeting. I was smiling from ear to ear as I walked out, past all my staring colleagues and to my future. Undetermined as it was, I wasn't phased.

I waited at Café Nero for Sakina and Tanya with my box of personal belongings and contracts that I had cleared from my desk. I hadn't spoken to either since our fallout, but as the reality of what I had done dawned on me, I needed their counsel.

"You did it," Sakina cried as I jerked around to find them both standing by the couch.

"You finally told the Bitch to 'piss off'!" Tanya added. They hesitated by the couch and I stood up.

"I'm sorry…"

"No, I'm sorry…"

"We're both sorry," Sakina joined in, as I hugged my friends. "It was unfair of…"

"No, I shouldn't be jealous…"

"We should've understood, been more sensitive about…"

"…your feelings for Jhanghir," Tanya finished, as we stood in a huddle.

"Who's up for cake?" she asked, reinstating our natural order.

"I can't believe I resigned – well, took voluntary redundancy!" I breathed as Sakina sat beside me and took my hands. "Just like that, with nearly a year's salary! Amma's really going to flip now…"

"Just tell her it was an office-wide thing, you don't need any more grief right now," advised Sakina, as Tanya went to place our orders. "You've lost a lot of weight Maya..."

"Well, I've been deprived of a month's worth of Devil cake!" Sakina smiled, but she wasn't convinced. "What am I going to do all day?"

"You're going to plan our bloody weddings, that's what!" Sakina threw in, as we laughed together. "You're so lucky, I wish I could stop working!"

"Vanilla machiatto with full cream!" We turned at Tanya's loud shout and saw her glaring at the counter assistant.

"You ok?" Sakina called out to Tanya.

"Yeah, the joker thinks that just because I wear a headscarf I don't understand English!" she shouted back, making the whole coffee house turn in attention. She shook her head before turning back to the humiliated, but now wiser, staff member.

"The upcoming wedding hasn't softened her up in the slightest?" I said with a grin.

"Not in the slightest!" Sakina agreed before we burst out laughing.

"So tell me, what are we going to do with you?" Tanya asked as she carried our coffees and customary slices of Devil cake on a plastic tray.

"You're going to help me lighten up and stop worrying so much..."

"I didn't mean what I said..."

"I know you didn't Tanya, but I've got my whole future ahead of me." I took my machiatto and looked at my dear friend. "Bangladesh changed me. I stopped believing that all my problems would get solved if I got married. But I need your help to continue believing that..."

"But you have to get married some day." Sakina murmured sadly.

"I will when Allah gives my lazy husband-to-be an A-Z to find me!" They laughed at my old joke, but I sobered up.

"I know you're going to hate me, but have you thought any more about Jhanghir?" Tanya asked after a nervous pause in the conversation. I no longer found the cake appealing. I played around with it until I forced myself to look up at Tanya. She had gone out on a limb to ask me, but she looked worried. I nodded and thought of Monsur. I had reached out to reconcile my friendship with the girls, perhaps it was time for me to take that step further.

"All the time," I finally admitted. "I go out of my head trying to figure out how everything got so confusing and messed up..."

"I had no business spreading the gossip," admitted Tanya.

"Tanya, I'm not blaming you," I corrected quickly as she leaned forward and took my hands.

"I just wanted to help you move on. I wanted you to believe the worst in him because I thought it would make it easier."

"The bit about the termination that was a lie, wasn't it?" I didn't need the answer to know the truth. Tanya and Sakina watched me as they tried to judge how much I wanted to know.

"I swear to you, that's what I was told..."

"I heard that too Maya," Sakina added. I was too scared to ask for more details, but I clenched my hands and waited. "It turned out that Preeya resumed her relationship with Jhanghir's cousin when they came over for that wedding."

"But she was too scared to call things off with Jhanghir," Tanya continued. "I don't pretend to understand it. I guess the family pressure, and the marriage being her father's last wish, it was just too much for her to deal with. Until she had no choice."

"What do you mean?"

Tanya looked at Sakina, before looking back at me. "Preeya was six weeks pregnant at the time she was to marry Jhanghir." She explained. I stared at Tanya, needing to know what Jhanghir had told her. "He flew out early because he was the first one she confided in…"

"He didn't deceive you about the date, Maya," Sakina pointed out before handing the story back to Tanya.

"Apparently he asked Preeya what she wanted to do…"

"She wasn't in any position to make a decision she wouldn't regret in the long run!" I guffawed.

"That's why Jhanghir advised her to keep the baby and marry his cousin instead." I looked at Tanya and ever so slightly shook my head.

"But she had a…" I began.

"No, she didn't." Tanya corrected. I breathed out ever so slowly and stared down at the cake I was unable to eat. "They cancelled the wedding and Preeya took her vows with his cousin. I heard that Jhanghir and his mother were the only two family members to attend the religious ceremony."

I sat in silence working through the events in my head. Though this was truer to Jhanghir's nature, I had my doubts.

"But he was still planning on marrying her," I pointed out to my friends.

"He took responsibility for the cancelled wedding Maya…"

"And all that stuff about the other woman, that was about…"

"If she had gone along with the wedding, would he be married now?" Tanya and Sakina stopped at my question. They floundered, avoided looking at each other and shrugged with uncertainty.

"But Maya, the stuff about him seeing other women…"

"You see, all the other rumours mean nothing if he still intended to marry Preeya after I begged him to choose me. But he didn't," I persisted.

"He went to his father, he took all the responsibility and all the blame for calling off the wedding," argued Sakina. "He didn't even use her affair as the reason for the cancellation, surely that counts for something?"

"You don't know that he didn't choose you," Tanya pointed out.

"You don't know that he did either." They both looked miserable. I knew they felt responsible for being unable to convince me, but for me that was the bottom line. Tanya and Sakina didn't have the answer, but I didn't expect them to. That could only come from Jhanghir. "It's ok, I'm ok, and in fact I'm more than ok. I know now that's he's not a bastard..."

"He's not Maya, he so isn't," Sakina quickly pointed out. "Will you call him?" I shook my head and chuckled at the thought. "Please, you just need to give him a chance to explain."

"He has my number and my email address, if he has something to say to me he knows where I am Sakina." I pointed out.

"Ego. God-given tool. And then logic. Have I taught you nothing about man's nature?" Tanya asked before giving me a serious look. "He asked for your hand in marriage Maya. In person. In front of all your family. Yet you didn't give him a chance to explain. What makes him think that you'll give him another one if he contacted you?" None of us had touched our slice of Devil cake. We had changed and the calorific cake had lost its importance as the answer to all our problems. Eight years I had given to this man. And that was just the start. I had laid my pride and soul on the line for him, and now I was being asked to do it again.

"If he wants me, he has to convince me." I was my own worst enemy. Tanya looked at Sakina and then turned to me with one last attempt.

"It's one question Maya. Do you really think it's too much for you to contact Jhanghir?"

"You're unemployed!" Amma's shriek could be heard at the end of road but that didn't phase her in the slightest. Tanya's questions resounded in my head but at this moment, I had a more urgent matter to resolve. "I've never had an unemployed child in my life!"

"I was made redundant..."

"Why? What did you do wrong? You back chatted your manager, didn't you? Why can't you keep your mouth shut, just be grateful for a job and stay out of troubles way!" She made it sound like I had invited some mystery curse on myself. "What do I say when I'm asked by interested families why you're not working?"

"Just tell them the company was closing down departments due to poor performance and my department happened to be one of them. It's happening everywhere. Tanya's brother was made redundant..."

"He's a lazy bum!"

"So was Leila's fiancé..."

"He has ants in his pants! That's why he's a contractor, and they always go first!"

"Amma, it's affecting a lot of people..."

"You're unemployed! What am I going to tell people in your bio data!" Before I could answer, she swanned off to find Baba.

"Your mother tells me you've been sacked." The quiet, steady words marked the first conversation he had initiated with me since Jhanghir's visit.

"I've been made redundant," I clarified, as he sat at the dining table facing me. Amma I could pull the wool over, but not Baba.

"Why?" I met the firm eyes that I had inherited, but was unable to hold his look.

"Because the office was..." And I couldn't lie to him. "Because I complained about discriminatory practices and they cut me a good deal."

"Discrimination is being told you're a sub-human and thanking white people for not beating you up..."

"Not any more, Baba, it's stopping the decision-makers humiliating and belittling us."

"So why cut a deal?" Baba asked.

My decision seemed contrary, but I stood by it. "Because it affects them financially and I save myself time and the costs of a court case, whilst gaining myself nine months' untaxed salary..."

"But you could hurt them more by getting a bigger payout..."

"I'm not after their money Baba, I can't work there anymore." He watched me and shook his head, failing to understand that work itself wasn't enough.

"What do you plan to do now?" He wouldn't look at me.

"I thought I could spend some time painting..."

"That will pay well." I felt the pain of his sarcasm, but smiled at his lack of confidence in me. I got up to leave the room before he could see the tears. But I was heartened by my resolve to be different. It was hard to resign. It was tough to make decisions alone. And it was near impossible to forget Jhanghir. But I needed to reconcile what I had to make the most of what I could have. We, single women, have to take control of our lives because if we don't, life will give up on us.

S: Shaadhi Season Means Shopportunities

Any opportunity for shopping is a shopportunity. And with three weddings on the horizon, shopportunities were coming along thick and fast. Now there are three dress codes that have to be adhered to if you're not the bride. First, never out do the bride, which means that crimson, blood or velvet red should be avoided at all costs, along with Mr T-type gold jewellery. Second, pay attention to grooming details, as it sets you apart from everyone else. And finally, always, but always, check what your friends are wearing.

With those rules in mind, I was ready to receive Leila in her full wedding mode, and for once, I welcomed her distracting, attention-devouring presence in our house. She arrived with Chachijhi and Mina who were loaded up with magazines, make-up books and samples. And soon after, Kala from Brighton, turned up with my cousins, Pana, Mana, Kara, Zarah and Farah.
"Wonderful! This is going to be the best wedding ever!" Leila squealed, as she took off her acid pink sandals and beckoned the girls. "Zarah and Farah, I want you to go through the samples and choose the colours you like, everything except blood red. I'm the bride and that's my colour." She was in her element, but before she could drag me into her world of no return, I escaped to the kitchen and instantly regretted it. Amma sat at the counter sobbing into her hands, as Chachijhi and Kala stood over her. Chachijhi speared me with a hateful look and, turning away, I walked into Jana who was closely followed by Hana.
"I need to talk with you." Since my chat with Tanya and Sakina, I had decided to get the truth from my sisters.
"That's a first," Hana remarked with pretend surprise. I hesitated. This was harder than I expected, but I had to stay focused.
"I need to talk to you about Jhanghir…"
"That's too little too late," Jana threw back at me as she brushed past me. I looked to Hana, who stood shaking her head.
"You've made your decision Maya. Live with it." I stared ahead as she followed Jana. I wanted to turn back the clock and revisit my conversation with Jhanghir. I wanted to give him time to explain, a chance to answer my questions without thinking the worst of him. I felt as if I had failed everyone. I returned to the busy living room and scooted down on the floor between Mina and Zarah.
"Have you thought about what we should be wearing?" I asked.
"I picked out six designs that I want you to choose from…"
"But we won't be able to tell how they look without trying on the outfits first," Pana pointed out, as Leila tutted in disagreement.
"We're having these custom made in India. Apparently it takes a week, so I'll have to get all your measurements today…"

"But Leila, the wedding's in four weeks. You don't have time to have it custom made in India!" Pana said, as we leaned forward to look at the designs magazine.

"You can't be serious about this one?" I blurted out as I picked up a cutting of a belly-baring strapless skirt suit. "You'll have two-thirds of the community walk out of your wedding on religious grounds!"

"I'm just giving you a choice, not that that style would've suited you as you really don't have a toned, flat stomach." I stopped myself from folding my arms to cover my stomach and caught Zarah's smile.

"She's on Planet Leila," she whispered, as we looked at some of Leila's choices. As the fourth of five daughters, Zarah was younger than myself and Leila. And whilst Leila was content on tying the knot ahead of me, Zarah took a more patient attitude to the entire matter.

"How about this?" I asked holding up a cutting of a matt-gold bias cut fishnet with a long trail. A short, fitted, Nehru jacket with ornate embroidered collar and sleeve edges completed the outfit. "Imagine forties-inspired strappy heels, and back-combed hair with ringlets cascading down our backs?"

"You're very good at this," Zarah commented as they looked at the cutting.

"Yes, yes, but you have to choose your colour samples!" Leila cut in, taping the cutting into her notebook. I moved over to where she sat. "Maya? Would you come with me to choose my wedding dress?" Leila's question surprised me.

"But Abdul Raquib's family are meant to buy it for you," I pointed out, as Leila snorted with derision.

"As if I'd let them choose an outfit for the biggest day of my life!" Leila dispensed with tradition when it didn't suit her. "But they are paying for it, so promise me you'll come? I really could do with your advice." I had no choice so I nodded, knowing full well that I was committing myself to wedding hell.

"One more shop, just Dhamini's." Two weeks later, I was ready to beg Brenda to take me back. Zarah, Farah, Mina and I trailed after Leila, ready to collapse with the number of bags of chooris, jewellery sets, shoes, clothes and decorations we had bought. By the time we stepped into the Southall store, Leila had two attendants at her attention.

"I need to know if you have anything like this, but I need it in seven different colours," Leila stated, showing the attendant the cut out design we had all agreed on, as we found any available place on which to park our butts.

"No, no, no, no, no. Listen to me, I'm having seven bridesmaids at my wedding. I can't have them wearing different styles. Maybe different colours, but not styles. I want one style, just one." Although we couldn't see Leila, we could hear her.

"Isn't that that couple? It is, isn't it? But he dumped her, why's she with him?" Mina whispered. I caught Zarah's concerned gaze and realised that Amma had told them about Jhanghir. So I looked to the furthest end of the store and froze.

"Oh my God, it is them!" Mina whispered as they approached the cash desk. "Oh my God, she's pregnant!" Mina's excitement at witnessing first hand gossip caused her to forget the need to whisper. As a result we faced the full force of Jhanghir's wilting look.

"Go and talk to him," Zarah muttered, pushing me obviously off the seat. I glared back at her before stepping forward in their direction. My stomach knotted, my heart raced and I lost my breath at the sight of him. As always, the man looked gorgeous in charcoal slacks and navy sweater. I tore my gaze away from him and looked in confusion at Preeya.

"Maya," he acknowledged but I couldn't meet his eyes.

"Jhanghir," I managed to mutter, feeling as if I would explode with unanswered questions and unspoken feelings.

"Leila! Leila! He's here! The man who ruined his fiancée and then came for Maya!" Mina cried, racing down the store to tell her sister in what she thought was a hushed tone and what the rest of us interpreted as a delighted chance to feed the Bengali gossip vines.

"Hello Maya." Preeya positively glowed as she leaned over to kiss both my cheeks. She was several months pregnant and still I felt dowdy and unkempt in my jeans and trainers. "How are you?"

"I'm well." I looked at her small bump and looked away as she self-consciously placed a hand over her abdomen. "I didn't expect you both…"

"No, I'm sure you didn't." I finally met his hazel eyes and fell for him all over again. I didn't want him to be able to make me 'feel'. I didn't want him to be the only one to affect my composure.

"Jhanghir's been my pillar of strength. I couldn't have gotten through the last few months without him," Preeya filled the silence between us. "And now that I'm settled here, it's so good to see a friendly face, even if it is between lectures and research forums!" Jhanghir continued staring at me, refusing to explain, absolutely refusing to give up the upper hand. He was forcing me to actually ask him.

"And you're happy with…"

"Jhanghir Rahman!" I closed my eyes at Leila's outraged shout as she marched through the open boutique. "You get away from my cousin…"

"Leila, it's fine…"

"Maya, you're an innocent sweetheart and much too forgiving. But I haven't forgotten what this man did to you. I know how these men work…" Leila trailed off as she stopped in front of Jhanghir, stunned by his striking looks. He had that effect on women and Leila, wide-eyed and speechless, was no exception.

"Leila, Preeya was just telling me she's settled here with…"

"Jhanghir Rahman…" Leila breathed out with a shy smile. "Nice to meet the very man who caused such a naughty controversy." A flirty giggle followed to confirm that my cousin was indeed clinically insane. I ignored her and looked to Preeya to finish.

"As you were saying, you're now settled with..."

"Mohibur Rahman." Every one of my cousins gasped with surprise and looked at Jhanghir in confusion. I turned to him, but Leila got to him first and kept him busy with the details of her wedding. "That would be Mohibur, Jhanghir's cousin." I turned back to Preeya and she smiled. She took my arm and led me away from my family. "I'm carrying Mohibur's child. Jhanghir had no idea we were seeing each other again and I was so afraid of my family that I thought I had go through with the marriage. But when I found out I was expecting, I knew I couldn't go through with it. I called Jhanghir and told him that I had doubts about the wedding. He flew out on the first flight..."

"I know all this already, Preeya," I whispered. It was now she who looked at me in confusion.

"Preeya, I've got to get back," Jhanghir called from the counter. We looked back at him to find him busily writing something down for Leila. Preeya waved her hand in acknowledgement, and then looked back at me.

"He called off the wedding, Maya."

"I know, Preeya."

"No, he called it off before I told him about Mohibur and my pregnancy." She revealed. I stared at her, and narrowed my eyes, evaluating why she was telling me this. "He'd been trying for weeks to convince his father that the wedding was a mistake..."

"Preeya, I've got to go if I'm to make it to the seminar," Jhanghir called out before Leila demanded his full attention. I looked back at Jhanghir, who watched me with contained suspicion.

"Why are you telling me this?" I whispered, shaking at the implications of what she had said.

"You know why." I met her wide brown eyes and I shook my head. "Meet me at Ajanti's in ten minutes." She waited until I nodded. Dazed by Preeya's revelation, we returned to my cousins and Jhanghir. I had judged Jhanghir in the worst possible way, and yet he stood before me without condemnation or hate.

"Promise me that you'll be at my wedding. I want you to meet my fiancé and if you're lucky I just might have a sister or cousin or two in mind for you!" I wanted to curl up and die at Leila's behaviour, but instead, I forced myself to smile.

"Leila, Maya." I nodded at his departure, but refused to meet his eyes.

"Preeya, it's lovely to see you." I leaned forward to hug her and she patted me on the back before following Jhanghir out.

"How could you reject him! Are you MAD?" Leila shrieked for the whole of Southall to hear. "He is a dreamboat, Maya, what's wrong with you?"

"Tell her to shut up," I told Mina, as I collected my shopping.

"What was wrong with the man? I bet some jealous ex made up the story!" Leila announced, following us out without any sign of giving up on her crusade for Jhanghir.

"We need to find the outfits..."

"You dumped him? Oh my God, no wonder your mother's been crying day and night!" It was a lost cause. 'Jhanghir-itis' caused women to believe that he was perfect in every way. And if I didn't have so much pride, I'd be the ringleader. In truth, I'd suffered for months because of Chinese whispers, and now I had to find the strength to admit that I was wrong.

I left my cousins trying on several outfits at Roop Ki Rani's, and as promised, I escaped to meet Preeya at the popular shoe shop. I paused as I found her waiting outside.

"I can't stay long, my cousins are waiting for me..." Preeya took my arm and led me into the shoe shop.

"But you've kept Jhanghir waiting long enough." I stopped at her remark and frowned. "You still don't get it, do you?" Preeya asked.

"I've heard so many rumours that I've given up trying to understand what happened." We sat down on a bench and I watched her try on various glitzy, gravity-defying high heels.

"So why haven't you asked Jhanghir?" The question was tinged with a touch of resentment. "Compared to asking him to walk away from his marriage, that should be a piece of cake for you." Preeya put the heels down to look straight at me. She knew everything. I felt embarrassed, ashamed and guilty, but I held her look. I wouldn't apologise for my actions.

"And he chose you, Preeya," I reminded her. She laughed, looking back at the shoe.

"You stupid girl." I raised a brow at the comment. Surprised by my quietness, she looked back at me and continued. "There was never a choice. I may have been the choice of our fathers, but I was never Jhanghir's choice."

"I can't account for his actions with other women..."

"There were no other women Maya." My heartbeat slowed. She was going to confirm the one thing I had longed for, but feared never to hear. "There was only you..."

"How... how do you know?" I whispered, refusing to believe her.

"Because he told me." Preeya turned to face me. "When he flew out to San Francisco, Jhanghir thought his father had told me about his wishes to cancel the wedding and that that was why I was upset. Before I could explain, he told me everything about your emails, and how he tried to convince his father to accept that he wanted to marry you after you had sent him your last email. Uncle Khan refused to listen and Jhanghir, being the son that he is, refused to give up trying to change his father's mind. He wanted his father's blessing..."

"But he still refused him," I finished, knowing how difficult that would have been for Jhanghir.

"He nearly gave up when he discovered that you had gone to Bangladesh to get married. Despite Uncle Khan's rejection, Jhanghir called your sister once a week, and she made your mother call you back to England."

"At which point, I rejected him," I finished, unable to meet Preeya's eyes.

"There were no other women involved, and Jhanghir didn't advise me to have a termination. In fact, he was the only one who stood by me when my family disowned me..."

"Why are you telling me this?" Preeya's silence made me look at her.

"I gave up a long while ago wishing he would forget you so that he could come to love me. Four years ago, I flirted with Mohibur hoping that would make Jhanghir realise that he wanted me. But Mohibur fell in love with me and I realised what it was to be loved. Truly loved. But I wasn't strong enough then to walk away from Jhanghir, and if I'm honest, there was still a tiny bit of me that hoped that maybe, just maybe he would fall in love with me after you refused him."

"I thought he was on the rebound," I explained, but she wasn't listening to me.

"He set the date after you told him you were going to get married. I knew that, the moment he started talking about dates. I even asked him about your wedding plans..."

"There was no wedding, I had no fiancé." Preeya chuckled and shook her head.

"That phantom guy of yours sure stirred things up!" But her smiled didn't last. "At Mohibur's sister's wedding, he was barely there. He closed up, refused to engage with anybody, hardly acknowledged me the entire weekend. I thought it was being around Mohibur that left him distracted. But it wasn't. It was you. He couldn't be here, so close to you and not see you."

"Ma'am, can I help you?" I looked at the store assistant, as Preeya asked for several pairs of size sixes to be brought for her to try on.

"Do you know how hard it is to be the second choice?" I had never thought I'd hear beautiful Preeya speak my deepest fear. "To want to be loved, but to know that you never will be, not in the way you love that person?"

"I thought I was the second choice." Preeya contemplated my answer and shook her head as if to forget her feelings for Jhanghir.

"And then Mohibur appears and showers me with attention and gifts and love." She laughed at herself. "Do you know what a revelation it is to find someone who thinks you're the most precious thing in the world?" Preeya didn't wait for an answer. "Of course you do."

"No I don't. I never had Jhanghir..."

"Yet you were always with him," she murmured. "Like a shadow he couldn't escape."

"I'm sorry." The assistant arrived with the shoe boxes and put them down in front of Preeya. "I had no idea…"

"Oh, don't feel sorry for me, Maya. I have a wonderful husband who totally adores me and that's the best feeling in the world." She was busy strapping on a pair of heels and I couldn't tell how fulfilled she was.

"Mohibur wasn't rebound for you, was he?" Preeya laughed and sauntered up and down the aisle. "Preeya?"

"I'm happy Maya, I have a man who sees me for me, someone who doesn't look through me searching for that other person…"

"Preeya, why didn't you tell him?"

"Because he didn't know he was doing it," she told me with a wide smile. "Because when I called him to tell him I couldn't go through with the marriage, he never once asked me to reconsider." Preeya sat down beside me and unstrapped the heels. She was hurting, but she refused to pity herself. I saw her in a new light.

"So why are you telling me this?" But this part, I still had to understand.

"He did nothing wrong. He tried to please everyone until his conscience failed him."

"I still don't understand. Why you are telling me this?" Preeya watched me and forced herself to speak.

"Because I love him and I want to see him happy." I thought I knew what love was until that moment. Preeya was making the ultimate sacrifice for the man she loved. She was letting him go. "You make him happy." This admission, the kindest act I had come across, brought tears to my eyes. Preeya looked away and turned to the attentive assistant. "I'll take these in the black satin and the rich bronze leather." And with that our conversation ended. My mobile shrilled to life and I pulled it out to find Leila's number.

"You had best not have sneaked off to see that scoundrel, Maya!" I answered the phone and watched Preeya walk to the counter to pay for her heels.

"I've picked up some cold drinks for us, I'll see you back in Roop Ki Ranis…"

"Don't bother, we're done here. We're walking back to the car. I think we're going to have to go across town to Green Street, there's absolutely nothing here." Leila called off and I looked up to find Preeya waiting for me.

"I have to go." Preeya nodded and I struggled to find a way to thank her. "It's nice seeing you, Maya. I hope to see you soon." She left without another word and I felt her pain. A few months earlier I had left England, feeling that I had lost Jhanghir to another woman. Now I was that woman and Preeya stood in my shoes. My mobile shrilled to life again and I groaned at my family's constant intrusion, which prevented me from sorting out my life. Still I answered the phone.

"I know you're in Ajanti's. I've spotted Preeya walking out alone. I want all the gossip, but most of all Maya, I hope you're not changing your gold heels. I know you think they're tacky but I want you all to have matching shoes. They're the only pair they had with seven pairs in storage." And so Leila went on, lost in only her wants and her needs for her wedding. I alternated between envying and hating her selfishness, but at times like this I simply loved her for making me cry tears of laughter.

We'd barely stepped through the front door before the shrieking started. And then Baba lifted me up in a rugby tackle, as I screamed with fear. Had they seen me with Preeya? Did they think I was going to run back to Jhanghir?

"I didn't do anything, but I promise I'll put it right!" But nobody paid the slightest bit of interest as I was carried into the living room with everyone screaming and dancing around a piece of card they passed around.

"Oh my God, are we going? Can we all go?" Leila took one look at the card and started to scream.

"You did it, you've done us proud!" Baba repeated over and over again as I stared in confusion, still holding on to my shopping.

"Done what?" Everyone laughed at my comment, as if I was teasing them. So I laughed along. It'd been a long time since I'd done anything right, and I wasn't going to prematurely end it by confessing it wasn't me.

"Why didn't you tell us? Why did you keep it a secret?" Amma asked rushing forward to pull me into a hug. "My daughter's going to meet a Prince! My daughter, my Maya and that's why she gave up working!" I liked Amma's style, but I was none the wiser.

"Can I come?" I faced the question over and over. I kept nodding until Amma took control.

"It says 'Invited Guests Only', and we can't take the entire kandan of fifty along!" She really was milking her position. "Maybe fifteen family members or so, that's acceptable." A debate took stock of who was most suitable to attend, as I finally grabbed the rich parched paper. The Khan-Ali Art Foundation had placed me in its 'top-ten annual newcomers' category and I was invited, with guests, to attend the ceremony at the Grovesnor Hotel in three weeks' time. I couldn't believe it. My hands started shaking and I looked up in search of Tariq. He had submitted my work without a word.

"Where's Tariq?" I shouted, looking around the crowded living room for my brother.

"I'm here." He was behind me and I jumped into his bear-hug. "Somebody had to keep your dreams alive." I laughed at his comment and gripped him hard until he shouted to be released. With Preeya's revelation and this development, I was the happiest single Bengali girl in the whole of the United Kingdom.

"I can't believe it, I can't believe they accepted my work…"

"Not just accepted it, you're in the top ten!" A cheer of support followed Tariq's comment. "And you're going to win!" Another cheer followed.

"Oh my God, what are you going to wear?" Leila cried out in horror. I dropped all my newly-acquired possessions, and together we screamed in excited delight.

T: Tandoori Nights Breed Temper Tantrums

"So, now what are you going to do with the rest of your life?" asked Baba, once Leila's wedding brigade had cleared out of our home and the hysterical ecstatic shrieks had dried up. I wonder how many times Bengali kids up and down the length of Britain had heard that question. And now I faced the question as a recently redundant, unemployed Business Art graduate, who had come in the top ten of the Khan-Ali Art Foundation. As I looked at their expectant faces, I realised I had no idea. No idea what the rest of my life would look like. Jana looked to Hana with a knowing look, Ayesha tended to Zara and Taj poured himself another mug of coffee.

"She's getting married of course!" Amma supplied, taking her place at the table.

"I meant in terms of work. Maya, what kind of job will this get you?" I looked away from the congratulations letter he held up to his wise, brown eyes. I wanted to tell him I was going to marry Jhanghir, which would make him happy. That would make everyone happy. But I had no idea how I was going to win Jhanghir back.

"No more studying, there's no point in any more studying." Baba let out a sigh of exasperation at Amma's interruptions and I skimmed the table to see if I had any allies. I caught Shireen-bhabhi frowning at Tariq and I realised that it was time to step up to Baba's expectations.

"I'm going into professional interior decoration... of restaurants, that is. Starting with Tariq-bhai's new restaurant that I'm going to invest my redundancy money in." I didn't know where that gem of inspiration had come from, but everyone looked stunned. "With my redundancy and savings, I'll have enough to invest so Tariq-bhai can buy that property in Ealing..."

"You don't have to do that," Tariq cut in immediately. "That's your money to start your life with..."

"And I'm doing that..."

"No, you're not. You're going to enrol into a good art school, and do what you're good at," Tariq finished. Amma almost dropped her teacup at the suggestion. "Who knows? Maybe you can win that art school bursary from the Khan-Ali competition..."

"Does anyone listen to me! She's not studying anymore, nobody will want an over- qualified woman as a bride..."

"Hear me out..."

"No, you're not going back to school!" Amma cut in, stopping as Baba put his hand on her arms to calm her. I realised I had Baba's total attention for the first time in my life and I couldn't fail him.

"I'm not giving away this money, I'm investing it because I know I'll get a good return and this will help me build a portfolio to start with. Tariq can save on the architect's and designer's fee because I have the training to turn your idea into a real design and I have the right contacts. I know furnishing wholesalers who've worked with all the best restaurants. And once it's up and running, I can work in the evenings to fund any further training I need." I explained with calm consideration.

"And I can get Shah to DJ on kicking nights!" Taj threw in only to freeze at everyone's dead reaction. "I mean for segregated disco nights…"

"Yeah, we can turn it into a glamorous must-be place to be in," I added. "We can host wedding receptions, theme nights…"

"Fantastic! And when do you plan on fitting in a wedding, or have you totally given up on that idea, since you reject every offer made for you?" Amma cried out before leaving the dining room with Ayesha in tow.

"With the profile I'll get from the Khan-Ali Foundation and this experience, I can do this." I insisted.

Tariq-bhai looked lost for words, but I knew – no, I felt – I was doing the right thing. It felt wonderful to start living a dream instead of just pining for it.

"And what about what your mother wants for you?" Baba's firm words burst my bubble. Jana and Hana shook their heads and left the table.

"I appreciate the thought, but that's *my* dream," Tariq muttered, reaching over to hug me, but I pulled back. "You have to start living your life."

I wanted to scream in frustration. I planned on winning Jhanghir back and starting a new life. I just couldn't tell them yet.

"Why can you take the twins' money but not mine?" I asked.

"Because they will still have their lives if I fail. You won't. I won't have that on my conscience…"

"Stop treating me as if I haven't grown up. I know what I'm doing…"

"Do you?" I stopped at Baba's calm tone that always meant he knew more than I ever would, but I still nodded. "Well, if you really want to do this, and you really want to know how glamorous it gets, I want you to do two weeks in Tariq's Marylebone takeaway. Six nights a week, evening shifts at reception with waiter salaries and no excuses." The reality of what I had gotten myself into sunk in, but I refused to back down.

"Fine…"

"This is ridiculous Baba, she can't be at reception…"

"If your sister has chosen her craft, let her graft for it," Baba insisted as Taj whistled and shook his head. I obviously missed the point of Tariq's interjection, but my credibility was on the line.

"That's suits me…"

"What suits her?" Amma asked having heard the development from bhabhi. "What is this talk about Maya working in a restaurant? Are you crazy? What will people say? Do you think any family will want a girl who works in a restaurant?"

"Starting from tomorrow night," Baba concluded, as Amma screamed and stormed out of the room. I nodded and felt proud of my stance. Tariq sighed and left. Baba followed suit. I remained in the dining room, and left to my thoughts, I started doubting my own decision.

I guess that is the advantage of having wisdom. Those who had aged with grace can see what we can't and whilst we think we're being smart, they already know the end game. By my third night, I wished Baba had told me how hard it really was.

"I ordered chicken korma not chicken tikka masala!" I stared at the well-dressed and obviously hungry businessman and waited for him to finish his tirade. "Are you listening to me!? Do you understand anything I'm saying? Why don't you just get back to your kitchen and get your mate Abdul out here?" I took the foil cartons out of the carrier bag, opened them up and emptied the contents into the bin, as the customer looked on in outrage. "That's my food you bitch!"

"Oh, now you want it?" My perfect English surprised him and I raised a brow. "Do you want me to pick it out of the bin for you because that's the only food you're going to get from this place ever again..."

"Maya, what are you doing?" Abdul cried rushing out from the kitchen.

"You want to replace her Abdul, she's bad for your business..."

"Sorry Mr Williams, she's doesn't know this job too well..."

"Abdul, don't apologise to this ignorant, sexist..."

"Ssshhh, Maya, he's a regular!" Abdul whispered, wearing a fearful frown.

"I'm a regular!" Mr Williams repeated with a self satisfied smile.

"Not any more. Abdul you are no longer allowed to serve Mr.Rude-Williams at this takeaway." Abdul looked like he wanted to die and Mr William's smile faded.

"You've had your chance Abdul. I'm taking my business elsewhere..."

"Yeah, don't forget to use that charming personality of yours elsewhere!" I called out, as he slammed out of the takeaway. My smile dropped as I found Abdul glaring at me, unable to speak his mind because his boss happened to be my brother.

"We shouldn't have to put up with that kind of behaviour..."

"You took down the order wrong..."

"He's white, what does he know about the difference between a korma and a tikka?"

"Maya, white people keep our business going, we can't afford to piss them off."

"Oh Abdul, we can choose who we serve..."

"But that's the tenth regular customer you've banned in three nights!" Abdul cried out. I looked at the skinny man and tried to empathise with his dilemma.

"Maybe we can invite a better customer base if we kicked out these rude ones..."

"Better customer bases don't take out, they dine out!" I cleared my throat at the logic and nodded. The door chime saved me from the guilt Abdul had imposed on me.

"Can I help you?" It was one of the customers I had offended on my first night.

"Evening Abdul, I'd like a pilou rice and lamb jalfrezi for two."

"I've got that," I smiled at Abdul before jotting down the order.

"That's two servings of pilou rice and lamb, not chicken, jalfrezi." I stared at the balding customer as he repeated the order slowly for my benefit.

"So, that will be two pilou rice and two lamb jalfrezi, Abdul," I mimicked to Abdul, who cried out in exasperation and raced back into the kitchen.

"That'll be eleven pounds ninety-eight." The customer looked insulted by my impersonation of him and walked out.

"Abdul?" He didn't reply from the kitchen. "Cancel that order, the customer's changed his mind."

"And Joe's definitely serious about getting back together with you?" I asked Clare, passing a new order through to the kitchen. "How apologetic is he?"

"Very! I've never seen him like this…"

"Yeah, right!" I derided, packing away the silver cartons and naans into the brown bag.

"Four naans, dhal and lamb vindaloo," I shouted, before handing the bag across to the waiting customer.

"He's not acting Maya. Apparently his mates saw me living it up in the pubs and bars, and Joe thought I was happy to be rid of him. He looks a mess, he says he's miserable without me…"

"Typical!" I blurted out in disgust. "The minute you have fun, he can't bear to live without you!"

"But I'm unhappy without him." Clare's admission stopped me and I toyed with the phone's chord. "I'm terrified Maya, I'm terrified of being vulnerable to him again." I rubbed the back of my neck, repressing the urge to advise Clare to kick her man to the curb. I had wronged Jhanghir and I was desperate for another chance to prove myself.

"No more what-if's Clare. Life's for living, give him a chance." My heart pounded at the thought and I waited at her silence.

"Maya, you're telling me to give him…"

"Yup, give Joe another chance. Tell him it's conditional on receipt of a Tiffany square-cut diamond wedding ring…"

"Maya, I'm serious!" I could hear the irritation in her voice.

"So am I." Clare's silence told me I had hit a nerve. I packed up another order. "Three samosas, pilou rice, chicken curry."

"I can't force Joe to marry me Maya!" Clare laughed as I passed the packed meal over.

"I know you want him back, I know you want to build a life together and to have his children. Do you want to be with him forever?" The door chime marked the arrival of a new customer. I handed the trendy young couple the menu and watched them discuss their choices.

"That's not the point…"

"So why are you taking him back, if it's not for the long-term?"

"You're obsessed with getting married! This is about trust Maya, rebuilding trust."

"You want some guarantee he won't do this to you again, this will protect you. If he screws up, you get to make him pay. Literally." The customer shook his head at my advice.

"You can be so cold Maya. You can't buy trust Maya..."

"Listen. I screwed up, Clare. I let my pride and ego knock back the one man I've dreamt of ever having..."

"You're talking about that guy aren't you? The one you called a 'nobody'?"

"I know what I want Clare, I would do anything for another chance." The couple were ready. I grabbed the pen and notepad. "Clare, I gotta go. Just know that if you're prepared to give him forever, expect nothing less from him."

"Hi." It was too late to stuff the Khan-Ali Competition outlines out of sight, so I looked up at Tariq and held up the papers.

"It's quite scary," I admitted as he leaned on the counter and took the documents from me. "There's so much to think about. Do I exhibit examples of my oil paintings and my pastel pieces? What should my theme be? How will I present it if I'm to have any chance at scraping into the top three of any of the three categories?"

"So you think you're going to win?" Tariq grinned as he flicked through the instructions, registrations, and outlines.

"Not in a million years! Khan-Ali winners tend to win across all the categories, I just don't want to embarrass myself by being so amateurish," I explained. "They've produced short bios of the twenty contestants on the back of the agenda, and everyone apart from me seems to be a genius..."

"Don't worry about it, you'll be judged on your work and that's all that matters." Tariq tidied up the papers and slid them back to me.

"I can't believe you sent in that female nude I did!" I laughed as I looked down at the small photo of it in the catalogue where my picture should have followed my bio.

"But your painting is amazing, Maya. All burning reds and molten oranges concealed behind a black veil. I can't figure out how you did it."

"Months, that took me months to perfect," I remembered, as I looked up at Tariq. I knew he could read my nerves.

"When I went through your work in the garage, I thought it was one of your best pieces." I smiled at him. "I just hope Amma and our aunts don't call it pornography when she sees it at the exhibition. You know they could end up collectively praying for your forgiveness."

"But you can't see anything..." I read the mischief in his eyes, and laughed at the image of their shock at the oil painting.

"You doing ok here?" I wondered whether frustrated Abdul, watching Baba or worried Amma had spoken with bhai.

"Yeah," I lied, avoiding Tariq's eyes.

"It's hard work Maya, you have to be patient and courteous. People underestimate how difficult it can be..."

"But only if you let people get away with treating you like crap." He grimaced at my attitude. "I'm fine, I can handle it."

"Don't rile my customers Maya, they keep this takeaway going." I frowned at bhai, but he held my eyes.

"I don't rile your customers, I just expect them to be polite and..." Tariq shook his head until I stopped talking.

"Look around you Maya. This is a takeaway, it's that simple. People come in here for good food to take home and enjoy." Tariq had no time for excuses.

"I know, but we can expect a little courtesy..."

"You expect the cold hard cash they hand over and for them to come back, that's it. That's your job here. Nothing more, nothing less."

"And to hell with the crappy, patronising attitude?" I couldn't believe Tariq didn't care about the way customers treated us.

"This isn't a centre for social racial behavioural studies, Maya. It's a takeaway." Tariq spoke quietly and slowly for my sake. "Unless it's physically threatening or seriously abusive, you ignore the rest..."

"No way! Some joker tried to teach me the difference between a korma and a masala, can you believe that?" He waited until I finished, but I hadn't. "I mean, didn't we bring the curry to England? I can't believe you expect me to take lessons on Bengali cuisine like that!"

"Maya, listen to me. The only thing you hear is the order customers put in, the only thing you do is hand over their meals, take their money and then wish them well in the hope that they'll come back to spend more of their money with us."

"Isn't this why we get walked over? Isn't this why every racist thug thinks they can belittle and humiliate us?" I threw back at Tariq, surprised by his priorities.

"I'm going to say this one more time, Maya." I stared at my brother. "This is not a centre for racial awareness or reform. This is my takeaway, this is my livelihood and the livelihood of every staff I employ here. I will not have you eating into my profits because the customer doesn't ask for a chicken korma in a way that panders to your standards of polite communication. Do you understand?"

"There's nothing wrong with expecting to be treated with some respect..." but I quietened down as Tariq stared at me. I understood his motives, I respected his desire to protect his business, but I struggled to accept the conditions he expected me to work under.

"If you don't like it, you know what you can do." Abdul returned from a home delivery and stopped at the tense silence between us.

"Everything ok, boss?" Tariq turned to Abdul with a broad smile and patted him on the back.

"Now it is Abdul, now it is." Tariq's intentions had been made clear. Abdul looked at me quickly, and I raised my chin defiantly. The door chimed open and a new customer walked in. Tariq and Abdul greeted the man with whom they seemed to be familiar.

"Alright darling!" I looked at the young city snapper with dead eyes and waited, knowing full well that Tariq was watching me.

"What can we do for you?" The customer chuckled and wiggled his eyebrows.

"I don't know about 'we', but I know what you can do for me!" The door chimed the arrival of his friends and they laughed at his innuendo. I waited without an inflection of emotion. "C'mon doll, crack a smile, I'm just being friendly."

"What would you like from the menu?" I handed over the small pamphlet and watched as he shifted uncomfortably at his friends' laughter. "We have our special today..."

"Tariq, you need to improve the customer service mate, a little hospitality won't go amiss here." I didn't even look at my brother.

"The kind of 'hospitality' you're after isn't on the menu..."

"Maya." I heard the warning in Tariq's tone and looked back at the grinning City twit. I had my pride.

"I've got a telephone directory here," I said, pulling out the thick directory onto the counter. "I trust you can find a number of gentlemen's clubs that will give you exactly the type of 'customer service' you're after." I ignored bhai's and Abdul's frustrated disappearance into the kitchen, and stared at the dumbstruck customers with a raised brow.

"You wouldn't let us tell you that there weren't any other women in Jhanghir's life," Tanya said as I took down a waiting customer's order and passed it through to the kitchen.

"It'll be fifteen minutes, take a seat," I told them, pointing towards the plastic seats where several other customers waited before turning my attention back to my phone conversation. "Preeya told me herself Tanya..."

"The girl's got a lot of strength, enough to make me feel bad for slating her reputation," Tanya cut in dryly.

"I felt so bad for her, because she still loves him. Tanya, I've really screwed up, somehow I've got to put it right..."

"You've fallen for him again!" I ignored her teasing comment and held the phone between my chin and shoulder.

"Shut up..."

"Admit it, you have..."

"You're really enjoying this, aren't you?" Tanya laughed away and I finally grinned. "So how am I going to get him back?"

"Excuse me, is there any chance I'll get my food before you sort your personal life out?" I stared at the smart alec, but he wouldn't leave without an answer. "Anytime today would be a good starting point!"

"Your order is..."

"Three naans with dhal and chicken korma." I shouted the forgotten order in Bengali through to the kitchen and asked for an estimated waiting time. The cook shouted back five minutes.

"You need to wait another seven minutes…"

"You said ten minutes before and it's been twelve minutes already!"

"I'll throw in a free poppadum if it takes any longer than seven minutes."
He accepted the offer, but continued to hover by the counter to watch
the clock.

"I can't believe you're still working there Maya…"

"I don't know how much longer I'll last. Tariq's given me a warning
because I offend the customers, Abdul's always shouting at me, I keep
mixing up the orders, and the customers hate me." I ignored the man's
nodding head and stared out of the glass walls onto Baker Street. "And
oh my God, I smell like a spice rack, even after sitting in a hot tub for
hours. Its in my hair, my skin and my poor, poor clothes. At this rate, I
have no chance of impressing George Clooney!"

"Maya, I hate to tell you this, but you don't have a chance regardless."
Tanya chuckled. "He isn't just going to breeze into your brother's
takeaway."

"Hey! You never know, the celeb magazines say he's going to be in
town soon to promote his new film. What are the chances that he's
going to want some Indian takeaway?" I asked with a chuckle.

"As good as zero if you're going to turn up looking the way you do as
his Indian takeaway!" Tanya threw back, as we both laughed at the
image. "What if he turns up at the hotel of your art competition?"
Several silent moments passed before we both screamed with
excitement. The man at the counter breathed out in exasperation and
turned his back to me.

"What if Maya?" Tanya asked again as I imagined several scenarios
that all ended with me being served with a restraining order.

"Don't get me distracted Tanya!" I laughed as I leaned back against the
counter. "I've got too much to do without hunting that man down at the
Grovesnor Hotel!"

"They must be working you bad if you can't make time for George
Clooney!"

"I'm so tired Tanya, it's not funny." I complained.

"So leave…"

"I can't leave, Baba will win," I stated as the customer listened in on my
conversation.

"Pack up and leave. You hate it…"

"I can't…"

"You think your dad doesn't know you hate it?" The cook called out that
the order was ready and pushed it through the window. I slipped it into
the carrier bag and handed it to the customer.

"No poppadum, but served in less than seven minutes!" He checked his
watch and didn't return my smile. "Tanya, it's not what I expected. I
clean up, check the tills, and do the figures so by the time I get to bed,
it's two or three in the morning!"

"Why can't you be normal and just leave?" The door chimed and I
looked up to see Abdul return from a home delivery.

"OK, thank you, we'll have your order ready shortly," I said, as he walked around the counter to stop in front of me.

"That was your friend again?" I shook my head and showed him the order I had taken down half an hour earlier. "I've been calling for the last ten minutes, and the line's been engaged…"

"The customer couldn't decide what they wanted…"

"Why are they always confused when you take the call?" he asked, taking the slip of paper I held out. "Whenever I take a call, they always know what they want." The phone rang again and I knew it was Tanya. Abdul raised a hand as I reached for it. I grimaced as he stepped forward and picked it up.

"Malik's takeaway," he introduced, watching me as I looked straight ahead. "No, this isn't Maryleborne Hospital, there is no Marylebone Hospital, you have the wrong number. Bye." Abdul returned the receiver to its holder before stepping back to look at me.

"Wrong number?" I asked, avoiding his eyes altogether.

"That's the third time this week, " he muttered, walking to the kitchen.

"She must be a community care patient," I offered. One look at him told me that he wasn't buying it.

It was near closing time and all orders had been tended to. Abdul, with the rest of the staff, prepared the ingredients and meals for the following day as I stared at my inbox.

"Any last minute orders?" Abdul called out from the kitchen, as I switched to the online orders that helped Tariq boost business. There were only two and my heart sank in absolute disappointment.

"Two have come through. There's an order of lamb tikka and naan to Baker Street and an order for two chicken kormas, pilau rice and raita to Lisson Grove." The combined groan from the kitchen made me grin, so I switched back to my mailbox. Monsur hadn't written since I wrote to tell him about my chat with Preeya. I had expected him to write back with dry comments about 'being lucky in love', and the merits of 'keeping hope alive', but there was nothing. I frowned and wondered if I was being insensitive to his loss. It would be about seven o'clock in the evening in Manhattan and Monsur would be hard at work keeping his diners happy. But I hoped that if he checked his email before he went to sleep, I could leave him with a few comforting thoughts. I hit the reply icon and started.

To: Monsur1@NYmail.com
From: MayaM@Instantmail.com
Dear Culinary King of Advice, I miss hearing from you, but I understand that that may be your polite way of asking for time and space. I apologise if my recent ramblings of 'what-if's', and 'how do I's' and 'can it be trues' failed to show you the sensitivity you deserve. I know you're still hurting. I know you crave, dream and still see Zina in your every

waking moment. And I know you long for the day when that empty hollow within you fills up with pure laughter and happiness.
I pray that you will love again. I wish that one day soon you will drift off to sleep with a smile on your face. But most of all I want you to have hope, because sadness in all its guises dims in the face of hope. I'm always here for you and I know I will hear from you again. Until then my friend, open yourself to life's next and enjoy every precious moment.

I had tears in my eyes as I hit the send button.

"These are ready to go," Abdul stated as he brought through the packaged meals. I switched screens and blinked away my tears.

"You want the addresses," I muttered, clearing my throat, but not before Abdul had seen my tears.

"Why don't you let me close up tonight…"

"No, I'm good," I smiled at his act of kindness. "You have kids to go home to see and I know they wait up to see you!"

"The little one can't stay up, but the other three, they come running to the front door, fighting to tell me what they did that day." I packed up some poppadums and condiments into a carrier bag. "They sit with me as I eat and then wait for me to tell them a story." Abdul added.

"I waited up for Baba every night and I loved it when he bought home poppadums for us," I told Abdul as I handed him the bag. He looked surprised and refused the bag, but I insisted. "I used to fall asleep on his knees, clutching a poppadum bigger than my face!"

"I'll come back and lock up," he offered as he took down the addresses of the customers.

"There's no need, I'll lock up. I've got the car outside, so I'll get home easily." He stared at me until he realised he had no chance of changing my mind. "I'll see you tomorrow." He rolled his eyes and laughed at the thought. I laughed too, as he walked out of the takeaway. This was a hard life, and I had more respect for my people than I'd ever had in the past. I thought about my dismissive ways, I thought about how I had tried to get as far away from my community's lifestyle as I could, and then I thought about Monsur. At one point, I had acted no differently to Zina. At one point, I thought I was better than this, and deserved more than this. What I didn't realise was this had made me who I am. I switched to my mailbox and saw that my message had been sent to Monsur. I wanted him to read it and find hope in it, but I didn't know if he would. It had been a while since I had heard from him and for some reason I doubted that I would. The truth was that I didn't know if he would ever overcome Zina's betrayal and love again, or whether he trusted himself to open up to life's next. I didn't know whether he could hear about how fate had given me another chance when fate had denied him. What I did know was that I had to win Jhanghir back. And I had to do that whilst he was still in London.

"Maya, would you go and have a shower!" Jerking awake at Leila's scream, I looked at my perma-perky cousin and groaned. "You look awful, you smell like you live in a restaurant, and I'm not taking you for a fitting in the condition you're in!"

"We're only going for a fitting Leila..."

"I can't believe you! I'm getting married this weekend and you have saddle bags beneath your haggard eyes. You're going to ruin my wedding pictures..."

"I'm exhausted, I've been up half the bloody night..."

"But you knew I had this fitting session, why didn't you get an early night?"

"I'm a working woman, I don't call the shots..."

"You just want to ruin my wedding!" Leila shouted, before bursting into tears.

"Don't start..."

"You can't stand to see me happy so you're going to ruin my wedding!" She added.

"You're mad, all the hairspray you've used is affecting your brain..."

"You're calling me brain damaged?" Leila cried, just at Amma rushed into the room.

"What an earth is going on?" Amma asked taking a sobbing Leila into her arms whilst shooting me an angry look. "This is a sensitive time for Leila, let's all try and be as helpful as we can."

"Can you tell Maya to go and have a shower so that she doesn't look like a tramp?" Open-mouthed I stared at the conspiracy against me.

"We're going for a fitting! I'm just trying on a stupid dress..."

"She called it a stupid dress!" Leila cried out between long, hard sobs, causing Chachijhi to race into the room. "She called it a stupid dress!"

"I didn't mean to call it stupid..."

"That's it Maya, you're not working until after the wedding..."

"You can't do that..."

"Leila needs all the support she can get, and you're going to make sure she gets it."

"I have a career to..."

"You're a waitress at a takeaway, and by all accounts, you're a bad one," Amma told me in a voice that tolerated no argument.

"But Baba said two weeks, with one night off..."

"You leave your father to me." Something in the way she said that told me she was giving me a way out. And her wink confirmed it. "You'll ruin your hands and your appearance working those ungodly hours. That's just not right for a woman, and I don't care a bit what you equal rights-demanding girls have to say about that!"

"But Tariq-bhai needs the..."

"Your brother's been trying to sack you since you started. He's got enough experience to find a way to fulfil his dreams. And right now I want you to help Leila fulfil hers ..."

"Why does she always get her way?" But I wasn't angry at Amma. With all the decisions I had in front of me, I needed time.

"Because I can influence you over this matter." Somehow, through all her tempers and tantrums she saw that, and she was giving me time. "I can't influence you on others, but I trust you'll use your good judgement with those." I knew Amma was talking about Jhanghir.

"No more tantrums, Amma." It was time to make things right with Jhanghir. It was time I apologised. Amma smiled and hugged Leila within an inch of her life and I knew it was because I'd have a bigger and better wedding. And that was the power of wisdom, the ability to turn a pointless tantrum into a personal victory.

U: Unexpected Unities Will Emerge

On the night before the wedding we walked through the dress-rehearsal and, as Leila's leading bridesmaid, I listened to Amma and Chachijhi debate whether or not I should lead, as it would draw attention to my single status. Whilst the debate raged and involved my sisters, aunts and cousins, I realised that the older you became, the more disturbing it was to always be the bridesmaid. Sure, as lead bridesmaid you got the best privileges, you dressed second best to the bride, and you even received thank you gifts from the glowing couple. But then you found yourself smiling the same smile, having the same conversations and telling the same jokes. And all the while, the only thought you had is that one day, just one day, you would be the bride. Up until that day, as the unemployed, cantankerous, oldest bridesmaid with far-too-much experience of other people's weddings, I spent most of the night working with the wedding coordinators to make sure every little detail of Leila's wedding was as she wanted. I didn't mind. Everyone had gathered at our home to make the most of Leila's last night as a Malik. There would be talking, laughing and non-stop eating. With the exception of Leila, who needed to rest for her 'unknown, but looming wifely duties', nobody would get any sleep. Throughout it all, I tried to ignore the fact that my life was going nowhere. Fast.

I walked into the house to find Amma and Chachijhi singing traditional Bengali wedding songs in the kitchen along with Kala and my cousins from Brighton. They sounded giddily happy and out of tune, but sang with all their hearts. I found my brothers on the Playstation in the living room, with Hamza sleeping on the floor. Abba nodded me a greeting as I looked in on the dining room where he debated Bengali politics with his counterparts. I crept out and tried to tip-toe past the kitchen.
"Take your coat off and come join us!" Chachijhi called out, bringing me to a stop.
"Let me go get changed first," I returned, making my way to the stairs.
"Maya! Leila's sleeping in your room and you know how she needs her sleep, try not to wake her." Looking back at Chachijhi, I watched her rush out of the kitchen.
"Of course," I agreed, inspite of the fact that I felt like I had no right to my life. Chachijhi gave me a warm hug before racing back to join the singing. I took the stairs, forgotten and invisible, feeling awful about feeling sad but unable to stop myself feeling like that. The bedside lamp was still on in my room, but I stepped into Amma's room and fell into her bed, exhausted. Tomorrow I would bump into the love of my life, and I would look haggard, jaded and unprepared.
"Hey." I opened my eyes to find Hana and Jana sitting on either side of the bed. I jerked up into a sitting position, convinced I had forgotten an errand.

"What have I done? What didn't I do?" But the twins shook their heads and smiled. "What's wrong?"

"Nothing," Jana answered, as Ayesha crept into the room and snuggled under the covers beside me. "We just wanted to check on you."

"We wanted to tell you that we're here for you," Jana began, as Leila walked into the room and sat at the end of the bed. "We haven't always agreed with your decisions or supported you, but we want you to know we've got your back at the wedding."

"Isn't Leila meant to be getting her beauty sleep?" I muttered, embarrassed by their concern.

"We stayed up for you," Leila said, as I felt the beginnings of a lecture, knowing that I had neither the energy nor the patience to listen.

"You know I'm really tired, I've got these awful bags and it's a big day tomorrow..."

"Maya, we were talking about you," Hana cut in, as I looked at my beautiful sister. We hadn't had a proper conversation since Jhanghir had walked out with his mother. Then I looked at Leila and realised she still wasn't happy with me being the lead bridesmaid.

"Leila, if you want me to walk beside you, I'll be there, if you want me to walk in last, I'll be right behind everyone, and if you want me to stand amongst the guests, I'll cheer as you walk by. Whatever you think is best, I'll do it, just tell me what you decide in the morning."

"I want you to be happy tomorrow." I stopped at her pitying tone. "I want you to do whatever you feel comfortable with." I preferred to be invisible and ignored rather than pitied.

"I don't want to walk in beside you, I'm too old to be the debutant, unmarried cousin." They all nodded in agreement.

"Fine," Leila accepted, as I looked at each in turn.

"I don't want to be sitting by your side on the stage as you receive the guests. It's only fair that Zarah and Mina should be there as they're next in line to get married." Needless to say, this would give me more time to spend with Jhanghir, who had been invited by a forceful Leila during our trip to Dhamini's.

"If that's what you want." Leila looked at my sisters before agreeing.

"And I don't want to wear those gold lamé heels..."

"But they match with your outfit!" I grinned as, true to her nature, Leila refused to give in on matters of appearance.

"What's this about?" I finally asked, leaning back against the bedhead.

"We know tomorrow's going to be very difficult for you," Ayesha began. "People will be asking why you're not married, whether you have any problems..."

"Some will ask you directly, others will gossip behind your back," Jana continued.

"You'll see some of the guys you rejected, many of whom may have gotten married since, others who'll still be single and smarting from your decision," Hana added.

"For example, Jhanghir and his mother will be there," Leila pointed out.

"...and we're not saying this is another chance," Jana clarified quickly. "We're just saying that it's going to be hard and that we've got your back."

Bengali family politics have no beginning and no end. Gripes are rarely understood, grudges are fiercely maintained, and nobody, but nobody is ever wrong. However, the best thing about Bengali families is that all family problems are put aside when you least expect it, and more importantly, everyone becomes united when you need it most. They were reaching out, and I knew it was time for me to meet them half way.

"I know about Jhanghir," I admitted. "The whole story..."

"Preeya told you, didn't she?" I looked at Leila and nodded. She wasn't as vacuous as she pretended to be. Then I looked to my sisters.

"I'm sorry I didn't trust your judgements..."

"We should've prepared you better," Ayesha cut in.

"And we know you were smarting after he snubbed your emails and this was payback, because you're such a hard-to-please bitch!" Jana added, as I stared at her with an outraged look. They all laughed and I grinned when Jana pulled me into a hug. "Just don't do it again!"

"He asked us not to tell you, you know." I looked at Hana in surprise and she nodded. "He said to leave you with whatever image you wanted to have of him." That sounded like him, obstinate and proud when he was angry.

"Will Jhanghir be there?"

"She's going to do it!" Leila was silenced by Ayesha's glare, but they all stared at me in excited anticipation. I cleared my throat and gathered my nerves.

"I need to put things right with him, apologise, and uh..."

"Do you want me to do that?" Hana offered, leaning forward to hold my hand. "I've spoken with Jhanghir and I can break the ice..."

"No, what if I approach him and break the ice as the oldest sister." Ayesha offered.

"But I can't do anything..."

"You're getting married," Jana reminded Leila who instantly quietened.

"We need to get him to agree before the family wedding pictures, that way he can be in them!" I watched as they excitedly discussed how they would put my life right and smiled at their enthusiasm.

"And he's bloody cute. I'm going to miss all the fun, aren't I?" We all looked at the petulant Leila before bursting out in laughter.

"It's my mess guys, I have to put it right." They quietened at my request.

"No!" Hana breathed out and I knew she was worried about my diplomacy skills. "You don't have to put anything right, you just have to agree to marrying him after we bring him round..."

"Hana, he called his wedding off with Preeya before he found out about her pregnancy." I had locked my sisters out of my life for so long that I felt awkward about revealing my feelings to them. But I was no longer afraid of their reactions, I wanted them to accept that I was their counterpart. They knew Jhanghir's story, it was long overdue for them to learn about mine. So I told them everything. I told them about the incident four years ago, about my emails, my failed trip to New York and my heartbreak at Jhanghir's rejection. I explained why I was so bitter when I saw him on my return from Sylhet. And as Ayesha and Leila wiped away their tears, I told them how Preeya had revealed to me how wrong I had been about everything.

"You plank," whispered Hana, as she shook her head before looking at Jana.

"But you didn't say anything," Jana said with a frown.

"Because everything I did went wrong. I always messed up." My excuse seemed pathetic compared to the pain I saw in my sister's eyes. "You guys never mess up, you're always perfect and I can never do any right…"

"We could've helped you," Jana insisted as I shook my head. "We can still help."

"Maya, we want the best for you, we can make it easier for you…"

"The easiest thing to do would be to allow you to mend the bridges for me, but how ungracious does that make me?" I countered.

"But he loves you, he'll forgive you…" Everyone looked at Leila and then ignored her. "Just promise me there won't be any spectacles or tears that will ruin my wedding pictures." We carried on ignoring Leila.

"I want him to hear it from me. He deserves that much after everything I've done."

"And what if it isn't enough?" Ayesha asked, but I could only shrug and smile.

"Then we wade in and force him to reconsider," Jana stated, grinning widely. "There's no way on God's earth he's going to turn our baby sister down!"

"Enough of the 'baby'!" I laughed as Jana pulled me into a bear hug.

"You lot are going to ruin my wedding, aren't you?" Leila realised in fear.

"No, we're finally going to sort out Maya's life." Hana laughed.

"But you're going to remember that it's my big day." I watched as my sisters teased Leila no end about her big day. But I caught her eyes and, ring or no ring, we both knew it was as much my day as it was hers.

Five hundred guests changed the conservative Holland Park Hilton into a myriad of Eastern colours and flavours as classic Indian music floated through the magical day. The hall was transformed into an Indian palace, with billowing silk canopies, and huge ice sculptures at every vantage point. Cousins Zarah and Mina led the rest of us bridesmaids into the flashing of bulbs and the whirring of cameras as we walked Leila into the hall. I felt my heart open up with joy as I imagined my own entrance in the not-too-distant future. For once, I did not dread the attention. Today, I would prove every whispering, gossiping, SLAAG derider wrong. I straightened up to my full height to make the most of my bronze silk diamante inlaid mermaid skirt and ornate Nehru jacket. I revelled in the attention, grinning stupidly as we walked through the hall and onto the stage where Leila was formally received. Once on the stage and standing behind the golden chaise, I searched for Jhanghir among the guests.

"Maya, put your head scarf on!" Jana whispered, as the Imam began the holy prayer. I pulled the bronze gauze over my sixties-inspired chignon and lowered my gaze enough to appear respectable, but I still searched for Jhanghir. I scanned the crowds until I caught the attention of Jhanghir's mother. I dropped my gaze into one of solemn concentration so that she wouldn't think I was brazen. However each time I looked up, there she was, looking straight at me. I listened as Leila exchanged vows, and then cheered with the guests at their union.

"Time to mingle," Jana told me purposefully. My sisters had released me from all my duties and replaced them with the duties of chief hostess. This meant I had to greet, chat and ensure that all the guests were having a good time. It was also a role that would force me to chat with Jhanghir, without being too obvious. I circled the floor with confidence, surprising my detractors with my friendly but steely attitude.

"It'll be you next!" I heard.

"Oh, you haven't got the invite?" I replied and watched as they floundered in a state of uninvited embarrassment. "Must go!" I called out before they could wrangle one.

"We can't wait for your wedding." my critics told me with calculated sincerity.

"You won't have to." They looked at me in confusion, angry that they hadn't been told of any developments.

"Who is he?" I locked my lips in false secrecy.

"What does he do?" I shrugged and giggled at their thirst for detail.

"When's the date?" I saw Jhanghir's mother turn and raise an eyebrow in interest. My false bravado shrivelled up and disappeared into nothingness.

"I can't possibly say," I breathed out, before greeting Mrs Khan.

"You look beautiful, Maya." Her warm compliment surprised me. "Are congratulations in order?" I looked back at the watching women, before returning my gaze to the elegant woman in front of me. She looked out of place amidst my Sylhethi people. My people were proud, but looked like they had grafted something out of nothing. Mrs Khan, on the other hand, looked like she had been born into a life of luxury and expected little else. I shook my head and heard the smirks of laughter behind me. She caught the interchange too, but I cleared my throat.

"Thank you for coming, Leila'll be very pleased you made the effort." I tried to speak Bengali with a Dhakayan accent, but even to my ears, it sounded awful.

"Jhanghir sends his apologies…"

"Oh, uh, right." We had spent hours rehearsing what I would say and how I would apologise, and now that all counted for nothing. I tried not to appear disappointed, but I was lost for words.

"He wanted to come, but he had other matters to see to." Mrs Khan spoke in English for my benefit and I forced a smile for her sake. "He has an important seminar to present on Monday, and his team came across a new development that they have to account for…"

"I understand," I smiled and nodded, needing to get away to compose myself. "Well, thank you for coming, and… and I hope you have a good time." I picked up the trail of my fitted mermaid lengha and quickly walked away.

"Maya!" Chachijhi intercepted my escape strategy and I stopped to look at the young man she had netted for my consideration. "This is Nasim, he's a lecturer at Islington College. I wanted to introduce him to you because he likes reading books about art." In sympathy, I smiled at the poor, balding, middle-aged man with the rather trendy Buddy Holly-type glasses. "When I found out about his love for art, I said 'you must meet Maya', and when I say must, I mean he will!" We all laughed at Chachijhi's humour, but I looked back at Mrs Khan as she wandered alone among unknown faces. I needed to know if Jhanghir would come to the walimah the following weekend, but more importantly I owed her an apology.

"So what do you say Maya, how does dinner sound?" I looked back at Chachijhi and then to the expectant, but silent, Nasim.

"Dinner?"

"Yes, well, you have so much in common!" Chachijhi blustered, as I checked on Mrs Khan again. My people didn't take to her kind at all, through no fault of our own. Dhakayans had always used their intellect to make Sylhethis feel inferior, and whilst Sylhethis were more hospitable, no-one was reaching out to make her feel welcome. I couldn't stand to see her drifting by herself.

"Maya, pay attention!" Chachijhi muttered, covering her irritation with a forced grin. I looked apologetically at Nasim.

"I'm sorry, I can't do dinner." I watched Chachijhi's smile fall. "Excuse me." I whispered before making my way around the tables and past familiar guests back to Mrs Khan. She saw my return and waited.

"I'm sorry." My long, meaningful, deeply, regretful apology appeared in the two word form. "I was judgemental and wrong, and, and…" I was flustered, trying to find the right words for Mrs Khan to understand how sorry I was.

"I'm sorry too, Maya." Her sincere tone told me that I was too late. I frowned at her words.

"I was hurt, not that that's an excuse, but I was wrong to offend you, both of you, in the way that I did." I continued.

"I see that now." Mrs Khan took my hands and looked directly at me. "But you've deeply offended Jhanghir, enough for him to ask his father to introduce him to his colleague's daughter." I looked away from her concerned gaze.

"Is that where he is today? I mean as well as preparing for his seminar?" Mrs Khan nodded at my realisation and I felt the sting of tears. "Will you pass on my apologies to him? Let him know that I know I made a mistake?" But Mrs Khan shook her head and pulled her hand away.

"He'll call me a 'meddling mother'," she explained pulling out her mobile phone from her Gucci handbag. Her remark annoyed me. I waited as she made a call to say that she was ready to leave and then she finished her call. "It'll sound better coming from you."

"I, uh, but where do I find him?" I finally asked, conceding to her authority on the matter.

"He's staying at the Olympia Hilton. Room 442. If you to find him, he's here for the Childhood Diseases Conference." I nodded in gratitude, stopping when she reached out to hold my face. "Don't make me regret this." In that instance, I realised her purpose for attending the wedding. A mother protected her own, even if it went against her own interests. And that's what Mrs Khan was doing. She was reaching out to me. I smiled hesitantly before nodding, and read her support before she turned away to leave.

"Maya, we heard you're getting married!" The sarcastic comment came from my regular detractors, and I turned to face them with a brilliant smile. Ugly Shapna and super slim Piara had dressed in brilliant red saris and had on far too much make-up. Nonetheless, they were married to rich husbands who afforded them a more than comfortable lifestyle, a fact they never let me forget.

"What took you so long to find out!" I waited around long enough to watch their smiles falter before waltzing past them.

"You mean it's actually true?" I saw Chachijhi beckon me with another poor fool she had netted and turned to walk in the opposite direction.

"You mean you haven't got the invite?" Shapna and Piara were on my heels and when I stopped they walked into me. I looked at each in turn.

"You mean to tell me, you haven't received an invite?"

"Maya Malik, you would not dare get married without us! How long have we known you? I mean, we're close enough to be sisters!" I grinned at the earnest explanation and shook my head. As I said, in Bengali families unity came when you least expected it.

V: Valuing Vanities And Virtues

As soon as Leila left with her groom for their three-day honeymoon in Venice, I called Jhanghir at the Hilton and left a message for him to return my call.

"Has he called yet?" Hana asked, as we took the groom's family the first post- wedding breakfast. But he didn't call. Not that night, or the following day.

"He's probably busy with the conference," Jana explained, as our parents greeted Abdul Raquib's family. "He'll call as soon as he's got a spare moment, probably at lunch."

But Jhanghir didn't call. Throughout the day, we received a never-ending stream of guests to support the near-mourning Chachijhi who had finally given away her daughter after wanting to get rid of her for so long. I was back on door duty, greeting guests and taking their coats before showing them in. Every time the phone rang, my heart rate went into overdrive as I ran to answer it. Not that it mattered, since it was never Jhanghir. But then Hamza appeared with the phone and I grinned as I took it from him.

"Hello?" I was nervous, excited and anxious at all once and I longed to hear his voice.

"Maya, it's me." It was Ayesha and I felt like a prize plank. "Has he called?"

"He might've, I don't really know. I've been busy with all the guests and everything."

"Right." She didn't buy a word of my explanation. "Jana, Hana and I have closed the clinic on Monday, we're going to spend it with you..."

"But what about your patients?" I couldn't spend an entire day being pitied.

"We've deferred most of the appointments and have an on-call locum to cover emergencies. We've got to have our beauty treatments and go shopping for your award ceremony because none of us have anything to wear."

"Oh my God." The award ceremony was only three days away. "I've got to be at the Grovesnor Hotel tomorrow morning to set up my exhibition..."

"Even better, we cover the clinic in the morning and shop in the afternoon," Ayesha continued. "We've decided Western shalwaar kameez, sixties inspiration, is that ok with you?" I agreed, but already dreaded finding anything suitable at such a late moment.

"How many of us are going?" Ayesha asked reluctantly.

"I've got to blag three more tickets from the organisers. It's fifteen at the last count." I answered with dread as Ayesha laughed at the figure.

"I'm not forcing the issue Maya, but have you thought of giving a ticket to Jhanghir?"

"He's not even taking my calls..."

216

"How many times have you called?" I bit my bottom lip and closed my eyes.

"Once."

"And what did you say?" Really, this was far too intrusive, but Ayesha knew me too well.

"I asked him to return my call." I revealed reluctantly.

"No reason as to why you called?" I didn't answer and Ayesha sighed. "Maya, I spoke to his mother at the wedding before she left and she told me he's under immense pressure to present the latest findings of his research programme as well as generate further funding. That means he's at seminars, round table meetings and sponsor dinners… Do you understand?"

"Did you put in a good word for me with his mother?" I asked hopefully.

"Maya, he flies out this week. If you want to put things right, if you really want a chance with Jhanghir, you've got to fight for it."

"Hi, I'm here to see Dr. Jhanghir Khan." I grabbed the car keys after Ayesha's call and headed straight for the Hilton in Olympia.

"A Doctor?" The receptionist looked at me with disdain and I knew I should have changed out of my baggy, plain, shalwaar kameez.

"Dr. Jhanghir Khan, I believe he's staying in Room 442" I told the receptionist in a loud, slow voice, refusing to be belittled on the basis of my appearance.

"Right, I'll be a moment." I waited as the perfectly groomed receptionist called up. She stared at me with the phone in her hand. "And you are?" The patronising tone rankled my nerves. I resisted the urge to pat my hair into place or apply a cover of lip gloss.

"Dr. Maya Malik." Her expression changed immediately, and I raised a brow at her presumptuous behaviour.

"Dr. Jhanghir, we have a Dr. Malik in reception for you." She put the phone down.

"He's not in," I assumed as the receptionist returned to the counter. "Do you have any idea what time he'll return?" The receptionist shook her head and looked at me with a blank expression. "Right, well, I'll just wait in the lobby." She turned away before I could finish. I found the washroom and smartened myself up. I regretted leaving the house on an impulse. My loose shalwaar kameez drowned me with its bland shapelessness, and my hair needed a good wash and blow-dry. I salvaged what little I could with lip-gloss, and pinched my cheeks red before returning to the lounge. The first half hour passed quickly, as I stared at the traffic heading for Kensington High Street through the glass walls. The following hour dragged. I stared down at the ticket and wondered if he would appear. I frowned, refusing to think otherwise. I refused to think at all. I watched hotel guests breeze in and out through the big circular door, before boredom forced me to buy the latest copy of *Heat*. I checked with the sour-faced receptionist if Jhanghir had arrived in my brief disappearance from the lobby. He hadn't, so I returned to my seat to finish reading the celeb magazine. Over the next hour, staff shifts changed and I watched 'Sour Face' disappear.

"Excuse me." A small Filipino receptionist turned to me. "I'd like to leave this for Dr. Jhanghir Khan in Room 442..."

"You waited all day for him." The bright announcement came with a brilliant smile that made me feel stupid. "You sure you no wait much longer?"

"No, if you could just hand this to him when he arrives..."

"Oh, so you're an artist!" The Filipino woman stared at my ceremony invitation and I wondered if she had heard my request. "But I thought you were a doctor?"

"I am - of art." I lied, as she read through the details of the invitation.

"But not a real doctor, like George Clooney in ER?"

"No, not like George Clooney in ER," I agreed, as she looked at me. "Could you give this..."

"I heard you, I heard you!" she trilled with a laugh, slotting the invitation into an envelope. "I'll give this to Dr Khan, don't worry." I waited long enough to see her write down Jhanghir's name before leaving.

I left my car in Olympia and took the bus down to Trafalgar Square where I made the short walk across to the National Portrait Gallery. I didn't understand why Jhanghir wouldn't return my call, if only to tell me to leave him alone. Why did men do that? Why don't men understand that one call, albeit to dash away any lingering hope of a reconciliation, is more preferable than silence? Although this may on the face of it appear to protect our feelings, it really and truly gives them a permanent escape from any 'difficult' situations. But most of all, I didn't understand how men could disappear, in the way Jhanghir had, when you were ready to give them what they wanted. What had Tanya said? Egos, God-given tool, and then logic. I had refused to believe that all men were the same, but the more I experienced the more I discovered what drove them. I walked through the late-Victorian period section, until I stared at her: Lady Campbell. The exquisite Lady Campbell. I knew nothing about her, except that Giovanni Boldini had painted her reclining in a black satin dress. The oil painting was dark, the flower on her dress and the tinge on her lips were the only colour to break up the painting. But it was her eyes and the tilt of her lips that arrested you. They told you she was in control. In the subtlest, calmest way, she was always in control. I wondered what her story was. How many suitors had she captivated? How many hearts had she broken? But above all, I wondered if she had mastered the mystery of what drove men? The tilt of her lips suggested that she had, but that didn't seem to matter. It seemed as if she wasn't afraid of life, with all its uncertainties and insecurities. She was confident. Assured of herself. I smiled as I remembered Nani. I remembered the freedom of conquering my fears and doubts and heartaches. I remembered what it felt to care about what I could control. Maybe I had lost Jhanghir. Maybe it was too late.

Maybe I had to start from scratch. But I had a lot to live for. Lady Campbell told me that, and for now, that was all that mattered.

"I'm here for the Khan-Ali Art Foundation Exhibition," I announced after the grey-haired uniformed receptionist finally chose to give me his attention. "The art exhibition…"
"Yes ma'am, but that's not until Wednesday. And today is Monday." I frowned at the patronising tone all receptionists seemed to be born with. Did they have some innate ability to smell wealth and privilege or estimate how much respect to give a person based on their salaries? As a Consultant, I had breezed in and out of five star hotels without a second thought, and now they could tell I wasn't a guest, and therefore a 'nobody'.
"I know, I'm one of the artists, Maya Malik. I'm here to exhibit my work," I said, noticing the chipped gold nail varnish manicure I had worn for Leila's wedding. I clenched my hands to hide their undignified appearance, but I was too late. He had caught the gesture before he turned to check his computer.
"Ah, the induction meeting, but you're late." Refined Terry shook his head at my tardiness. "You should be in Meeting Room 5." He said that as if I knew the Grovesnor Hotel well.
"Directions would be useful?" I asked as the wealthy booked in all around me.
"Take a right just through here, right again until you see a stairway. Take the stairs up, then it's right until you arrive at Meeting Room 5." I thanked Terry, then raced towards my destination. Not that it did me any good. Finding the meeting room amidst the rabbit-warren of rooms meant I became lost in an instant. After three requests for directions, I burst into the room, which was filled with my competitors and representatives from the Khan-Ali Art Foundation. I murmured an apology before making my way to a vacant chair. The competition had three categories: Best Painting, Best Newcomer and Overall Winner. Though I had been nominated for the second category, my work would be considered for the other two categories. I looked around the room at my twenty-odd attentive peers and knew that there was no way I'd ever win the competition.

After two sessions outlining the objectives of the Foundation, the competition and judging process, the exhibition, and the awards, we paused for a coffee break. I remained in my seat and watched the competition make their way to the coffee area. I felt like a fake; that at some point the organisers would realise that they had made a mistake in selecting my piece, and would ask me to leave. I felt out of place amongst my peers and sought out the restrooms to retreat to. There I found ladies of leisure touching up their make-up in the sumptuous rooms filled with dressing tables, ornate mirrors and tasteful Molton Brown toiletries. With a wry smile, I looked at the Khan-Ali Foundation pack. There was a welcome note, followed by instructions, an artist's entry tag, a schedule of events and an outline of the prizes for the competition. I looked at the awards list and read through the list. The overall winner would receive a comfortable prize of twenty thousand pounds and an autumn show at the Khan-Ali Art Galleries in London and New York. I looked for the prize given to the winner of the Best Newcomer category and sighed over the traineeship as a curator at the Khan-Ali Art Gallery in New York. That would be a dream. I skimmed over the runner-up prizes, which ranged from being given artist coverage in the Foundation's magazine to hundreds of pounds worth of art products and materials. Realising that the sessions would have commenced, I stuffed the documents back into the jacket cover and raced back to the meeting room.

"...the artist who fails to appreciate the importance of time." I didn't want look at the speaker I had walked in on and disturbed, but I peeked up with an apologetic smile.

"Some say only an artist understands the true meaning of time." I returned.

"And the artist seems to be a wise ass." I couldn't pretend to be invisible as my fellow competitors filtered back to their seats holding coffee cups and biscuits. The speaker stood before me and though he had all the demeanour of a mature playboy, I couldn't place his origins.

"And who might you be?"

"Somebody who now has no chance of winning, right?" The speaker exploded into booms of laughter.

"That's good!" he said between spurts of laughter, as he caught sight of the prize list I had reviewed. "You seem particularly taken with the competition's rewards."

"I didn't know how good the prizes were." The contestants behind me sniggered at my naiveté, and I promised myself I would keep quiet from now on.

"And you're particularly pleased with…?" The speaker refused to let me blend into the background. I skimmed through the list of prizes.

"First prize of course! The chance to show your work at a proper gallery, that's pretty amazing. I think the special prize is really interesting, in that it would probably be the most productive training artists can get. So I guess that they'll want someone really good and I'm not saying that that's me at all, but seriously, this is an amazing deal. It's like winning the lottery for artists." I stopped talking because I sounded like a kid with a new toy. I put the piece of paper down and renewed my promise to remain quiet.

"So Ms Nobody, do you have a name?" The speaker hadn't forgotten me and I knew that with my name acknowledged I had no chance of winning.

"Maya Malik. And you would be?" I asked, looking up with my chin jutted forward. When those around me gasped, I already knew.

"Isaac Khan-Ali, Chief Executive of the Khan-Ali Art Foundation."

"So what happened next?" Jana cried, taking another serving of chicken vindaloo. We were waiting for Ayesha and Hana to join us at Kebabish on the Ealing Road.

"What's the point?" I muttered still agonising over my deplorable introduction to the founder. "Can you eat that when you're pregnant?" I asked Jana.

"Shut up! I've been craving a vindaloo since Leila's wedding, but you're bloody brother-in-law refuses to make me one. The lousy, good-for-nothing, rotten..."

"Jana, your child is eating a vindaloo right at this moment." She was in the first trimester of her first pregnancy. Whilst we were overjoyed at the prospects of having a new Malik added to the family, her pregnancy wasn't common knowledge.

"If it's a boy, it'll make him a man and if it's a girl, I'll bloody well make sure she knows how to cook a good vindaloo!" Something had obviously happened to her senses and as she looked dangerous, there was no way I was going to stop her.

"Your mother-in-law would have a fit if she saw you now..."

"She doesn't know yet," Jana told me between mouthfuls. I stared at her until she looked at me, ready to give me more details. "We decided against telling her because she'd announce it to the Gants Hill Bengali community and it's too early for that..."

"But it's her grandchild, surely she..."

"Surely nothing! This is my first baby. I'm not putting it under any family or community scrutiny before I get through the first trimester," Jana explained before grinning. "And seriously, do you think we could manage any more celebrations at this point?"

"You know Baba and Amma would take on your in-laws to throw a party!" We both laughed at the thought, and then she looked at me.

"Jhanghir hasn't returned your call yet, has he?" I shook my head, feeling embarrassed and unwanted. "Do you want me to try?"

"Can you imagine how that would look?" She laughed with me.

"I'm older than you, I don't need your permission to do what I think is right!" I warned her off and she teased me until we both felt bad that Jhanghir hadn't called. "You're not going to give up are you?"

"I don't want him to take out a court order against me for stalking!" But Jana didn't laugh along with me.

"Are you?" she repeated.

"I've called, I waited hours for him at his hotel. I left him an invite to the Khan-Ali Art ceremony. Don't ask me to do anymore." I asked quietly.

"Ayesha said that he's really busy Maya..."

"You don't have to make excuses for me..."

"I'm not, I'm just telling you not to give up..."

"I'm not giving up, I'm just giving him time to come to me." Jana assessed me and for the first time ever, simply accepted my decision. Curbing all my silent fears about Jhanghir, I held her eyes. When she nodded and returned to her meal, I breathed out, relieved at finally being listened to. "So what happened next at the Grovesnor Hotel?" I groaned, holding my head in despair.

"We each had to talk about our submitted piece in turn, and I had nothing to say…"

"Nothing?" Jana paused to look at me in disgust.

"Well, as good as. I just said I love sunsets and the play of sunsets on people's appearances." Jana almost gagged on her food. "I know, corny. But the others are all real artists, they talked about their inspiration, their favourite artists, abstract expressionism and, and… by the end of it, I knew I didn't belong there."

"Hey, you're in the competition because you're good," Jana pointed out. "Not because you can bore everyone to death talking about the Renaissance period or the emergence of Surrealism…"

"They even dress like artists, all angst and un-coordinated with weird, funky hairstyles. They're all so fresh out of art school and so ambitious, I feel so old and square." Jana laughed at my description. "I have to find two or three other pieces to support my central piece, but I don't have two or three other pieces that are good enough…"

"Well you must be one shite artist if you've only ever produced one good piece."

"That's not what I mean, I don't belong to any one school of art. I love modern art but I hate conceptual art, I don't like Gaughin, I think Turner's bland, I love Cezanne and Opie and Rothko…"

"Ignore all that bullshit, that's you trying to be pretentious and it doesn't work." I stared at my sister and understood why she was respected. It was because she didn't mince her words. "Bloody, what's his name, the sunflower man…"

"Van Gogh?" I supplied.

"Do you think bloody Van Gogh did these 'deep and meaningfuls'? He cut off his bloody ear because he was loopy and inspired and his passion moved him enough to drive him loopy. That's art and that you can't explain." Jana poured the last of the vindaloo on to her rice. "Don't you dare apologise for your feelings. If the sunset influenced you, then say the sunset moved you, but let your art do the talking for you." I wondered if the vindaloo gave Jana her all consuming passion. I picked up a fork and took a mouthful.

"What are you doing?" Jana cried, as I gulped down water to cool the fire in my mouth.

"But I'm no Van Gogh," I breathed when the fire relented.

"Neither was Van Gogh, until people recognised a Van Gogh." Jana reading my confusion, put her fork down. "What makes a vindaloo different from a jalfreezi? The ingredients are similar, they're both Indian dishes, and though the spices differ, how do we know one from the other?" I began to understand where she was taking her analogy.

"They have a label and that's why we know they're different."

"I'm an unknown artist Jana, barely that…"

"Only a cook knows what he's using for his masterpiece, but one thing's guaranteed and that's that some diners will hate it and some will love it. You're not a diner Maya. You're the cook and your only job is to present your best creations."

Once Ayesha and Hana turned up, we tried Dhamini's, Season's, Menhdi's and Punjab's. And whilst each of my sisters found themselves a classic outfit with shoes and accessories to boot, I was left empty-handed with not a stitch to wear. I wondered what Isaac Khan-Ali would think if I decided to greet the judges and invitees buck-naked. My smile disappeared when I remembered that most of my family in England would be attending.

"You found nothing," Amma stated, as we piled into the house and filed through to the kitchen. "How could you all buy something and leave Maya without a single piece?"

"She's too fussy!" Hana muttered, walking straight to the fridge to pull out a carton of mango juice. "If it's not too Western, it's too bud, if it's not too long, its too short. Either her bust looks too flat or her butt looks massive. There's no pleasing your youngest daughter!" Hana handed out the glasses and I took mine whilst checking the phone for any messages.

"We got you a sari with matching blouse and accessories, " Ayesha said, handing Amma the gift wrapped box from Punjab's.

"Did you remember to buy Shireen something?" Jana pointed to one of the bags and Amma shook her head at the expense. "But Maya still doesn't have anything."

"Maya looked lovely in the shimmering sari from Variety Silk House, but she said it was too expensive..."

"And before you scream at us, we offered to buy it for her," Ayesha pointed out. "But she refused, saying it was obscenely expensive."

"Oh Maya!" Amma cried shaking her head. "You deserve to treat yourself."

"Did you take any calls for me Amma?" I asked, avoiding everyone's eyes as I checked the pots and pans.

"Sakina called. She said to call her to let her know what to wear on Wednesday. Clare said she's taking off a day to be at the Grovesnor Hotel with John." I looked at Amma and waited. "And Tanya rang to check how your morning went."

"Your sari's beautiful mom," I told her as I grabbed an apple and headed out of the kitchen towards the garage.

"Maya?" She seemed concerned by everyone's silence and I stopped to look back at her. "Is everything ok?" She deserved to know, but I didn't want to wallow in self-pity. If Jhanghir refused to answer my calls or even acknowledge me, then I had to accept his decision and focus on the good aspects of my life.

"I need to pull out two or three more pieces if I'm to have any chance of winning. I won't be long." She nodded, unconvinced, and I looked at my sisters confident that they would honour my decision to stay quiet.

"Don't be too long. Remember we've got everyone booked into RCK Beauticians for seven," Ayesha said as I headed out to the garage. But for the moment, I passed the furniture and sealed boxes to get to my work; I was lost to time. I uncovered my paintings and surveyed them. One by one, I assessed each work of art. I checked through my oil on canvas paintings, the poor replicas of Reubens' oil on plywood experiments, and then my favourite pastel portraits and landscapes. I pulled out large canvasses and small pastel boards to assess what theme I could use to compliment my veil-obscured female nude oil painting. I made mental notes about mounts and positioning, and deselected certain paintings only to re-select them. Before long, I had a dozen pictures propped up in different parts of the garage. I imagined each piece under different lighting and on different mounts until I stared at five short listed pieces. They were vibrant, striking and rich in colour. I wondered how I could have given up the brilliance of colour for the mundane greys, navy blues and blacks of city folk.

"Maya, it's time to go!" I looked through the window at the main house from where Ayesha called me and held up my hand. "No, not in five minutes, everyone's ready and we're leaving now." She disappeared into the house and I stared back at my work. This was my life. Always chaotic, uncontrolled and interrupted. I shook my head and began walking back to the house, promising myself that I would return to the garage. I stopped and smiled.

"Life!" I breathed out just before entering the house.

"About time!" Amma muttered, putting on her head scarf as she walked with me to the car. Life. That was my theme, that would be my exhibition and this was my life.

But to have a shot, I had to give myself every advantage, which began with looking and dressing the best. Hana had booked us all a total body work over at RCK Beauticians, so that we could spoil ourselves to our hearts' content. And my heart was contented soon enough. After I had been waxed, soothed and oiled into smoothness, I was vanity incarnate.

"You're having your hair done next," Jana said, as I gave her my place before walking across to the hair care section. Such self-indulgence was simply divine! Amma sat leafing through Asian magazines with a myriad of tin foil on her head and as I took a seat beside her, one look warned me against making any sassy comments.

"This is going to cost a fortune…"

"Your father's a proud man, and you've made him very happy, Maya. He insists you treat yourself so that you can enjoy yourself," Amma said as I looked at her. "You've worried us both recently. You have sadness in your eyes." I looked away not wanting to think about the empty longing within me.

"It's tiredness Amma, so much has happened with the wedding, and this..."

"You don't have to pretend with me." I caught her eyes and immediately regretted it. I didn't want pity or compassion. I didn't want to admit I had failed.

"It's out of my control Amma."

"You're a good girl Maya..."

"Baba calls me his 'royal headache'," I pointed out, eager to change the topic.

"And he's right! And you do make him laugh when you get going, but believe you me he wouldn't have you any other way." I laughed with Amma, but I looked straight ahead when the hairdresser arrived and started finger-combing my hair back.

"I just want it trimmed and blow-dried, but could I see how that Julia Robert's chignon looks on me?" The hairdresser nodded and tested the weight of my hair before telling me to sit straight and very still.

"What will you be wearing Maya?" The hairdresser asked as she twisted my hair back to assess what it would look like.

"I'm not too sure..."

"She's wearing a nude tone sari." I turned to Amma in surprise and winced when the movement pulled my hair from the hairdresser's hands.

"You got me the silk sari from Variety Silk House..." I stopped as Amma shook her head.

"Your father took Ayesha to buy it for you." Tears stung my eyes and I was lost for words. Amma reached over and wiped my tears. "Artists may enjoy looking like unemployed tramps, but no daughter of mine is going to the Grovesnor Hotel in ripped clothes." I burst out laughing at her comment and leaned over to hug her. I caught Ayesha watching us from the massage chair and grinned.

"You got me the sari?" I called out as Amma laughed at my delight.

"Baba got you the sari." She told me.

"Baba got me the sari, he got me the sari!" I shouted dancing across the tiles floor to Hana and Jana who peeled back their cucumber slices to look at me. "I got the sari, the beautiful one, I got the sari!" I said, leaning over between them. "Jhanghir's not going to know what's hit him!" I whispered to my sister who groaned and laughed at the same time. "You watch me! With a little help, I am going to be so ravishing he's going to come to me on his hands and knees!"

"Focus on the competition, you don't want to be a drop dead gorgeous loser, albeit courtesy of great make-up," Hana said dryly, curbing a cheeky smile before replacing the cucumber slices over her eyes and leaning back to relax. My smiled faded. I turned to Amma and slowly walked back.

"Hana stop teasing your sister!" Amma chastised, reading the panic in my eyes. "You're going to look beautiful Maya and you're going to win!" But it was too late. The doubts had set in. What if I went to all that trouble only to end up losing in front of everyone I loved? What if I let Baba down after all that he has done for me? But there it was. That beast called hope. The beast that misled everyone.

"Will you be very disappointed if I don't win?" I asked Amma as the hairdresser gave up on me sitting still and moved on to Amma.

"Oooph be gentle, I'm an old lady!" Amma winced pulling away from the hairdresser. "There's no way you're going to lose in that three-hundred pound sari with your entire family watching." I had tried to reign in everyone's expectations. I had told everyone that there were better artists than me and that I had only the slimmest chances of winning. I stared at Amma, feeling the cold fear of pressure. "Given that half the family don't understand English and the other half will be blown away by the setting, if you don't win, just run up on to the stage and hug one of the winners. They won't be any the wiser!" I stared at Amma for a millisecond before bursting into laughter, before long she joined me.

Taj had taken the day off to help me set up my canvasses in the Grovesnor Hotel. Whilst he was dressed in his designer casual best for the location, I turned up in jeans and a mini dress, much to Terry, the receptionist's, disdain.

"Ms Malik," he greeted me as I stopped at reception to rest my canvass.

"I need directions to get to the exhibition." Terry looked to Taj who was on his mobile trying to convince Shah he'd just seen a Juventus footballer. "He's with me, he's my assistant."

"Of course," Terry agreed checking his computer. "Two rights down the same corridor, take the stairs on your left down and you'll be at the ballroom." I was about to leave, but hesitated.

"I'm not the first one, am I?" Terry shook his head and I grimaced.

"The first one arrived at sunrise," he offered, putting my attendance into perspective. I was already behind, but I refused to panic.

"But I'm the best dressed one, right?" A Versace-cloned lady paused while checking in to stare at me.

"It would be improper of me to comment ma'am." I winked at Terry and the aghast lady. Terry almost cracked a smile as I grinned before leaving the reception hall. I led Taj through to the ballroom. I walked into what looked like a work factory. Mounts, canvasses, materials, tools, and easels were scattered at every vantage point.

"You've finally decided to turn up." One of the Mr Khan-Ali's 'suits' appeared at the entrance. "I take it that you've brought the extra pieces?" The condescending smirk told me I needn't have bothered, but I nodded.

"Where do I go?" The 'suit' grinned and I knew I had been assigned the worst position in the ballroom. I looked around the hall and found the only unclaimed spot where a lonely, packaged canvass lay at the furthest corner of the room.

"Back of the hall on the right side, just before the stairs..."

"Can't she put her paintings up by the stage?" Taj asked, finally ending his call.

"As you can see Mr..."

"Malik," Taj supplied, misunderstanding that his presence was not welcome.

"Mr. Malik, the more conscientious and competitive artists have staked their positions early. It really was a matter of first come, first served," 'The Suit' explained. "But don't worry, the judges will circulate each exhibit and consider them individually."

"That's bullshit Maya, you're at the back and they'll see your work last," Taj muttered as The Suit disappeared and we walked past my competitors. We all had twenty four hours to produce an exhibition using our best portraits, but they had brought themselves extra hours with sheer dedication. Some greeted me, others hovered around their pieces protectively, whilst others went for anonymity by completely covering their works. There were classic portraits, Cubist craziness and romantic expressionism. I stopped by Kate, a pale, gaunt girl with haunted eyes, with whom I had grabbed a coffee break on Monday. She was from a troubled background and her pieces of dark expressionism disturbed the senses. But she didn't have the pretentious angst that the others had. Since I had no chance of winning, I wanted her to win.

"It's not too bad Taj. I've got great lighting here." The darkened spot with dimmed lights seemed perfect, but my brother's point about being at the back still worried me.

"We'll make a winner of you," Taj said supportively, pulling off his sweater. We spent most of the morning mounting the canvasses on the large black board every contestant had been given. It wasn't until we had secured the canvasses and stepped back that we realised that the lighting worked against the paintings.

"Taj, you need to get to Argos and buy me three projection lights..." I muttered, grabbing my bag to draw him a sketch of what I meant. "We've got to be able to secure it on the floor, so I need a staple gun..."

"You can't be drilling things to the floor or affecting the ballroom in any permanent way," advised The Suit, appearing from nowhere. I waited until he wandered off.

"Pop into Smiths and buy some red acetate, sticky-back Velcro..."

"What are you going to do?" asked Taj, pulling on his sweater, as I pulled my hair back into a pony.

"I'm going to try to win," I realised with a shaky smile.

"This is all your fault," I muttered, as Tariq picked us up on his way home from work.

"What are you talking about?!" he grinned, as I stretched out in the back of his Toyota while Taj dropped off into exhausted sleep. "What have you done to Taj?"

"He deserves half of everything if I win anything," I yawned, as we drove through the empty midnight roads of Park Lane. "He helped me set up today and we did a good job."

"You think you can win?" I caught Tariq's eyes in the rear-view mirror and shook my head.

"I've got a really bad spot and the other artists have some great collections. By the time the judges get to me, they'll have decided their favourite." He looked straight ahead, contemplating my words.

"Or you could change their minds." I grinned at his fighting attitude as we cut through Edgware Road to join the A40 West. "That's why I'm picking you up past midnight, because you're not giving up without a fight."

"The whole place is flooded with white light. I've just given my pieces some atmosphere. That's my fight, that's all I have left in me!" I chuckled with Tariq until he threw me some of Hamza's sweets.

"I've bought the Ealing restaurant, I got a silent city investor and the deal's going through this week." I reached around the seat to hug my brother as I screamed with joy for me. Taj mumbled for us to 'shut up' before nodding off again.

"You could've taken my money." Tariq laughed and shook his head.

"There are no short cuts in life Maya. You take the short cut and you sell yourself short." Tariq headed for Acton and I sat back. "What do you think Baba will say about my ideas?" Tariq's question was the first admission I heard about his insecurity.

"He'll be very proud of you," I told him, without hesitation.

"You think so?" he laughed, but I knew it was important for him to hear those words.

"I know so." He didn't respond, but his question made me realise that I too wanted to make Baba proud of me. It wasn't until I got home and walked into my room that I realised how much I wanted that. I had yet to see the sari I had wanted, but there it was on my bed waiting for me. The sari I had so desperately wanted but couldn't afford to buy. The small note had 'Baba' written on it. I sat on my bed and opened the box. I peeled back the cream tissue paper and stared at the sari. I smiled down at it. I had a lot to prove. I had a lot to gain. I had a lot of hope for tomorrow's promises.

W: Want It To Win It

The Khan-Ali Art Foundation had booked each contestant into a room at the Grovesnor to help us prepare ourselves for the event. Jana and Hana had dropped me off early at the hotel to help me get ready. They left soon after, having pinned me into the sari and painted me as close to perfection as my looks allowed. I emerged from my room in the shimmering nude sari that moulded itself to my body with every step that I took in my four-inch heels. With my hair pulled back into an elegant chignon, an intricate, designer, brown-glass necklace around my neck and immaculate make-up, I felt confident. I refused to acknowledge my insecurities. I refused to think about Jhanghir. I refused to realise what I had lost. I promised myself that I would enjoy today and deal with my empty life tomorrow. So I sashayed across the lobby like a budding star and enjoyed every double-look and hushed whisper I caused. As I approached the reception desk, Terry looked once, and then again, in surprise.

"Do you think I have a slim chance Terry?" I asked, as he walked over to me.

"You have more than a slim chance, Ms Malik." I held his eyes in understanding. We were cut from the same cloth and he wished me genuine success. "I've arranged cover to allow me time to watch the announcement." With a wide smile, I stepped back and made my way to the ballroom to receive the judges.

"Ms Malik." I looked back at Terry and waited. "Good luck." I nodded before walking on with a heady rush of anxious excitement. The suits stared in awe, as I breezed in and walked towards my exhibition. I paused to speak with my competitors who had revealed their exhibitions and were now happy to talk to anyone and everyone about their work. But, with each bit of information gathered from the other contestants, I felt more empowered to market mine just that little bit better.

"Maya?" One of the suits approached me, grinning in appreciation. "You look stunning…"

"Thank you. Everyone seems to have made an effort," I said, leading the way to my stand. "Do you think the judges will like what they see?" I indicated towards my paintings, but the 'suit' stared at me, understanding my intention to use every possible means to get recognised. When he grinned, I smiled. It was all about labels and I think I had just been tagged.

Within an hour, the ballroom was buzzing with the excited chatter of judges, journalists, contestants and collectors. I spoke to countless people, some hard and critical, others enchanted and complimentary. The atmosphere thrilled me, and for the first time, I began to relax.

"Ms Malik!" The loud, familiar call stunned me. I recognised the humorous tone, and excused myself from an interested buyer. "Don't you scrub up well!" The raucous laughter was uninhibited and I smiled at his playfulness.

"Mr Khan-Ali, it's good to see you," I returned, meeting his laughter-filled eyes.

"You stand out from the others." I stood beneath his intimidating appreciation, refusing to blush or to break.

"I intended to." He watched me, nodded and turned to my exhibition. That's where his expression came alive. I smiled.

"Who do you think should win?" The question threw me.

"I'm not qualified to judge..."

"You've never held back from sharing your opinions Maya, don't start now." I looked back at my paintings and stared at the sunset. Such beauty was missed by this fast-moving, blind world.

"I love my sunset," I breathed, looking back at the burly Mr Khan-Ali.

"Who do you think should win?" he repeated, as the 'suits' noted down every word. I looked down the hall to where Kate stood, all nerves and quietness, as she tackled the art-lovers and critics. She had no family present. No proud parents or boasting siblings.

"Kate Jones," I stated, looking directly at Mr Khan-Ali. "I find her work both disturbing and compelling." I stared in wonder when he chuckled. He combed back his hair before leaning forward.

"That's interesting." I frowned as I looked into his piercing grey eyes.

"Kate said she craved your ability to paint Utopia." Mr Khan-Ali disappeared after that statement.

"Utopia! He called her work Utopia!" Chachijhi's screech of excitement heralded the arrival of twenty family members and friends. "Maya! Look how beautiful you look!" I smiled self-consciously as bystanders stopped to stare at my descending family.

"The lovely man at reception let in your Ayesha's in-laws," whispered Chachijhi. "Hana and Jana have brought their in-laws too." She added with a wink.

"But we're spreading apart so that we don't look like we're all here together," Amma whispered in conspiracy.

"Aaaahhh, we need a picture, we have to get a picture!" Kala cried out rushing forward to hug me before snapping away at every opportunity. In an instant I was surrounded by twenty family members, all leaning in, bending over, and crouching around me to make it into the picture.

"Everyone together, that's right, yes together. Look at me, look at me."

"I've looked at the others," Amma announced, as she hugged me before posing for a picture. "You're the best, the others don't know how to draw. They paint squares and spots, and distorted faces with the noses in the wrong place, and God forbid there are even pictures of shameless, naked people with their bits showing..."

"Where? Which artist?" Amma clipped the back of my young cousin's neck and Sadek concealed his sudden interest in the competition. I winked at him and pointed to the exhibition stand in question. I saw his short smile and then felt the smack of Amma's admonishment. But then she smiled. "That's why you're going to win."

The morning disappeared through a series of informal interviews with journalists and judges. Every so often, I spotted a family member dragging anyone remotely connected to the world of art to my exhibition, and I stood back and laughed. Tanya and Sakina's loud greeting marked the arrival of my friends and I hugged them warmly as they squealed with excitement.

"Oh my God, Maya, you did all this?" Sakina breathed, standing back to stare at my work. I greeted their fiancés in turn before looking at my proud friends.

"You wouldn't believe it, would you?" Tanya pulled me into a hug, as we both laughed.

"And you look so beautiful! Where did you get that sari!" Asked Sakina, stroking the sheer material.

"Baba got it for me, I feel amazing in it!" The girls teased me and I took it on the chin until they stared at my work.

"You're going to win Maya," Sakina stated, as she looked around the ballroom.

"You're different, your work stands out." Tanya agreed without hesitation.

"You haven't seen the others properly yet!" I remonstrated. But there was no convincing my friends.

"You did a nude?" Tanya demanded, with wide eyes and a naughty smile. "Who did you get to pose..."

"Shut up Tanya! Amma and every one of my aunts have pretended not to notice, so don't you dare give them any ideas!"

"Why didn't you do a guy? That's what I'd like to see more of!"

"Hear! Hear!" We turned to find Kala standing back to admire the picture. We all stared at each other with uncertainty as my aunt stared at my oil painting. She turned to Tanya and nodded, as if deep in thought. "The male body is beautiful, Maya. I think you should do more of those for next year." And with that she walked away. A moment of surreal silence followed before we burst out laughing.

"Are you ok?" Tanya asked as Sakina discussed my work with her fiancé.

"Yeah." I refused to think about Jhanghir. Tanya knew I had invited him, and she knew he was always at the back of my mind. "I've been so busy, I haven't had a spare moment..."

"Brainwashing the journos and bribing the judges to let you win?" I laughed at her comment until it faded.

"Somebody's got to win right?" Tanya nodded in agreement.

"He doesn't know what he's giving up." I smiled at her comment and again felt the ache of loneliness. I saw a photographer approach me and breathed a sigh of relief.

"There's no such thing as happy ever after, Tanya. That only happens in fairy tales," I said as I walked towards the beckoning photographer. But Tanya caught my arm.

"So promise me you're happy now. In this moment, promise me he won't make you sad, because you've earned this. You deserve to be happy." I hugged my friend so that she couldn't see the tears in my eyes.

"I'm happy," I whispered. By the time I stood back, the tears had gone and I was perfectly composed to meet the photographer.

Later that afternoon, I saw Baba and Tariq approach with a bewildered Clare and an even more bewildered journalist. Out of respect, I quickly pulled my sari around me to cover my arms and abdomen and smiled at the journalist.

"This is definitely the best exhibition of the evening." Baba pretended not to know me, and I looked suspiciously at an innocent Amma. "I've offered Ms Malik five thousand pounds for it, but she flatly refuses me," Baba added grandly, as I balked at his display.

"That's because every Khan-Ali endorsed piece has a flat rate asking price of fifteen thousand pounds." The journalist pointed out, realising Baba's ploy.

Kala's squeal pierced through the ballroom and I held onto my smile as Chachijhi helped Amma into a seat. The journalist walked away unimpressed.

"Did you hear that?" Tariq whispered. "Maya, do you realise how much you've earned tonight?"

"Oh my God, oh my God!" I breathed, holding onto Baba's arms for support. "Oh my God, it was just a stupid competition!" Baba burst out laughing at my comment and before long we were all laughing.

"You're ruining the viewings!" Jana announced as she hugged me before herding my aunts together. She grabbed my cheeks and stared into my eyes. Like Tanya, Jana had expected Jhanghir to turn up, and like Tanya, Jana couldn't find the words to comfort me. I had looked out for him, found myself staring at the entrance for him, but now I accepted he wasn't going to come. I smiled and nodded. I was strong enough to see today through. She kissed me on the forehead and walked away. "You're going to win," Jana called back with a cheeky grin before leading my aunts away. Hana appeared with several art lovers and discussed the merits of my work without a passing greeting. Tariq and I watched until she turned to me as a stranger would and asked about the interest I'd received.

"The Khan-Ali Art Foundation has found buyers for every piece, but I believe there's some debate over the value of the pieces!" Hana led the chortle of amusement before leading the group on to the next exhibition. Tariq and I burst out laughing as we watched our family work the floor like rabid animals.

"Ladies and gentlemen, the winners of the Khan-Ali Art Foundation competition will be announced in fifteen minutes. Joseph Hamstraf of the International Art Commission will commence the ceremony after which Chief Executive Isaac Khan–Ali will announce the winners." My family cheered at the announcement while the more conservative art lovers clapped in appreciation. "Once again, ladies and gentlemen, the winners will be announced in fifteen minutes." Tariq and I laughed nervously before looking at our family. Baba plagued journalists, Amma followed the judges with Chachijhi, and the twins circled the floor with panache.

"They're criticising all the painters," Taj muttered in outrage. "Every exhibition they stop at, Ayesha, the twins and Shireen-bhabhi find flaws and problems as if they were buying..."

I thumped Taj's side as a journalist asked me to pose by my paintings. I smiled at the journalist as he snapped away. It was then I saw Jhanghir. But as soon as I saw him, he disappeared among the crowds.

"Maya." I ignored Tariq's call. I left the journalist standing to wonder among exhibitions to find Jhanghir. But I couldn't find him. Instead, I found Jana discussing the merits of a Cubist impression of a car.

"Why have you left your stand?" Jana cried out, leading me back to my stand.

"Did you see him? Did you call Jhanghir to tell him to come?" She looked at me with confused concern. "Did you remind him to come?" But she shook her head.

"I'm sorry he's not here sweetheart, but you're doing great. Everyone's talking about your work..." I looked around and caught Jhanghir leaving through the main hall. I looked back at my exhibition as Tariq and Taj beckoned me to return. I closed my eyes and knew I had no choice.

"Maya, you have to go back..." I didn't hear the rest of it. I lifted up my sari and raced out of the hall.

X: Don't Knock The X-Factor

He had just walked out. Jhanghir, the love of my life, had turned up on the biggest night of my life only to walk out again without even a passing 'Congratulations'. Wasn't it enough that he had denied me my last chance to be married? Wasn't it enough that he'd made me cry through endless nights and lose my precious appetite? Still, that didn't stop me running through the packed lobby, past journalists and photographers to get to him. As I couldn't run in my heels, I grabbed the service lift to the ground floor, but it took me up to the first floor. I raced through corridors, losing my way in the circular tunnels that led to oak-panelled conference rooms with expensive imported conference tables that were topped off with bowls of cheap mints.

"Excuse me, where are the elevators?" The passing steward wasn't impressed with my sudden question. He looked at my stage pass and changed his expression to one that was more accommodating.

"Behind you ma'am." Of course they would be. There wasn't time to think about how stupid I appeared so I thanked the man with humility.

"Ma'am, one push is sufficient." I jerked around to glare at him. I had just walked out on everything, and close to a hundred thousand pounds, for a man I couldn't find. I wasn't in the mood to be made to feel stupid.

"No fucking shit." The smug grin dropped as the elevator doors pinged open behind me. I didn't care that he just stared in open wonder. That, for all those who've been subjected to the 'you're unworthy for concierge concern' treatment, felt bloody good. Without another word, I turned around and walked into the lift.

And there he stood. It was him. It was the man who had comforted me and countless others, through all those lonely nights. It was only George bloody Clooney, standing in all his manly gorgeousness before me.

"How Alanis Morrisette ironic."

"Excuse me, ma'am?" *Ma'am? Was he speaking from a script?* I checked the lift to see if there were any other people but there weren't, and I realised that he was talking to me. It would be too easy to let Jhanghir disappear from my life. In two days' time, he would wake up to see Gorgeous George and I splashed across every tabloid - that would teach him to walk away from me! It was then I realised I was staring at George. I shut tight my eyes, spun around and pressed for the lobby. Ignore the temptation, ignore the temptation. He was probably on his way to see some gorgeous model for a few drinks in the Red Room. But how was this fair? I know Allah created all things to tempt us, but he really must have been having a laugh with me. I agonise for years to find my soul mate, and the minute I realise who that is, he sends Gorgeous, one-off, smouldering George into my hands.

"You are so mean!" I muttered heavenwards.

"Ma'am?" As usual I was louder than I had intended to be. Should I ignore the gorgeous man's query and ruin my moment by appearing to be a complete nut? Hell no.

"This is such bad timing," I said turning to face the divine man, who raised his brows in confusion. But I shut my eyes and carried on. "Two months ago, when I was a crushed spinster who'd lost her soul mate to a 'Twiglet', you would've been great for me. But your timing sucks!"

And yet the Adonis refused to speak.

"No, I have your number Mister," I said pointing a firm finger at him.

"Uh-huh." He looked at the LCD monitor before fixing me with a worried look.

"Yeah, Mr Smoothy with the dreamy eyes, and the quirky, lovely smirk, and the..." God he looked utterly scrummy. No! Stay focused! "... but the man I love who dumped me, who I then dumped just walked out on me again. But I know he loves me..." And that's when I realised what I was doing. I was passing up on the man of my dreams for Jhanghir.

"I love him," I whispered with a big wide grin. And then he smiled. Oh my God, this man had the ability to make the butterflies in my stomach indulge in a mass orgy with that smile. The doors pinged open and I turned to leave, but not before I could ask. "You were going to hit on me, weren't you?" I asked, holding the doors open to take one last look at my soon to be virtual ex-husband.

George, the sexiest man in the world, winked. He delivered every time. It didn't matter that he looked more than relieved at my departure. What mattered was that I'd given George up for Jhanghir. Jhanghir, oh my God, Jhanghir. I had to find him.

"Did you win Ms Malik?" Terry asked as he saw me race towards him.

"Terry, did you see an Asian man, a very good-looking Asian man about five feet nine inches tall, short cropped hair, deep American accent..."

"But your competition Ms Malik..."

"Terry, I have to find him, he just left without a word and I can't lose him again." I was close to tears, and Terry rushed around the counter to escort me towards the revolving doors. It was the wrong time to throw me out but I didn't have the energy to fight or argue with him.

"Mike, have you seen a young Asian gentleman, about five foot nine inches with a ..."

"...American accent?" The doorman finished as I smiled at Terry. "He asked for directions to Bond Street. He just turned around the corner." I had pulled off my heels and was racing off by the time Mike finished. I shouted back my thanks before turning the corner. I saw his three-quarter-length mac. He wasn't too far ahead of me so I yelled out his name. He continued walking and I called out again. When he stopped, I felt my heart thud with purpose. We met halfway until we stood before each other. He looked uncertain, but handsome and strong, and all the things I loved him for and more.

"Why did you leave without a word?" I demanded. "Without even a goodbye?"

"You looked beautiful," he breathed out, stunned by our proximity.

"Without even a goodbye?" I repeated as he met my eyes.

"And ruin your moment of glory?"

"You're just going to walk out of my life again, after everything that's happened?"

"You refused me Maya…"

"You withdrew the bloody proposal…"

"That's called pride Maya, it's the only thing I have when you're around," Jhanghir shouted, as if he were angry with himself. He finally looked at me with narrowed eyes. "You disarmed me from the moment I met you and you think it's easy for me to breeze out of your life?" I avoided his hurt eyes and frowned.

"I just turned down George Clooney for you." The corners of his eyes creased as he suppressed a grin.

"At least try to have a serious conversation Maya…"

"He's actually staying at the Grovesnor. Come back with me, you can check that I'm telling you the truth." Jhanghir raised a brow. "We met in the lifts and he fell for me instantly…"

"Instantly?" He repeated with false interest.

"And I turned him down," I declared, wishing he would believe me.

"Why?" I faltered at the telling question. "Why turn him down?"

"Because I must be the craziest woman alive," I muttered. "I'll regret it in the morning, I'll wake up knowing that I could've been bedded by the greatest…"

"Maya, why did you turn him down?" I finally met his searching eyes.

"Because he wasn't you." Jhanghir grinned at my admission. "He's not as arrogant or condescending, and he doesn't denigrate my background quite as well as you do," I grinned as he chuckled. "You called me an unwanted, disposable, overaged woman…"

"And you presumed the worst in me. Maya, I handled every form of condemnation from family, friends and the community because I gave my word to protect Preeya's reputation, but your judgements were the harshest."

"You broke my heart. You ruined my future and my dreams with your silence." Jhanghir reached out and cupped my jaw as he stepped closer. My legs felt watery, but I refused to avoid his intimate gaze. "I hated you for that and yet…" I could feel his warmth and thought I was going to pass out. "…yet I'm absolutely hooked on you." I felt his lips against mine. The gentle caress was the briefest, most beautiful touch I'd ever felt. Before I knew it, he pulled away and left me wanting.

"Maya." Jhanghir held my shoulders, forcing me to look at him. "If we don't get back now, you might as well come with me." It took me a while to realise his intentions.

"Oh…" I breathed out as I licked my lips and tasted him. Words failed me and all coherent thoughts disappeared.

"Your family will kill you and then they'll come after me." I frowned at his words because my intentions mirrored his. He grinned before crying out in frustrated exasperation. "Your ceremony Maya, you need to get back..."

"The ceremony?" I breathed and then gasped in clarity. "The ceremony!"

"Don't panic, we'll make it back in time..."

"Oh my God, we're never going to make it!" Before I knew it, Jhanghir was dragging me back to the hotel.

"We're going to make it," he shouted as he held onto my hand. I clutched my shoes against me and tried to keep up with him. We turned the corner, ran along the taxi rank, dodged arriving guests and jumped over cases.

"You got your man!" Mike laughed holding the door open at our arrival. "Good luck!"

"I've got him Terry, I got him back!" I called out as we raced into the lobby where everyone stopped and stared.

"I see that you did, Ms Malik," Terry smiled as he stood behind the desk. It was then that I spotted Gorgeous George amidst a group of businessmen who were also watching us.

"I got him!" I said, holding up Jhanghir's hand and smiling at George who chuckled.

"You weren't kidding!" Jhanghir muttered, pulling me round to look at me.

"I may obsess about the guy, but I'm not crazy!" I grinned as Terry coughed.

"Your presentation..."

"Terry, what's the fastest way to get to the ballroom?" Jhanghir and I were already racing through the lobby by the time Terry had finished. The guests and visitors gasped and jumped out of the way, but we didn't stop. Grasping my heels against me, I followed Jhanghir out on to Park Lane. We took a left until we found the entrance to the ballroom and then took the descending stairs.

"Do you have a pass?" We came to a sudden stop in front of the entry guards.

"I'm one of the contestants, I need to be in there!" I could hear the introductions being made for Isaac Khan-Ali as I held out my ID tag.

"And sir, where's your ID?" The thick burly man with no neck stared at Jhanghir.

"He's with me." The guard didn't even blink. "Jhanghir, where's your invite?"

"I threw it away..."

"You threw it away!" I shouted in disbelief.

"I didn't need it once I was in there." Jhanghir shouted back. "It's in that bin over there, if you'll just let me get to that ..."

"You threw the invite away!"

"Maya!" Leila's screech of acknowledgement nearly pierced my ear drums. "What are you doing here?" She came to a stop beside us with Abdul Raquib, and stared at my hand, which Jhanghir clasped. Self-consciously, I pulled mine free and folded my arms, before reaching out to hug her. "But why aren't you inside?"

"He's announcing the winners!" I cried out taking the invites from Leila's hands. "You're going to have to leave your husband here..."

"Maya, have you gone mad?" she demanded trying to grab the invites back.

"Leila, Jhanghir doesn't have an invite..."

"Sir, I thought you said you threw it away." We ignored the guard as Leila snatched the cards and we scrabbled for them. Jhanghir pulled me back while Abdul Raquib restrained Leila.

"I can't believe you want Abdul Raquib to stay out..."

"I don't mind waiting outside..."

"We can bribe the guard!" Leila shouted, which made us all freeze.

"We don't have to bribe the guard, Abdul Raquib doesn't have to wait outside," Jhanghir insisted as he forced me to look at him. He cupped my cheeks and grinned.

"You have to go inside, Maya. Right now..."

"I want you with me..."

"Terry will show me in, but you have to go in." I shook my head and stared at him.

"Maya, come on!" Leila called out, taking my arm to lead me in. I looked back and caught Jhanghir racing back up the stairs. Taking a deep breath, we rushed past the guard, through the lobby area and burst into the darkened ballroom.

Y: A Simple Yes

The entire hall came to a standstill as Leila and Abdul Raquib burst in behind me and pushed me forward. Isaac Khan-Ali paused and looked over to where I stood and I tightened my grip on my heels out of fear. I saw three of my fellow contestants on the stage, with Kate holding the golden envelope. She had won the overall competition, and I felt disappointed for not coming in the top three. The silence was unforgiving, the hundreds of pairs of eyes were intimidating and I couldn't meet a single pair.

"Your timing is unbelievable," Mr Khan-Ali announced with a solemn expression.

"Put your heels on," Leila whispered behind me. Slowly I lowered my heels before bending over to slip them on.

"Ladies and Gentleman, the Khan-Ali Art Foundation Best Newcomer bursary goes to Maya Malik." I froze at the announcement and then winced as the spotlight near blinded me.

"Stand up, stand up!" Leila breathed out, gripping my arm to drag me up. The feeling in my legs disappeared and I could hardly breathe.

"Maya, he wants you on the stage." As I stood up straight, I realised I couldn't move, I knew that if I moved I would collapse into a mass of jelly. Mr Khan-Ali read my disbelief and broke into a wide grin.

"She's won, my baby's won!" Amma cried out racing through the ballroom towards me. Slowly the clapping started and as Amma enveloped me in her arms, my family burst into thundering cheers.

"She's my daughter, she's my baby, I knew she'd do it, I knew she'd win!" she cried out, leading me down the stairs where I was lost amongst my grinning, cheering, hugging family beneath a sea of flashlights.

"What's happened to your lipstick?" Jana cried out pasting lip gloss on my lips. "Where have you been?" she whispered as I was pulled away into Tariq's arms. I was passed from sister to brother, from parent to uncle, to aunt and cousin and friends until I laughed with unbridled joy.

"Ladies and Gentlemen, Maya Malik told me that only artists appreciate the meaning of time." Isaac kept everyone amused as I made my way to the stage. "Needless to say, I'm sure even she's pleased that she made it in time to accept her prize!" The crowds laughed as I walked on to the stage and congratulated my fellow winners. I looked at Isaac Khan-Ali and grinned stupidly. I felt he had been rooting for me from the beginning because I was the underdog. He held out his hand, but I walked up to him and hugged him until he enveloped me in a bear hug.

"Thank you," I whispered, as he rumbled with laughter.

"You deserve it," Isaac returned before we separated. "Maya Malik everyone." I gripped his hand as I stared out at the sea of faces and flashing lights. My legs felt like jelly and I wished there was a podium instead of just a mike that I could hold on to. I looked at Isaac and he gently patted my hand before indicating the mike.

"I don't have a speech. I didn't think I'd win," I whispered to Isaac, but the mike picked it up and everyone laughed at my disbelief. I thought of Nani, I thought of Monsur, I thought of all the introductions I'd had, I thought of all my fears and insecurities, tears and tantrums, until I could think no more. All my senses deserted me and I looked around until I found Jhanghir at the back of the hall. He was brimming with pride and cheering with the best of them. I was happy. And lucky. And blessed beyond my imagination.

"A few words about your paintings Maya," Isaac encouraged as the clapping quietened down.

I nodded at him before looking out at my family and friends. I blinked back tears of happiness and cleared my throat so that I could speak without breaking down.

"Tha.. Thank you." I hesitated and looked round at the projections of my paintings on the wall behind me. I stared at my Nani's village in the sunset, and I knew what I had to say. "That's my grandmother's village. I learnt a lot there. She said to me, 'There are only so many times you can reject life before life rejects you'." I looked back at the silent audience and smiled.

"'Embrace life' she said, 'and life will embrace you'. I tried to embrace life in my work, you know, capture perfect, timeless, treasured moments to keep believing in life. And I really think that life is embracing me now, so I want to thank you all for allowing that to happen." I took in a sudden breath when the hall erupted with applause and I shook my head as I looked at Mr Khan-Ali in surprise. I wished Nani was here to see how far I had come with her help. With a small smile, I looked back at my family. I waited until the applause faded and smiled wider than I had ever smiled in my life. I had one more thing to do to complete my perfect moment.

"Of course, if I forget to mention my family, I'll never capture such moments again." The crowd laughed, but I caught Amma sniffing with pride and felt the sting of tears. "Tariq, you're my rock, so thank you for believing in me when I refused to. And my beautiful family, I owe you everything. Amma, Baba, Taj, my beautiful sisters, I've tested your patience, love and kindness this past year and I'm humbled by your resilience. So I want to thank you by telling you your days of waiting, praying and pleading for my marriage are over." I grinned as the confused murmurs waved down the hall. Jhanghir froze at the back of the hall, but this was it. This was my moment to end my stint at stifling spinsterhood.

"She's lost it!" Amma muttered to Ayesha who ignored her and kept on smiling whilst looking straight ahead.

"It's too much pressure," Chachijhi pointed out. "She's broken beneath the pressure!"

I took a deep breath but couldn't stop grinning as Isaac frowned at my break with convention.

"Jhanghir Khan, will you marry me?" My heart thundered and my hands shook as I looked across the surprised gasps of pleasure to my man at the back of the hall.

"Taj catch me!" Amma called out as she nearly fainted at my forwardness.

"She's broken, she's pining for that boy!" Chachijhi muttered tearfully amidst the silence.

"Oh my God, I've pushed her too hard, so hard she's up on stage asking a man who's in America for marriage!" Amma cried out holding her head in her hands. "All she had to do was take the prize, thank us and walk off. That's it. That's it and even that's too much to expect of this crazy girl..." But their embarrassed whispers died down as the crowds parted to make way for Jhanghir.

"He's here!" Kala cried. "Where's my camera? Give me my camera!"

"When did he get here?" Chachijhi demanded. "Who told him to come today?"

"My camera, which mongrel has taken my camera?" Kala demanded.

"How dare he turn up after everything he's put my Maya through..."

"Get your sandals off, we'll teach him to respect the Maliks..."

"Amma, stop it!" Leila interrupted, stopping Chachijhi from taking off her slippers.

"Our Maya's about to get herself a husband!" Tariq remarked with a beaming grin.

"Oh my God, my baby's getting married!" Amma realised, pushing Taj back to watch Jhanghir walk up to the stage. I looked away from my approving, smiling father to the man who walked towards me. He was grinning in disbelief and I smiled.

"Do you think that looks like a man who wants to say yes Mr Khan-Ali?" Isaac nodded in agreement before roaring with laughter. I looked back and found Jhanghir in front of me.

"Yes, I will marry you." The whirring of cameras and lighting of flashes took over as I stared at the man who had saved me. All my yesterdays were over. With one 'yes', Jhanghir had saved me from the litterbin of spinsters and SLAAGs.

"You know I can't hug you in front of my parents until you give me that diamond first!" The crowds laughed at my warning and burst into applause when Jhanghir folded me into his arms. I looked up into his hazel eyes and everything faded away but the scramble of my mother clambering on to a table.

"My Maya's getting married, it's going to be the best biggest Malik wedding ever and you're all invited!" Amma shouted at the top of her lungs and the whole hall erupted with laughter.

Z: Zindaghi

Zindaghi means life. Actually it means more than that, Zindaghi means the willingness to embrace life. Just as I thought I was getting a grip on life, the discussions about marriage that follow terminated spinsterhood are designed to throw you back into the pits of singledom. After my public marriage proposal, the gossip vines of the Bengali community were singed with differing accounts of the event. It started off with the much outraged:

"She got so desperate she even asked him to marry her! In public. In front of her parents for everyone to see and hear. The world is changing, the old ways of the alaap are dying."

This developed into the hushed suggestion that I had:

"...only accepted the proposal because nobody else wanted Khan's son. How else would she end up with such a good looking, educated doctor - albeit a scandalous one?"

And then there was the version that spread like the plague through Bengali kitchens;

"Reena's mother's nephew is the third cousin of Maya's Kala in Brighton, and I've been told that Maya's been ruined! Ruined, I say. She's in the family way and she's forcing him to marry her!"

The gossip, albeit creative, became the source of contention for both families when our parents met the following day. In true Bengali style, everyone left work early to contribute to the discussion, as I sat nervously facing my future in-laws.

"Maya did your son's duty for him and looked like a million-dollar Bollywood star!" Baba bragged, sitting down on the garden bench to enjoy the warm, hazy June evening. He had left Taj and my brothers-in-law to man the barbeque in true caveman style. "Though the question isn't why she did it, it should be why she didn't accept in the first place!"

"Maya was misinformed about the events..."

"She listened to the gossip without question, and now she's the source of the gossip!" Mr Khan interjected, as Ayesha sat shaking her head. "People are saying much worse things about Maya than they ever did about Preeya."

"Why should it matter what people are saying?" We all looked around to find Jhanghir step into the garden with Leila and Abdul Raquib. He looked at me briefly with confident, smiling eyes before turning to our parents. Amma coughed in her discreet obvious fashion until I caught her indicate that I leave the table in true shy bride-to-be fashion. She then smiled widely at a frowning Mrs Khan. I left Baba's side to sit with the twins on the grass as they listened whilst looking through *Asian Bride*. Hamza raced over and found his place beside me.

"The fact remains that we're getting married. And given that we'll be living in Manhattan, I don't see why this should matter anyway..."

"It matters because my daughter's being gossiped about," Baba threw back, now siding with Jhanghir's father, who looked like he appreciated the support.

"The phone hasn't stopped ringing since we came home with people asking..."

"...asking about how Maya did at the ceremony," Ayesha finished off calmly.

"And let's not forget that people have been talking about Maya for a long time now, but the gossip only seems worse because of Jhanghir's broken engagement." Leila's comment drew offended silence from the Khans, causing Amma to drag her away.

"Don't let her move or speak," she ordered Jana before returning to the table.

"We accept that Maya broke with convention by proposing in the way that she did and without consulting us first," Tariq interceded, delivering the first tray of tandoori chicken and warm naan to the garden table. "But Jhanghir has accepted. We have to get past the community gossip and start planning the wedding." I grinned at Hana as Tariq controlled the situation with a maturity that belied his age. And then Amma ruined the temporary calm.

"Yes, now about the wedding and where the kids will live," she began, as Ayesha tried to put her off continuing. I covered my face in disbelief as Amma tapped at the corner of her eyes. "Why don't we agree that they should move to London?" Amma concluded.

"But Jhanghir's training is in Manhattan..."

"But he could transfer here," Amma pointed out, as Tariq sighed in exasperation.

"He could even join the family practice with Ayesha, Hana and Jana," Baba added.

"Jhanghir's a trainee surgeon, why would he want to join a GP practice?"

"Because it's the best GP practice in Britain," Leila piped out before Hana could gag her.

"But how can I live with my baby living so far away from me?" Amma said quickly before bursting into tears. We all stared at each other in shock as Amma covered her face with her sari and cried out with long, heart-breaking sobs. This was incredible. "Who'll iron her clothes, or make her bed, and what will she eat? She can't even cook!" I covered my face in despair, because Amma made me sound as incapable as a newborn baby.

"Stop her! Will you stop her before they change their minds!" I whispered to Jana.

"Jhanghir is a responsible boy, and Maya's not a stupid girl, so they'll manage." Mr Khan stopped as Mrs Khan glared at his insensitivity.

"We'll watch over her," Mrs Khan offered, taking Amma's hands. "We'll make..."

"But you live all the way in Canada! What if she doesn't feel well, who's going to make sure she takes her medicine?" Amma asked between her tearful sobs.

Baba, despite having four daughters, had never learnt how to deal with overt displays of female emotion, so he led Jhanghir's father to the barbeque just as Chachijhi ran out to comfort Amma.

"We've all prayed to see Maya married off, why are you crying?" she asked, holding Amma's crying form. Jhanghir strolled over to us with Tariq and a tray of grilled meat.

"Can we at least have both the wedding and walimah here?" Amma continued.

"But our family in the States will want to celebrate Jhanghir's marriage too..."

"Well they can come over, and stay with us!" Amma suggested. "We'll have enough room in the house if we move all the furniture out to the garage," Amma insisted.

"If you came over for the walimah you could spend some time helping Maya to settle into the apartment." Mrs Khan's suggestion eased some of Amma's worries.

"What about their honeymoon? There's no reason why they can't stay with me." We gave up listening to Amma as she continued to negotiate our honeymoon in London.

"Hey Dr Khan!" Leila grinned as he sat down beside me. "You're not married yet, so no fooling around!" Leila's voice carried, which caused everyone to stare at us.

"Shame you're married Leila, or who knows what would've happened?" Jhanghir returned, sidling in between Leila and me.

"Oh you are naughty!" Leila returned, before collapsing into a fit of giggles. I exchanged looks of wonder with my sisters as we helped ourselves to the grilled chicken. Before long all the cavemen joined us on the grass as Leila told us about her blissful honeymoon. I looked around at each of member my family and felt like the luckiest girl in the world.

"I've still got two open tickets to the Maldives." Jhanghir spoke only to me, and I looked at the man who would be my life. "We could have a secret secluded beach wedding and create enough gossip to last us a lifetime."

"We'd be disowned," I said as I piled food on to his plate.

"Good! Let's just get married on the beach, alone ..."

"You can't steal my foopi away!" Hamza shouted, causing everyone to freeze.

"Hamza, that's not what Jhanghir meant..."

"Yes it is, he wants to marry you in secret, I heard him!" I felt like dying beneath the scrutiny. I gathered the courage to look at Jhanghir and watched as he burst out laughing.

"Who's marrying who in secret?" Amma demanded, storming across from the patio area.

"It's not funny, he's stealing foopi!" Hamza shouted as I pulled him into my arms. Ayesha, Tariq and the twins joined Jhanghir with the ribbing. At that precise moment, I knew my wedding would be an utter nightmare to organise, but I wouldn't have it any other way.

My name's Maya Malik, and I'm no longer a twenty-eight year old SLAAG. I still buy every issue of *Asian Bride* in preparation for my imminent wedding, but I no longer have to hide from my mother's groom-searching techniques, or sit through patronising pep talks from well meaning friends. My biggest fear isn't being a failed artist. It's the realisation that at my ripe old age, I found a perfect man from the diminishing stock of eligible bachelors and I still have to turn him into my husband. I've had my fair share of disastrous alaaps, community pressure, tears and heartaches, but it's now that the real work begins. Well, you didn't think this was a simple love story? In reality this should serve as a wake up call to remind you that finding the right man isn't the end. Oh no. After that comes the pre-nuptial agreement, your relationship with the in-laws, and if you can get past that, then, and only then, do you get to the wedding. I have no doubts there will be tears and tantrums about the venue, outfits, living arrangements, gold sets, and everything else that has come to dominate weddings. But as our families danced around these issues, my fears about arranged marriages dissipated. I now had Jhanghir, and more importantly I could see the beginning of the next stage in my life. I'm sure there is a guide to planning marriages, but for now I was just glad that zindaghi had given this ex-single, lonely, aging, Asian girl a happy ending.

About the Author

Rekha Waheed is a writer with a sharp eye for Brit-Asian fusion and redefining cultural stereotypes. Born and raised in West London and of Bengali origin, Rekha makes her first contribution to contemporary Brit-Asian fiction with 'The A-Z Guide to Arranged Marriage'.

Rekha is a writer, an analyst with an academic background in Economics from SOAS, University of London. She is also an active promoter of improved literacy programs in the British- Bengali community.

Lightning Source UK Ltd.
Milton Keynes UK
21 December 2010

164712UK00001B/187/A